To Marilyn

Peter Bernhardt

I want to express my gratitude to the members of the Sedona Writers Critique Group, the Internet Writing Workshop, and YouWriteOn.com for their constructive criticism that improved this novel beyond measure.

Kerry Taliaferro, former role coach (Korrepetitor) at the Stuttgart Opera, provided expert advice that was invaluable, and the management of the Stuttgart Opera and the Stuttgart Opera School were generous with their time and personnel. Thanks to soprano Theresa Plut I gained a deeper appreciation of the challenges awaiting an aspiring opera diva.

I especially thank the readers of my early drafts for valuable feedback. My appreciation to Helma Boeck and Karl Ganter for their recollections of the atmosphere in Berlin at the time the Wall fell, and I am indebted to Claudia Käsbohrer for enabling me to authentically sketch the scene in the Congress Hall in Garmisch-Partenkirchen.

There were many others who made significant contributions to this work. They are too numerous to name, but I express here my deep appreciation for their help and support. They know who they are.

The Stasi File

Opera and Espionage— A Deadly Combination

Peter Bernhardt

Peter Bernhardt

Published in 2009 by New Generation Publishing

First Edition

Published by New Generation Publishing

Chapter One

Sylvia Mazzoni stepped out the stage door of the Big House, the locals' name for the Stuttgart Opera Theater. In her blue jeans and sweatshirt, she looked more like a member of the cleaning crew than a soprano leaving a rehearsal called solely on her account. She took several deep breaths, releasing the lingering tension with each exhalation. A gust of November wind whipped the trees around, causing shadows to thrust and parry in the dusky Schlossgarten Park. She shivered, pulled a long wool scarf from her shoulder bag, and wrapped it, Pavarotti style, around her throat. Anything to protect The Voice. She removed her hair clasp to allow heavy, dark tresses to cascade around her shoulders.

The music director had engaged her for two performances as Micaëla in *Carmen* after seeing her in the part at the regional opera in Ulm. She had done well this evening, but would she pass the real test tomorrow? Her debut at the renowned Stuttgart Opera could make or break her career. If she failed to impress, she'd be relegated once again to bit parts in provincial houses. She vowed not to let

5

that happen. She had worked too hard for too long to fail now.

The park adjoining the theater, brimming with life all day, was deserted. Sylvia thought of waiting for a colleague to accompany her, but eager to catch the next streetcar, she ignored her intuition and stepped onto the cobblestone promenade along the lake. A glimmer of city lights filtered through the bare branches of giant oaks and sycamores. Dim sidewalk lamps cast long, crooked fingers across the dark water. To shake the foreboding image, she looked for the soft ripples that would precede swimming mallards and swans, but it was late even for them.

Sylvia peered up the dark path. A few meters ahead, the desiccated leaves of a giant poplar rustled in the night air. From there it was only a few minutes to the shopping arcade and the streetcar stop. She pressed on.

A burly man came around the bend, his right hand tucked inside the front of his leather jacket. Startled, Sylvia felt an adrenaline rush. She clutched her umbrella and stepped to her right to give him a wide berth. Out of the corner of her eye she caught a sudden movement, a lunge toward her. She spun around. Glinting metal ripped through her sweatshirt and slashed her left upper arm. She winced with pain as she jammed the metal tip of the umbrella as hard as she could into the attacker's chest. He grunted. The impact jarred the umbrella from her hand and sent it clattering to the ground. Warm liquid trickled down her arm. Sylvia staggered onto the damp lawn. She fought to regain her balance but slipped and fell hard.

Frantic, she looked for the umbrella, but it had rolled down the path, beyond her reach. Get up, she exhorted herself in a panic, but too late. The towering figure came at her again. Heart thudding, Sylvia skidded backwards on the grass. She heard herself scream, "Help, help . . . help me!"

The man drew back the knife and slashed downward again. She rolled. Her face, covered by her tangled hair, flattened against the wet ground. She clawed the hair aside and saw the knife plunge to its hilt into the ground where she had been a second ago.

"Damn you, traitor!"

She'd heard that guttural voice before. She raised her head and found herself staring into hate-filled eyes. Could it be . . . ? Before she finished the thought, his massive body crushed her, knocking the breath out of her. She opened her mouth to cry again for help, but could only spit blades of grass. Cold fingers dug beneath her scarf and closed around her throat. Muscular thighs straddled her hips, pinning her so that struggle was useless. She brought her hands up, trying to loosen his grip, but the vise only tightened.

"Ple . . ." Sylvia's voice trailed off in a gurgle, her trachea compressed in his grasp. Blood rushed in her ears. The man's menacing face became a distorted blur. Panicked, she fought for a breath. Her limbs went numb. Darkness swallowed her.

Then a sharp thump penetrated the void. Dead weight slumped against her chest. The vise at her neck loosened.

She gulped for air, fighting the crushing weight. One small breath came, then another. She opened her eyes. The attacker's face pressed at an unnatural angle against her chest. Blood trickled from the man's slack mouth. Repulsed, she pushed the stubbly face away and struggled to shove the corpse aside. It tipped for a moment, then rolled back on top of her. She shuddered.

Sylvia took several more ragged breaths, gathering her strength, but before she could make another attempt, someone lifted the body off her. Her chest heaved with relief.

"Frau Mazzoni, are you all right?"

She stared at the man. Then she recognized Intelligence Officer Dieter Schmidt.

"Herr Schmidt. What are you—?"

"You're safe now." He took her right arm to help her sit up, then pointed at the blood-soaked clothing on the other. "Can you move your arm?"

Sylvia gingerly lifted her left arm. The pain was tolerable. The sweatshirt's damp sleeve clung to the wound, stemming the blood flow. "I guess it's okay."

"Good." He motioned toward the lifeless body lying in the grass next to her. "Do you know him?"

She forced herself to look. "He's with . . ." She took a deep breath. "He was with the RAF, a friend of Horst." She shivered. For years she had looked over her shoulder expecting the Red Army Faction terrorists to come for her. They never had. Why now, twelve years later, just when she'd begun to think she was safe from their revenge?

Schmidt nodded. "I was afraid of that." He bent down and felt for a pulse. After a few seconds he said, "His terrorist days are over."

Sylvia stared at Schmidt. "Did you shoot him?"

He steadied her on her feet. "We'll talk about this later. You have to get away from here now—before the police arrive."

He scrutinized her face. "Can you make it back to your hotel by yourself?"

In a daze, she nodded.

"I have to take care of things here, but I'll check on you as soon as I can." He collected her bag and umbrella and thrust them toward her. "Frau Mazzoni, not a word about this to anyone. Go. Now!"

Sylvia stumbled in the direction of the shopping arcade.

Chapter Two

Deep in thought about the motion for summary judgment he needed to finish today, Rolf Keller mumbled a hasty good morning to his secretary on his way into his office. She put up a hand. Startled, he stopped. His Friday would not go as planned.

Her expression a mixture of curiosity and concern, Betty said, "Mr. Stein's secretary has already called twice. She left word to send you up to his office as soon as you came in."

Betty Crandall had a checkered twenty-year history with Stein & Weston. She'd been continually reassigned from senior partners to junior ones, then to associates. As one of the new hires in 1982, Rolf was not given a choice. Betty became his legal secretary.

In her forties and unmarried, she was considered odd. Thinning red hair framed her high forehead and hollow cheeks. A sharp nose protruded over lips so thin they were almost invisible. At a few inches below six feet, she stood almost as tall as Rolf. She wore clothing she must have bought in the sixties, as age had not yet thickened her gangly frame and spindly legs. Rolf couldn't decide whether she was motivated by frugality or simply lacked a sense of style.

He soon realized why the other lawyers didn't like her. She was outspoken and dared to question word selection and grammar in legal documents. Occasionally, she even committed the unforgivable sin of calling attention to a mistake. The overblown egos of most lawyers couldn't abide what they considered interference by an underling, but Rolf loved her directness. That's why seven years later she was still his secretary.

Her voice interrupted his thoughts. "You're not in trouble, are you, counselor?"

Rolf appreciated the quip. In contrast to the formal culture pervasive in the firm, Betty and Rolf had been on a first-name basis for a number of years. They abandoned that practice only in professional settings or to tease one another.

Harry Stein, founding partner, did not make it a habit of asking associates to his office. Of course, Rolf knew where it was—in the southeast corner of the twelfth floor—yet in seven years he'd been there only twice. Stein governed the firm with an autocratic hand through the other partners. Except for the annual Christmas party, he didn't mingle with associates.

"Any idea what he wants, Betty?"

She shrugged. "Not a clue."

Rolf's eyes fell on the legal pad next to the inbox on his desk, yet he made no move to pick it up. Instead, he glanced at the coat hanger where he kept a dress shirt, coat and tie for court appearances or other occasions requiring last-minute changes to business attire.

"Are you changing for the big boss?"

Rolf sensed the challenge in her question. "Business casual should do, don't you think?"

Not chancing another satiric remark, he stepped into the hallway and walked past support staff cubicles and lawyers' offices. When he reached the interior spiral staircase that connected the three top floors of the downtown Washington office building Stein & Weston occupied, he hesitated, then decided to take the employee elevator instead. He couldn't help speculating about the reason for being summoned. In his eighth year with the firm, he would be under close scrutiny for a potential partnership. The unspoken rule was that associates who hadn't made partner by the end of their tenth year never would, and they were expected to leave of their own accord.

During the elevator ride, Rolf recalled the stories Betty had told him about associates who stayed on after they'd been passed over for partnership. They found themselves being assigned first-year lawyer duties like library research and shunned by partners and associates alike. Whispers eventually grew so loud even the most oblivious and stubborn got the message.

Rolf was determined not to let that happen to him. Vestiges of law partnership not only included prestige and marketability, but most important, increased financial rewards—crucial for him. He couldn't keep paying alimony, child support, the house mortgage and his apartment rent on an associate's salary. He had to make partner, and long before his tenth year.

When Rolf stepped from the elevator into the twelfth-floor wood-paneled corridor he considered the idea that Stein summoned him to tell him he made partner. He knew he'd performed well, but well enough to make it after only seven years? Not likely.

The generous size of the partners' offices on the twelfth floor emphasized that not all lawyers were created equal, at least in Stein & Weston's view of things. When he had wound his way to the southeast corner, Rolf spotted a brass name plate engraved with Harold Stein, Senior Partner, and one below bearing the inscription Mildred Reid, Secretary. The dark wooden door stood ajar.

All roads to Stein lead through his secretary, Rolf thought, as he peeked inside while giving the wood panel a half-hearted knock. And the roads were not necessarily smooth, judging by the piercing look Mildred shot his way. Assessing his status in the firm within a nanosecond, the woman in her fifties with the short-necked physique of a linebacker gave a slight nod in his direction, which he interpreted as a sign that his presence would be tolerated.

"Have a seat, Mr. Keller. I'll let Mr. Stein know you're here." Her tone made the invitation a command. Lowering himself onto the edge of one of the black leather chairs facing her cherry-wood desk, he couldn't help wondering what would happen if he didn't comply. While he hadn't seen her job description, he felt pretty sure it didn't include being nice to associates.

He had hardly registered her voice on the phone announcing his presence, when he heard, "Mr. Stein will see you now." She walked to a tall door behind her desk, opened it and motioned for him to pass. As she closed the door behind him, he fought the feeling of a schoolboy entering the principal's office.

His shoes sank into the thick beige carpet of an office so spacious that, in addition to the usual desk and visitors' chairs, it easily accommodated a conference table with six leather chairs and an oversized sleeper sofa, leaving plenty of room to maneuver in between. The room was bright, thanks to floor-to-ceiling windows spanning two walls.

Rolf squinted against the morning sun streaming through partially open blinds. The senior partner swiveled his leather chair in Rolf's direction and rose from a reclining position. An easy smile spread over a gaunt face that was accentuated by a long nose, large ears, and a high forehead. When Harry Stein stood to offer a firm handshake, Rolf noticed how fit he looked in his custom-tailored navy suit, especially for a gray-haired man approaching sixty. Rolf guessed that at a couple of inches below six feet, he didn't weigh over 160 pounds.

"Good to see you, Rolf. How are you?"

Surprised by the warm welcome, Rolf stammered, "Fine . . . sir."

"Have a seat. Coffee?"

Following a hunch he'd be there for a while, Rolf replied, "Yes, please."

Back behind his huge desk, Stein pressed the intercom button on a multi-line phone. "Mildred, coffee please." Without awaiting a response, he turned and looked at Rolf. "I was sorry to hear that you and Lynn divorced. It's tough to be back on your own, even if it's for the better, isn't it?"

Taken aback, Rolf groped for a response. He hadn't imagined that his personal life would be a meeting topic. Mercifully, they were interrupted by a knock on the door, and Mildred wheeled in a coffee service cart. She served black coffee to her boss then moved the cart next to the visitor's chair. Rolf poured from the carafe and stirred cream and sugar into his cup. He waited until the door closed behind her before he answered Stein. "Actually, I haven't had a lot of time to think about it."

"Your billable hours for the last quarter are among the highest in the firm. Of course, the partners like to see that for obvious reasons." Stein leaned forward, resting his arms on the mahogany desk surface. "But I'm curious about the sudden increase."

Rolf felt blood rush to his head and hoped to God he wasn't blushing. He didn't appreciate being made to feel like a witness under cross-examination. He set his cup on the cart to give himself time to think. Stein was no fool and would see through any attempt to placate. His response had to include a good part of the truth.

"To be honest, these last few months have been pretty rough. There's been no reason to go home to an empty apartment, so I've been burying myself in work. And I started to think that now would be a good time to increase my billable hours."

Stein leaned back in his chair to let the response sink in. He lifted his coffee cup from the desk pullout and took a sip. Resting the cup on the armrest, he swiveled his chair toward the corner window, apparently studying the vast array of office buildings bathed in early sunshine.

Rolf wondered if his answer, truthful as far as it went, would satisfy. He saw no point in volunteering how much he needed the partnership.

The senior lawyer swung back and replaced his cup on the pullout. "You're an independent sort, aren't you?"

The way Stein looked him over, Rolf almost wished for his coat and tie. Definitely no partnership offer here, he thought, feeling foolish for having even entertained the idea.

Thus Stein's next words surprised him all the more. "From what I hear about your courtroom practice, you stand your ground against tyrannical federal judges. Your briefs are excellent, thoroughly researched, well written, and show creative thinking."

Rolf was thoroughly confused. Was partnership in the offing, after all?

As if he'd read Rolf's thoughts, the senior lawyer continued. "You've been with this firm seven years now. As you know, the firm's general practice is to wait ten years before an associate is offered partnership."

Rolf's heart sank.

"However, in your case I'm making an exception."

Rolf had the distinct impression there was significance in the fact that Stein referenced the firm when he spoke of the usual practice, but referred to himself alone as the one deciding to deviate from the norm.

"A senior associate on the brink of partnership is usually assigned a complicated case." Stein gave him a stern look.

"The assignment I want you to handle is extremely sensitive. It's not really a legal matter, but the skills it calls for are exceptional—the kind I'd like to see in a partner, and you're uniquely qualified for the task. If you handle it well, you'll be our newest partner." He did not need to specify what would happen if Rolf failed.

Harry Stein's voice took on a note of gravity. "Before I go into details, I need to ask you how you're doing in your recovery program."

Rolf's mouth fell open. Was there anything this man didn't know about his personal life? Before he could suppress his anger, he burst out, "Alcoholics Anonymous is just that, anonymous. I'm not going to talk about it." He felt his body propelling itself out of the chair.

"Please sit down. I'm not prying into your AA program. But I do need to know what the odds are of your staying sober."

How had Stein found out about him going to meetings? Had someone from AA broken his anonymity? Rolf fought his anger. Stein knew. Walking out of this office wouldn't change that.

He struggled to regain his composure, taking his time to sit back down. "Well, a good percentage of people who practice the twelve steps stay sober. The ones who don't work the program usually relapse."

"I'm familiar with the statistics. I'm asking *you*. Are you going to stay sober?"

Stein had a litigator's stare. Rolf could not avoid his eyes. He took a deep breath and lowered himself onto the chair. "One day at a time, you bet I am."

He knew he had spoken the truth, and the lawyer behind the desk seemed to sense it too.

Harry Stein stood, walked over to the wood-paneled side wall, and slid two panels apart revealing a sizable safe. His upper body shielded the combination wheel from view. After a series of clicks and the sound of moving hinges,

Stein reached into the open safe. He closed it and carried a manila folder to the conference table, motioning for Rolf to join him.

"Rolf, when did you give up your German citizenship to become a U.S. citizen?"

Although he suspected that Stein already knew the answer, he dutifully replied, "In 1982."

"Do you still feel an allegiance to the country where you were born and grew up?"

Rolf tried not to let it show that he was caught off guard once again. "Well, not the kind of allegiance I feel toward the U.S., but I do follow what's going on over there, the way one keeps up with an old friend after moving away. Of course, with the fall of the Berlin Wall, there's been much speculation whether the two Germanys might be united."

"What do you think? Will Germany be reunited?"

"I'd say chances are pretty good, provided the Germans can convince the World War II Allies that a united Germany poses no threat. But it'll take astute political maneuvering on Chancellor Kohl's part."

"And do you think he's up to the task?"

Rolf was surprised and flattered by Stein's question. Although he was a native German, that did not make him an expert on German or global politics. "All I know is what I read in the newspapers. I gather that Helmut Kohl is quite a skilled politician. If anyone can do it, he can."

Harry Stein nodded. "Yes, my client agrees that German reunification is imminent."

Rolf noted that Stein had erroneously referred to *re*unification, as if Germany would be restored to its pre-World War II borders. In fact, there was no possibility of that. Only the states comprising Communist East Germany, the German Democratic Republic, were on the table, so it was more appropriate to refer to German unification. Rolf let it go.

Stein's voice interrupted. "You need to catch this evening's flight to Frankfurt, then fly on to Stuttgart in the morning."

"But this is the weekend for me to have Ashley . . . my daughter." Rolf suspected the clarification was superfluous, as Stein had shown he was intimately familiar with Rolf's family life.

"Sorry. This is urgent."

Rolf knew the firm did not tolerate refusal of any task, no matter how onerous to the associate's private life. He realized Stein had arranged things without even considering the possibility that Rolf would refuse. Short of quitting the firm, there was no realistic alternative to going.

"You can make other arrangements for your daughter, can't you?"

Rolf supplied the expected answer to the rhetorical question, "Yes, sir," all the while dreading the thought of having to tell Ashley he was canceling their weekend visit. She'd grown distant lately, causing him to wonder whether she blamed him for the breakup. If there was a way to explain divorce to a seven-year-old, he hadn't discovered it. Perhaps he lacked the courage.

When Stein walked over to the desk to retrieve his coffee, Rolf seized the opportunity to steal a glance at the file facing away from him. He strained to read the capital letters on the label and got as far as determining that there were three when Stein's voice boomed across the room.

"I assume you're familiar with the Stasi?"

Rolf spun around and noted with relief that Stein had his back to him.

Trying to sound nonchalant, Rolf responded, "Yes, the East German secret police."

"What do you know about them?"

"They're using blackmail and bribes to coerce East Germans to inform on one another. Spouses on spouses, children on their parents. They read the mail and listen in on phone calls. They've taken the Gestapo's methods of extracting confessions from enemies of the state to new levels of sophistication. Torture is not just physical but psychological as well."

Stein returned to the table, placing his cup and saucer next to the file. "You know they're not just a police force?"

Rolf nodded. "They're into domestic and international espionage, maybe terrorism as well."

"You do know quite a bit." Stein looked as pleased as a schoolteacher whose pupil has just passed the test. "You're wondering what that's got to do with your assignment." He took a swig of coffee and returned the empty cup to its saucer with a loud clink. He rested his hands on the closed file. "There is a Stasi official who's reached the same conclusion we have about the likelihood of reunification. He's contacted the West German Federal Intelligence Service and offered to supply documents from the Stasi files."

Rolf wondered how a law firm partner would know about matters of international intelligence but asked a different question. "What does he want in return?"

"I'm not privy to the negotiations. My guess is he wants to protect himself in the event Germany is united and the communist government and the Stasi are disbanded. Maybe he's about to defect."

"Why would the intelligence people want to involve a private person in espionage matters?" There, he had asked the question in a way that his boss wouldn't take personally.

"Well, they really don't, of course. It seems this Stasi informant insists on his terms regarding when, where and to whom he is willing to pass these papers."

"I don't follow how that relates to me."

"The West Germans apparently have some information that leads them to believe you're the ideal person to keep an eye on the receiver of these documents."

"I still don't get it." Irritation crept into Rolf's voice. "Why do they need an American lawyer to watch over the transfer of files?"

Stein was patient. "I understand your frustration. It sounds crazy, I know. It'll make more sense once you know the details."

"And when will that be?"

"A Mr. Schmidt will contact you at your Stuttgart hotel."

"And who am I supposed to be watching?"

"Schmidt will tell you that."

"I don't suppose you know what's in the Stasi documents."

"No, and that's what you need to focus on. My client needs to know and your job is to find out."

"How do you expect me to accomplish that?"

"You'll use those exceptional skills a partner would have."

"Does this Schmidt know that I'll be looking at these papers?"

"No. As far as he's concerned, you're just making sure the recipient delivers the documents to him. There's no need to tell him otherwise. Follow his instructions, but at some point you'll need to figure out a way to learn what these documents contain—even make copies." Stein's eyes bored into him. "But even more important, you must ensure the safety of the receiver."

"Why is your client interested in that?"

"That's confidential. And Schmidt is not to know that you're keeping a watchful eye on more than the documents."

Rolf put up his hand. "Mr. Stein, do you have any idea how ruthless the Stasi is? Why would I want to risk my life playing spy games in Communist Germany? I'd rather cut my partnership teeth on a thorny legal assignment."

Stein looked straight at him. "I'm offering you a partnership three years early. That's worth taking a risk, wouldn't you agree?"

Rolf shifted in his chair. "I'll think about it."

"I must have your answer now." Stein's tone softened. "Look, I know you're under some financial pressure. Who wouldn't be after a divorce? When that plane takes off for Frankfurt this evening with you on board, there'll be a hefty advance on your partnership earnings deposited in your bank account."

Rolf studied the ceiling. He needed to think, but there was no time. He stared at Stein. If he was going to be bought, he might as well find out the price. "How much?"

"50,000 is a nice round number."

"Okay, but not as an advance."

Stein studied him, the firm set of his chin spelled no. Then, a smile warmed his eyes. "You're a tough negotiator. I appreciate that. Here is what I will do for you. If you perform as I expect you to, the money is yours outright. If you don't, you pay it back."

Rolf realized he had Stein's final offer. He nodded. "Fair enough."

"Good." Stein motioned for Rolf to sit. "With that settled, I need to give you some ground rules. You are to report directly to me and to no one else in the firm. I want to be informed of all developments immediately, day or night, at one of these numbers." He produced a card out of his coat pocket and handed it to Rolf. "Memorize these. Use the first number during office hours; at other times, the second. And call me every day, even if you have nothing in particular to report."

"How do I know what to report, when I don't have any idea what I'm supposed to be doing?" Rolf protested.

"You'll know."

Stein clearly meant to discourage Rolf from asking further questions. Rolf probed nevertheless. "What client name do I use for keeping track of my billable hours?"

Stein's face was stony. "Send your hours to me and I'll take care of it." He rose. "Well, you'd better be going. Mildred has made the necessary arrangements." He extended his right hand across the desk. "Good luck."

During their handshake he added in a low voice, "Rolf, you're clear about your mission then. Keep the receiver safe and find out what's in these papers—every last detail. I don't care how you accomplish that. Just make sure you do."

"Yes, sir." Rolf felt an enormous weight descend on him. He retreated toward the door, each step seeming more like a hike in wet sand than a walk on soft carpeting. Halfway to the door he turned. "How long will I be over there?"

Stein looked amused. "No telling. Be sure you pack more than casual clothes, perhaps something suitable for attending the opera. You like opera, don't you, Rolf?"

Chapter Three

Colonel Heinz Dobnik leaned against his fourth-floor window, observing the Friday evening exodus of the workforce from the Stasi headquarters in East Berlin. The figures below huddled against a stiff November wind that whipped through Normannenstraße. Dobnik remembered with a touch of cynicism that he now worked for the Office of National Security, not the Stasi.

In the face of mass demonstrations—until a few weeks ago unimaginable in this totalitarian state—the East German government desperately clung to power. Last Friday, eight days after opening the Wall, the parliament had changed the name of the Stasi, the most feared and hated state institution, to Office for National Security, and dismissed Erich Mielke, head of the Stasi for thirty-two years, in the hope that these cosmetic changes would ward off the citizens' fury.

The public was not so easily duped, however, and its demands grew bolder by the day. With the Communist Party distancing itself from the Stasi, Mielke had tried in vain to stem the wave of demoralization sweeping the agency staff. Mielke's successor, ever mindful of the unstable political environment, ordered the field offices to destroy mountains of documents containing information gathered through tapped phone lines and intercepted mail.

"Do you need anything else before I leave, Herr Oberst?"

Colonel Dobnik turned and looked at his secretary with a weary expression. "No thanks, Frau Ammer. Have a good weekend."

"Good night."

Dobnik nodded an absent-minded goodbye, his thoughts already having returned to the plan. He went over it in his mind once again, wondering if he'd overlooked anything. The tiniest mistake could negate months of planning, raise suspicion among the West Germans, and expose him as a traitor. He did not want to take a bullet to the back of the head like the two Stasi officers and the navy military intelligence captain who had recently been caught attempting to make contact with the West.

With darkness setting in, his reflection in the window supplanted the view of the street below. He did not like what he saw: a short, stubby figure, bloated face, heavy pouches, double chin, and a receding hairline. He looked a decade older than his forty-four years. Years of being a workaholic had taken their toll, not only on his body, but on his marriage as well. Of course, in light of the precarious nature of his current undertaking, he considered himself fortunate to be free of family responsibilities.

The heels of his shoes clicked on the parquet floor, following a habitual path between desk and window. The cleaning crew could not seem to restore the dulled wood in this section to match the polish of the remainder of the floor. Dobnik had started the pacing a few years ago when he'd discovered East Germany was harboring and training terrorists. Mere hard work had turned into an obsession as he tried to find ways to put an end to his country's coddling of terrorists. Yet how could he expect to effect policy changes in a political system that did not tolerate dissent?

Dobnik stopped in front of his desk and ran his fingers through his thinning hair. He wondered why he'd been picked for this project, ostensibly the brainchild of Brigadier General Holger Frantz, the head of counterintelligence. Dobnik recalled how stunned he was by the brigadier general's remarks when summoned to his office that humid afternoon last September.

"Colonel, you're one of our brightest officers, so what I'm about to tell you will not come as a surprise."

Dobnik didn't trust compliments from superiors. They were often followed by a "but" leading to unpleasant consequences. Since he didn't know how to respond, he didn't.

"For some time now we've been keeping an eye on the situation in the Soviet Union. Unfortunately, glasnost and perestroika are not mere slogans. Gorbachev seems to mean what he says."

Dobnik held the general's gaze. He too had been following the clues pointing to the decline of communism. When Mikhail Gorbachev intimated that the Soviet Union would no longer use its military power to prop up the totalitarian East German regime, Dobnik surmised that the days of the German Democratic Republic were numbered. But he would never have dared to express this sentiment to anyone.

The general continued, "We cannot afford to ignore the possibility that our government may fall or, at the very least, have to make radical changes."

Dobnik could hardly believe the general would speak about a subject considered taboo in East Germany. Dobnik glanced around the room. Was someone listening, waiting for him to give himself away? He kept his mouth shut.

Frantz rose from his desk chair and approached Dobnik who remained seated and waited for the general, towering over him, to speak.

"There is already talk of uniting the two Germanys." Dobnik heard incredulity and contempt in the general's voice.

Returning to his chair, Frantz slammed his fist on the desk top. "We cannot let that happen! Do you understand?"

"Yes, sir." Dobnik hoped his response sounded sufficiently emphatic.

Frantz lowered his hefty frame into the chair. Even sitting down, he presented an imposing figure. Dobnik was struck by the contrast between the general's heavy, dark horn-rimmed glasses and his shiny bald head.

"Colonel, you're going to help us stop this nonsense. There'll be no unification."

Dobnik's heart sank. Whatever Frantz had in mind, it could ruin the personal plans Dobnik had been preparing for months.

"You are to pass information to West German intelligence."

"I am to do what?"

The general appeared to relish his shock. "You'll give them secrets we want them to have."

"Disinformation?"

"Exactly. But first, we have to make sure they trust you." Frantz's demeanor turned pensive. "You'll give them good information at first. Earn their confidence and whet their appetite for what you bring when you 'defect.' "

Dobnik squirmed in his seat.

"Before I go into details, I need to make sure you understand one thing. There are only three who know about this, General Mielke, you and I. As you know, we have a few spies embedded in the West, and we have to operate under the assumption that they may have infiltrated us as well. So, you cannot talk to anybody about this. You are to make all the arrangements yourself. Not even your secretary is to know. Is that clear?"

"Understood."

The general drew an envelope from the center drawer and tossed it across the desk. "Here are your travel papers. You're on a morning flight to Trieste. I have you booked on a return flight the next day."

"I'm going to Italy?"

"Yes. To be credible, you'll have to initiate contact from outside East Germany. The West Germans surely know about our tapped telephone lines."

"What if it takes me longer to establish contact?"

Frantz stared at him. "The agent I want you to contact is Dieter Schmidt. I know he'll be at his headquarters during the next few days. But if you have trouble reaching him, call me."

On his way home to pack, Dobnik thought about how certain the general had sounded when he talked about the West German agent's whereabouts. The information must have come from a Stasi mole inside the Federal Intelligence Service. That meant Frantz might learn of any deal Dobnik tried to make with the West German spy agency.

Sleep deprived, Dobnik felt ill at ease when the airplane lifted off Berlin-Schönefeld's runway the next morning, a feeling that stayed with him for the duration of the flight. He could have blamed the bumpy ride, but he knew better.

While his taxi driver fought the downtown Trieste traffic, Dobnik thought about the kind of low-budget hotel Frantz likely had reserved. He could hardly believe his eyes when he saw the lobby of Hotel Lombardi. Its dark wood-paneled walls and salmon-colored granite countertops spoke of luxury, almost opulence. He unpacked his carry-on to a growling stomach, reminding him he had not eaten lunch. Yet he wouldn't find a restaurant open for dinner at a quarter to five. He hadn't planned on contacting Schmidt until the next morning but the thought popped into his head that he might still be able to reach him before closing hours.

Dobnik picked up the phone next to the bed only to put it back on its cradle. Frantz's arrangements for this fancy hotel might well include bugging his room and the phone. His room key dropped off, he crossed the hotel lobby, bypassing the phone booths off to the side. He joined the bustling crowd on the sidewalk. The rich display of wares in the shop windows caught his eye. Nothing like it could be found in all of East Berlin unless you were a party functionary living in Wandlitz.

Short on time, he quickened his pace and soon found what he was looking for: a hotel with private phone booths in the lobby. He had the operator call the number for the West German Federal Intelligence Service, known as the "BND," in the small Bavarian town of Pullach near Munich. When he heard a female voice answer "Bundesnachrichtendienst," he asked for Dieter Schmidt. By all accounts—and the Stasi had volumes of information on its sister spy agencies in West Germany—long-time BND agent, Dieter Schmidt, conscientious rather than brilliant, would suit their purposes.

"Who may I tell him is calling?"

Dobnik hesitated. "Tell him I have the information he's been looking for."

Static filled the line. He thought about what else he could say to persuade her to put him through, when she said, "Hold, please."

After listening to canned music for what seemed several minutes, Dobnik expected the female voice to inform him that Schmidt was not available. Just when he concluded that his teaser hadn't been explicit enough, a husky male voice asked, "What information do you have?"

"Herr Schmidt?"

"Yes. And who are you?"

Dobnik ignored the question. "I can provide files on several subjects of interest to you."

"Such as?"

"Where you can find the terrorists you've been looking for."

Schmidt's sharp intake of breath sounded over the line. After a second, he asked, "RAF?"

"Yes."

"And how would you know that?"

"I have copies of files that show where they trained and what they're planning."

The long pause told him Schmidt was trying to assimilate the information. Then his voice came over the line again. "Stasi files?"

Dobnik was impressed. Perhaps the Stasi analysts had underestimated Schmidt's capabilities.

"Yes," Dobnik responded.

"How would you have access to those?"

"I work there."

"Give me some proof of that."

"The proof will be in the first drop."

Another long pause. Would Schmidt bite?

"What do you want?"

Dobnik responded without hesitation. "I want to relocate. Bavaria would be nice with a few amenities we can discuss later. And immunity."

"Are you ready to relocate now?"

"Not for a few weeks. What about the immunity?"

"I'd have to see what you've got first." Schmidt's voice was firm.

Dobnik thought for a moment. "Okay. I'll set up an initial drop. I'll call you with the details."

"Don't wait too long. The communist regime's days are numbered."

Dobnik took a deep breath. When his annoyance at Schmidt's dig had passed, he responded with an even voice, "I wouldn't be so sure."

"How soon can you make the drop?" Schmidt pressed.

"Soon," Dobnik replied.

Apparently sensing that Dobnik was about to hang up, Schmidt said, "Wait. Call me at this number."

Dobnik fumbled for a pen. He wrote the number on a page of the phone book spread out before him. "Got it." Dobnik cut the connection and tore off the corner of the page containing his scribbles. Entering East Germany with the piece of paper was out of the question. He'd have no trouble memorizing the five-digit phone number and the four-digit area code for Pullach.

His mission accomplished, Dobnik treated himself to a sumptuous Italian dinner of several courses—cover, he told himself, rubbing his stomach. Afterwards he strolled through Trieste, digesting his meal. He found a bench on the promenade from which he could observe the busy port while licking the flavorful raspberry gelato he had bought from a street vendor and enjoying the late summer sun. Every time his thoughts turned to the problem of setting up the drop, he suppressed them. The planning could await his return to East Berlin. He would not let it spoil the rest of his visit.

The briny breeze, the cries of the sea gulls as they dove between the masts of fishing trawlers and sailboats dancing on the oily water, and the vitality of the Italian people fascinated him to such a degree that he lost track of time. When he noticed the shadow from the bench stretched across the path he stood, having soaked up as much atmosphere as he could. Returning to his hotel, he reflected on a successful and most agreeable day.

Back in East Berlin, Dobnik began planning in earnest. The more he thought about the details, the more his concern grew. He couldn't put his finger on what exactly bothered him. Perhaps it was the way Frantz had presented the idea. His was a high-risk mission. Exposure as a fraud by the West Germans and possible betrayal by his own agency were real possibilities.

Smuggling the documents into West Berlin was too risky. If Frantz had it in for him, he would have him arrested as a double agent. He had to make the drop in East Berlin. But who could he use as recipient? Certainly no BND agents. He had no reason to trust Schmidt or whomever he might send. And the chances of a Western spy slipping into East Berlin, unnoticed by the Stasi, were remote. He had to find someone else. But who?

Weeks of racking his brain failed to produce the name of a suitable recipient. Then in the late afternoon of another day wasted in a fruitless search, Dobnik found himself reminiscing about his college days, mostly spent drinking with Horst Kreuzer and his leftist friends. No sooner had he thought of Horst than Sylvia Mazzoni's image popped into his head. She probably didn't even remember him. After all, he'd been just one of the countless drinking buddies of her boyfriend, Horst, during their wild student years in West Berlin. She wouldn't have had any reason to suspect that he and Horst shared more than a taste for *Berliner Weiße* beer—a political view considered radical left wing in the eyes of capitalist West Germany. They had chosen different paths to act on their political convictions. Kreuzer joined the Red Army Faction to fight West German society through terrorism. He, on the other hand, defected to East Germany and became a Stasi agent.

What had ever become of Sylvia? Since she'd been the lover of an RAF terrorist, the Stasi would have kept a file on her. With that thought Dobnik bolted from his office. The file room clerk took less than a minute to locate her file. Dobnik carried the folder to his office and closed the door. He flipped open the file cover. The document filed on top answered his question of what had become of her: an aspiring opera diva with a key performance scheduled at the Stuttgart Opera.

Dobnik leaned back in his chair and studied the ceiling. Could she be the intermediary he'd been looking for? He rifled through the rest of the file, which tracked her and Horst's activities since their student days in the seventies. He smiled. She'd be the perfect carrier. An idea began to form how to get her to East Berlin. If she resisted, her file provided him with ample ammunition to coerce her. He sold Frantz on the idea of using Sylvia as an intermediary by embellishing her left-wing associations at the Free University Berlin, leaving the brigadier general with the erroneous impression that Sylvia was in on her boyfriend's terrorist activities. Dobnik needed her and was willing to do whatever it took to ensure her participation.

A Communist Party convention held in Belgrade in mid-October provided Dobnik the cover he needed for contacting Schmidt with the arrangements for the first document drop. Frantz approved the travel. Eager to phone Schmidt, Dobnik had to endure the usual first night social hour and dinner. He could not afford to miss it, lest he arouse suspicion. On the second day of the convention, he skipped the afternoon session and walked to a nearby downtown hotel. He recalled from a previous stay that it had phones in the lobby.

From memory, he asked the operator to dial Schmidt's number. To his surprise, a female voice answered, "Wiedenmaier."

Startled, Dobnik asked, "Is this Dieter Schmidt's number?"

"It is, but he is out of the office. May I take a message?"

Dobnik didn't know what to say.

"Hello, are you there?"

"Uh . . . yes. When do you expect him back?"

"In the morning."

"Tell him I'll call him tomorrow afternoon with news about relocation."

He slammed down the phone. Another day wasted. Instead of returning to the convention, he walked a few blocks until he found another hotel with lobby phones for tomorrow's call.

Wednesday afternoon, Schmidt answered on the first ring.

Dobnik got right to the point. "I've got everything arranged for the first drop. It'll be on Monday, November 27 at the East Berlin Opera."

"At the Opera?"

Dobnik relished Schmidt's amazement and could hardly wait to hear his reaction to what he'd tell him next. "At the opera and to an opera singer."

After a considerable pause, Schmidt said, "You are serious."

"The singer's name is Sylvia Mazzoni." Dobnik waited. The long silence told him he'd delivered a shocker. He continued, "You remember her. Horst Kreuzer's girl. You got to her and she turned him in."

"She paid her debt twelve years ago." Schmidt sounded angry. "Even if I wanted to go along with this ludicrous scheme of yours, how in the hell do you suppose I could persuade her to play spy in East Berlin?"

Dobnik had anticipated the objection. "Your outfit has never shied away from using appropriate methods of persuasion. She's on the brink of a promising opera career. If her past association with an RAF terrorist became known . . ." He didn't finish, letting Schmidt draw his own conclusion.

"Blackmail?" Schmidt's voice held a tinge of disgust. "But I still don't see how we get her into East Berlin."

"Leave that to me. You just make sure she knows what happens to her career if she fails to cooperate."

"Look, this is insane. Use a professional instead of an amateur."

"It may be crazy, but that's the only way you're going to see what I've got."

After another silence, Dobnik heard a faint sigh. "All right, have it your way. I'll work on things at this end. Since you are an opera buff, use the code name 'Mozart' when making contact."

"I'll be in touch." Dobnik hung up and left the hotel.

Colonel Dobnik hadn't liked Brigadier General Frantz's scheme back in September, and now on this Friday evening in November, again running his fingers through his hair as he stood in the center of his office, he cared for it even less. He didn't trust the general's motives. Perhaps the West Germans were not the only ones being set up. He'd been careful to copy files after hours. But the high number of copies on the machine's counter could have given him away. His secretary could well be an informant for Frantz.

Something else bothered him. Was this an official operation, sanctioned by Mielke? If so, had his successor been properly briefed? He had to find out whether they had authorized this mission or whether Frantz was pursuing an agenda of his own.

Reflecting on the relative ease with which he'd been able to plan the document drop for next week, Dobnik locked his desk, took his heavy overcoat off its hook on the back of the door and left his office. As he waited for the elevator, he thought about Sylvia's performance in Stuttgart tomorrow evening. Hopefully, she'd sing well enough not to raise any questions about the engagement he'd arranged for her at East Berlin's Staatsoper Unter den Linden.

Dobnik had no qualms about involving an unsuspecting Sylvia. Nor would he hesitate to use her in case he had to run.

Peter Bernhardt

Chapter Four

Sylvia emerged from Schlossgarten Park and headed toward the shops. Her senses magnified, she was determined not to miss the slightest movement or sound. Heightened perception created the sensation of moving in slow motion, while in fact she had broken into a race walker's stride. Her mind darted in many directions. Did the Red Army Faction still seek revenge for her betrayal twelve years ago? What had brought Federal Intelligence Agent Schmidt onto the scene? Was she under his agency's surveillance and had he shot the terrorist?

Sylvia touched her throat and swallowed. Her voice seemed to have escaped the stranglehold without any serious damage. She thought of tomorrow night's performance. Her voice would be there for her—it had to be. Approaching her mid thirties, she'd not likely get another chance to break through. Years of music school by day, waiting tables at night, singing at weddings and funerals—her hard work had to pay off tomorrow. Nor did she dare disappoint her mother, without whose monthly checks and unfailing emotional support she'd never have gotten this far.

Peter Bernhardt

Chapter Four

Sylvia emerged from Schlossgarten Park and headed toward the shops. Her senses magnified, she was determined not to miss the slightest movement or sound. Heightened perception created the sensation of moving in slow motion, while in fact she had broken into a race walker's stride. Her mind darted in many directions. Did the Red Army Faction still seek revenge for her betrayal twelve years ago? What had brought Federal Intelligence Agent Schmidt onto the scene? Was she under his agency's surveillance and had he shot the terrorist?

Sylvia touched her throat and swallowed. Her voice seemed to have escaped the stranglehold without any serious damage. She thought of tomorrow night's performance. Her voice would be there for her—it had to be. Approaching her mid thirties, she'd not likely get another chance to break through. Years of music school by day, waiting tables at night, singing at weddings and funerals—her hard work had to pay off tomorrow. Nor did she dare disappoint her mother, without whose monthly checks and unfailing emotional support she'd never have gotten this far.

She passed the streetčar stop and hurried toward the taxi stand alongside the park, shielding her blood-stained sleeve with the bag and umbrella. Her trembling fingers clutched the door handle of the Mercedes at the front of the line. She managed to open the door and slid into the rear seat, careful to keep her bloody arm from the shiny leather upholstery.

"Hotel Schwäbischer Hof, bitte."

The heavy-set man in the driver's seat turned around until his beer belly pressed into the steering wheel, his face straining from the effort. He gave her a quick look, nodded, started the engine, and sped away from the curb. By the time Sylvia turned to look out the window, Upper Schlossgarten Park had vanished like a bad dream. But thoughts of the attack had not. Grotesque images of the knife-wielding assailant, his stranglehold, his bloody corpse flashed unbidden into her mind. She couldn't shake them. They haunted her for the duration of the ten-minute taxi ride.

Schwäbischer Hof, a traditional German hotel, stretched along the east side of the lower part of Schlossgarten Park. As the cab drew up to the entrance, Sylvia pressed a ten-mark note into the driver's hand, stepped out and managed to slip inside the revolving glass door before the doorman noticed her. Now, if she could just make it through the lobby and collect her room key without questions.

Sylvia made eye contact with the young woman behind the teak-wood counter and, in a voice designed to discourage chitchat, said, "Room 785, please."

She snatched the key, turned, and headed for the bank of elevators across the lobby. Just when she thought she'd gotten away unnoticed, she heard a baritone voice. "Frau Mazzoni, what have you done to your arm?"

Sylvia cursed under her breath, wondering what the manager was still doing at the hotel at this hour. She said through a forced smile, "Oh, it's nothing, Herr Grell. Just a slight mishap."

"Would you like to have a doctor look at it?"

"No."

But her brusqueness did not deter the balding man in his fifties. "The staff nurse is still here. I'll have her come up to your room."

Realizing that protest might draw suspicion, she tried to sound gracious. "Thank you, Herr Grell."

He nodded and returned to the front desk.

In her room, Sylvia cautiously removed the blood-covered sweatshirt and undressed for a quick shower. Her tight grip in the taxi must have staunched the bleeding, and the water's spray washed most of the blood from her arm. The wound was not serious, and the blood had begun to clot. She fought her fears and tentatively sang a few scales. Relief poured through her. Miraculously, her voice seemed unscathed by the ordeal.

Minutes later, wrapped in the terrycloth hotel bathrobe, Sylvia answered a knock on her door. A plump woman wearing a white nurse's uniform and flat-heeled shoes gave her an appraising look before entering.

"Let's take a look at that injury of yours." It was not a request.

Sylvia bared her left arm.

The nurse inspected the wound, tugging at the surrounding skin from several directions. "Ah," she exhaled. "You're lucky. Not too deep. Knife?"

Sylvia nodded.

"What kind?"

"Kitchen."

"Dirty?"

"My friend had been slicing cucumbers when she accidentally turned into me."

Sylvia thought she caught a look of disbelief on the woman's face but, without a word, the nurse reached into her bag, pulled out a bottle of iodine, and applied a few drops to the cut with a cotton swab. It reminded Sylvia how, as a child, she used to scream when her mother daubed it on her many scuffs and scrapes.

The nurse covered the wound with a cotton bandage. "Keep this on overnight," she instructed. "I will look at it again tomorrow." Her expression did not invite objection.

"Thank you."

"And stay out of your friend's kitchen," the nurse muttered and disappeared.

Chapter Five

"Would you care for a cocktail, sir?"

The question caught Rolf Keller off guard. He didn't usually fly first class. The inviting manner of the stewardess seemed to admit only one answer, and he almost blurted out a yes. It had been a hell of a day and scotch and water sure sounded tempting. He could already feel the burning sensation traveling from his mouth down his throat, hitting his stomach, spreading relaxation into every cell. Trouble was, he knew only too well what would follow, and he could not afford that.

He forced "No, thank you" from his lips, hoping his voice didn't signal regret. "Just water, please."

The flight attendant nodded and turned toward the window passenger. His striped tie hung loose at the open collar of a starched white shirt—his concession to the rigors of the upcoming eight-hour flight. Rolf guessed late forties, either a business executive or perhaps even a fellow member of the bar. Rolf enjoyed being comfortable in his T-shirt and jeans. Why let his wardrobe advertise that he was a lawyer, a profession the public held on a level with politicians and used-car salesmen?

The Boeing 767's steep ascent into the evening sky above Dulles Airport pressed Rolf into the seat. He tried to relax, but there were too many unanswered questions for his mind to cease churning. To begin with, why would the firm that preached flying tourist class book him to Germany in first? Why had he agreed to take on this crazy assignment? Rolf reclined his seat and closed his eyes, but he still could see Harry Stein's inscrutable smile when telling him to dress for the opera.

♬ ♬ ♬

The faint light of dawn filtered into the first-class cabin through partially drawn window shades. Passengers began to stir. Rolf awakened from a brief slumber and rubbed his tired eyes. While three or four hours of napping didn't amount to a good night's sleep, he hoped it would be sufficient to hold jet lag at bay or at least to minimize its effects. From his prior travels he knew sunrise over the ocean meant breakfast would soon be served, with the descent to Frankfurt to follow in a couple of hours.

The flight attendant made her way down the aisle handing out care packages, which to Rolf's surprise contained toothbrush and toothpaste. Being unfamiliar with the amenities of first class, he'd brought his own. When he returned from the restroom, his neighbor, a large man with coarse features, greeted him with a friendly, "Good morning. Looks like you've managed to get some decent rest."

Rolf settled into his seat. "Yes, not bad. How about you?"

"No, I can't sleep a wink on these flights. I'm envious." The man stretched out his hand. "I'm Kent Ferguson."

"Rolf Keller, pleased to meet you." During their handshake Rolf noted that yesterday's striped tie was gone—no doubt a casualty of a long night of chasing elusive sleep, as was the formerly crisp white shirt, now wrinkled and partially untucked over a protruding belly.

A flight attendant inserted snap-on tables into the armrests of their seats. After spreading white cloths over the tables, she took their coffee orders and left. The stranger turned a fleshy face, accentuated by thick lips and a pug nose, toward Rolf. "What takes you to Germany?" His eyebrows rose quizzically into a large forehead made more prominent by a receding dark hairline.

"Business." Rolf expected the usual follow-up questions quizzing him about his occupation.

But Ferguson nodded. "Yes, November is not the season for holiday travel in Germany, is it?"

The stewardess returned carrying trays, which she placed on their tables. The steaming coffee, scrambled eggs, ham, croissants and orange juice looked inviting. As Rolf dug in, his seat mate mumbled between bites, "I gather you're German."

"I didn't think I had an accent."

"If you do, I didn't catch it. It's the way you use your knife and fork. Unlike us hand-switching Americans, you Continental Europeans keep your fork in the left and knife in the right hand while eating." As if to demonstrate his point, he cut a piece of ham, put down his knife, and moving the fork from his left to right hand, scooped up the ham and scrambled eggs.

"I suppose that's one habit I've kept." European table manners felt so natural that Rolf couldn't imagine eating any other way. "You're very observant," he complimented Ferguson, wondering what his profession might be.

"Well, I've traveled a fair amount in Europe. And I remember the old movie with Jimmy Stewart, *The FBI Story*, where the spy-in-training is taught to differentiate the table manners of Americans, Continental Europeans and the British."

The chitchat ceased while they finished their breakfast. Afterward, Ferguson asked. "What part of Germany are you from?"

Rolf pushed back his tray. "Stuttgart. Do you know it?"

"All I know is that it's in southwest Germany near the Black Forest and that Porsche and Mercedes are made there."

"Yes. It's the birthplace of the modern automobile. Gottlieb Daimler started kind of a handyman tradition among the local Swabians when he put together the world's first motor car with an internal combustion engine. You can still see it in the Daimler-Benz Museum." Enthusiasm permeated Rolf's voice. "But what I love most about Stuttgart is the city's atmosphere."

Ferguson raised his eyebrows. "What do you mean?"

"The way it stretches across valleys and hills, the old houses and castles, the forests and vineyards—such a large city but with a small town's ambiance." Describing his former hometown gave Rolf a peculiar sense of pride. "You know it is almost as hilly as San Francisco."

Ferguson handed his tray to the flight attendant while addressing Rolf. "Sounds like a nice place. Why did you leave?"

Rolf became pensive, not sure how much detail to tell the stranger. His words were measured. "Oh, after I finished university, I wanted to experience a different culture. I've been fascinated with the U.S. ever since I can remember. When I had the chance to get a visa, I jumped at it."

"So you still have family in Stuttgart?"

Rolf thought he detected more than a casual interest in Ferguson's tone. "No one I've kept up with."

He hoped his brief response would discourage further questions about his kin. Rolf didn't care to mention his deceased parents. Nor was it any of the stranger's business that there had been more behind his decision to emigrate than an adventuresome nature. He was not proud of the way he had left in the face of Sylvia's pleas for help. He had tried to drown the gnawing guilt, and for a while alcohol had helped. But no matter how much he drank, the feelings returned when the booze wore off. Then AA took away his excuses for getting drunk, forcing him to face his remorse and deal with it in some other way.

He had been apprehensive about returning to Germany. Now, for the first time, he considered the possibility that this assignment might offer him a unique opportunity to make peace with his past. He knew he couldn't undo the pain he'd caused, but perhaps there was a way to make amends in some form.

Ferguson's voice jolted Rolf back to the present. "What kind of business are you in?"

"Uh . . . I'm a lawyer."

Ferguson's chin dropped. "Oh, really? I never would have guessed."

Rolf knew the reaction was not just based on his informal dress. When people learned of his profession, they often expressed disbelief. Some even told him he seemed too nice to be a lawyer.

Now that the stranger had broached the subject, Rolf felt free to ask, "What about you, what do you do for a living?"

"I'm a foreign correspondent covering Europe for several news organizations. That's how I get to travel all over." Evidently noticing Rolf's surprise, he added. "Granted, I don't dress like a journalist. But you aren't exactly wearing a lawyer's uniform either."

"No, I hate to wear a suit and tie."

They chuckled as their eyes met.

Rolf recovered first. "What do you report about?"

"As you know, German reunification is the hot topic. Right now I'm on the lookout for human interest stories, how people's lives might be affected, both East and West Germans."

"And what are you finding? Is everyone excited about the prospect of living in one Germany again after more than forty years?"

"I'd say most are, but not everybody. Some in the East are worried about losing their jobs, and West Germans are concerned about how high unemployment and reconstruction costs will affect their economy. So, there is a fair amount of opposition to reunification."

"It's always about the old pocketbook, isn't it?"

Ferguson nodded. "Not only that. Some folks are quite nervous about what the Stasi files might hold. They'd just as soon spoil Chancellor Kohl's bid to reunite Germany. Failing that, they wouldn't mind a bit if there weren't too many Stasi documents left by the time reunification comes around."

The mention of the Stasi files caught Rolf off guard. He studied the stranger for any sign that this was more than a chance encounter. However, remembering the numerous news reports during the last few weeks speculating whether and when Stasi documents might be made public, Rolf relaxed. Of course, as a journalist Ferguson would be right on top of that story.

Trying his best to sound nonchalant, Rolf probed, "Making Stasi files public likely would blow the cover of many an East German spy."

Ferguson looked around, and then spoke in a hushed tone, "Not only spies, but terrorists and other collaborators with the communist government. No one knows for sure how many there are, but the word is that the infiltration of West German society is widespread."

Rolf puckered his lips into a silent whistle. "Looks like you're well informed."

"I do have my sources." He exuded confidence without sounding arrogant. "I'd say Chancellor Kohl has a tough job selling the idea of a united Germany to the French and British. They are quite nervous at the prospect of their

World War II enemy becoming powerful once again, both politically and economically. I hear Margaret Thatcher is dead set against it, and Gorbachev is lukewarm on the idea as well."

After unbuckling his seatbelt, Ferguson strained to twist his massive body, which filled most of the first-class seat. He managed to reach into the back pocket of his slacks, pull out his wallet, and hand Rolf a card. "If you come upon anything newsworthy, give me a call."

Though he couldn't imagine that he would run across anything of interest to a journalist, Rolf glanced at the card before sticking it in his jeans pocket. "You're in Berlin."

"I just moved there, since that's where the action is these days. How about you? Where is your legal business taking you?"

Rolf thought it a stretch to call his mission legal business. "Stuttgart, for starters," he disclosed. Ferguson probably thought him secretive, but in fact Rolf didn't know where his assignment would carry him.

Apparently not put off by Rolf's reticence, Ferguson remarked. "Sounds like you may be over here for a while."

"I really don't know."

Although that was the truth, Rolf intended his reply to signal that no more information would be forthcoming.

Ferguson obliged and closed down their chat. "Well, whatever your undertaking may be, I wish you good luck."

"Thanks. I'll need it." Rolf surprised himself with the fervor in his voice, and he began to brood over just how much luck it would take to successfully complete this strange assignment. His apprehension had not abated by the time the pilot announced the Boeing 767's approach to the Rhein Main Airport.

Chapter Six

Between the closing elevator doors Sylvia spotted to her horror Horst Kreuzer. But hadn't he died in prison? He sprinted toward her across the hotel lobby. Their eyes locked. His stare of recognition paralyzed her. He lunged forward but too late to trigger the sensor. In the split second before the doors clicked shut, she saw him spin and race for the stairs.

The elevator began its sluggish climb. Could he beat her to the seventh floor? She held her breath, hoping that this would somehow propel the ancient contraption faster. The side panel light labored from numeral to numeral. At last, the motor whined and slowed, the number seven lit up, and the car jerked to a stop. She restrained herself from pulling on the retreating steel doors, fearing she might cause a jam. Keys in hand, Sylvia squeezed through the opening and peered up and down the corridor. Not detecting any movement, she turned right and ran past the door leading to the stairwell. Her room was the third on the left.

As she turned the key, she heard the stairwell door smash against the wall. Sylvia charged into her room, slammed the door, and threw the deadbolt. In an instant, he was pounding on her door. She shut out the ever louder thumps. The door seemed to buckle. Terror filled her. There was no place to go.

Sylvia awakened with a start, her skin bathed in sweat. For a moment she didn't know where she was. Then her eyes fell on the nightstand clock. It read 11:37. Before she could sink back onto the mattress, a noise at the door jolted her. Someone actually was knocking. Still woozy, she lowered her feet to the carpet, snatched the hotel bathrobe from the closet to cover her nightgown, and shuffled over to the peephole.

When she recognized Dieter Schmidt, she unlatched the chain and pressed down on the handle. The stocky man in his forties leaned into the door, charged across the threshold, and shut the door behind him.

He put up his hand. "Sorry to bother you this late. I was hoping you'd still be up."

Protest caught in her throat. When she switched on the light, she saw rain droplets glistening on his moustache and fine brown hair. He shed his gray raincoat and folded it over his arm. His rumpled shirt and stubbly chin attested to a long day.

"Are you okay?"

Sylvia touched her upper arm. "A flesh wound. I guess I should thank you for shooting him. You saved my life."

"I didn't shoot him."

"What?" She glared at him. "Then what were you doing there?

"I was trying to catch you after the rehearsal to talk to you about Berlin."

"But if you didn't kill him, who did?"

He ran his fingers through his wind-tousled hair in a feeble attempt to untangle it. "We're working on it, but it's better you don't know about that. It's who he was that matters. You called him a Red Army Faction terrorist."

"He spent a lot of time with Horst Kreuzer." Her cheeks flushed at the thought of her former lover.

"Do you think he wanted to settle a score?" Schmidt looked worried.

"I expected them to come after me. But why would they wait twelve years?"

He paced back and forth on the well-worn carpet. "If it's not for revenge, then it's possible the terrorists have found out about your mission."

She clutched her bathrobe tight, as if to fend off his chilling words. "If that's true then . . ." She gathered strength. "You're going to have to get someone else to do your bidding."

"You know we can't. It has to be you. But we are going to implement the highest security measures for this operation." Schmidt draped his coat over the high back of a chair by the window. He circled the chair and sank into its corduroy cushion.

"Does that mean you're going to be here a while? I've got a big day tomorrow and would like to go back to sleep."

"We need to talk."

She sighed. "What about?"

"Have you told anyone about our conversation last week?"

"No way." Sylvia's posture stiffened. "How many at your end know that you've pressed me into service? Have you asked them the same question?"

"You know the Stasi defector insists on dealing with you and no one else. I did what I had to do."

"And that makes it okay for you to blackmail me?"

Sylvia knew she had no option but to cooperate. When first approached by Schmidt to act as an intermediary, she had rebuffed him. "No, I don't want any part in this."

She could still hear his threat. "Seems to me someone with your past is not in any position to refuse."

Her stomach tightened. "What do you mean? I've done nothing wrong."

"You may have managed to forget your association with the Red Army Faction, but I can assure you we have not."

Rage welled up inside her. "Who are you? Who are you working for?"

"My job has to do with national security. I'm with the Federal Intelligence Service."

"If you really are in Intelligence, then you know perfectly well that I was never associated with any leftist terrorist group. Not with Baader-Meinhof and not with the RAF."

"Does the name Horst Kreuzer ring a bell?"

"He was a college friend, so what?"

"Come now, Frau Mazzoni. We both know he was an RAF member . . . and your lover."

"Since you're so well informed, you'll recall that I'm responsible for his getting caught." She tasted bile as she recalled her betrayal.

"Yes, that's why you were let off easy."

"I had no idea what Horst was mixed up in. When I learned about it, I broke it off."

Schmidt appeared as unmoved by her claim of innocence as the police had been twelve years earlier. Without acknowledging her assertion, he continued in a matter-of-fact voice. "I understand you're scheduled to sing at the Stuttgart Opera." His eyes narrowed. "We would not want to do anything to jeopardize that."

Sylvia understood. Blackmail never ended. How could she have been so naïve as to think that the bad choice she'd made at twenty-two wouldn't come back to haunt her? The police threatened to have her prosecuted as an accessory because she was the girlfriend of a terrorist. Her protestations that she knew nothing at all about Horst's activities went unheeded. So she'd tipped them off to her ex-boyfriend's lesser-known hangouts.

Now, twelve years later, she found herself bullied once more. This intelligence agent had coerced her into spying by threatening her. The management of the Stuttgart Opera would not look kindly on her past indiscretion, no matter that she viewed it as mere youthful folly. To make matters worse, the opera was 85 percent state subsidized, and the wishes of Schmidt's employer would undoubtedly be heeded. In other words, if she didn't cooperate, she could kiss her opera career goodbye, at least in Stuttgart. Sylvia slumped into the empty chair, cradling her aching arm.

Schmidt adopted a confessional tone. "There is something I haven't told you, but it's time you knew. I'm hoping the Stasi papers will provide us with clues about an assassination plot. Perhaps we can prevent the murder of yet another industrialist or government official." He hesitated in an apparent search for the right words. "We must get our hands on these documents. Germany's future may depend on it."

"Yeah, right. I bet you tell that to all your recruits."

They fell silent. Through the partially open window they heard the soft sound of falling rain, periodically interrupted by tires splashing on wet pavement below. The rain had a hypnotic, soothing effect.

Sylvia broke the silence. "I assume you have a plan as to how this document exchange is going to take place?"

There was a long pause. Schmidt shook his head as if to clear it. "That's what we need to talk about. The Stasi informant is secretive. He will make the drop while you're in East Berlin to sing at the Staatsoper. I don't know when or where. Nor do I have any specifics about the materials you're to receive."

"You have no idea who he is?"

"No. I gave him the code name 'Mozart,' since he seems to be enamored of opera."

"Do you know why he picked me?"

"No, not really. Maybe he knew you in college. Is that possible?"

Sylvia shrugged. "Horst had lots of friends, and they all liked to party. Some of them had leftist tendencies. So I wouldn't be surprised to learn that one of them crossed over to East Germany. Could be anyone." Deep in thought, she leaned back. "When were you first contacted about the Stasi documents?"

Schmidt hesitated, apparently weighing whether to answer her. At last, he said, "In September."

"And when did this Mozart first mention my name?"

Even more perplexed, Schmidt replied, "It's been a month . . . Have you appeared in East Germany before? Isn't that unusual for a singer from the West?"

She ignored his first question. "I was flabbergasted when the Stuttgart Opera Director told me that I'd been requested to cover two performances in East Berlin. I naturally assumed they wanted me because I'm singing that role here."

Sylvia's mind was racing. "There is something you haven't told me." She scanned his face for clues. "How could your informant know that . . . Oh, but of course! The arrangements for my appearance were made last month, about the time he gave you my name. *He's* the one who set up the whole thing."

Schmidt stared at her in amazement. "Not bad. An opera singer with a knack for intelligence."

"I suspect intelligence is a bit like opera. Either you have natural talent for it or you don't. Plenty of sopranos can sing the notes of Madama Butterfly's aria 'Un bel dì vedremo.' But it takes an artist to fully communicate the geisha's desperate longing for Pinkerton's return."

"Are you such an artist?" Schmidt probed.

"I'd like to think so. I hope so."

The light-hearted moment provided a welcome relief until reality set in again. Sylvia shifted forward onto her elbows, causing the table to tilt a bit. "I cringe at the thought of an East German secret agent approaching me."

"We're concerned about that too."

"You're concerned? Oh, that makes me feel a whole lot better."

Schmidt fidgeted. "There will be someone working with you, to keep an eye on things."

"Who is that?"

"You'll meet him tomorrow."

Sylvia regarded him with suspicion. "Are you sure he'll be looking after me rather than the merchandise?"

"Look, we want this transaction to go without a hitch," Schmidt said, his voice gruff. "We will do our best to make sure of that."

He stood and pulled his coat off the chair. "I've kept you up long enough. Get me your schedule for East Berlin—performances, receptions, dinners, personal errands. I need your itinerary down to the minute."

"I'll see what I can do."

Schmidt opened the door and turned. "Get some rest. Tomorrow promises to be quite a day. Gute Nacht, Frau Mazzoni."

As he stepped into the hallway, she caught a peculiar expression on his face. Climbing back into bed, she couldn't help but think that his parting comment referred to something other than her performance tomorrow evening.

Chapter Seven

Schmidt's black Mercedes climbed out of the basin in which Stuttgart nestled, ascending the Neue Weinsteige. This scenic southern route afforded breathtaking views of vineyards and the city panorama during the day and sparkling city lights at night. However, on this Friday night Schmidt was too preoccupied to take in the scenery. Instead, he focused on the rain-slick uphill curves. Vineyards gave way first to deciduous trees, then to pine forest as the road crested the hill and straightened. He could smell the fresh scent of rain-soaked pine trees through the car vents. Strobe lights on his right informed him that he was passing the Fernsehturm, "the television tower," a Stuttgart landmark.

Schmidt breathed a little easier when he spotted the autobahn entrance. As soon as he cleared the tight curve of the entry ramp, he floored the gas pedal and steered into the left lane. This time of night he could stay in the passing lane most of the way to Munich, going close to 200 kilometers an hour.

As he mulled over his conversation with Sylvia Mazzoni earlier that evening, agitation fueled his tired body, keeping him alert for the drive on the wet road surface. In his twenty years with the Federal Intelligence Service he'd done his job with pride, even when defending the Federal Republic of Germany required unorthodox methods. There was no question he'd done his share of dirty work, but he had convinced himself that the greater good of society sometimes justified employing drastic means.

Who said intelligence services should play fair? Even though Sylvia had paid long ago for her ill-chosen romance by giving up her boyfriend to the authorities, Schmidt had to use it against her once more. Otherwise he'd never get his hands on the Stasi documents.

Yet his irritation persisted. He had a bad feeling about this case. "Why in hell do we have to use a couple of amateurs?" The sound of his voice reverberated through the car's interior, drowning out for a moment the hiss of the radials hugging the wet pavement. Given Sylvia's past, he doubted she could be trusted with the documents. Had she really been unaware of her lover's terrorist connections? He had his doubts. She certainly had plenty of reasons to harbor resentments against the West German authorities. That's why he had decided to have her watched. He just hoped that American lawyer was trustworthy and would not mess things up.

Bright headlights flashed in his rearview mirror, causing him to move over into the right-hand lane. The force of water crashing against his windshield from the passing sedan startled him, demanding his complete attention until several passes of the wipers cleared his vision.

Schmidt's thoughts returned to his conundrum. Based on recent intelligence, he suspected some terrorist plan was in the offing—perhaps another in the growing number of murders of West German politicians and industrialists. Unfortunately, the data was too general to be useful. He hoped the Stasi documents would provide enough details to enable him to take countermeasures. Would the informant heed Schmidt's demand for specific information about left-wing terrorists in West Germany who'd received training in the East?

He again maneuvered into the left lane to pass a slow-moving Volkswagen van. While he eased back to the right, Schmidt wondered whether the defector could identify Stasi spies who had infiltrated West German institutions, especially its three major intelligence services.

Schmidt's mood darkened even further when he considered the checkered history of the Office for the Protection of the Constitution in Cologne, which reported to the Ministry of the Interior, and its numerous scandals providing fodder for the sensationalist press. Since its creation in 1950, five of its six presidents had resigned, were retired early or disappeared. One had absconded to East Germany, and upon his return was sentenced to a jail term. Others resigned for reasons like discovery of a Nazi past, the exposure of Chancellor Willy Brandt's top aide, Günter Guillaume, as a Stasi spy, and the defection to East Berlin of a group leader in the agency's counterespionage department.

The reflection of lights crawling up the hill from the opposite direction diverted Schmidt's attention. When the approaching truck negotiated a curve, its headlights hit Schmidt full force, blinding him. He flashed the Mercedes' lights, ready to step on the brakes. What was a truck doing on the autobahn at this hour? He tried to catch a glimpse of the driver when the vehicles passed each other. Then he caught himself and laughed, his adrenalin level subsiding. In his profession constant suspicion went with the territory.

He flicked the light switch again, watching with satisfaction the far edge of the high beam devouring the distant roadway ahead. His contentment gave way to repugnance as his thoughts returned to the West German intelligence services once more. Schmidt shook his head in disgust. No doubt the Stasi also had moles in the Military

Counterespionage Service and with his employer, the Federal Intelligence Service. The attack on Sylvia could mean that the Stasi knew about its agent's attempt to bargain secrets for immunity from prosecution in the West. Or were there others who did not want Stasi records to fall into the hands of the West Germans and who somehow had gotten wind of Sylvia's role?

He frowned while pondering the likely reasons for the collaborator's insistence on using an opera singer as a go-between. Schmidt never had liked the idea. There were far less risky ways of passing information. But the instructions were clear: the transaction would take place according to Mozart's specifications, or not at all.

These thoughts so consumed Schmidt that he almost missed his Munich exit. The dashboard clock registered one thirty. Ellen would be surprised to see him. She woke up no matter what time of night he came home. In his line of work, he couldn't always let her know when the workday would stretch into the wee hours of the morning. He smiled, thinking about how he'd teased her over the years that her boyfriend must have extrasensory perception since Schmidt could never catch him. In intelligence, trust was not easy to come by, so he was especially grateful to have plenty of it at home.

He considered, and promptly rejected, the idea of calling his boss tonight. The phone call would wait until the morning. Besides, he wasn't at all sure what to tell him. Perhaps a few hours' sleep would restore the clear thinking and energy he'd need for what promised to be a frantic Saturday.

♬ ♬ ♬

Karl Bauman put down the morning paper and pushed back his chair. He was on his third cup of coffee, and the morning sun had begun to peek out from behind the remnants of last night's rain clouds promising a sunny, if cold, Saturday. But far from being content, he stood and stepped over to the bay window surrounding the breakfast nook. Through wire-rimmed glasses his eyes swept the park-like expanse of the backyard without looking at anything in particular.

When he began to pace, he heard his wife's voice. "You're thinking about work, aren't you, Karl?"

He'd been fidgety all last evening and this morning, worrying whether something had gone wrong in Stuttgart. It was not like Schmidt to fail to check in without a good reason.

Bauman gave his wife a sheepish grin. She was on to him. They'd been married too long. He was about to change the subject when the kitchen phone rang. His wife answered and hung up. "You'll have a call in your office in a minute."

Without a word, Bauman snatched his coffee cup from the table top, and strode across the den to the far end of the house. That had to be Schmidt calling back on his secure line. He arrived at his desk in time to pick up the receiver on the first ring.

"Hallo." Even though his agency assured him the line was secure, Bauman never answered with his name.

"I'm going for some fresh air. Care to join me?"

Recognizing Schmidt's voice, Bauman replied, "See you in half an hour," and depressed the hook to cut the connection. He stared at the receiver before replacing it. Why was Schmidt being so secretive? They hadn't used their prearranged out-of-doors meeting place in a very long time. Something must be worrying him.

Thirty minutes later—after some backtracking and driving through a few yellow lights made him reasonably sure he hadn't been followed—Bauman parked his dark blue BMW at the far corner of a mostly empty lot, passing up several vacant spaces too close to Schmidt's black Mercedes.

Bauman strode along the pedestrian side of an asphalt trail featuring painted profiles of walkers and bicycles. He spotted a green felt hat above the third bench from the parking lot and upon drawing closer recognized Schmidt, sitting with legs crossed, seemingly engrossed in watching crows chasing each other across a distant empty field.

"Mind if I join you?"

Schmidt looked up. "Please do."

"Nice hat," Bauman mumbled as he lowered his hefty frame onto the bench, his long legs stretching almost to the edge of the trail.

"Well, it is Bavarian after all."

Bauman pulled his gray overcoat tight. "It's a bit chilly for outdoor get-togethers, don't you think?"

"Karl, we may have a problem at the agency. A man tried to stab Sylvia in the park after rehearsals yesterday evening. I was coming to her aid, but just before I got there, someone shot him. Sylvia recognized him as one of her RAF boyfriend's buddies."

Bauman let out a whistle. "They're trying to kill her after all these years?"

"That would seem the obvious answer." Schmidt turned to face Bauman. "Perhaps too obvious."

"What are you saying, Dieter?"

Schmidt got up and extended his gloved right palm upward. "You're right. It's a tad nippy for sitting. What do you say, shall we walk?"

Without waiting for a response, Schmidt peered in both directions prior to stepping onto the trail. Bauman drew next to him, brushing against his elbow.

"So what is this about?"

Schmidt didn't respond. He was either stalling for time, or he had heard the labored breathing of a group of bundled-up runners on the path behind them, Bauman couldn't tell. They moved aside to let the joggers pass.

Finally, Schmidt said, "Karl, do you think we could have a mole in our department?"

Bauman let out a deep breath and watched its cloud hang in the frigid air, hesitating before it rose skyward bit by bit. "What gave you that idea?"

"I just don't buy the scenario that the RAF would wait twelve years to avenge her betrayal of Horst Kreuzer. I think they might have gotten wind of the East German spy's plan to defect with Stasi documents that could expose them. So, they decided to kill the carrier, Sylvia." Schmidt resumed his stroll.

Bauman walked alongside. "You may be right. If the defector didn't exaggerate, his documents could finger RAF members and their next terrorist attack. But, Sylvia might have told someone about her assignment."

"I've considered that, but I have a pretty good truth gauge, and I believe her when she says she hasn't."

Years of working with Schmidt gave Bauman a deep appreciation for his instincts. "That's good enough for me. Who else knows about this crazy plan? The Stasi informant of course, you and I, and, as you know, everything we plan has to go through Analysis."

Bauman's demeanor darkened as he thought about Department 3, the Analysis Section. "And Department 3 may or may not pass it on to the Chancellery in Bonn or, heaven help us, the Constitution Protection Office in Cologne—I wouldn't know. They would tell me, however, if we're supposed to coordinate with the Cologne bunch, and so far I haven't heard a word."

"Don't forget, there is our Stasi comrade, Mozart, himself. Who knows whether he's playing straight?" Schmidt slowed as the trail narrowed.

Stepping ahead, Bauman continued with his train of thought. "Yeah, it's a mess. You're right about being extra cautious. I'll do some snooping with Lederer in Analysis. Perhaps he'll tell me if anything's been passed on and to whom." Bauman stopped abruptly, causing Schmidt to bump into him. "Sorry. Don't know why this didn't occur to me earlier. Those American lawyers . . . can they be trusted?"

Schmidt shrugged. "The partner in Washington is the only one who knows about Sylvia. He assured me the associate he's sending is clueless. It's my job to spring the plot on him . . . probably this evening."

"Given the history between those two, that should be quite something to watch," Bauman quipped.

Not amused, Schmidt responded, "He's going to be in for quite a shock. I'm not looking forward to that part of the evening."

"You're right, it's no laughing matter. Do you think we ought to pull the plug on that part of the arrangements? You can still decide not to use this lawyer."

"It's risky, I know, but less so than leaving whatever Mozart decides to deliver in Sylvia's hands alone, especially in East Berlin. You know, we can't really do much over there yet. Maybe in a couple of weeks our agents will be able to operate more effectively."

They turned back. Bauman could tell Schmidt was still unsettled and assured him, "I'll leave it up to you. Use your best judgment."

When they reached the bench, Bauman shook Schmidt's hand. "Go ahead. You need to get back to Stuttgart. Keep me informed."

"I will."

Bauman watched Schmidt hurry down the path. Lowering himself onto the bench, he shook his head in disbelief at the peculiar setup the Stasi spy had demanded. He was in complete control. But the information he'd promised was too valuable for them not to play along. Still, Bauman hated the many loose ends, and especially amateur operatives. The arrangement might prove too chaotic even for a professional of Schmidt's caliber.

Chapter Eight

The shrill ring of the telephone woke him. He fumbled the receiver, almost dropping it, put it to his ear and said, "Hallo," before he remembered that German custom called for saying one's name when answering the telephone.

A hesitant female voice inquired in accented English, "Mr. Keller?"

"Yes."

"You requested a wake-up call, sir. It's three o'clock in the afternoon."

"Yes, thank you."

After arriving at his downtown Stuttgart hotel late that morning, he'd managed a second nap. He was about to hang up, when he realized she was speaking again. He interrupted, "I'm sorry, did you say something else?"

"Yes, sir. You have a phone message. Would you like for me to read it?"

Woozy from jet lag and his nap, Rolf wondered who would call him so soon after his arrival. Could it be Stein?

The voice at the other end interrupted his thoughts. "Mr. Keller?"

"Uh . . . yes. What is the message?"

He heard the muffled sound of paper rustling. "A Mr. Schmidt called at a quarter to two. I told him you were resting. He did not want to disturb you and left the following message: 'Welcome to Stuttgart, Mr. Keller. Please meet me in the hotel lobby at five thirty this afternoon for an early supper. I have opera tickets for us this evening.'"

"Fräulein, did he leave a phone number?"

"No, sir."

He felt a twinge of resentment. How presumptuous of this Schmidt to plan Rolf's evening without affording him the courtesy of leaving a call-back number. Rolf considered and rejected the idea of trying to locate him. Even assuming the person lived in the area, he'd never find him in the phone book without knowing his first name. The Stuttgart phone directory likely contained hundreds of listings for Schmidt.

While it would make for a long day, it never occurred to him to turn down an invitation to the opera, even though he had no idea what was on this evening's program, let alone who would be singing. Recalling Stein's parting quip, Rolf concluded that he must have made these arrangements.

"Will there be anything else, Mr. Keller?"

"Do you by any chance have a map of suggested jogging routes?"

"The concierge in the lobby has one."

Rolf thanked her again and hung up. He donned his running clothes and shoes. The thought of lifting the remainder of the jet lag cobwebs with an easy run cheered him. On his way out he stopped at the concierge's desk to check the jogging map, which showed routes traversing Schlossgarten Park. Since his dinner appointment was less than two hours away, he hurried across the lobby to the rear door exiting into the park. He'd only have time for a short run.

The park, stretching for kilometers, provided a welcome oasis for Stuttgart's city dwellers, the way Central Park did for New Yorkers. Rolf ran along the asphalt path, dodging an occasional puddle left from recent showers. A boy on a bicycle pedaled past, the luggage rack above the rear wheel clasping a soccer ball. Rolf remembered how as a teenager he used to ride his bike through here on his way to town to catch the latest Hollywood movie. Back then he wasn't a runner, and he certainly didn't pay much attention to nature. Now, jogging on the trail that meandered through the park, traversing meadows and winding around trees and lakes, he basked in the natural beauty surrounding him. The park's giant beech, oak and plane trees had shed their leaves weeks ago, but that did not diminish their grandeur in Rolf's eyes.

He passed an elderly, bow-legged woman shuffling along the path. The way her bony legs protruded below the hem of her dress in an odd angle reminded Rolf of the stick figures he drew as a child. Her attire was typical of the garments worn by the elderly female population of the region: black three-quarter length dress, black head scarf, and black shoes. It was as if after attaining a certain age, the local Swabian women went into permanent mourning. Rolf enjoyed watching the people in the park, yet he was the subject of much ogling himself, for the sight of a jogger was still not as commonplace here as in the States.

Tree shadows grew longer in the fading late afternoon light. Approaching the end of his run, Rolf felt a relaxed appreciation of the rhythmic movement of his limbs and the bite of brisk air. He arrived at his hotel with flushed cheeks and pearls of sweat on his brow—testimonies to an invigorating workout. A hot shower dispelled the last remnants of jet lag.

Remembering Stein's dress code admonition, he had brought the khaki slacks and navy blazer from his office coat hanger. Opera was no longer the stuffy affair it used to be. So in lieu of dress shirt and tie, he selected a blue open-collared shirt to wear under his jacket.

Rolf exited the elevator and crossed the lobby toward the front door when he remembered that European hotel custom called for him to drop off his room key at the reception. He stopped abruptly to change directions and felt hands pushing against his upper back. He spun on his heel, instinctively raising his arms in a defensive stance. A young man in blue jeans mumbled an insincere apology, looked away and scurried past. Rolf relaxed when he realized that his sudden halt had caused the collision. Still, something about that fellow struck him. Had he seen him before somewhere? He hadn't really gotten a good look. Besides, what stuck with him was not the man's appearance but the way he'd moved. Rolf shook it off.

Rolf hurried to the desk and handed his room key to the female clerk. He glanced at an imposing clock hanging above oak cubbyholes that lined the rear wall of the reception area. The noisy, insistent ticking of the second hand drew his attention, conjuring the image of a countdown—to what, he did not know. But he had a strong premonition that his life might take a major turn this evening, and—like the seconds ticking away as he watched—he could only go forward. There would be no turning back.

Rolf, feeling uneasy now, moved away from the counter. Not knowing what the person meeting him looked like and not seeing any likely candidates, he sat down in an armchair facing the main entrance. His mind began to churn. According to Stein, Schmidt would fill in the details about his task, perhaps tonight. Yet that seemed inconsistent with an outing to the theater, surely not a place for a private conversation which might include highly sensitive information.

Maybe the intent was to soften him up by catering to his passion for opera or to make him feel obligated in some way. No, there had to be another reason, one he could not imagine no matter how hard he racked his brain. And what was the rush in going to the opera on the very day he arrived? Rolf was still speculating when a stocky man emerged from the revolving glass door, slowed his steps, scanned the lobby, and meeting his gaze walked straight up to him.

"Mr. Keller?"

Chapter Nine

Though she did not consider herself superstitious, Sylvia kept to a firm routine on performance days. She would sleep in, exercise, shower, eat a late lunch in her room, drink lots of water, and arrive at the theater at least two hours prior to curtain time—a habit cultivated during the five years she'd been singing minor roles in small European opera houses.

No matter how minute the part, Sylvia prepared as if she were singing the starring role. Early on, her voice coach instilled in her the belief that her soprano voice was a gift, one she had an obligation to nurture and develop. Even though it was part of her body, she regarded her voice as a separate instrument she was allowed to play. And whenever the temptation arose to take her ability to sing for granted, the voice somehow would not behave as expected, reminding her of its independence. Experience had taught her the futility of attempting to subjugate the instrument by brute force. Instead, she'd learned to let her voice inform her how it wanted to be used that day.

Since the Schwäbischer Hof did not have an exercise facility, and since jogging in the park did not appeal to her after last night's experience, she opted for an hour of yoga in her room. During that time she attuned her mind to her body. Without singing a note, she knew the state of her voice by the sensation in her nose and throat. All felt well today. Except for singing a few scales in the shower, she would wait to warm up until after she arrived in the theater dressing room.

With an hour to go, she had managed to stick to her performance-day habit. Sylvia recalled her promise to call the hotel nurse but was loath to deviate from her routine. After all, the wound seemed to be healing well. There were no ill-effects from removing the bandage and taking a shower, and fortunately the costume for this evening's role would cover her upper arm. Besides, she didn't need the distraction a nurse's visit was sure to bring. Just when her rationalizations were succeeding, the phone rang.

Startled, she answered, "Mazzoni."

"Frau Mazzoni. Treulich here . . . Gertrude Treulich . . . I'm the nurse who treated you last night."

Sylvia blushed like a schoolgirl caught in a deception. "Yes . . . uh . . . I was just thinking about calling you." She recovered her composure. "You want to know about my arm. It's fine. There's no need—"

"I'd better have a look. I'll be right up."

Sylvia was still trying to think of what she could say to dissuade her when she heard a click on the line. She couldn't decide whether to be annoyed or to admire the woman's persistence.

The nurse entered a few minutes later, holding a folded newspaper, which she laid on the coffee table. "Do you mind if I put this here while I have a look at that wound of yours?"

Sylvia nodded her assent. Frau Treulich had an antiseptic odor about her, reminding Sylvia of hospital corridors. Yet, she did not appear as brusque as she had yesterday evening. Instead of an intrusion, Sylvia began to regard the nurse's visit as a welcome diversion from her intense focus on the upcoming performance. In her shocked state the previous evening, she had probably misjudged the woman.

Ostensibly satisfied that her patient was indeed all right, the nurse turned to leave, only to hesitate as if to gather courage.

To her own surprise, Sylvia encouraged her. "Did you have something else?"

"Well . . . yes I do, actually. I've heard that you're singing at the opera this evening."

"Yes, I am. Do you like opera?"

"Oh, yes." Her voice and face exuding enthusiasm, she gushed, "I've loved all the operas I've seen, which unfortunately hasn't been very many."

"Have you ever seen *Carmen*?"

"On TV once, but never in the theater. Is that what's on tonight's program?"

"Yes. Would you like to attend as my guest?"

"Oh, that would be wonderful."

Her immediate acceptance surprised Sylvia. Most Germans of Frau Treulich's generation felt traditional courtesy required several polite refusals before any gift could be properly accepted.

Evidently sensing Sylvia's hesitation as she tried to decide whether more than one ticket was appropriate, Treulich piped up. "If you happen to have two tickets . . . I'd like to take my daughter. She's twelve."

Sylvia retrieved her purse from the bed and pulled out two tickets. She felt a strange satisfaction at the nurse's grateful expression. "You know, when I was twelve, my mother took me to see *Aïda*. I decided that day that I would become an opera singer."

Sylvia became wistful. She'd gotten the tickets for her mother. Intellectually, she understood why Anna couldn't come all the way from Milan to attend tonight's performance. Her good luck phone call earlier today would have to suffice. Without her mother's emotional and financial support—paying for Sylvia's studies and voice lessons—her aspirations for a career in opera would have forever remained a daydream. She had no business feeling sorry for herself. Still, she felt a void: her first performance on a big stage—perhaps career defining—and no one she knew or cared about would be there to watch.

"Are you the lead?" Treulich's question interrupted Sylvia's rueful reflection.

"No." Sylvia walked the nurse to the door. "But I'm one of the main characters. You'll recognize me."

On her way back into the room, she saw that the nurse had left her newspaper on the coffee table. Sylvia picked it up, but when she opened the door and looked down the hall, Frau Treulich was nowhere in sight.

While putting the paper back on the table, her eyes were drawn to a front page headline. "Murder in Schlossgarten Park." She skimmed the short paragraph reporting that the body of a man who had been shot was found late Friday evening in the park near the lake. The bulletin described him as a male in his mid-twenties, medium build, five foot eleven, clad in a black leather jacket and jeans. No identity papers were found on the body. The article requested anyone with information to contact the police at the listed phone number.

Sylvia started to shake. She flopped onto the sofa. That had to be Manfred Klau. Why hadn't Schmidt identified him to the police? Was he covering for the killer, perhaps himself? Or was he protecting her? Should she contact the police? She stared off into space, unable to focus. Questions kept swirling in her head.

Then she jumped to her feet and made for the bathroom. She splashed cold water on her face. Toweling off, she looked in the mirror. Get yourself together! A determined face stared back at her. She would not go to the police. That criminal got what he deserved. She could not afford to lose her focus. This evening would be the most important in her professional life as a singer, and she would let nothing interfere.

She left the hotel a half hour ahead of schedule. She rode the streetcar and exited at the Staatsgalerie, a brisk five-minute walk from the theater. Checking her watch, she opted to stroll around the Schlossplatz. She thought of last night's attack and the murder, but her apprehension subsided as she noted how many people were still in the castle square area.

Her eyes settled on the imposing structure of the Neues Schloss, "the New Castle," built in the eighteenth century in rococo style. After it burned to the ground during World War II, the palace was rebuilt in Louis-XVI-style and later altered to Empire style. She knew the huge complex, once the residence of dukes and kings, was now used chiefly for state receptions.

One by one, the street lamps lit up. Sylvia watched the chain reaction of soft illumination along the walkways and boulevards. After lingering for hours, twilight at last succumbed to the dark. The historic buildings, glowing in the beams of muted floodlights, lent the downtown area a romantic air—a quality which the artist in Sylvia had always loved about Stuttgart.

Catching sight of the distant opera house, its festive lights reflecting in the adjacent lake, she turned her attention to what lay ahead. She walked toward the theater, her purposeful strides quickening. A brief glance up at the tower of the Stiftskirche informed her of the time, a quarter after five—time to get to the theater and shift her focus to the character she would portray a few hours from now. Sylvia began the mental and emotional process of transforming herself into Micaëla, a multi-faceted character. The first act alone called for her to be innocent, yet clever, in deflecting the soldiers' advances, and then become sweet and self-effacing in her duet with Don José. In the third act she had to be resolute and courageous, risking her life to "rescue" Don José from Carmen and the band of smugglers.

The woman who walked through the artists' entrance a few minutes later, nodded to the stage doorman, and entered the dressing room, was more Micaëla than Sylvia. In that frame of mind she began to warm up the voice, a few scales at first, followed by various parts of her role. The practice confirmed her earlier appraisal. She was indeed in good voice today.

Micaëla's costume was hanging on the back of the dressing room door: a simple blue dress as specified in the libretto, befitting a peasant girl from Navarre, Spain. Sylvia slipped into the garment, noting with satisfaction the precise fit achieved by the opera tailor shop. For the next hour theater professionals perfected her makeup and hairstyle. While the soprano who usually sang the role used a wig for the plaits indicated in the score, Sylvia chose to have her long, dark hair braided for the occasion. Although she knew that all this activity was part and parcel of an opera production, she felt self-conscious about so many people making a fuss over her appearance.

Her thoughts drifted to last night's mysterious comment by Schmidt, alluding to something of import that might transpire today. No, she would not waste energy on speculating about matters over which she had no control. Better to focus on what she needed to accomplish this evening. Though she felt nervous, it was not the panic that paralyzes, but rather a mixture of fear and adrenalin—the kind a marathoner might experience waiting for the starter's gun. She had read about the terrible stage fright Franco Corelli used to experience, despite having been gifted with an exceptional tenor voice and movie star looks. He did not, however, let his angst keep him from becoming one of the greatest tenors ever to grace the opera stage.

Her musings were interrupted by the stage manager's intercom announcement, "Five minutes," followed by the names of the singers who had to be on- or backstage when the curtain went up. When she heard her name, Sylvia closed her eyes and bowed her head, embracing a deep stillness within. Confidence welled up inside her. A few moments later Micaëla, garbed in her blue dress and braided hair, strode down the corridor toward the back of the stage.

Chapter Ten

In the lobby of Hotel Königshof, Rolf rose from his armchair and extended his hand to the stranger who had addressed him. "Herr Schmidt?"

"Yes, I'm Dieter Schmidt. Pleased to meet you and welcome to Stuttgart."

While processing his first name and firm handshake, Rolf noted with relief that Schmidt too had found it unnecessary to dress up for the opera. He wore a black turtleneck under a herringbone jacket, mostly covered by a gray overcoat, with black slacks and shoes.

After a few perfunctory questions about Rolf's flight and accommodations, Schmidt glanced at his watch. "Well, we'd better be going. I thought we'd walk to the restaurant. It's only a few minutes, but you'll probably want to put on your coat."

Rolf complied and hurried to catch up with Schmidt, already halfway to the rear door. They stepped into the cool evening air. The street lamps spread muted light down the walkways, lending the park a pleasant atmosphere.

Taking the footpath that meandered behind a shopping arcade, Schmidt remarked, "The café is just around the corner."

Rolf was too busy keeping up with Schmidt's purposeful stride to respond. The walkway curved, and a gate leading onto a terraced area came into view. Two lamps illuminated the words Café Bravo on a sign hanging from an iron arch above the entryway. As they crossed the empty patio, Rolf imagined how full of life this garden restaurant would be during the summer season.

Inside, he was surprised to find that most of the tables were occupied. Germans loved their afternoon coffee klatsch, a ritual of relaxing, gossiping and people watching in a cozy café while sipping strong coffee and nibbling delectable pastries, especially Torten and Kuchen. However, by this time of day, most eateries were empty, the coffee hour just past and the dinner hour not yet underway.

Across the park from Stuttgart's two main theaters, the Little House, designed for plays, and the Big House, for opera and ballet, the café was popular with theatergoers. Schmidt had managed to reserve a table tucked away in the corner, but affording a view from the expansive front window onto the park. When Rolf spotted the illuminated opera house across the lake, excitement began to build in him until he remembered he was there on business.

Just before the waiter reached their table, Schmidt asked Rolf in a low voice, "Do you mind if I order a beer?"

While responding, "Oh, of course not," Rolf computed the underlying message—Schmidt was familiar with the details of his personal life, just as Stein had been.

Ordering beer or wine in German restaurants was easy. On the other hand, asking for noncarbonated water required a little perseverance. No upstanding German would ever think of drinking tap water, and no restaurant would dare to serve it. In no mood to shock the server with such an outlandish request, Rolf settled for a bottle of lightly carbonated mineral water.

With their drink orders out of the way, Schmidt remarked, "I understand you're quite an opera fan."

"Yes, you might say I'm passionate about opera. How about you?"

"I enjoy a performance once in awhile, but I'm not smitten as you are."

Rolf wondered when Schmidt would broach the real topic. In the meantime, he continued with the opera talk, a subject he could discuss all evening. "In school we had to attend plays, classical music concerts and operas, and write reports for a grade. Back then I wanted to listen to the Beatles and Elvis Presley—certainly not opera. Now I'm glad the seed planted during those years has sprouted."

While their drinks were being served, they studied the menu and ordered before the waiter had a chance to leave. Schmidt settled for the daily special, a southern German meat dish with dumplings in a rich sauce, which sounded too heavy to Rolf. Wanting to stay alert for the performance, he decided on two of his favorite Swabian specialties, soup with meat-and-spinach-filled raviolis, called *Maultaschensuppe*, and a buttered pretzel with lox. He could always eat something at the theater during intermission if he became hungry.

His thoughts were interrupted by Schmidt. "I'm sorry. I haven't even told you what's on tonight. *Carmen.* You've seen it, no doubt."

Rolf's eyes lit up. "Yes, many times. It's one of my favorites."

Schmidt's face took on a serious expression, signaling a change in subject. He took a sip of beer, set down the glass, and looked around. Satisfied that they were a safe distance from the neighboring tables, he spoke in a hushed tone. "I expect Mr. Stein has told you about your task?"

"Only that I'm to observe the transfer of certain documents . . . and that you would fill in the details for me."

"I see. May I presume that you know the source of these documents?"

Even though they were out of earshot of the other tables, Rolf understood the wisdom of being circumspect. "I've been told the institutional source but not the individual."

"Unfortunately, we don't have that information yet," Schmidt acknowledged with a shrug.

The server approached with the entrées, and substantive talk ceased, as both offered the traditional German, "Guten Appetit."

After a few spoonfuls of soup, Rolf resolved to take the initiative by asking direct questions, as if interrogating a witness. "When and where is the exchange to take place?"

Schmidt stopped eating. "Sometime next week in East Berlin. There will likely be two deliveries on different days."

"I gather the first is to establish credibility." Judging by Schmidt's expression, Rolf's deduction had impressed.

"Yes, I think so."

"And what exactly am I supposed to do?" Finished with his soup, Rolf took a big bite out of the chewy pretzel, his teeth tearing the fibrous, salty lox, while he waited for a response.

His companion did not seem in a hurry to answer. Schmidt scraped the last morsels of pork from his plate, wiped his mouth with the white cloth napkin, and took a healthy swig of beer. He fixed his eyes on Rolf.

"The East Berliner providing the merchandise is dictating the terms. We haven't had any say. He's made all the arrangements, and we know only what I've told you. The drop will be made next week in East Berlin."

Schmidt paused for another gulp of beer, then continued. "He did tell us who will receive the materials."

Rolf saw his opportunity. "And who is that?"

"You'll find out very soon."

Rolf shook his head in frustration. Stein must have known the recipient's identity too, yet like Schmidt had refused to tell him. Why were they so secretive? He discarded politeness. "So, are you going to answer my question and tell me what my role is, or is that a big secret too?"

The sarcasm appeared to take a bite out of Schmidt's composure. He picked up his glass but set it down again without taking a drink. After an awkward pause, he offered, "I can understand your frustration. Here is what I can tell you. The Stasi agent—his code name is 'Mozart'—insists on passing his information to an opera singer who will be performing at the East Berlin Opera next week."

"An opera singer?" Rolf cocked his head to one side. "Actually, I don't know why I'm so surprised. After all, opera singers bring plots to life that are sometimes implausible and always full of twists and turns. Maybe such an artist is the ideal person for this job."

Schmidt continued, "You asked about your assignment. It's simply to watch over the transaction and ensure that everything that is delivered finds its way to me."

"In other words, you don't trust the singer."

"Let's just say I'm more comfortable knowing you'll be there." Schmidt cupped his hands around the bottom of his glass, as if to warm his beer, and leaned forward. "Your mission is very delicate. Mozart is not to learn your true role. We don't know why he insists on using this singer as a carrier. You're there to guard against a double cross."

Rolf also leaned forward. "You know, I'm a lawyer, not a spy. You must be nervous having to rely on amateurs."

Schmidt grimaced. "Believe me, that wouldn't have been my choice."

"How do you propose that I defend myself, as an unarmed civilian?"

Even though they had been conversing in voices too low for anyone to overhear them, Schmidt lowered his to a whisper. "I don't expect you'll need a weapon, and I strongly suggest that you don't obtain one. As an agent of the Federal Intelligence Service, I am not permitted to carry a gun nor can I give you one." He leaned back and switched from a whisper to a low volume, "Besides, from what I've read, you're not exactly defenseless. I understand you're proficient in martial arts."

No longer surprised by how much this agent knew about him, Rolf said, "I've attended self-defense classes, sure. But I'm no James Bond. Though, given the element of surprise, my training might help me out of a tight spot."

Schmidt relaxed. "Good. The last thing I need is to have a bunch of armed amateurs running around East Berlin." He turned somber once more. "Since we're in a reactive mode in this deal, you may have to do some improvising. How are you at extemporizing?"

"You can't be a good trial lawyer without being able to think on your feet. Take the witness who's told you one story during all the interviews and at trial rolls out a whole new version you've never heard before. You either learn to ad-lib or get out of the courtroom."

Schmidt appeared satisfied with the response. "You should know we have reason to believe someone is trying to foil this plan."

"What makes you think that?"

Ignoring him, Schmidt called for the bill, leaving Rolf to stew about this disturbing news. Schmidt insisted on paying from his government expense account. They reentered the park and strolled around the lake toward the opera house.

"Since you are such an opera buff, perhaps you can give me some insights on what to look for in tonight's performance," Schmidt remarked.

Rolf brightened. "Everybody knows Carmen's "Habanera," and the toreador song. But my favorite is the sublime music Bizet composed for Micaëla—the way he captured her charm and innocence, the sharp contrast between her lyrical passages and Carmen's passionate tunes. Watch for her first act duet with Don José. But, the whole opera is full of magnificent music, a true masterpiece. Are you familiar with its background?"

"I've read that the poor reception the opera received may have caused Bizet's premature death."

"There's no question that the 1875 premiere at the Opéra Comique in Paris was a scandal. The audience, expecting family entertainment, was shocked by the 'immoral' subject—sexual passion and jealousy involving a seductive gypsy who is brutally murdered on stage. And worst of all, smoking factory girls!" Rolf became more serious. "The Paris press panned the score as too Wagnerian, if you can believe that. Three months later a disconsolate Bizet died at age thirty-six, thinking his opera a failure. There are those who call that a legend, pointing out that the opera scored thirty-seven performances in its first season and that Bizet died of a heart attack. But there is no disputing the fact that only after his death did *Carmen* become one of the world's most popular operas."

While they ascended the flight of steps that curved across the front of the theater, Schmidt commented, "A tragic opera and a heartrending real-life story behind it."

The chandelier-lit foyer evoked a feeling of familiarity in Rolf, though twelve years had passed since his last visit to the Stuttgart Opera. He followed Schmidt weaving through the audience. His attention on the theatergoers' dress, which ran the gamut from blue jeans to evening dresses and tuxedos, he bumped an elderly lady's elbow. When he bent down to pick up the program she had dropped, he glimpsed a man turn away and disappear into the crowd. Something about his movement reminded him of the young man who had bumped into him in the hotel lobby. Distracted, he mumbled, "Entschuldigung," while returning the program to its owner. He was still wondering whether he was seeing ghosts, or someone was indeed following him, when chimes beckoned patrons to their seats.

He approached a coatroom attendant to buy a program, but Schmidt hurried him along. Rolf decided to forego the purchase. He knew the plot inside out, and if he wanted to learn about the singers, he could always buy one during the first intermission.

As they settled into the fifth row of orchestra seating, Rolf murmured, "I'm impressed. You must have connections to get these seats."

"It helps that the government pays for most of the theater's operating expenses."

Rolf turned to survey the performance hall and soaked in the intimate atmosphere. The king's box, roofed by a huge crown, protruded from the center of the first balcony behind him. As a student, he used to sit high up in the third balcony, called *Zwetschgendörre* by the locals for its semblance to a hot summer attic used by farmers to dry plums.

"Great place, isn't it?" Schmidt seemed to take pleasure in Rolf's enjoyment. "Do you know how King Ludwig II of Württemberg paid for the construction of this theater?"

"No, I don't."

"Back before World War I, he sold honors and titles to German industrialists for one million Reich marks apiece."

Rolf studied Schmidt's face for signs that he was kidding. Seeing none, he remarked, "How ingenious!" The house lights dimmed, stifling his urge to follow up.

The musicians in the orchestra pit ceased tuning their instruments, and the buzz of myriad conversations died down. Stillness pervaded the house, creating a suspenseful air that evoked a nostalgic feeling in Rolf. He recalled how he used to eagerly await his mother's reading of Brothers Grimm fairy tales to him at bedtime. As an adult, opera transported him into that imaginary world, just like fables had when he was a little boy.

The spell was broken by applause descending from the balconies, signaling that the conductor had entered the orchestra pit. Moments later Rolf saw him ascend the podium and, after several bows to the audience, turn toward the stage and raise his arms. The exhilarating orchestral prelude conveyed Rolf straight away to the opera's opening scene, a square in Seville.

On the stage, soldiers outside a guard house fought boredom, watching the goings-on in the square, when Micaëla, in blue dress and braids, appeared looking for Don José. Rolf could usually foretell from this scene of the country girl deflecting the flirting soldiers whether the part was well cast. So far so good, he thought. This performer portrayed the peasant girl's charm and innocence and had a lovely soprano voice. Of course, the upcoming duet with Don José would tell for sure.

Beneath Micaëla's sweetness Rolf sensed an undercurrent of sensuality so strong that it brought a sudden flush to his face. The feeling was powerful and disturbing, but even more unsettling was the odd sense of déjà vu, almost as if he knew her. He attributed the notion to an overstimulated imagination. Opera did that to him.

The women from the cigarette factory entered the scene, and Carmen, wearing a low-cut, provocative red dress, sang her captivating "Habanera." But Rolf remained distracted, anticipating Micaëla's return. He sensed Schmidt's gaze when she reappeared. Perhaps he wanted confirmation that this was indeed the duet mentioned earlier. Rolf gave him a thumbs up.   Micaëla was bringing news to José from his mother. Rolf became so enthralled by the warmth and sheer beauty of the singer's voice caressing Bizet's soul-stirring tune that tears came to his eyes. If he had ever heard "Parle-moi de ma mère!" sung any more expressively than by this Micaëla, he couldn't remember. Again, a feeling of recognition emerged. Had he seen her perform before?

Out of the corner of his eye, Rolf saw Schmidt studying him. There was something disturbing in his demeanor, as if he were expecting a reaction. When Rolf looked at him, Schmidt turned toward the stage. For an instant, Rolf wondered what Schmidt was up to, but then returned his attention to the opera.

The timid kiss Micaëla planted on Don José's forehead, a present from his mother, conveyed perfectly her shy nature. Could this possibly be . . .? He didn't dare to think her name. No, it couldn't. And yet, the round face, the dark eyes, the shapely figure filled out by a few more pounds over the years, and the way she moved—there was no use in denying it—he was looking at Sylvia.

Rolf felt his stomach tighten as anger welled up. That's why Schmidt had been watching him. He and Stein had set this up. They had led him on the whole time, knowing he would never have agreed to come had he known he'd face the woman he had deserted so many years ago. He pushed the anger down for now and focused instead on Sylvia. Seeing her on the stage brought feelings of awe and relief: awe at what Sylvia had accomplished, and relief that abandoning her had evidently not been as devastating as he'd imagined for all these years.

He watched Don José embrace Micaëla to plant on her cheek a return kiss for his mother. Another feeling welled up in him, whether caused by the poignancy of this scene and the glorious singing, he couldn't tell. He recalled his premonition on the airplane that this trip might give him the chance to make amends somehow. Perhaps he was looking at that opportunity. Would he have the courage this time not to disappear?

The thunderous applause showered upon the singers at the end of the duet jolted him. He joined in, clapping with enthusiasm, noting that Schmidt followed suit. He even heard a few shouts of "Brava," obviously meant for Micaëla, which astonished him, coming as they were from a reserved Stuttgart Opera audience.

Rolf barely followed the remainder of Act I with Carmen's beguiling "Seguidilla," bewitching Don José with her promise of love at the tavern of Lillas Pastia near the ramparts of Seville. Having won Don José's complicity, Carmen escaped detention as the red velvet curtain closed. The audience waited until the heavy curtain's gold fringe stretched across most of the stage before responding with another round of resounding applause. When the ushers opened the exit doors for the first intermission, Rolf could restrain himself no longer. Rising abruptly, he squeezed around the patrons on their feet and clapping. He sensed Schmidt following. Rolf crossed the foyer and headed out the front door and down the steps toward the lake promenade, stopping only when he reached the edge of the water.

He heard Schmidt's solicitous voice behind him, "So, what do you think?"

His anger boiled over. He shouted out over the lake, "What do I think? I think you and Stein are two conniving bastards! Sylvia is the carrier, isn't she?"

He heard Schmidt's sharp breaths but stared out over the water, as if in its soft ripples he could find the solution to his predicament. Once again, he replayed in his mind, as he had so often during the twelve years since he left Germany, how Sylvia had sought his help in ending her relationship with her terrorist boyfriend, Horst Kreuzer. Not wanting to jeopardize his pending visa to the United States, Rolf had refused to help her, whether out of cowardice or jealous revenge for her preferring Kreuzer to him, what did it matter? He hated himself for it.

"Herr Keller. Listen to me. I don't like this any better than you do. But it's the only way, given the Stasi agent's demands."

Rolf turned to face Schmidt. "How in the hell did you persuade Sylvia to get involved in this?"

It was Schmidt's turn to study the lake. "As you know, she kept some bad company at the Free University Berlin."

"Blackmailed her, did you?" He heard the contempt in his voice but didn't care.

"Like it or not, in this case it was necessary."

"The end justifies the means, huh?" Rolf surprised himself with his derisive laugh.

Schmidt fidgeted. "The situation in Germany is not black and white. Things would be a lot easier if it were. We're dealing in shades of gray." After a pause, he looked at Rolf. "I have decided to go ahead with this venture. I'll take the responsibility."

Despite his anger, Rolf felt impressed with Schmidt's forthrightness. Still, he couldn't get over the deception. "You could have told me."

"We couldn't take the chance. We had to get you over here."

"I can still walk away, you know."

"I realize that. But before you decide to do so, you may want to consider a couple of things."

"Such as?" Rolf crossed his arms, partly against the evening chill and partly to defend against whatever persuasion Schmidt was about to try on him.

"First, by refusing this assignment, you'll guarantee the end of your practice of law in Washington. Stein will see to that."

Rolf knew he was right. Still, he could probably get on with some law firm in Bismarck or Amarillo, or hang out his own shingle somewhere. He stared at Schmidt. "You said 'first.' What's your other point?"

"From what I know about your character, when someone pushes you, you push back harder. I don't expect you to go along just because we're pressuring you. But, what I'm about to say will probably make your decision, one way or the other."

Second message, Rolf thought. This German intelligence officer had checked out his background. Like Stein, he probably knew more about his past than he himself remembered. Rolf turned to face Schmidt. "Well, *this* should be interesting."

"This plan is going forward with or without you. We wanted you to be part of it for two reasons. The first, and I admit, the primary reason is the one I gave you at dinner: to keep an eye on the documents and make sure I receive them. There is a secondary consideration, however. Your job is also to watch out for Frau Mazzoni. She was attacked yesterday evening in the park by a young man with a knife."

Rolf glared at Schmidt. "What?"

"She's all right, but someone seems determined to scuttle this operation. What they know about this plan, or who they are, I have no idea. Nor do I know what our Stasi accomplice has up his sleeve." Schmidt hesitated in an apparent effort to choose his next words with care. "Sylvia needed you once before when she was in trouble. What is your choice going to be this time?"

Rolf understood another message had been sent. "You've been over my life with a microscope, haven't you?"

"That's my profession."

Rolf opened his mouth to tell Schmidt about the young man in the hotel lobby and the theater foyer, but something made him hesitate. Could he trust him? He heard the faint sound of electrical chime tones and started to move, but stopped when Schmidt spoke again.

"Mr. Keller, I realize you're an American citizen now. But you spent the first twenty-two years of your life in Germany. You will always have a place in your heart for your country of birth."

"That's true," Rolf acknowledged, wondering where Schmidt was headed.

"Let me assure you that the mission we are asking you and Frau Mazzoni to undertake is of vital importance to a democratic Germany. Mozart has intimated that he may provide some information on terrorists operating in West Germany. As you know, the Red Army Faction has been targeting leaders in industry and government since the seventies. Based on recent intelligence we have reason to believe that it may be planning an assassination in a matter of days. If these documents fill in enough details, we might be able to prevent it."

Not waiting for a response, Schmidt walked toward the theater. As they reentered the foyer, Rolf said, "You realize that Sylvia probably hates my guts."

"We'll find out very soon."

The second act unfolded as Rolf tried, without success, to make the difficult decision. Even the toreador song and Don José's flower aria could not captivate him this evening. He asked himself why he was so looking forward to Micaëla's third-act aria and realized it really mattered to him how well she did. Would she measure up to the world-class sopranos he had seen and heard in this role?

During the second intermission Schmidt excused himself, mumbling that he had to take care of some business, as Rolf stood in line at one of the counters selling refreshments. The most popular drinks were *Sekt*, "German champagne," and a drink consisting of equal parts *Sekt* and orange juice, called *Sekt-Orange*, a "German mimosa." A small voice in his head told him his nerves could use a soothing drink about now. By the time he reached the counter, he had convinced himself he could handle one glass of *Sekt*, just one. As he caught the server's eye, he heard his AA sponsor, "Never trust that voice. It will always lie to you," and out of Rolf's mouth came the words, "A butter pretzel and mineral water, please." Rolf reached for a paper napkin and dabbed perspiration from his upper lip.

The first half of Act III couldn't go fast enough for Rolf. He almost blushed when he realized he was nervous for Sylvia. Schmidt had told him when they returned to their seats this was her first appearance on a large opera stage, after singing minor roles in small houses since her graduation from music and opera school five years ago. In other words, tonight's performance could launch her career. At last, she entered the mountain scene and began to sing about overcoming her fears as she looked for José among the smugglers. Rolf's nervousness gave way to excitement and, realizing she did indeed measure up, turned to exhilaration. Perhaps bias clouded his judgment. Yet the audience seemed as mesmerized as he. The tumultuous applause and several bravas that rang out after the last note confirmed he was not alone in his appreciation. Who would have thought when he last saw her twelve years ago in West Berlin that she'd end up a first-rate opera singer?

No matter how often he'd seen the opera's tragic ending, Carmen's courage in facing death always touched him. The audience heaped lavish applause upon the artists during multiple curtain calls. Rolf was struck by the fervor of the clapping and shouting for Sylvia who glowed in the adoration showered upon her. At that moment, Rolf decided to do his part in helping with this crazy undertaking. Whatever the obstacles, this time he intended to stay the course.

After they retrieved their overcoats from the checkroom Rolf started toward the exit. Schmidt took him by the shoulder. "Not so fast. We've got an appointment in Sylvia Mazzoni's dressing room."

"Now? At this hour?"

"Yes, right now. Come on, it's this way." Schmidt headed for a side exit.

"Does she know about me?"

"Not yet."

Rolf hurried after Schmidt. He was more nervous than when he had been summoned to Stein's office. But he was not running away, at least not yet.

Chapter Eleven

Sylvia wound her way around the sets stored backstage for the upcoming acts—a tavern, mountain scenery, and a plaza in front of a bullring. She took care to stay clear of the massive stage elevator. It frightened her. There were no safety railings to prevent a fall or to avoid being crushed by the giant apparatus. The only warning consisted of a broad yellow stripe designating the edge of the platform. She stood off to the side where she could see the director's assistant, a young man in rumpled green corduroys, who would cue her to take the stage.

Applause told her that the conductor was entering the orchestra pit. She looked up into the cavernous space that comprised the backstage area, several stories high, akin to a modern hotel atrium but without decoration. Given her small-opera house experience, she felt overwhelmed—the way she imagined she'd feel standing in the empty hold of a huge cargo ship. The orchestra struck up the prelude, and at the first few bars an intimidated Sylvia transformed herself into the peasant girl Micaëla.

She heard the soldiers' derisive comments about the people in the square. Her entrance was only seconds away.

The assistant stage director pointed in her direction, then toward the stage. She entered and assumed the hesitating steps of a shy country girl looking for Don José without quite knowing where he might be.

For a moment the sheer size of the audience, filling the auditorium's fourteen hundred seats, flustered her. Then she glued her eyes to the stage. Once the soldiers had begun their flirting banter, she lost herself in the role and the audience disappeared from her awareness. After her quick retreat from the pursuing soldiers, she lingered backstage listening to Carmen bewitch José.

When she took the stage for the second time, she did not look into the audience but only at Don José. Her voice was relaxed in negotiating Bizet's lyrical passage. The stout tenor's acting was stiff, but his singing superb. Their voices blended perfectly. She left the stage elated. All these years of studying, practicing, waiting tables to scrounge up enough money to continue, and singing bit parts in out-of-the-way places had been worth it. Her challenging third-act aria was yet to come, but deep inside she knew she would do well.

The first few times she had performed the role, she'd been at a loss as to how to spend the long interval between her first- and third-act appearances, a span of almost two hours. Sometimes she hung around backstage and listened to Act II, or went to the theater canteen or a rehearsal room, but most of the time she just relaxed in her dressing room. She tried to do so this evening, yet after only a few minutes, she put down her novel, too excited to concentrate. A walk in the fresh air sounded enticing, but management did not permit artists to leave the theater during a performance.

She settled for the next best thing: a backstage stroll. Walking along the side stage, she happened upon a long, narrow corridor that connected the theater storage area to the main stage. Curiosity beckoned her to explore. As she entered the conduit, constricted by towering stage sets propped against both walls, claustrophobia assailed her. The cramped passageway, three stories high to accommodate the flats, evoked in Sylvia the feeling of trudging through a gorge. Dim lighting and chill underscored the eerie effect. How easy it would be for someone to hide in the shadows and trigger an accident. She rejected the thought. That she was about to embark on a precarious mission—coerced by the West German authorities—didn't mean she had to imagine a spy lurking around every corner. Nevertheless, she retreated to her dressing room.

She decided to give the novel another try. As she struggled to get into the plot, she heard a faint knock and looked up from her book. Unsure whether the sound had come from her door or from across the hall, she held her head still and listened, but heard nothing. The noise must have been something else. She usually had no visitors between acts, and was certainly not expecting any this evening.

There was another, stronger knock followed by a female voice. "Frau Mazzoni. A Mr. Schmidt is here to see you."

Sylvia jumped up, her book hitting the floor. She pulled the door open and looked straight into Schmidt's eyes. "What are you doing here? And how did you get past the doorman?"

Ignoring her questions, he stepped inside before any thought of protest came to her. "The person who will accompany you to East Berlin is with me this evening. I'd like you to meet him later."

"You picked a fine time to interrupt. I have another act to sing, and I need to prepare."

"Yes, I know. So let me get to the point. Could we meet you here after the performance?"

"I'll be here." She wanted to ask him what he knew about the murder in the park, but this was not the time.

"See you then. By the way, we're both enthralled by your singing and are looking forward to the third act. In my lay opinion, you are the accomplished artist you described last night." With that he was gone.

She was surprised at the sincerity of his compliment, then felt a stab of curiosity as to whom he had chosen to watch over her and the pilfered Stasi papers.

The intercom broadcast the end of the second intermission, and Sylvia began testing her voice and reassuming Micaëla's identity. All felt well. She closed her eyes in reflection and a feeling of gratitude washed over her as she realized how fortunate she was. Sylvia felt the urge to call her mother to share the wonderful experience.

Working as an Italian guest worker in a Stuttgart tool manufacturing plant, Anna had raised Sylvia alone. After a long day at the factory, she would fix them dinner, and no matter how tired, was always ready to help her daughter with homework afterwards.

When Sylvia would run home from school crying because her schoolmates made fun of her olive complexion and black hair and taunted her about not having a father, Anna never failed to offer comforting words and hugs. She told Sylvia her father had left before she was born and she would understand when she was a little older why he couldn't be with them. In later years, when Sylvia's questions about her father became more insistent, her mother resorted to changing the subject. She simply refused to discuss him. Finally, Sylvia quit asking, but never stopped wondering who her father was and what he was like.

Opening her eyes, Sylvia realized she'd run out of time. The phone call would have to wait until after she'd met the role's final challenge. She reached the backstage waiting area during the gypsies' fortune-telling scene. As soon as it ended, the assistant director gave her the nod. Sylvia felt the paradox of gathering confidence to depict a scared country girl venturing into the smugglers' hideout, and she was struck by the similarities between the role and her own trepidation about the Berlin escapade. Would she find the strength to emulate Micaëla?

Sylvia willed the doubts from her mind and slipped into the role. Expressing Micaëla's anxiety through Bizet's melodic lines in the aria, *Je dis que rien ne m'épouvante,* felt natural. "I say that nothing frightens me," she sang without straining for the extended high notes; she simply let them happen. Everything seemed effortless, and when the scene ended, the intensity of the applause and the bravas surprised her. She marveled at the joy in her heart, even as she dragged José off to see his dying mother.

Once offstage, Sylvia hurried toward the dressing rooms. With twenty minutes until the end of Act IV and the final curtain calls, she'd have enough time for a quick phone call to Milan. Anna was the person she most wanted to tell of the public's enthusiastic response to her major stage debut, though one never knew what the critics would say, or if they had even bothered to attend. Since she was only a substitute, chances were they hadn't.

She swore under her breath when she spotted one of the smugglers from the previous act using the backstage pay phone. He showed no signs of getting off. She really wanted to share her good news with Anna, who would be so pleased and proud. Sylvia made herself conspicuous, pacing by the phone for several minutes, but the caller kept his back to her. Then she recognized the irony in seeking her mother's approval, just as Don José had done in the opera, and she felt foolish. She'd call Anna tomorrow.

The final curtain calls felt like a dream to Sylvia. The enthusiastic reception she received during her solo bow overwhelmed her. She returned to the dressing room in a trance and, having forgotten all about her visitors, shed Micaëla's blue dress and began to undo her braids. A knock on the door jolted her back to reality. She caught a glimpse of herself in undergarments in the dressing table mirror, dark strands of hair hanging loosely down on one side and a tight braid still on the other. She spun toward the door and bumped into a chair, knocking it against the wall. What a mess! How could she have forgotten?

"Frau Mazzoni. Are you all right?" the dressing attendant inquired from the hallway.

"Yes."

"Two gentlemen to see you. They say you're expecting them."

"Tell them to wait just a minute." There was no time to put on her street clothes. She tore her black silk robe off the hanger behind the mirror, tied the belt around her waist and, after a quick glance to confirm that she was decent, called out, "Come in."

Schmidt entered with his usual self-assuredness, but his companion seemed hesitant. A shy watchdog? Then he stepped into the room and Sylvia gasped. His hair was now more brown than blond, still neatly parted on the left, with no signs of thinning. His face and forehead bore a few more character creases, but there was no doubt: it was Rolf Keller.

She had no idea how long she'd been standing there, staring, trying to comprehend what she was seeing. No one spoke, her gasp the only sound.

Finally, Schmidt broke the silence. "I believe you two know one another."

His words shook Sylvia out of her daze. "Is this some kind of joke?" She heard the anger in her voice.

"I'm sorry to have sprung this on you."

"That's it. The deal is off." At that moment she meant it, no matter the consequences.

She lurched at the door, flung it open and hissed, "Get out of here, both of you!" Braid swinging, silk trailing, unintended flesh flashing, Sylvia faced the two men with all the wrath of the wildest Valkyrie.

"Frau Mazzoni, please hear me out." Schmidt moved toward one of the chairs across from the dressing table and sat. "I can explain."

Neither she nor Rolf made any move to follow his example, maintaining their standoff.

"You conned me. Why should I listen to you?" She was livid, her anger more directed at Schmidt than Rolf.

Schmidt floundered. "Would you two sit down? Let's talk about this."

Sylvia did not move from the door. "What possessed you two to cook up this scheme, and what in hell makes you think I will go along?"

Rolf stepped toward her, put a gentle hand on her shoulder, and looked her in the eye. "Sylvia, I didn't know you were involved until this evening."

Rolf's deep baritone voice sounded more mature than she remembered. His sincere demeanor and the energy behind his words persuaded her to close the door and edge onto the stool in front of the mirror. As she did, Rolf took the chair next to Schmidt.

Struggling to rein in her doubts, Sylvia glared at Schmidt. "I'm not so sure I *will* be involved. This whole affair is beginning to look a lot more dangerous than you led me to believe. You owe me an explanation about last night's murder in the park."

Schmidt looked startled. "What about it, Frau Mazzoni?"

"The newspaper says the police can't identify him. I told you his name. Why didn't you give it to the police?"

Rolf jumped up. "What's this about a murder? Why haven't you told me about this, Schmidt?"

"Sit down. I'll tell you what I can." Schmidt waited for Rolf to return to his seat. "It's for your protection, Frau Mazzoni. We cannot let anything interfere with your assignment. The last thing we need is the police snooping around. I intend to find out who shot him and why. There's no need to get the police involved until after you've accomplished your mission."

"Sylvia, don't go. This is too dangerous." Rolf turned toward Schmidt. "Just tell your Stasi spy to deliver his documents to me. Though I still don't understand why you brought me into this."

Schmidt cleared his throat. "Frau Mazzoni must be the recipient. That is not negotiable. As for your role, I explained that to you earlier. You are to assist her and to watch out for any foul play by the Stasi."

"But with all the wily professionals for you to choose from, why select me, an American lawyer who doesn't know the first thing about the spy game?" Rolf's biting sarcasm surprised Sylvia whereas Schmidt seemed unperturbed.

"The reason is simple. We needed a cover to explain why Frau Mazzoni has a traveling companion. We know that there existed a . . . relationship between you during your student days."

Sylvia felt herself blushing and averted her eyes. As she shifted on the stool, the neck of her robe fell open to reveal considerable cleavage. She clutched it closed and caught Rolf hastily looking away. How dare he? Yet, her annoyance didn't quite cover the tiniest pleasure she felt in his attention.

Schmidt seemed to sense that neither one of them wanted to talk about their past involvement. He forged ahead. "Your cover is that you are renewing your liaison."

"Very clever."

Sylvia detected a touch of irony in Rolf's comment. Her pulse slowed. "Isn't that kind of farfetched, given that we haven't seen each other since our student years in West Berlin?"

"Mozart, the Stasi spy, doesn't know that. Your story is that after Mr. Keller's recent divorce, he reestablished contact with you, attended some of your performances, and the two of you rekindled your romance."

So he got married. No sooner had the thought entered her mind than she quelled it. Why should she care? Yet, as she regarded his hard-edged face, clean shaven except for a neatly trimmed mustache she didn't remember, and his blue eyes that held her gaze, she couldn't deny she still found him attractive.

Schmidt's voice interrupted her reverie. "There is another wrinkle. I suspect Mozart chose you, Frau Mazzoni, because he remembers you from the Free University Berlin. Maybe he was one of Horst Kreuzer's drinking buddies. Perhaps he even thinks you shared Kreuzer's extremist left-wing political views."

"So he may know me too." Rolf leaned forward.

"If that's the case, so much the better. That would certainly make the student romance story more believable."

"That's all well and good," Sylvia objected, "but Mr. Keller here doesn't exactly have a good track record of sticking around when the going gets tough."

"I did cut out on you, didn't I, Sylvia? Perhaps I can make it up this time."

She felt like a louse. Why did he have to be so damned fair about it? He should be making excuses. But then, she of all people had no business judging him, considering that she hadn't been a model of loyalty herself so far as Horst Kreuzer was concerned.

Schmidt rose from his chair. "Frau Mazzoni, this is a lot to digest. It's late, and I'm sure you'd rather revel in your splendid performance this evening. Sleep on it and we'll talk tomorrow. This plan is going forward with or without Mr. Keller, but I do think you'd be much safer with him on board."

Rolf stood up as well and caught her eye. "Sylvia, hearing you sing tonight was worth the trip, even if you don't want me to go with you to Berlin."

She was too stunned to respond. Schmidt was right. She promised herself she would enjoy the rest of the evening thinking about her Stuttgart debut. At the same time, though she tried, she could not suppress the niggling feeling that there was something else Schmidt was not telling her. She wondered whether he knew more about the murder than he had divulged. Did he not trust her to deliver the documents without an escort? And what about Rolf? He certainly had shown himself to be unreliable in the past. Why should she trust him now? Yet part of her wanted to, and that made him even more dangerous.

Chapter Twelve

Rolf woke early. The combination of jet lag and incessant thoughts of what might await Sylvia and him, or whether he would even accompany her to Berlin, made for a restless night. He pondered the dangers of traveling to communist East Germany. Was Sylvia's opera career or his partnership worth the risk of languishing in an East German prison cell, or worse, facing execution? And what if Sylvia decided to go it alone? No, he couldn't let that happen. Though he didn't know how he could protect her, he had to persuade her to let him come.

If Sylvia balked at his presence, he'd just have to tell Stein the bad news. Damn the partnership! Ah, yes, Stein. He owed him a phone call, but not until Sylvia made up her mind. When would she? Rolf stared at the ceiling, attempting to quell his impatience. He hated not being in control. There had to be a way for him to take the initiative. But what could he say to sway her?

He fumbled for the phone book on the nightstand and leafed through its pages. Schmidt had told him where Sylvia was staying. He located the number and dialed.

The operator at the Schwäbischer Hof took a few seconds to locate Sylvia's room number. Rolf's courage waned with each ring.

He was about to hang up when she answered in a sleepy voice, "Mazzoni."

"Sylvia, it's Rolf. Did I wake you?"

"What do you want?"

He grimaced. Had she decided already? "Sorry to call this early, but I need to talk to you."

The line went silent, and he wondered if she would hang up on him. Then her protest rang in his ear, "At this hour?"

"I have something to tell you about the papers you'll be receiving in Berlin." Not knowing how much Schmidt had divulged to her, Rolf hesitated but then forged ahead. "What I want to tell you will help you make up your mind about my coming along."

Her sigh was barely audible over the phone. "All right. I'm listening."

He knew he was close. "Not over the phone. Can you meet me this morning?"

"Where?"

"You still run, don't you?"

He thought about his years of heavy drinking and how he'd quit running until the divorce, when he had taken it up again with a vengeance.

"Yes. Why do you ask?"

"Let's go for a morning jog." He checked his watch. "How about meeting me in your hotel lobby at eight?"

After a long pause he heard her hesitant, "Okay."

"See you then." Rolf cut the line before she could change her mind.

He climbed out of bed, stuck his head out the hotel window and felt a crisp morning breeze. Thin, broken clouds chased each other across the sky. The low eastern sun did not yet dispel the early morning chill but gave promise of warmth to come—a good day to dress in layers.

Rolf knew the Schwäbischer Hof was somewhere on the other side of the park but thought it wise to ask the gray-haired man behind the front desk for directions. The clerk's sleepy eyes and disheveled hair bore witness to haphazard nightshift sleep. No more than a fifteen-minute walk, the clerk told him, which meant he could cover the distance in an easy five-minute warm-up jog. Rolf donned his billed cap, put on his running gloves and headed for the park.

Though he arrived early, Sylvia was waiting in the lobby. Her dark hair, gathered in a pony tail, fell down the back of a burgundy jogging suit. Rolf produced a small plastic bottle of water from his jacket pocket. "Here, I've got another one."

"I didn't know you had a marathon in mind."

"You haven't lost your sense of humor, I see."

"Can you get to the point?"

Her resolute tone told him she had her guard up. This could be a long morning. He started toward the exit. "Let's go." He noted with relief that she was following. Once outside, he didn't take the overpass leading to the park but walked down the sidewalk instead.

She called after him. "Where are you going? Aren't we running in the Schlosspark?"

"No, too many eyes there. Come on." He crossed over to the median and headed for a U-sign.

"We're taking the streetcar?"

Instead of answering, he ran down the row of steps. She caught up to him at the lower platform alongside tracks. A monitor protruding from the wall flashed the news that the next Stadtbahn No. 1 train would arrive in one minute.

Rolf fished a five-mark coin from his trouser pocket and inserted it into a ticket machine. They found two empty seats in the first car. Rolf caught the drift of alcohol and turned around. The rancid smell of stale liquor mixed with sweat came from a man, mumbling to himself. Rolf knew that stench. It was ever present the mornings after he and

Lynn had partied through the night. Of course, he could only detect the disgusting odor on Lynn, never on himself. No doubt, she'd found him just as revolting.

"Daydreaming?"

"Uh . . . I guess so. That man behind you reminded me of something." Rolf hoped he'd never have to experience that again. Sylvia looked out the window as the streetcar climbed out of the tunnel. Even though baggy runner's garb concealed her figure, one glance reminded him why he found her so attractive. He'd always had a weakness for Sylvia's type. Her Mediterranean complexion, round face, and the black sheen of her long, thick hair had made him weak-kneed in his twenties. Now in his thirties, he appreciated the spirit reflected in her intelligent, dark eyes almost more than her considerable physical attributes.

Sylvia interrupted her study of Stuttgart's street life to look straight at him. "So, what can you tell me that'll convince me to trust you this time around?"

He felt blood rushing to his face. "Trust is a two-way street. You weren't exactly upfront with me back then about your steady boyfriend Horst Kreuzer."

Her eyes flashed. She started to speak, but Rolf put up his hand. "Please, let me finish. That doesn't excuse my behavior. You came to me for help when you discovered how deep Kreuzer was into terrorism. But I was a coward. I didn't want to jeopardize my visa application to the States. I'm not proud of what I did, and I've had a lot of years since then to regret it."

"Well, as you can see, I managed without you. All I had to do was rat on Horst, quit the university, and get the hell out of Berlin."

Rolf looked away. Their outing was off to a rocky start. What could he say? He stared at the passing buildings and the light Sunday morning traffic for the rest of the ride. The conductor's announcement of the end of the line provided a welcome distraction.

Sylvia stood. "Let's go. Looks like we both need to run off some anger." They were in Fellbach, a small town just east of Stuttgart. She pointed toward the wooded hills to the south. "Don't tell me we're going to run up there."

"What's the matter? Not in shape for a few hills?"

Again, she ignored his invitation to banter and took off running. He fell in behind her. They traded the city streets for a footpath winding through pine forest up to the Kappelberg. The pine needles on the path glistened in the few spots of the forest floor where sunbeams managed to penetrate the tree tops. Their labored breathing attested to their exertion on the gradual uphill slope as the soft thud of their carbon soles striking the compacted clay echoed through the woods. Rolf inhaled the fresh forest air, its aroma intensified by recent rains. It helped expunge the memory of the man's odor in the streetcar.

When they reached the hilltop, Sylvia slowed to a walk, and he sidled in beside her. "You know, Rolf, I did not lead you on. I never pretended you were the only one I was seeing."

She was right, of course. "I understand that now, but I didn't want to then. What did you do after you left Berlin?"

"I came to Stuttgart to live with my mom for awhile until she went back to Milan to help her uncle manage a small hotel."

Sylvia broke into a jog. At a relaxed running pace, Sylvia took about one and a half steps to each of his strides, but her breathing seemed as easy as his.

When they neared the edge of the forest, she said, "You still haven't said why you wanted to talk to me, and we probably should turn around."

"No. We're on a five-kilometer course to Untertürkheim, where we'll catch the streetcar back. Rotenberg is coming up. I'd planned to stop there to talk."

"Yes. Rotenberg is a charming place."

Was she softening? he wondered. They left the forest and ran along a path that meandered through hillside vineyards. Even in November, the view of villages nestled between hills and patches of woods interspersed with vineyards provided a pleasant backdrop to their vigorous exercise. He remembered childhood family hikes to the Rotenberg Mausoleum. King Wilhelm I of Württemberg had the memorial erected in the early 1800s for his young queen Katharina who had died after only three years of marriage.

Sylvia stopped in front of a rotunda, crowned by a towering cupola. "Did you know that the queen was the daughter of a tsar?"

He nodded. Reflecting on the king's devotion to his Russian wife, Rolf felt romantic at first, but then saddened when he realized she had died at thirty—four years younger than Sylvia's age.

"The shrine is closed during the winter." She stretched her arms wide. "But the panorama is open all year."

A momentary enthusiasm penetrated her suspicion. She unscrewed the top of her water bottle and took a few sips, reminding Rolf to do the same. The sun broke through the scattered clouds, and for a while they watched the light show of sun and shadows playing across the hills and valleys, with the Neckar River below. Morning mist and patches of ground fog hovering over the low-lying fields added a transcendent quality to the atmosphere.

Sylvia turned from the iron railing that lined the edge of the chapel plaza to face Rolf. She dabbed at pearls of perspiration on her forehead. "Rolf, it's time you told me what you got me out here for. I want to know why you're involved in this venture and everything you know about it."

It was his turn to wipe sweat off his brow—from the running, not from her question, he told himself. He recounted his conversations with Stein and Schmidt but left out his suspicion that Schmidt might not trust her, as well as Stein's admonition for him to review, or even copy, whatever documents were passed.

When he'd finished, Sylvia gazed at the panorama without seeming to notice it.

"Do you honestly think Schmidt gives a damn about my safety?"

"I don't really know."

"All he cares about is getting the documents. He doesn't trust me. You were brought in to keep an eye on me."

Impressed with her astuteness, he said, "Schmidt doesn't trust anybody, not the Stasi spy, not you, and not me."

Still looking out over the fields, Sylvia demanded, "I'm still waiting to hear why I should even consider relying on you."

He took a deep breath. "Has Schmidt told you anything about the contents of the Stasi documents?"

"Only that they may provide information about an assassination plot."

"Yes. Apparently, he's been promised details of a planned assassination by terrorists. But what you need to know . . . ," Rolf paused until Sylvia turned away from the scenery to look at him, ". . . he means the Red Army Faction. That's what I wanted to tell you. He's hoping to arrest the ring leaders before they can kill another prominent figure."

"The sooner they catch them better." She glared at him. "You think I'm still involved with them, don't you?"

He held her gaze. She had cut her connection with Kreuzer, but he had to know if she had disentangled herself from his cause. "You're not, are you?"

"They tried to kill me. Does that tell you anything?"

His trial lawyer instincts told him she told the truth. He put up a hand. "Sorry, but I had to tell you."

"That Schmidt's after the RAF is not exactly a revelation, now is it? I hope that's not the reason you got me out of bed."

"No." He'd said it too fast, then caught himself. He didn't want to lie to her. "Actually . . . yes . . . one reason." He felt like a fool and fought to regain his composure. "But I wanted to ask you about Schmidt blackmailing you. He's threatening to destroy your career, isn't he?" Her brooding expression let him know he'd hit a nerve.

After a considerable pause, Sylvia nodded. "Yes. But even if I cooperate, there's no guarantee that will end the blackmail."

"No, it usually leads to more." Rolf took her by the shoulder. "Sylvia, that's what I wanted to talk to you about. This mission is huge. The way Schmidt talked about the planned assassination . . . he's worried to death it may derail unification for good."

"Rolf, you're hurting me." She grabbed his hand and he released his tight grip on her shoulder.

"Sorry, the thought of how they're using you . . . I got carried away. But, you shouldn't just go along. You must bargain with Schmidt. In exchange for your cooperation demand an agreement that the intelligence services won't use your past against you ever again."

"Do you really think they would do that?"

"You should push for it. Schmidt will do whatever he can to keep you. I'll do anything I can to help, if you want me to."

"Maybe you're right." Her reserve seemed to have lessened. She glanced at her watch. "We should be going. But before we do, I need a straight answer from you, Rolf. If I sense you're holding anything back, you're not coming to Berlin with me. Can you be honest with me?"

He felt her piercing gaze. Dreading what she might ask, he responded, "Yes, I can do that."

Sylvia kept her eyes fixed on his. "There are other reasons for your taking part, aren't there? Schmidt and Stein have ulterior motives, and your job is to carry out their plans. Am I right?"

Rolf broke away from her stare. She had a way of putting him on the spot. Stein, no doubt, would expect Rolf not to disclose the special charge he had given him. Still, Schmidt was the only one he'd said to keep in the dark. Rolf's intuition counseled a forthright response. But could he trust her? He had to take the chance.

"Sylvia, have you ever thought about law school? With your sizzling cross-examination skills, you'd make a great trial lawyer."

She did not break her intense stare. "So, what's the answer?"

"Will you give me your word that what I'm about to tell you will stay with you? Not a word to anyone, and especially not to Schmidt?"

"Yes, of course."

"My boss wants me to learn what's in the Stasi papers before they're passed to Schmidt. If possible, I'm to make copies. That's it, or at least that's all I know about."

Sylvia paused for a long moment, seeming to consider his fate, before she spoke, "Since I'm handling the risky part of this operation, it seems only fair that I'd get a peek at these materials too."

He grew suspicious. "Why are you interested in these papers?"

"The way I see it, we are pawns in this operation, at everyone's mercy—the Stasi spy, Schmidt, Stein. The only time we're in control is when we have the documents. I want to know what I'm passing along . . . what I'm risking my life for."

His first thought was to object—to argue that she'd be safer not knowing—but he couldn't fault her reasoning. As they resumed a slow-paced jog, he said, "All right, we'll look at them together. I won't tell Schmidt or Stein, if you won't."

"It's a deal." She ran ahead of him on the downhill trail toward the Untertürkheim streetcar stop. Before long, they were on board a yellow car, No. 13.

After they had transferred to Stadtbahn No. 1, Rolf asked, "So, what time is the flight?"

With arched eyebrows, Sylvia answered, "Seven thirty on Air France. I bet Schmidt's already arranged for your ticket."

Rolf relaxed. He had succeeded. "And tickets for your two Berlin performances, I hope. Speaking of which, I'm curious. What made you decide to become an opera singer?"

She gave him a wistful look. "That's a long story. Maybe some other time. Enough about me. Your turn to tell what you've been up to during the last twelve years."

Rolf spent the rest of the ride talking about law school, the firm, getting married and divorced, and his daughter Ashley. He generally didn't volunteer on the subject of his drinking, but when she asked him about the breakup, he thought for a moment and then responded, "Lynn and I both had a drinking problem. I quit, she didn't. I've been in a twelve-step recovery program for several months now and have been staying sober. AA has taught me that I can't control my ex-wife's drinking." He shrugged. "But I'm worried the toll it might take on Ashley." He shuddered at the thought of Ashley riding in the car with Lynn."

Sylvia caught his eyes. "I'm sorry. That's a terrible predicament for a father who loves his daughter."

They fell silent. Sylvia got up for the stop at the Schwäbischer Hof but motioned for Rolf to stay seated. "The next stop is closer to your hotel. I imagine you have some packing to do."

"Shall I pick you up at your hotel?"

"No. I'll see you at the airport."

The streetcar door swished closed behind her. Rolf watched her stride along the platform toward the stairs. He hoped he hadn't misinterpreted Schmidt's comments and, as a result, exaggerated the importance of the contents of the Stasi documents. Would she press Schmidt for a deal guaranteeing her a future free of coercion, and would he deliver if she did? The streetcar approached the stop near his hotel. For awhile he became preoccupied with exiting the underground station and locating Hotel Königshof.

Once he set out across the park, he resumed his speculations. Had he done the right thing in leveling with her? He didn't really know how deeply she'd been involved with Kreuzer. Perhaps she'd known more about his terrorist activities than she let on, even shared his extreme political views, possibly still did.

Well, he had cast his lot by trusting her and he couldn't reverse his decision. At the same time, there was no sense in being a blind fool. He'd stay on the alert for any signs of betrayal.

Chapter Thirteen

By late afternoon Rolf had run out of excuses to put off the call to Stein. He pulled the black phone off the nightstand and onto the bed while calculating the six-hour time difference between Stuttgart and Washington. Thinking his boss would be at the office at ten in the morning, he dialed the first of the two numbers he'd committed to memory per Stein's instruction. Then he remembered it was Sunday. He disconnected and called the number for non-business hours—a mobile phone, judging from the prefix. He listened to the successive clicks of the rotary phone laboring to transmit the signal.

After the fifth ring, just when he thought he'd get out of having to talk to his boss, Stein answered with a hello.

"Mr. Stein?"

"Yes."

"It's Rolf."

"It's about time you called. Hang on a moment while I pull over."

Rolf listened to background traffic noises, then tires slowing on pavement.

"What took you so long?"

Rolf heard the annoyance in the senior lawyer's voice, but he resisted the urge to defend himself and launched into his status report instead. Stein sounded pleased that everything was on course for Berlin. No surprise there. What did surprise Rolf were Stein's questions about Sylvia, her Stuttgart Opera performance and the degree of concern in his voice when told about the attack in the park.

He recalled Stein's admonition to watch out for the person slated to receive the Stasi papers. He must have known about Sylvia all along. That meant Schmidt's explanation for keeping her involvement a secret—to get Rolf to Germany first—was probably true. But if it were not, there must be more to Sylvia's role than he had been led to believe, something the senior lawyer hadn't divulged. Stein and Schmidt certainly had a penchant for keeping secrets.

Stein's voice interrupted Rolf's train of thought. "When you get to East Berlin, you know not to call me from your hotel or anywhere else, don't you? All the phones are tapped. Call me from West Berlin."

Washington traffic noises—a blaring car horn followed by faint police sirens—filled the momentary lapse in conversation. Rolf struggled to temper his irritation at Stein's condescending advice. It didn't take a master spy to be aware of the communist government's sweeping measures to keep tabs on its citizens. Rolf recalled telling Stein about the Stasi's domestic spy network. Either he had forgotten, or he was just being extra cautious.

Nevertheless, Rolf felt the need to disabuse his boss of the notion that he was dealing with an idiot. "Yes, I'm aware of the tapped phone lines in East Germany."

If Stein caught any hint of Rolf's frustration, the tone of his response didn't reflect it. "Good luck in Berlin. And next time, don't wait so long to call."

Rolf replaced the phone but remained seated on the bed. Something about the conversation bothered him. He stood and walked to the window overlooking the park. Stuttgart's citizenry was out in full force, soaking up the rare late November sun. The phone call kept gnawing at him. Was it the interest Stein had shown in Sylvia that puzzled him, or was there something else? If so, what could that be? Nothing came to him. He shrugged, refusing to rack his brain. The more he stewed, the less likely he was to find the answer.

♫ ♫ ♫

After terminating the connection, Stein glanced at the Sunday morning Arlington traffic. He reached for his checkbook and leafed through the register until he found the string of numbers he had written under one of the entries. Starting with the second numeral, he punched every other number into his cell phone and pressed the dial button.

A male voice answered on the first ring, "Yes?"

"I just heard from Rolf Keller."

Chapter Fourteen

"Hotel Drei Sachsen, bitte."

Sylvia's directions to the taxi driver jolted Rolf. While climbing after her into the Mercedes' rear seat, he failed to duck his head in time, banging it against the top of the door frame.

As the cab pulled away from the curb of the Berlin Tegel Airport, Sylvia asked, "Are you all right?"

Rolf touched the side of his head. "Yes. It's not that I'm a klutz. I just figured out what's been bothering me about the phone conversation I had with my boss."

Her dark eyes met his. "Well, are you going to tell me?"

"Are we staying in West or East Berlin?"

"East."

"When did you learn that?"

"Schmidt made the arrangements. He told me when I called him after our run this morning."

"Did Schmidt agree to a guarantee against further blackmail?" Rolf asked in a low voice.

"He was noncommittal. He agreed to request it, but wouldn't make any promises."

"What's your impression of how hard he'll pursue it?"

"I believe you're on to something about how badly Schmidt wants these papers. My sense is that he'll try to convince his boss to give me assurance against further coercion. Do you . . ."

She stopped talking when the driver slammed on the brakes and yelled "Arschloch!" His herringbone cap bounced up, down and sideways with his wild gesticulations toward a small sedan that had cut them off. He glanced in the inside rearview mirror with a contrite expression and muttered, "Entschuldigung."

Rolf laughed. "Well, he was kind of an asshole." He appreciated how closely the German's driving habits matched those of New York and Washington cabbies.

Sylvia broke into his thoughts. "You still haven't told me what's troubling you."

"I wanted to make sure of something before saying anything. I didn't know where we were staying until you told the driver, yet Stein knew our hotel was in East Berlin. I'm supposed to keep him informed, but he seems to do a darn good job of that without me. He's three thousand miles and six hours away, and he knows what's going on over here before I do."

Sylvia nodded. "Makes you wonder about Stein and Schmidt."

Rolf studied the glittering city lights as their taxi wound its way through evening traffic. Congestion ahead slowed them to a crawl. Pedestrians crowded the sidewalks.

He asked the driver, "Is there something special going on this evening?"

The cabbie gave him a quizzical look. Apparently realizing that his passengers were clueless, he responded, "We're approaching the border. Ever since the Wall was opened, it's been like a carnival around here. Berliners still can't believe it."

"Nor can I," Rolf said. "I never expected the Wall to come down during my lifetime."

Sylvia leaned forward. "It didn't even occur to us to ask you whether you're allowed to take us to the eastern sector."

"That's no problem. The Volkspolizei hardly check anymore."

A few minutes later the driver's pronouncement proved true. A young East German policeman leaned against the wall of the guard station, a red rose sprouting from the barrel of his rifle. After a cursory glance at their taxi, he waved them through.

Once they were in East Berlin, Rolf decided to broach a subject that had been much on his mind. "You asked me this morning to tell you everything I knew about this venture, and I did. Now I want to ask you the same thing. Is there anything you haven't told me?"

She met his gaze. "No. You know everything I do. What makes you think otherwise?"

"Stein asked a lot of questions about you, what you were like, how the performance went, and details that for the life of me I couldn't connect with my mission. It made me wonder whether there is a link that escapes me."

Sylvia shook her head. "Strange. I don't know the man and have no idea what he may be up to." Her expression changed from consternation to curiosity. "And what did you tell him about me and the opera?"

Rolf recalled how he had marveled to his boss about Sylvia's stunning performance, her lyrical voice and wonderful acting. Embarrassed to repeat his glowing comments, he was groping for a response when the driver pulled into the circular drive of a five-story hotel. A uniformed young man opened the door on Sylvia's side, then collected their bags from the trunk. Rolf motioned for her to follow the bellboy inside while he paid the fare.

When he entered the lobby, Rolf saw Sylvia turn away from the front desk and walk over to a lounge area, motioning to him. He sensed something was wrong.

"What's the matter? Don't they have our reservations?"

"They have a reservation, all right. Schmidt booked one suite for the two of us."

For a second Rolf fantasized keeping that arrangement but then caught himself. "I suppose he was thinking of our cover."

"You'd think he'd at least mention it, or God forbid ask us! How are we going to change it without drawing attention or arousing suspicion about our relationship? Any ideas?"

"Let me handle this."

He strode to the desk and asked for the manager. A short, bald-headed man in a blue business suit appeared from an office behind the counter. "Is there a problem with the reservation?"

Rolf moved to the far side of the counter, waiting for the manager to join him. When he did, Rolf spoke in a hushed tone. "Not a problem, exactly. It seems there's been a mistake made in booking one room only. You see, Frau Mazzoni will need some privacy to prepare for her opera performance. So, one room, even a suite, won't do. Do you understand?"

While listening, the manager's demeanor changed. Ostensible concern turned to puzzlement, followed by understanding, which in turn changed into an expression Rolf interpreted as somewhere between condescending and conspiratorial. Rolf wasn't sure whether the manager felt gracious in helping out a fellow male, or if he recognized he'd been given a line and was willing to play along.

"But of course. I understand." He walked behind the counter and rifled through a large card file. After what seemed like several minutes, he looked up. "I have a suite on the top floor and an adjoining room. Would that be satisfactory?"

Rolf wasn't sure why, but he asked, "Is there a connecting door?"

"Yes."

"That's perfect. We'll take it."

He motioned Sylvia over to help with the paperwork, detailed as was usual in German hotels. As they stepped into the elevator, she eyed him with suspicion. "Looked to me like you two were cooking up something. Did you manage to keep us decent and moral without blowing our cover?"

Rolf grinned. "You'll see."

Although they were expected to act like a couple, common sense dictated separate rooms. Nonetheless, he couldn't suppress a tinge of regret.

Chapter Fifteen

Brigadier General Holger Frantz extended a large white envelope across the surface of his huge desk. "Colonel, here is the material for your first delivery."

He made no attempt to get up from his chair, obviously expecting Heinz Dobnik to do so. Jumping to his feet, the colonel reached for the packet. In doing so, he glanced up at the gallery of photographs decorating the wall behind the general. Many of the pictures portrayed a smiling Frantz shaking hands with party bosses. One photo depicted former Party Chief Erich Honecker pinning a medal on Frantz, probably when he was promoted to brigadier general.

Envelope in hand, Dobnik returned to the black leather chair and took stock of his surroundings. The spacious room and the carpeted floor indicated he was in the office of a department head. Yet the size of the office and its carpet did not completely dispel the dreariness that pervaded the atmosphere. After all, Stasi headquarters was a huge gray building complex, populated by comrades and bureaucrats under the thumb of a nearly bankrupt communist regime. The ill-fitting cabinet doors flanking the side wall and the cheap grade of carpeting reminded Dobnik of his country's limitations. There was no hint of luxury or opulence of the kind he'd seen in some offices in the West.

When the general spoke again, Dobnik wondered whether his momentary hesitation had telegraphed uncertainty about when he should review the envelope's contents. "You can look at these later. It was difficult to decide what to include. We need to give the West Germans information they find valuable, and which they can verify as genuine. But we don't want to give away secrets unnecessarily, do we?"

"No, sir." Dobnik summoned his courage. "How did you manage to strike that delicate balance, sir?"

Frantz seemed pleased by the question, apparently unaware that its admiring tone was feigned. "I believe you'll agree these will be sufficient to lend you credibility. But if you see something that shouldn't be there, or something that should be but isn't, let me know right away."

Merely intimating that the general might have made a mistake would involve a greater risk than Dobnik was willing to take. Yet he dutifully replied, "Of course, sir," all the while pondering whether Frantz was plotting to blame him for leaking state secrets.

Frantz studied him for a moment. "I assume you'll make the drop at the opera this evening?"

"That's my plan."

"Very well. Make sure nothing goes wrong."

The veiled threat caused Dobnik to stammer, "Yes . . . sir."

Frantz stood but remained behind his desk. Dobnik took the hint and headed for the door when the general's voice stopped him. "One more thing. I've thought of a name for this project. Let's call it 'Operation Independence.' Has a nice ring to it, don't you agree?"

Frantz's smirk made Dobnik shiver. He forced a "yes" from his lips and retreated into the outer office. As he passed Frantz's secretary, her phone buzzed and he saw the intercom button light up. Dobnik slowed his steps. While closing the door, he heard her hushed, "Yes, sir. I'll get him."

The timing of the intercom call reawakened his suspicions about Frantz's intentions. What if the call had had some connection with his task? Of course, it could be something entirely unrelated, or if related, Frantz might handle it by phone. Yet he could not shake his strong intuition that the general was summoning someone to his office to carry out a clandestine plan. Dobnik decided he needed to nose around.

He walked across the dingy linoleum floor, badly faded with edges curling in a few spots. How symbolic this gloomy, windowless corridor was of the run-down East German economy. Where could he go to observe without being conspicuous? He passed the elevator. The hallway continued for a few meters before turning ninety degrees to the left. The person visiting Frantz would likely be coming up the elevator, unless his office happened to be on this floor of higher-ups. Dobnik decided to take that chance. If he was wrong, he'd just have to make his presence appear unsuspicious. Rather than standing in place, he paced up and down the side corridor, listening to the faint sounds of the elevator as it circulated between floors. If anyone approached him, he would simply keep moving, as if he were on his way to another office.

Since he hadn't checked his watch at the start of the stakeout, Dobnik had to rely on his sense of time. He estimated he'd been there close to ten minutes. Five more, he told himself, and he'd write off his hunch to wild imagination. Just then the elevator noise grew louder. Dobnik peeked around the corner and saw the light above the steel door illuminate. He moved out of sight as the motor whined to a stop.

When he heard the door retract, Dobnik walked down the side hallway away from the elevator to give himself cover in case the person came his way. He listened to the sound of boot soles clicking on the hallway floor, loud at first, then growing more distant. Whoever had gotten off was heading the other way, in the direction of Frantz's office. Dobnik reached the corner in a few quick steps and peered down the corridor. What he saw produced feelings of satisfaction and then of fright—satisfaction that his instincts were proved right, fright because he was looking at the burly back of Major Boris Schlechter.

Disturbing rumors collected around Schlechter like flies around rotting flesh. He was reputed to do the bosses' extreme dirty work when it came to internal matters. Dobnik thought about the suspected traitors who had not been prosecuted, either because the party bosses didn't have the scant proof necessary for a show trial or considered a trial politically too risky. Escaping prosecution definitely did not equate with being out of harm's way, as a large number of those spared the ordeal of a trial died under mysterious circumstances. Some fell out of upper story windows or onto tracks in front of onrushing trains. Others overdosed. Some had fatal automobile collisions. Still others died of gunshot wounds.

Watching Major Schlechter disappear into the brigadier general's office, Dobnik reflected how with each case the whispers grew louder that Schlechter was somehow linked to the deaths. Dobnik suspected the Stasi bosses might even have fueled the gossip in order to convey to the lower echelon what awaited those who betrayed the East German state. Most of those who'd been fingered as traitors would undergo a show trial with conviction a foregone conclusion. The only question was whether the punishment would be a lengthy prison sentence, or death. Of course, if the convicted was so unfortunate as to end up at Bautzen II, the prison dubbed the "Yellow Misery," tortures administered by Stasi officers often turned a prison term into an actual death sentence. Dobnik stiffened as he recalled last year's "suicide" of double agent Horst Garau at that prison.

Dobnik caught the elevator. As the cab descended, he considered the incidents in which Schlechter was said to have had a hand. If even a fraction of the rumors linking Major Schlechter to those deaths were true, Dobnik realized his life depended on escaping to the West at the first opportunity.

♫ ♫ ♫

Deep in thought about what needed to be done, Frantz motioned Major Schlechter toward a chair. Dobnik appeared to have bought the story he'd been given about Operation Independence. The colonel might just manage to pull it off without the West Germans suspecting a setup. But things could go wrong. Frantz had to protect himself, and that would best be done by exposing the colonel as a counterspy.

Frantz returned his attention to the room. He studied the major's hard eyes sunk deep into a baby face that seemed out of character with a graying military haircut. The creaking of the chair, straining to hold the beefy six-foot frame, reassured him he'd chosen the right man. Not only did Major Boris Schlechter possess the physique to dispose of enemies of the state, but his dedication to the cause and his personal loyalty to Frantz could not be doubted.

The general congratulated himself for having plucked Schlechter's file out of hundreds of prisoners' records years ago. The selection pool had been limited, since the majority of jail inhabitants in East Germany were there for political reasons and therefore not suitable for the tasks Frantz and the Stasi had in mind. Schlechter had served the first of his fifteen years on an armed robbery conviction when the general offered him the chance to put his penchant for violence into service for the good of the state. He seemed smarter than his criminal record suggested, and in the general's estimation, cunning enough to rid society of those who would endanger the communist way of life. Schlechter had not disappointed. The prospect of fourteen more years of hard prison labor provided strong motivation. He always followed orders.

"Major, if I needed to plant information with one of the Western Allies' intelligence services, could you do it and make it appear genuine?"

Schlechter shifted in the black leather chair. "If it doesn't matter to you which one. We're a bit thin right now with the Americans and French. They've caught a couple of our agents. But the Brits think they are getting great intelligence on our government from a spy who's actually a double agent working for us."

The general beamed. "The MI5 would be perfect."

"May I ask about the nature of the information and what time frame you have in mind?"

To make his failsafe appear credible, Frantz knew he needed to lay some groundwork with the major. Of course, he wouldn't tell him any more than he needed to know.

"Major, I require your word that you will keep secret what I'm about to tell you."

"Of course, sir."

Frantz sighed and contorted his face into what he hoped conveyed a worried expression. "Regrettably, I have reason to believe that we may have another traitor among us. Someone who may be delivering documents to the West Germans."

Schlechter showed no surprise. No doubt he was aware that the number of defectors in the Stasi ranks had grown considerably since Gorbachev's ill-advised policies had put the East German government on shaky footing. With the Wall open, it was only natural to expect defections to the West to increase.

"Who is it, sir? Let me take care of him." The major's response rang with indignation, his vehement tone leaving no doubt how much he would relish an assignment to dispose of the traitor.

Frantz was satisfied. "We haven't been able to identify the turncoat yet. I hope my suspicions will be proved wrong." He paused for emphasis. "I have reasons to believe that the defector plans to pass state secrets to a Sylvia Mazzoni, an opera singer from the West who is singing at the Staatsoper in two guest performances this week."

"An opera singer?"

"Hard to believe, I know."

"Do you have any more details about the drop, when and where?"

"No, not yet." Another pause. "Major, have our double agent find a way to tip off British Intelligence that sometime this week Frau Mazzoni is expected to receive a top secret Stasi file exposing a high West German government official as a Nazi collaborator. The Brits should love to get their hands on that, don't you think? Anything to scuttle the West Germans' grandiose ideas of unification."

Schlechter returned the general's smirk. "When do you want this planted?"

"Today."

The major jumped to his feet. "I'll take care of it right away."

He turned to leave but stopped when Frantz spoke again. "As for the traitor in our midst, I hope to have some evidence as early as tomorrow. When I do, I'll have a job for you."

"Understood."

Frantz rose to shake the major's hand and walk him to the door. "Major, I know I can count on you."

Alone again, the general strode over to the window, pleased that everything was proceeding according to plan. He could hardly wait to unleash Schlechter on the unsuspecting Dobnik and Mazzoni. Patience, he counseled himself. Better to wait until after the leak to the British. By the end of this week he'd not only have exposed a traitor in the Stasi ranks as well as a western spy, but the West Germans could forever bury their ambitions to swallow East Germany. Once they saw the Stasi documents, the Allies would see to that.

Chapter Sixteen

Heinz Dobnik stared in disbelief at the papers spread out over the large desk. His first thought was that Brigadier General Frantz must have made a mistake. Surely, he didn't mean to give this kind of information to the West Germans. The colonel studied the text and map coordinates over and over until he could no longer deny that they disclosed West German missile sites considered top secret by NATO and the Pentagon. He contemplated calling Frantz per the general's invitation, but resisted the impulse and instead took up his habitual worry walk between desk and window.

After a few moments, he interrupted his pacing to ponder the potential reasons for giving over this information. First, the general wanted to impress upon the Federal Intelligence Service that he, Dobnik, had access to top-level secrets. Second, the West Germans could verify the accuracy of the information from their own sources or those of the United States. That still didn't fully explain why the Stasi was willing to release this information, because its value would fall to zero the instant it was leaked to the West.

Dobnik rubbed his chin and resumed his trek. The significance had to be in the timing of the release. Perhaps one of the Stasi moles who might have betrayed this top secret had been caught, making it only a matter of time before the Western Allies found out about the security breach on their own. Or could it simply be a matter of thawing relations between Gorbachev's Soviet Union and the United States, rendering this information less crucial?

Whatever the reason, he would not second guess the general. No sooner had he reached that decision than a frightening thought popped into his head. If his suspicions about Frantz and Schlechter were justified, and he were caught passing these papers to Sylvia . . . ? He did not want to finish the thought. Eyeing the envelope and papers, he walked to the door and threw the deadbolt.

Dobnik returned to the desk and retrieved a writing tablet and pencil from a side drawer. He needed to organize his thoughts. Backstage access having been cleared with opera house security, he had planned on delivering the documents to Sylvia Mazzoni in her dressing room after this evening's performance. Now, in light of Schlechter's visit to the brigadier general's office, Dobnik rejected that idea as too risky. Frantz might have set a trap to catch him handing over the top-secret materials. He needed to find a way to get the documents to Sylvia without being present when she received them. But how? Dobnik was drawing circles on the lined writing pad when the intercom buzzed.

His secretary's voice echoed through the room, "Herr Oberst. Just a reminder that everyone is gathering for coffee and cake in the conference room on the eighth floor to celebrate Major General Rittmeister's birthday."

"Thank you, Frau Ammer. Go on ahead. I'll be there in a few minutes."

As much as he didn't feel like going at that moment, all the big shots would be there, and his absence would be noted. Perhaps an idea about the document drop would come to him during the boring party. He gathered the loose papers and stuffed them in the envelope, which he placed in the open wall safe behind him. Closing it, he reminded himself once more to change the combination. It felt ridiculous to continue using his wedding anniversary date a year after the divorce.

Dobnik's mood improved thanks to a tasty chocolate cake, strong coffee and only a few short speeches. While Rittmeister expressed his appreciation for the party, Dobnik recognized the opportunity this presented. Subsequent to Mielke's dismissal as the Stasi chief, Frantz had assured Dobnik he would personally brief Major General Rittmeister on Operation Independence. This was Dobnik's chance to find out whether Frantz had kept his word. Colonel Dobnik maneuvered himself toward the group surrounding the major general, ostensibly to shake his hand. When the other well-wishers moved on, Dobnik addressed Rittmeister before anyone else could join them.

Remembering the recent flood of memos generated by Rittmeister prescribing the types of documents to be kept and the ones to be destroyed, Dobnik said, "Herr Generalmajor, may I express my appreciation for your recent measures to safeguard our sensitive files?" Dobnik hoped he didn't sound phony.

"Thank you, Colonel. We all will have to do our best to save this great institution."

Colonel Dobnik tried to think of a way to steer the discussion toward his current assignment, hoping to find out whether the major general knew anything about it. To Dobnik's delight, Rittmeister filled the awkward lull in the conversation with an innocuous question. "Working on anything interesting, Colonel?"

Dobnik glanced around before answering, "Sir, I'd rather not say . . . here." Seeing the general frown at his insolence, Dobnik added in a whisper, "Operation Independence, sir."

"What is that?"

Even before the major general's question, Dobnik could tell from his blank look that he had never heard of Operation Independence. In and of itself, that might mean nothing. Frantz probably invented the name and would not necessarily have shared it with Rittmeister. Dobnik needed to follow up. "You know, the misinformation project Brigadier General Frantz assigned to me."

Before Rittmeister could reply, several partygoers joined them to wish the general a happy birthday. Although Dobnik didn't have the major general's verbal response, his facial expression had been unmistakable: Rittmeister had not been briefed about the document drops. As soon as he could do so without calling attention to himself, Dobnik left the conference room and returned to his office.

Feeling agitated, he opened his safe. Instead of retrieving the envelope, he reached for the bottle of schnapps, poured a generous portion into a coffee cup and took a gulp. The burning sensation distracted him temporarily, but it quickly subsided and the worries returned. He tried hard to think of reasons explaining Rittmeister's lack of knowledge. Perhaps the tumultuous events surrounding Chief Mielke's firing and the briefing of his successor on ongoing projects had the Stasi brass so preoccupied that this project had fallen through the cracks. Or Rittmeister had been told but had forgotten.

Dobnik took another sip and shook his head. Neither one of these explanations would do. This mission was too important and too unusual for the higher echelon not to have been informed, if it was indeed an officially sanctioned undertaking. Besides, Frantz had promised to inform the major general. Nor was Rittmeister likely to forget this kind of undertaking. Dobnik did not like the conclusion he reached: he and Frantz might be the only ones who knew about this scheme. If so, Frantz could do as he pleased—a chilling thought.

There was one more trail he could follow. If Frantz had lied to him about informing Rittmeister, then his assertion that former chief Mielke had been in the loop was likely false as well. Dobnik had previously considered contacting Mielke, but had rejected the idea as too risky. Deposed leaders in a totalitarian state usually did not fare too well. Once the most feared and hated man in East Germany, Mielke became more vulnerable with each passing day as the people began to vent their anger against the Stasi and its officers. He was not the person to be seen with these days. Nevertheless, Dobnik made up his mind to pay him a visit, and soon, since he might be arrested at any time. He simply had to find out whether Mielke knew about this operation.

Colonel Dobnik emptied his cup, resisting the temptation to refill it. Now that he'd reached a decision about Mielke, he needed to turn his attention to this evening's task with a clear head. He stashed the half-full bottle in the safe. A plan about how to make the drop began to form. It was amazingly simple. He wondered why it had taken him so long to think of it.

He carried the white envelope from the safe to the copier on the credenza and copied all the pages to add to his collection, just in case the papers he'd drop off for Sylvia this evening somehow didn't find their way to Dieter Schmidt. Dobnik put both sets of documents back into the envelope, which he slid into his attaché case. He shut the safe, glanced around the office to make sure nothing was left out that shouldn't be, retrieved the briefcase from the desk and strode out to his secretary's workstation. She had not yet returned from the birthday party.

Her desk was neat as usual, pens and pencils arranged by color in a clear-plastic cube. Dobnik took out a red pen and wrote in large handwriting on a note pad next to her phone that he'd be gone for the rest of the day. She was used to him leaving the office without telling her where he was going. It came with his job. He had made it a practice to tell his secretary only what she needed to know.

After returning the red pen to its place, Dobnik walked out into the hallway. His stride became more energetic as he anticipated all he had to do this afternoon to arrange this evening's drop. Not only did he like the simplicity of his plan for the delivery, but also the message he would leave for Sylvia Mazzoni, unbeknownst to Brigadier General Frantz. Dobnik congratulated himself for his foresight on insisting that Sylvia be the recipient. It was becoming more and more likely that he would indeed need to use her for his own purposes.

Chapter Seventeen

"Taxi, Frau Mazzoni?"

Surprised that the doorman knew her name, Sylvia responded, "Uh . . . looks like a nice morning for a walk. How far is it to the opera house?"

"Only a few minutes, ma'am." He pointed to the right.

She crossed against heavy morning traffic to stroll along the center promenade of Unter den Linden, named after the beautiful trees that used to line the broad walkway. Incredibly, Adolf Hitler had many of the old linden trees cut down and replaced with poles displaying Nazi insignias and swastika flags. And the bombs of World War II destroyed most of the boulevard along with its remaining trees. Sylvia shook her head at the insanity. The replanted lindens still had a lot of growing to do before the boulevard would regain its renowned magnificence. Though East Berlin looked dreary in comparison to the western sector, she could feel a certain excitement in the air. People were anticipating freedoms they hadn't known since before Hitler came to power in 1933. The impetus to unify Germany seemed stronger here than in the West. After decades of deprivation, East Germans seemed eager to partake of the economic riches of its western neighbor.

When she caught sight of the Staatsoper Unter den Linden, her thoughts turned to what lay ahead. According to management's message requesting her appearance this morning, this would simply be a brief orientation session. She located the artists' entrance without difficulty. The stage doorman waved her straight through. He'd obviously been told to expect her.

On her way to the assistant director's office, Sylvia reflected on Rolf Keller's urging to let him accompany her. With this morning session already impinging on her usual performance-day activities, she didn't need the added distraction of having Rolf around. Not wanting to be reminded of matters unrelated to opera, she'd insisted on coming alone, although as much as she hated to admit it, she would welcome his presence during the delivery of the documents.

The door to the office to which she'd been directed stood open and she entered. She noted with unease that the man greeting her appeared to be younger than she. Short, brown hair, not cut by an expert barber in a long time, if ever, hollow cheeks and an old-fashioned dark brown suit made for a drab appearance, reminding Sylvia more of a bureaucrat than a musician.

He extended his hand, offering an impersonal, limp handshake. "Werner Braun. Welcome to the Staatsoper, Frau Mazzoni."

His tone belied the words he spoke. He sounded anything but welcoming. He averted his eyes, leaving Sylvia with the impression that the Stasi agent must have really pressured theater management into engaging her. Being disliked by directors, and probably colleagues, was not exactly a recipe for success. The meeting turned out to be nothing more than orienting her to the peculiarities of the production, and peculiar it was. There was a growing trend in German opera houses, fueled by young directors eager to make names for themselves, to arrange productions in modern settings.

She feigned interest as Braun explained the director's brilliant concept of transporting *Carmen* from the early nineteenth century to contemporary times. At least it still took place in Seville, Sylvia thought. The gypsy band had been replaced by a street gang in black leather jackets. Instead of entering a mountain scene in the third act, Micaëla would find herself exploring back alleys where gang members congregated.

Her apprehension about Braun's tender age appeared justified, and from what he was telling her about the production, she surmised she'd not likely spot any gray hair on the director either. She kept her opinion to herself, however. She couldn't afford to turn down any opportunity. No matter how crazy its concept, as long as the production didn't interfere with her ability to sing and act, she'd manage.

An hour later, Sylvia entered the lobby of Hotel Drei Sachsen. The front desk clerk handed her the room key along with a phone message. She shook her head in disbelief when she saw the caller's name, Ursula Sommer. Now that was a switch—her agent calling her! During all the years Sylvia had telephoned her to enquire after engagements, most of her calls had gone unanswered. The note asked Sylvia to contact her immediately for important news. She wasn't sure how difficult a call to Frankfurt might be, but the hotel operator achieved the connection without delay.

"Frau Mazzoni. Good to hear from you. I didn't know you were singing at the Staatsoper until I talked to the Stuttgart Opera Director. I would have hoped you'd steer the Berlin engagement my way."

Sylvia found the woman insufferable. "Well, Stuttgart management made the arrangements. I was told they'd get in touch with you."

"Never mind. That's not why I called earlier. You must have done something really special Saturday evening."

Before she could stop herself, Sylvia interjected, "You could have seen for yourself, if you'd used those complimentary tickets I sent you."

Line static filled the ensuing pause. Then Sommer's voice, a little less sure than before, rang in Sylvia's ear once more. "I wish I could have come. But what I wanted to tell you is that you received great reviews in the local press, and Stuttgart Opera is offering you a two-year contract. Shall I fax it to you?"

Sylvia thought for a long moment. Signing a contract right away sounded tempting. Yet something told her to hold off. "No. Let's wait till I'm back in Stuttgart later this week."

Sommer signed off with a parting shot. "It's your career."

This time Sylvia did not voice her irritation but let the challenge pass, recognizing the agent's eagerness to collect her percentage. After replacing the phone, Sylvia sang out a wall-shaking "Hurrah!" Critics not only had attended but had liked her—amazing.

She heard a knock on the connecting door. "Sylvia, is everything all right?"

She unlatched the lock and let Rolf into the suite.

"Yes, I was so excited, I couldn't help myself. Things couldn't be better on the professional front. Stuttgart has offered me a two-year engagement."

Rolf's face broke into a grin. "Congratulations." After a pause, he added, "How did this morning's rehearsal go?"

"Well, it was more of an orientation session." She wanted to add a comment about the lukewarm welcome and the modern staging, when she remembered not to say anything she didn't want the East German authorities to hear. Sylvia touched her lips with her index finger.

Rolf nodded. "Do you want to grab a quick lunch?"

Sylvia told herself she probably should opt for her usual room-service meal on performance day. Still, she felt prepared for this evening, with the pressure off to some extent, given the news from Stuttgart. Besides, they hadn't yet discussed the logistics of Rolf's presence during a potential document drop.

"Yes, as long as we make it short."

They chose a small restaurant halfway between the hotel and the opera house. The place looked clean and was less likely to be bugged than the hotel restaurant or the opera café. Rolf took a table by the window, far away from the door. They selected from the daily specials and were served within a few minutes.

Rolf looked up between bites. "So, what's the scoop on this evening's production?"

"For one thing, I got the definite impression they don't really want me here. The Stasi must have put some pressure on the director to engage me."

"That'll make it quite a challenge to do your best, won't it?"

"Well, I can deal with it. What's more, the staging is dreadful. I only met the assistant to the director, but from what he told me, I'm afraid we've got another young genius on our hands who knows better than the composer. He has Micaëla looking for Don José among gang members in back alleys instead of the mountains in southern Spain, for heaven's sake!"

She realized she'd been pointing her fork at Rolf. "Sorry. I get worked up when I think about these arrogant directors, modernizing plots at all costs in order to make a name for themselves. The critics love this crap, and the German public seems to tolerate it, or the theaters wouldn't keep dishing it out."

"My, my—someone has strong feelings about that. We've coined a phrase for it in the States: Eurotrash."

Sylvia chuckled. The waitress cleared the table, stacking empty dinner and salad plates on her arm. She looked surprised when they ordered coffee, a beverage usually consumed with cake in the late afternoon rather than after a German lunch. Sipping the strong brew, Sylvia noticed Rolf's wistful look. She followed his gaze at the neighboring table and saw a thirtyish woman and a bony girl, no doubt mother and daughter, eating in silence.

"Thinking about Ashley?" Sylvia asked in a soft voice.

Rolf turned toward her and his eyes refocused as if returning from far away. He seemed embarrassed. "Yes, that little girl is about her age."

"You feel like talking about it?" Sylvia asked with an even voice, trying to convey her willingness to listen without prying.

Rolf studied her, hesitated, then relaxed. "Yeah, I guess so. I've been feeling guilty. Lynn and I divorced and instead of seeing Ashley every day, we're down to visits every other weekend. From her perspective, I'm the one who disappeared from her daily life, not her mom."

Sylvia reached across the table and squeezed his hand. She didn't know what to say.

"And then I take off for Germany without saying goodbye," he continued. "But when I look at these East German families, I realize how well off Ashley really is, even with divorced parents." He raised his hand as she withdrew hers. "You know the communists have brainwashed children to inform on their parents. They are taught it's their patriotic duty to turn their parents in to the Stasi for suspicious activities or criticism of the state."

Sylvia shook her head. She couldn't imagine.

"Do you like children?"

His question startled her. "Well . . . yes. But in my line of work, it's best to postpone having a family, if that's what you're asking." His look told her she'd guessed correctly. "Being an opera singer means constant travel around the globe." She laughed. "But I'm getting ahead of myself, daydreaming about an international career."

"You'll make it," he reassured her.

She wanted so much to believe him. Suppressing her doubts, she sought his eyes. "I hope you're right." After a moment she said, "Don't beat yourself up. I'm sure you do your best to be a good father. Sometimes it's healthier for a child to grow up with divorced parents than in an unhappy marriage. Children sense the discord among spouses who white-knuckle it to stay together at all costs."

Rolf nodded and stared out the window for several minutes, then turned back abruptly. "When and where do you think Mozart will give you the documents?"

"Your guess is as good as mine," she said with a shrug.

"Let's assume he'll do it sometime during the performance." Rolf raised his eyebrows. "He must know you have about a two-hour time lag between your first- and third-act appearances. Perhaps he's planning to come to your dressing room then."

"Mozart may not make the delivery himself, you know."

"Not likely that he'll involve someone else. A man in his position, betraying his country's secrets, can't afford to trust anyone within the Stasi. If he doesn't come himself, the papers will arrive by some innocuous means. The carrier won't know what he's delivering."

She knew he was right. "So, what do you suggest?"

"I'd like to be in your dressing room before and after the opera and during your two-hour break."

She studied his face looking for a clue whether he sought more than admittance to her room. Wary of his prior desertion, she pondered whether by acceding to his request she would let him back in her life. But could she handle the Stasi agent without Rolf's presence? To buy time, she drank the last drop of coffee, almost slurping the aromatic brew. One cup was all she would allow herself. After that, she'd sip water until curtain call. Setting the empty cup down, she made her decision.

"All right. I'll tell the stage doorman and the dressing assistant to let you pass."

During their walk back to the hotel, Sylvia told Rolf she needed to be alone to prepare. Before she could cross the boulevard toward the Drei Sachsen, Rolf stopped her. "Will you let me know when you're ready to leave for the theater this evening? I'd best accompany you."

"Yes. I'll collect you about five thirty," Sylvia replied. Though it likely was none of her business, she asked, "How will you spend the afternoon?"

"I'll probably give Stein a ring." He waited until several pedestrians had passed and then added, "But first, I'll be looking for a self-service copy shop."

Rolf turned and walked toward the underground station.

Chapter Eighteen

Locating a vocal score for *Carmen* turned out to be more difficult than Heinz Dobnik had imagined. Calling around to the various shops had not been an option, unless he wanted Brigadier General Frantz to learn the details of his plan, thanks to bugged phones. Unsuccessful searches at two bookstores and a music shop had eaten up half the afternoon. As he entered the shop at the Staatsoper, he realized this likely would be his last chance to find what he needed in East Berlin. There'd be plenty of stores in the western sector of the city that sold just about anything relating to this popular opera. Although he felt reasonably certain he hadn't been followed, he did not want to chance going to West Berlin unless absolutely necessary.

Dobnik was in luck. Because of an afternoon function in the café the opera shop had opened early and it was stocked with *Carmen* paraphernalia. Among the books, recordings, t-shirts and libretti, Dobnik spotted several copies of the musical score, available in soft cover and hardback. For his intended use, only the hardback would do. He carried two copies to the cash register. The young woman behind the counter informed him in a high-pitched voice that the total came to thirty-five. Handing her forty Ostmarks, he took in long blond hair, a round face, and a full figure, bordering on plump, and wondered whether she might be an aspiring opera singer earning some extra money. Then he realized his thoughts were guided by the stereotype about overweight divas.

"Have you seen the current production?"

Her question caught him off guard. "Uh . . . no, I haven't. I'll be going this evening." As an afterthought, he asked, "Have you seen it?"

"Yes. It's wonderful, especially the way it's been updated to our time."

As an occasional operagoer, Dobnik preferred traditional over modern performances. He hoped her comment didn't mean he'd have to sit through some nonsensical contortion cooked up by an eccentric director of the new generation.

She handed him a plastic bag containing the two books. "I hope you'll enjoy it. You won't be seeing the soprano who's been portraying Micaëla. They've brought in a guest artist to sing her role for the next two performances." As she held out her hand with his change, she added in a low, secretive voice, "People around here question why they would bring in a singer from the West when our regular has been performing so well."

He did not like the idea of Sylvia Mazzoni attracting extra attention, which could make his job more difficult. With a noncommittal retort of "Who knows why artists do what they do?" Dobnik pocketed his change and hurried from the shop. For a brief moment he considered visiting the opera café downstairs, but decided he couldn't afford the time. He still had much to do. Twenty minutes later he exited the underground at Alexanderplatz. After a brisk walk down a side street, he stopped in front of a row of free-standing garages. Except for an elderly couple crossing the intersection at the end of the street, the neighborhood was deserted on this workday afternoon.

Dobnik inserted a key into the lock of a brown wooden door bearing a faded green "D." After glancing up and down the street once more, he turned the rusted handle and heaved the reluctant garage door up. He crouched to step under the overhead door before wrestling it back down from the inside until only a crack remained, admitting enough daylight for him to find the light switch.

A light bulb in the center of the ceiling illuminated badly cracked plaster that looked as if it might fall any moment. Dobnik pushed the door down the rest of the way and locked it. Walking around the gray Trabant sedan, he noted with relief that the tires seemed to be properly inflated. The car often sat for weeks, since he used public transportation to get to work and around town. East German Trabants were not known for their reliability. Depending upon how things went this evening, he might have to drive the car out to his cottage in Wandlitz tomorrow.

Satisfied by his visual inspection, Dobnik moved to the back of the garage. Plywood shelves housed oil cans, various fluids, and cleaning supplies. Cobwebs would have alerted a careful observer that these items had not been used for quite some time. Nor would they be today.

The colonel crouched in front of a tall wooden cabinet that spanned the lower portion of the wall and worked a combination lock holding together two door handles. In the dim light emitted from the single ceiling bulb, he managed to turn the dial to his wedding anniversary date, this time thinking he would definitely change it to his divorce date—but not today. After removing the lock, he swung open the doors and reached into the spacious opening, retrieving a red toolbox, grimy towels of various colors, frayed at the edges, and a black plastic tarp of the type one might spread on the floor while working on a car. Dobnik used it, however, to cover up the piece of luggage that he now pulled from the cabinet.

Exhaling sharply, Colonel Dobnik hefted the molded plastic suitcase onto the top of the cabinet. His biceps burned under the heavy load. After he conquered the suitcase lock by once more dialing the same combination, Dobnik flipped open the gray top, propping it against the plywood shelves. Looking over the pile of papers, he now wished he had organized them in some form, but it'd be too time consuming to start now.

He stared at the copies of documents, all of which had crossed his desk during the last year. He'd been rather selective in what to duplicate, concentrating on information implicating the communist government in supporting and training terrorists. Though his job did not directly expose him to data relating to Stasi spies in the West, he had copied memos containing hints about the identities of some of them. In the right hands, like the West German intelligence services, the vague references might be sufficient to finger a double agent. In addition, he had made notes from conversations he'd either participated in or overheard, yielding clues about the Stasi spy network in the West.

Dobnik reminded himself he'd left his briefcase and plastic bag leaning against the sidewall below the light switch. He retrieved them, took the set of documents copied from the papers Frantz had given him out of the attaché and deposited them in the suitcase. After adding one of the *Carmen* scores from the plastic bag to the stack, he started to close the case but stopped. Instead, he peeled back one corner of the paper pile and ran his free hand along the right inside side panel until he felt a crease. He pulled on the panel and it opened to a small hidden compartment. A quick look confirmed that the Makarov pistol and the magazine were still fitted snugly in place. He pushed the panel back, closed the case, and returned it along with the tarp, towels and toolbox to the cabinet.

Locking the door behind him, he reflected on how fortunate he'd been to find this garage for lease when he moved into the apartment around the corner after his divorce. Though he'd been thinking about starting a personal collection of Stasi documents for quite some time before that, he'd put it off until he had a good hiding place. He was now glad he'd waited, since his ex-wife might very well have turned him in if she'd found out about his illicit stash. Stasi informants were known to include spouses who reported on each other.

While he could have parked his Trabant on the street like so many other residents, keeping it in the garage provided a perfect cover for his real purpose. Still, as his thoughts turned to Frantz and Schlechter, he was no longer sure this was a good storage place. But he'd worry about that tomorrow. Today he needed to take care of the delivery.

When he reached the end of the street, Dobnik turned the corner and crossed the roadway to enter a gray building. He did not wait for the notoriously slow elevator, which scared him anyway as it often broke down, but climbed the eight flights of stairs to his apartment directly across from the staircase. Out of breath, he fumbled for his keys and finally managed to open the door. Even considering his seniority at the agency, he'd been lucky to have been allocated a two-bedroom apartment after the divorce, the second bedroom serving as his study. He knew families with children that made do with a one-bedroom.

Dobnik laid the satchel and bag on his desk in the study and proceeded to the corner window in the living room. From there he could see the road outside the apartment building as well as the street leading to the row of garages. Not seeing anything out of the ordinary, Dobnik returned to the study. To make it to Sylvia's hotel before she'd leave for the opera house, he needed to get started.

More and more he'd ignored the prohibition against working on secret papers at home, figuring that being caught violating this rule was the least of his worries. He sat in the swivel chair behind the desk and pulled out several drawers, depositing scissors and adhesive tape on the desk surface. Next to those he laid the *Carmen* score book and then lifted from his briefcase the set of documents Frantz had given him. He searched through the desk once more, finding the tape measure in the back of the center drawer.

Dobnik folded the papers in the center and measured the thickness of the stack at about one centimeter. The score, at over two hundred pages, was almost two centimeters thick. He opened the book and picked up the scissors but then furrowed his brow. Scissors wouldn't work, at least not initially. He thought for a moment, jumped up from the chair, causing it to swivel, and rushed through the bedroom into the bathroom. A hasty search through the cabinet under the sink yielded the desired box cutter.

Back at his desk, Dobnik opened the score to page twenty-five, placed the folded stack of papers in the center and outlined its perimeter in pencil. He laid the documents aside and started to cut along the outline. Fifteen minutes later he had cut the center out of most of the pages, leaving intact only twenty pages at each end of the vocal score. With Frantz's papers deposited in the cut-out section, Dobnik's thoughts turned to the message he needed to compose.

♫ ♫ ♫

Colonel Dobnik was pleased with the Café Franken on Unter den Linden. The coffee and cake were quite good and the location was even better—diagonally across from the Hotel Drei Sachsen. He'd been there since five and was on his third cup of coffee. The colonel checked his watch yet again. Five thirty, and still no sign of Sylvia Mazzoni. He knew the only regular hotel exit was on Unter den Linden. Surely she wouldn't take the rear emergency exit. Though it was a bit chilly in the café, beads of sweat formed on Dobnik's forehead when he considered the possibility he might have missed her.

He hadn't seen her in twelve years. Was it possible she'd changed so much he wouldn't have recognized her? Then he saw a dark-haired woman in a black overcoat exit the hotel. He exhaled when he recognized Sylvia. She still looked as attractive as he remembered her, at least from a distance. But who was that with her? Her manager or agent, perhaps. Yet something about the tall man in the gray coat struck him as familiar. To his surprise, they did not take the hotel limousine or a cab but walked toward the opera house.

Dobnik paid the waiter, watched Sylvia and her companion disappear, and waited a few more minutes before exiting the café and crossing over to Drei Sachsen. He entered the lobby and walked straight up to the reception desk. The lone clerk on duty turned toward him, white blouse buttoned up to the chin over a flat chest.

"Is your manager in?"

"Yes, I think so."

"I need to see him now."

Dobnik's firm tone elicited a nod and a quick retreat by the gaunt young woman into an office behind the reception area. Moments later a short man in a white shirt, striped tie hanging loose to one side, stepped up to the counter. "May I help you?"

Colonel Dobnik showed his ID. "What's your name?" Working for the Stasi had its advantages, such as getting absolute cooperation from the public, though Dobnik wasn't sure how much longer that would be the case. Since the opening of the Wall a growing number of citizens had begun to complain about the Stasi. It was only a matter of time before identifying himself as a Stasi officer in public would draw an adverse reaction. But this day it still achieved the desired effect.

"Kurt Brummer." The manager said in an unsteady tone.

Dobnik demanded, "Herr Brummer, I need to take a look at your guest list."

The bald-headed manager lifted a huge book, placed it on the countertop in front of Dobnik, and rotated it. It took the colonel only a minute to locate Sylvia Mazzoni's suite on the fifth floor. He was getting ready to bark his orders at the manager when he noticed the name on the room next to Sylvia's—Rolf Keller. That's who he saw with Sylvia. What in hell was he doing here? What was Sylvia up to?

Dobnik caught himself. "Herr Brummer, I assume you have a master key to all the rooms." Without waiting for a response, he continued, "Please get it."

The manager hesitated. Colonel Dobnik stared him down. "What are you waiting for?"

Brummer shrugged and walked into an office in the rear of the reception area, reminding Dobnik of a dog trained to obey its master's commands. A few minutes later the colonel opened Sylvia's suite on the top floor. He'd taken the stairs so the manager wouldn't be able to tell from the elevator lights which rooms Dobnik was checking. Herr Brummer appeared to have bought the explanation that following up on a tip required a search of a few rooms, and he'd seemed properly intimidated.

In quick succession, Dobnik traversed the living room, bedroom, and bathroom, with only one thought: where could he hide the papers so Sylvia would find them but no one else? True, the vocal score provided good camouflage, and someone stumbling onto it would think it only natural to find a score of *Carmen* in the room of a cast member. Nonetheless, he hated to rely only on that. A busybody maid might just flip through the pages and discover the subterfuge.

Once again he paced around the suite. His eyes swept the rooms, looking for nooks and crannies. He didn't have much time, and nothing occurred to him. Think, he told himself. What is the diva likely to do when she returns after the opera? Singing and acting in a heated theater produced a lot of sweat. She would probably shower or take a relaxing bath. He walked into the bathroom, but then rejected the idea. If the maid came to turn down the bed, she might well check on the towel supply and the bathroom.

Returning to the bedroom, he stopped in front of the chest of drawers and began to look through them. The third drawer held what he was looking for: a lavender nightgown rumpled from sleep was lying on top of panties and stockings. In his early days he might have felt self-conscious about invading someone's privacy by rummaging through lingerie drawers, but he had given up those sentiments many years ago.

He spread the gown on the bed. The briefcase holding the papers had not left his hand the whole time he'd been in the hotel. He took out the score book and opened it to make sure the documents and his note were still in place. He slipped the book into the upper part of the nightgown and folded the remainder of the garment around it several times. Then he carried the nightwear with its secret contents back to the drawer. To guard against discovery by a nosy maid, he slid the gown underneath the lingerie. Sylvia might have to search for a while, but she would find it.

The drop made, Dobnik started to leave, but stopped when his eyes fell on the door connecting to the adjacent room. He reached for the door handle. This was his chance to determine whether Sylvia's companion was really the Rolf Keller from their West Berlin student years. The handle gave but he did not open the door. He'd find out soon enough. There was one more arrangement to be made, and he'd better hurry to pick up his special order at the flower shop before it closed.

Peter Bernhardt

Chapter Nineteen

Now and then the sun broke through a thin cloud cover, enticing Rolf to cover the kilometer from the Hotel Drei Sachsen to Checkpoint Charlie on foot. He watched the black puffs of smoke from the exhausts of the East German cars rumbling along the boulevard. Passing between East and West Berlin used to involve strict border controls. The opening of the Wall two weeks ago had changed all that, and he was given only a perfunctory check.

Even when tempered with occasional sunshine, November in Berlin did not invite long walks. Thus, once in West Berlin, Rolf boarded a yellow double-decker bus and climbed the stairs to the upper compartment from where he had a great view of Tiergarten Park. Perhaps he'd find time for a scenic run through the park tomorrow.

After a twenty-minute ride past many of the famous city sights, Rolf found himself strolling once more, this time along West Berlin's major shopping street, Kurfürstendamm, popularly called Ku'damm. Caught up in comparing the scene to what he remembered from twelve years ago, Rolf lost focus until he remembered he needed to find a self-service copy shop. He brandished his camera

150

like the Japanese tourists around him, while he scanned the storefronts on both sides of the street. The search yielded a grand total of two, which would do for his purposes, except that they both closed at six in the evening. The Stasi papers needed to be copied as soon as Sylvia received them, which most certainly would not be before six. The thought of Sylvia having to safeguard the documents overnight until the copy shops opened Tuesday morning spooked him.

Transcribing the information by hand was out of the question. The drawings and charts he'd seen were too intricate for that, and Stein would not be satisfied with an approximation of the contents. Rolf recalled his boss's emphatic statement that he wanted to know every last detail. His automatic Fuji camera might work, but he couldn't think of a safe place to have the film developed. He now regretted not having kept up with anyone he knew in college. As he approached one of the many cafés lining the Ku'damm, he slowed his steps. Perhaps he could get some information while warming up with a hot cup of coffee from his long walk in the biting air.

The coffee needed some accompaniment, of course. After ordering a slice of almond torte, he asked the waitress if she knew of a copy shop that was open evenings. The look she shot him telegraphed he was pursuing a hopeless cause. Sure enough, she professed ignorance of any copy shops in the area, let alone any with extended business hours. He'd become so Americanized during the last twelve years that he'd completely forgotten about the quixotic practices of German merchants.

While devouring the delicious pastry and sipping the steaming coffee, Rolf considered his options. Between now and the end of tonight's performance he needed to think of a secure storage place for the documents. Keeping them in the hotel overnight was too risky since the Stasi might search their rooms at any time. He left the café in a hurry and hailed one of the many cabs whizzing along the

Ku'damm. On the ride back to the hotel he realized he'd neglected to call Stein. Never mind his boss's admonition to call every day, tomorrow would be soon enough. By then he should have something to report.

He'd barely made it back to his room when a knock on the connecting door let him know Sylvia was ready to leave for the opera house. Rolf slipped on his gray overcoat. She wore a black coat over her jeans. He wondered about her casual dress before it dawned on him that she would be made up as Micaëla at the theater. Given what she'd said about the production at lunch, he did not dare to venture a guess as to the nature of her costume.

After exiting the hotel, Sylvia walked to the curb to hail a taxi. Rolf nudged her arm. "Do you mind if we walk? There are a couple of details we need to discuss."

"Okay." She pulled her coat tight against the evening breeze. As they broke into a brisk pace along the sidewalk, she declared, "You've got five minutes. Once I'm at the theater, Micaëla is all I can afford to think about."

"Have you given any thought about what to do with the documents until we can deliver them to Schmidt tomorrow?" he asked in an urgent tone.

"No. I thought Schmidt gave that job to you. He doesn't trust me, remember?"

Rolf took a deep breath so that he wouldn't take the bait. She had every right to be angry and frustrated. He waited until after they crossed the first intersection before he spoke in an even voice. "The copy shops all close at six. I don't like the idea of having the papers on us overnight. What if this is a Stasi setup, and they come barging into our rooms in the middle of the night?"

Sylvia stopped and looked at him. He saw apprehension in her eyes. "I hadn't thought of that. We could rot in an East German prison cell, or worse."

She did not specify what would be worse, but Rolf could imagine what she was thinking.

"What do we do?" she pressed.

The sidewalk overflowed with pedestrians streaming out of office buildings along Unter den Linden. Quitting time, Rolf thought, and stores would soon close as well. The throng of office workers was swallowed up by the jubilant crowds milling about. Strangers hugged one other and exclaimed, "Wahnsinn! Wahnsinn! Das ist ja irre!"—total madness, sheer insanity. More than two weeks after November 9, the East German populace still could not fathom that the Wall no longer imprisoned them.

Beneath the excitement, Rolf could see the marks decades of oppression had left on hard-etched faces. Some seemed unable to cast off their serious expressions, eyes cast down or staring straight ahead, faces displaying resignation. Few were taking the time to look at the linden trees. How hard the lives of the ordinary East German citizen must have been! His musings were interrupted by people bumping into him as he stood with Sylvia at the curb by the traffic light. Rolf jogged her elbow, encouraging her to resume their trek.

After they cleared a throng of pedestrians, he suggested, "As soon as you get the files, give them to me, and I'll put them in a storage locker overnight." He saw her doubting look. "You can come with me if you want."

"You've checked this out?"

"Yes. I've got several possible places in mind, all in the western sector, of course."

They'd reached the Staatsoper, and Sylvia led the way to the artists' entrance. Rolf decided to take her lack of response to his last remark as a sign of her assent, especially since there seemed to be no alternative. He hung back while Sylvia made arrangements with the stage doorman to assure Rolf's unfettered access to her dressing room. The man in gray uniform behind the sliding glass windows repeatedly glanced in his direction with a suspicious expression, but judging by the man's final shrug, Sylvia's persuasive powers had worked.

When Rolf saw Sylvia motioning to him, he hurried past the guard window to catch up with her in the narrow hallway around the corner. She hissed, "They are rigid and rule-bound around here, but I insisted."

"Good. I imagine there is a passageway between backstage and the auditorium. I'll see if I can find it so I won't have to pass through this guy's fiefdom again."

Instead of answering, Sylvia turned the next corner and strode up to a young woman in a white apron sitting on a wooden bench alongside the wall. A dressing assistant, Rolf concluded. After learning Sylvia's name, the woman directed her to a door at the end of the corridor.

Sylvia asked, "Am I sharing my room with anyone?"

"No, you've got it all to yourself."

"That's great, because I need my manager here a good part of the time. That's not a problem, is it?"

Rolf endured more scrutinizing, followed by a tentative, "I suppose that's all right."

Sylvia was not to be deterred. "Would you tell Mr. Keller how to get from here to the stage and the auditorium while I get ready?"

The dressing assistant looked at Rolf. "It's like a maze around here. I'll need to take you."

The short-haired woman rose and beckoned Rolf to follow her to the end of the hallway while Sylvia entered her dressing room. The route from the dressing rooms to backstage was straightforward, a wide hallway populated with theater employees striding to and fro seeming to concentrate on the challenging task of setting up the stage flats, the lighting and whatever else might be involved in getting the performance underway.

The dressing assistant walked to the left side of the backstage area, proceeded along a gray painted wall and after a few strides stopped in front of a metal door that blended into the wall to such a degree that Rolf probably would have walked right by without noticing it. She depressed a stainless steel handle and stepped over the threshold. She waited for him at the top of a flight of stairs, gray metal as well. He couldn't help but wonder whether the opera house's productions were more colorful and imaginative than the backstage decorations in someone's favorite shade of gray.

As soon as he caught up to his escort, she bounced down the stairs. Rolf counted ten steps before finding himself at the beginning of a narrow corridor that appeared to go on forever. The sparse lighting from fluorescent bulbs placed along the low ceiling about every thirty steps and sidewalls so close together that people passing each other had to turn sideways, reminded Rolf of walking through one of the temporary tunnels rerouting a sidewalk along one of the many Washington construction sites. This passageway gave him the same creepy feeling, a premonition of something caving in on him without warning.

After they had passed the third light fixture the hallway split. As she took the right fork, the woman pointed to the left one. "This goes to the café in the basement after another flight of stairs down."

Without waiting for a response, she pressed ahead. Rolf counted four more fluorescent lights before the pathway split once more. This time she followed the left branch, muttering over her shoulder that the right corridor led to an emergency exit. By now Rolf was lost, a laboratory rat running through an endless maze. He tried his best to remember all the twists and turns, the stairwells and doors, even as the woman's explanations confused him more than helped. They couldn't have walked for more than four minutes, but the ups and downs and multiple changes in direction made it seem much longer. Finally, his guide opened a door. "Here we are."

Rolf expected to see the auditorium. Instead they were standing in the foyer. His disappointment must have been palpable, as the assistant volunteered, "From here you have to cross the foyer to get to the auditorium, just like the general public." As if reading his thoughts, she continued, "The doors to the auditorium remain closed until an hour before the performance."

With that she turned toward the unmarked door through which they had come. "This door usually stays unlocked during performances, but you can't always count on it."

She held the door open for him. Stepping through, Rolf asked, "What if I have to get backstage, and it's locked?"

"You'll have to exit the foyer to the street and walk around to the artists' entrance."

Envisioning having to pass the doorman again almost brought a sarcastic "great" to Rolf's lips, but he restrained himself. He felt warm in his overcoat after their brisk walk and shed it, folding it over his arm. When he did, he felt the little notebook and pen he was keeping in the inside breast pocket. He took them out and made notes while they retraced their steps. This seemed to make the employee uncomfortable, but Rolf didn't care. There was no way he'd find his way through here without a memory aid.

When they returned, one of the other dressing assistants blocked him from entering Sylvia's room, indicating she was in the middle of changing. While he waited, he sketched the backstage route in his notebook. There were several things he did not like. If he wanted to hang around Sylvia's dressing room during the two-hour break between her appearances, he'd either have to sneak out in the middle of the first act, or miss the opening act altogether. Since his seat was close to the front, leaving before the act ended was not a realistic option. Just as one was not seated once an opera began, so one was not to leave during a performance, especially not in Germany, where many audience members still regarded opera as a formal affair.

Reluctantly, Rolf resigned himself to missing Sylvia's initial appearance. He'd have to be satisfied with catching her in Act III. His mood did not improve as his thoughts returned to the passageway. There were too many places inviting a wrong turn despite his sketch and notes. At least the foyer door was open this evening, unless some employee were to come along and lock it.

"You may go in now." The dressing assistant who had shown him around earlier spoke in such a low voice that it took him a moment to comprehend. She knocked and opened the door for him. The room was small and felt crowded with two dressing tables. His eyes were drawn to Sylvia sitting in front of the mirror of the near dresser. She was decked out in sleek black leather pants and a tight lace-up bodice. He couldn't help but stare at her curves.

"I told you this was ultramodern."

Sylvia's words brought him back, and he strained to catch his breath. Apparently, she had misconstrued his reason for staring: she looked stunning, the tight slacks and low-cut top hugging her curves and accentuating her voluptuous figure.

"Uh . . . yes, it's modern all right," he stuttered, feeling like a tongue-tied idiot. Now, if he could just keep from blushing. If the director had chosen this provocative outfit for innocent Micaëla, Rolf couldn't imagine what sensual Carmen would look like.

"Rolf, I need to warm up my voice a bit, and they'll be doing my hair and makeup in a little while. Is there anything else we need to talk about before you leave?"

As he focused on practicalities, he could feel the blood rush recede and his face cool down. "Yes, I'll have to miss the first act. Otherwise, I can't get back here when you leave the stage. Perhaps I can catch a glimpse of the performance from backstage if they let me hang around there while you're on."

"Okay," was all she said.

Rolf turned to leave. "I'll get out of your hair. See you at the break. Good luck!" He wasn't sure she'd heard him. She seemed far away, in another world.

♫ ♫ ♫

The first act went without any problems. Despite feeling more like a motorcycle mama than a country girl, Sylvia managed to convey the lyricism in Bizet's music. Yet she did not feel as inspired as she had on Saturday night, whether owing to the strange production or because tonight was anti-climactic after her Stuttgart debut, she did not know. She was just glad the audience didn't express derision at the director's concept of *Carmen* à la twentieth century.

Rolf gave a thumbs-up when she came off the stage. "I couldn't really see and hear too well from backstage, but judging from the applause, your performance must have been wonderful."

While they walked back to the dressing room, Sylvia nodded. "Yes, they seemed to like it, modern and all."

"Never underestimate the tolerance of operagoers, at least in German theaters."

Sylvia chuckled. He dispensed his sense of humor with wit and a light touch, something she had always liked about him. Once inside the dressing room, she slipped her silk robe over her outfit. It made her feel uncomfortable to strut around in a body-hugging costume that invited leers from men and disapproving looks from women. If Rolf had any intentions, he hid them very well. She wasn't sure what she thought of his apparent nonchalance.

For a while they speculated anew about when and how the documents would be delivered. Then the conversation turned to opera and Sylvia's prospects. Waiting and filling time were not her strong points, and she sensed Rolf felt awkward too. Having talked themselves out, they repeatedly glanced in the direction of the door as if expecting someone to come bursting through at any moment. After a while Rolf scooted his chair closer to hers and peered into her eyes.

"Sylvia."

The way he said her name caught her attention, a signal perhaps that he was about to raise a sensitive subject.

"There is something I'd like to tell you."

She did not like the sound of that. Some kind of confessional or rehashing of the past was the last thing she wanted to hear before she'd have to get back into her performance frame of mind. "Rolf, this may not be a good time for—"

"Don't worry. This won't take long, and there may never be another time."

Was he referring to potential danger? She wondered.

Rolf went on, "I told you after our run yesterday that I'm a member of Alcoholics Anonymous. It's a spiritual recovery program promising me I'll stay sober if I continually do my best to work the program's twelve steps."

"Yes, I've heard of it." Where was he going with this?

"Step nine requires me to make amends to all those I've harmed, and you're certainly on that list."

Sylvia could tell this was not easy for him. "Listen, there's no need to dredge up the past—"

Once more, he interrupted her. "These amends are not for you but for me. If I don't make them . . . well, they say I may drink again, something I won't take a chance on."

She sensed that there was no stopping him now. Indeed, he picked up the pace, as if he were afraid that too long a pause might prevent him from finishing.

"I've made amends to my ex-wife, to my daughter and to all the other people I've hurt. You're the only one left on my list. Making amends isn't simply to say sorry and go on. It's to repair what damage I've caused, if that's possible."

He'd been studying the ceiling while firing these words in rapid succession. Now he looked straight at her. "Sylvia, I never expected to be able to make amends to you in person. For that reason, this assignment has been a piece of good fortune, no matter what happens."

Once more she detected an ominous note. Did he know something she didn't?

Rolf spoke again. "You're right. There is no need to drag out every last detail of my shabby behavior twelve years ago. But there are two things I want to talk about." He took a deep breath. "It was wrong of me to spy on you and Kreuzer, and I was a coward in refusing to help when you needed to get away from him. I can't undo those things, but I want you to know that I'll do my best to never repeat them."

His words brought anger to the surface that she thought she'd shed long ago—not so much about his refusing to help her escape from Horst Kreuzer, but about his following her to see who else she might be dating.

Unprepared to voice her forgiveness, she was still groping for a response when Rolf spoke up. "Sylvia, you don't need to say anything. I told you earlier, amends are for the person making them, not for the person receiving them. While it might make me feel good to have you accept them, it's not necessary."

His words astonished her. They conveyed a meaning so different from societal convention, which required acceptance of an apology in order for it to be effective. Yet she could sense the deep truth in what he'd stated. Whatever she said would sound trite. So she simply responded, "Thank you."

They fell silent once more until he asked the question that was on her mind as well. "Do you think the Stasi spy knows enough about opera to realize Micaëla is idle for a couple of hours?"

Sylvia shrugged. Act II had just ended. The second intermission and the first part of Act III would take about forty-five minutes. It was time to refocus on the performance.

"Rolf—"

A knock on the door interrupted. "Frau Mazzoni, there is a delivery for you." She recognized the dressing assistant's squeaky voice. Rolf was closer to the door and reached to open it.

A young man who looked like one of the stagehands she had seen around entered, holding out a bouquet of lavender roses. "These were delivered by a florist a few minutes ago at the artists' entrance, with instructions to bring them to you right away."

Sylvia stared at the flowers, then at the stagehand. "In the middle of the performance?"

Surprised, she accepted the bouquet while Rolf pulled some bills from his wallet and pressed them into the man's hand.

When they were alone, she remarked, "That's odd. Flowers before the end of . . ." Rolf's quizzical look stopped her. Could this be the delivery?

Rolf was already at her side inspecting the bouquet. He removed a yellow envelope from among the stems and handed it to her. "Frau Mazzoni" was scribbled on top and in big letters underneath "Personal and Confidential." She tore it open and unfolded the single sheet of typewritten paper. It bore a cryptic message: "Enchanting voices and roses are to be treasured. Lavender becomes you. Tonight, may it bring what you're seeking."

She handed the note to Rolf. He appeared as perplexed as she. "What in hell does this mean?"

As if reading her thoughts, he parted the dozen stems she was still holding but turned up nothing. The intercom called out the names of the singers to assemble backstage for the start of the third act. Sylvia forced her attention back to the opera. "Rolf, I need to get ready. Would you please leave now?"

"Sure. I'll be in the audience for the third act. It's a pretty safe bet we won't see anything of our friend this evening. But just in case he does show, I'll risk the spectators' wrath and sneak out between acts. I'll meet you back here then. Perhaps in the meantime I can figure out what that message means."

He reopened the half-closed door, "I can't wait to watch you looking for Don José in the motorcycle gang."

Maybe he was more a smart ass than a wit, she thought, adjusting her earlier assessment.

♫ ♫ ♫

Rolf remained in her dressing room while she took her bows. Although satisfied with her singing this evening, she perceived the audience response was not as enthusiastic as in Stuttgart. That had something to do with the production, she imagined, or with the way she had been inserted into an established cast. It took her fifteen minutes to change from Micaëla back into her street clothes while Rolf waited in the hall. As they had suspected, there were no more visitors.

After saying good night to Rolf, Sylvia entered her hotel room at eleven thirty. She filled the vase she'd picked up from the nightshift clerk with water and arranged the roses, admiring the glorious sheen on the blossoms. Did the Stasi spy know that lavender was her favorite color? These roses had a scent so faint it took all of her imagination to detect it. Raised in a greenhouse, she surmised. She set the flowers on the coffee table and went to the bathroom to brush her teeth.

Usually she would shower after a performance, but not this evening. She took off her jeans and crawled directly into bed in her long-sleeve t-shirt, too tired to bother with a nightgown. Closing her eyes, she recalled Rolf's parting admonition to let him know immediately, no matter the hour, if something came to her about the message. She'd not think about it any more tonight. All she wanted to do was drift off, but she kept tossing. Maybe she was still wired from performing. Relax, she told herself, and sleep will come. As drowsiness finally washed over her, the thought of lavender came into her head. Her upper torso jolted straight up as if pulled on a string. Of course!

She jumped out of bed, raced over to the chest and pulled open one drawer after another. Where had she put it? It had to be with the lingerie. She folded back her underwear and spotted the lavender nightgown at the bottom. It was wrapped around something. Sylvia picked up the gown with both hands, carried the load over to the bed, and unfolded the garment. To her surprise, she was looking at a vocal score of *Carmen*. Realizing this would be no ordinary score, she opened the cover and then stopped. Should she call Rolf first? No, not until she made sure this wasn't some kind of joke.

She began flipping the pages. There was no doubt this was the musical score of tonight's opera. She had held ones like it many times before, reprising the role of Micaëla. But this book had a different feel. When the next few pages turned over, she knew she had the Stasi papers in her hands. As she stared at neatly folded pages nestled in the book's cut-out center, her initial excitement turned to chill. The Stasi agent had been in her room this evening. He had rummaged through her lingerie, fingered her nightgown. Sylvia dropped the book on the bed in disgust.

After a moment she decided there was no time for feeling creepy and violated. She picked up the book once more, opened it to the middle and peeled off the adhesive tape that held the loose pages in place. When she unfolded a stack of paper, her eyes fell on a handwritten note resting on top of the pile.

"Sylvia. Unexpected difficulties. Future performance in doubt. Critical that we meet Tuesday afternoon at four, corner Charlottenstraße and Unter den Linden by Humboldt University (for old times' sake). Come alone!"

She stared at the words in bewilderment, as if the longer she looked, the clearer they'd become. Quite the opposite occurred. Giving up for the moment, Sylvia glanced at the rest of the papers. She counted twenty-seven pages containing drawings, numbers and typewritten text. Scanning the papers shed no light on their meaning. Her thoughts kept returning to the handwritten note.

The nightstand clock showed a few minutes past midnight. She thought of Rolf's fears of the Stasi bursting into her room in the middle of the night. Should she wake him? It was now or not at all.

Chapter Twenty

Responding to a soft touch on his shoulder, Rolf strained
to open his eyes. Through half-closed lids he perceived a
fuzzy round face encircled by long, dark hair, bending over
him. He murmured a satisfied "Ah" at the marvelous
dream, letting his eyelids droop.

"Rolf, wake up!"

The urgent whisper startled him. This was no dream.

"Sylvia. What are you—"

"Shh!"

Her index finger moved toward her full lips. For the
briefest instant Rolf imagined she'd come to climb into his
bed. Then he saw her sweatshirt and jeans. What was she
doing in his room and how did she get in? Too dazed to
ask, he propped himself on his elbows and stared at her.

As if reading his mind, Sylvia spoke in a low voice,
"You didn't lock the connecting door on your side."

She repeated the signal to remain silent and moved
toward the door, which was standing ajar. Had she found
the Stasi papers? He tossed back the covers, hitched up his
gray flannels and followed her, barefoot, across the
threadbare carpet to her suite. Sylvia stood next to a small

round table in the living room. She pointed to a book and loose papers strewn across its surface. No sooner had he recognized the *Carmen* score than Sylvia opened it, revealing a hollow center. Rolf let out a faint whistle.

He burned to know when and where she'd found it, but Sylvia might not be the only one listening. He did not speak. Instead he sifted through the documents, trying to comprehend what information they held. As best he could tell, the descriptions related to some kind of weapons system. He broke off his study, aware of the risk in keeping the materials in the hotel suite. Analysis could wait until after he'd made copies. There wasn't a moment to waste in getting the papers to a safer place.

As he straightened, he caught Sylvia's quizzical expression. He bent toward her until his mouth almost touched her ear and whispered, "I'll store these as we discussed. No need for you to come unless you want to."

She did not react for what seemed the longest time, testing his patience. Just when he thought of pressing for a response, she shook her head. Her tentative acquiescence to have him handle it stirred up mixed feelings. Initially, he appreciated her trusting him with the documents, but then felt regret at having to navigate the city on his own in the middle of the night. Even so, it was better that way. He'd attract less attention alone than if the two of them were to leave the hotel at this hour.

Sylvia folded the pages and returned them to their hiding place. She handed him the score book, mouthing a silent, "Be careful."

He returned to his room and dressed in a hurry. Finding his overcoat pockets too small to hold the book, he placed the score in the small of his back so that it was covered by his shirt and held by the belt of his jeans. A few minutes later, Rolf rang the bell on the front desk. An elderly man shuffled out of an office behind the reception counter. "I need a taxi right away," Rolf demanded.

The clerk dialed a number and after a short delay said, "A taxi will be here in ten minutes."

Rolf pressed a ten-mark bill into the clerk's hand, generating a profuse, "Thank you." It couldn't hurt to have this fellow's gratitude in case he had to repeat this late-night excursion after Wednesday's drop, Rolf thought as he headed toward the front door. He stayed inside the lobby, keeping an eye out for the taxi. During a wait that seemed endless, he wondered whether, with the Wall open, East Berlin cabbies would drive into the western sector. By the time a gray Wartburg taxi pulled up in the driveway, Rolf had made his travel plans.

Through a half-burnt cigarette dangling from the corner of his mouth, the young driver mumbled that he could take him to any place in West Berlin. Rolf was tempted to deviate from his plan. It would be so convenient not to have to change taxis, especially at this time of night. But prudence counseled against staying with the East German cabbie, who could very well be one of the 170,000 Stasi informers among the East German populace. After they crossed the border at Potsdamer Platz, Rolf spied a Mercedes taxi pulling into a hotel driveway and told his driver to follow. He handed him twenty marks, more than enough to cover the fare for the short distance they had driven. With the book nestled against the small of his back, he reached the Mercedes in time to keep the exiting passenger from closing the rear door.

As he slid onto the leather seat, Rolf looked around but did not perceive any cars that looked suspicious. Apparently no one had followed his taxi from the eastern sector. Facing forward, he responded to the bearded driver's expectant look with, "Bahnhof Zoo, bitte." He had decided to look for a locker at the popular Zoo train station off Ku'damm. If that didn't work out for some reason, he'd try West Berlin's other train stations and airports.

The car's sharp acceleration surprised Rolf, reminding him he no longer was riding in a Wartburg. He felt as if he had switched from riding a tired old donkey to a thoroughbred racehorse. The driver did not seem concerned with speed limits at this time of night, and with no traffic to speak of, he pulled up in front of the train station after only a few minutes' drive. He reached to stop the meter, showing a fare of six Marks and forty Pfennigs.

Rolf handed him a ten-mark bill. "Keep the meter running. I'll be back shortly. Will you wait?"

The man studied him for a moment. "Okay."

Rolf climbed out of the car and once again peered in all directions, seeing nothing but a few passing cars. Satisfied, he hurried into the station. There were a few men in shabby clothes milling about the main hall, probably using the building as a shelter from the cold night. They certainly did not look like passengers, and he doubted any trains were running at this hour. Rolf let his eyes sweep the building for signs pointing to lockboxes. Not seeing any, he followed the directions to the bathrooms, calculating that lockers would be close by. When he spotted them, he kept on walking and entered the men's room down the hall.

A quick glance around assured Rolf that he was alone in the washroom. Not having to pretend to need the facilities, he walked back to the entrance, hoping to catch a glimpse of anyone who might have observed him disappear into the bathroom. He peeked out into the hall, trying to remain invisible by hugging the side wall. He saw nothing to cause him concern. Forcing himself not to appear hurried, Rolf strolled back to the locker area. He noted with relief that the boxes covered the walls of a side hallway open on both sides. With no one around, he deposited two one-mark coins in a slot at the far end, turned the key and swung open a steel door. Looking both ways and still not seeing anyone, he pulled the book from the back of his jeans in one quick motion, laid it on the lockbox's metal floor, shut the door, and withdrew the key as he heard the coins drop.

He stuck his hand with the key into his coat pocket and made a mental note of the number on the box. The key should contain the numerals as well, but he hadn't taken the time to look, and even if it did, they might not be legible. Rolf left the deserted locker area, exiting the end of the hallway opposite the one he had entered. The passageway fed into a wide corridor with a bakery on one side and a flower shop on the other, both closed. After a few meters, he found himself once again in the main hall, which appeared the same as he'd encountered it a few minutes ago.

As he hastened across the gray stone floor, worn uneven by countless footsteps, Rolf wondered if the cabbie had decided to pocket the ten marks and call it a night. Even at a major train station like this, catching another one could take a while. He was relieved to see the dark blue Mercedes with the motor running in the same spot as he had left it and jumped into the back.

"My hotel is on Unter den Linden. Can you take me there?" Rolf asked with some hesitation, not sure whether West Berlin cab drivers had any reservations about driving into East Berlin.

"No problem. What's your hotel?"

"Drei Sachsen."

Rolf took the man's nod as a sign he knew the hotel. He leaned back and felt himself relax for the first time since setting out on this escapade. Being a spook seemed a lot easier than Hollywood led you to believe. But then again, having things fall into place this easily made him wonder if he'd overlooked something. The taxi turned onto the Street of June 17th, named for the populist uprising by East Berliners against the totalitarian regime in 1953—a revolt brutally crushed by Soviet tanks.

A huge hotel complex spread along the right side of the boulevard. Following intuition, he called out, "Would you turn in here for another quick stop?"

Without answering, the driver slammed on the brakes to negotiate the curve at the far end of the driveway and turn back toward the hotel entrance. Rolf let go of the key he'd been holding inside the coat pocket all this time to retrieve his wallet from his rear jeans pocket. The cabbie waved him off.

"That's all right. You can pay me later. How long will this take?"

"About ten minutes."

"I'll be here." With that he reclined the driver's seat and closed his eyes.

Rolf entered the hotel and scanned the lobby—not a person in sight. He spotted a row of telephone booths across from the bank of elevators. He slipped into the first one, folded the glass door closed behind him, and looked at his watch. One forty-five. That meant it was a quarter to eight Monday evening in D.C.

He reached into an inside coat pocket and pulled out a notebook. Leafing through its pages, Rolf appreciated Betty's foresight in insisting that he record her unlisted home phone number. During all the years she'd been his secretary, he'd not used it once. As soon as he located the entry, he dialed the number. What he wanted to ask of her precluded him from calling her at Stein & Weston. There, as in communist East Germany, someone else might be listening.

She answered on the second ring. "Hello."

"Good evening, Betty."

After a momentary silence she responded with an exuberant, "Rolf. What a surprise! Are you calling from Germany?"

"Yes. I'm in Berlin. I'm doing okay. Listen, Betty. I don't have much time to explain. It's almost two in the morning here and I need to get back to the hotel." He paused, not knowing exactly what he wanted to say. Doubts about the trustworthiness of his intuition began to surface.

"I finished the motion for summary judgment and brief you left for me Friday. But that's not why you're calling, is it?"

Good old Betty. She could read his mind three thousand miles away. "No, it isn't. I need your help, but I'm not really sure in what way." He collected his thoughts. "Has Stein or his secretary told you anything about my assignment?"

"Mildred called me. She would say only that you're in Germany on a personal mission for Mr. Stein that could take several weeks."

"I'd like to tell you more, but I'm not supposed to say a word to anyone in the firm about what I'm doing. And it's better for you not to know."

"That's all right. You'll tell me if necessary. What can I do?"

An old lawyer had told him many years ago never to let go of a good legal secretary. He had recognized the wisdom in that back then, but now it really came home to him how fortunate he was to have Betty.

"Harry Stein keeps a file on my assignment in his office safe. I suspect he's holding something back, and it's crucial that I learn what that file holds. Otherwise, I'm operating in the dark over here." Rolf paused, giving her a chance to interject. When she didn't, he continued. "But I have no idea how to go about that. I'm sure he puts it back in the safe every time he leaves the office. He may even lock his office door."

"What's the name of the file?"

"I saw the label for just a second. Look for three capital letters."

"You don't believe in easy tasks do you, counselor?"

Relieved to hear the tease in her voice, Rolf retorted. "No, only the toughest task will do for you, Mrs. Crandall."

"Well, I'm going to have to think on this one. Can I call you?"

"No. I need to call you. I'm staying in East Berlin where the phone lines are tapped. I'm talking to you from a West Berlin hotel right now." Rolf thought for a moment. "What time do you leave for the office in the mornings?"

"At seven thirty."

"I'll call you around seven in the morning."

"Okay."

"Thanks, Betty. You're a sweetheart."

"Yeah, yeah. Take care of yourself."

Rolf hung up and left the hotel in a hurry. He tapped on the taxi's window. When he heard the click of the power door locks, he climbed back into the cab. "Thanks for waiting. Drei Sachsen and no more stops."

When they arrived a few minutes later, Rolf gave a handsome tip. On impulse, he asked, "Can you pick me up at ten in the morning?

"Sure." The cabbie reached into his shirt pocket and handed him a card. "You can reach me at this number."

Rolf watched the cab drive off. "Bernd Schlosser," he mumbled and put the card in his wallet.

On the way up to his room, Rolf wondered whether he had done the right thing in calling Betty. He had no idea how she would be able to help, but he'd sure like to learn the contents of Stein's file. It might explain some things about this assignment the senior lawyer had not bothered to share.

Chapter Twenty-One

Heinz Dobnik wished he could wipe the smirk from Brigadier General Frantz's face. He wondered if it had been there during the twenty-four hours since he'd last seen him. While the general droned on about the importance of the mission, Dobnik, half listening, gazed through the office window at a gray Tuesday morning. Sylvia Mazzoni's mellow soprano from last night's performance of *Carmen* still rang in his ears. Had she found the score book?

"Colonel, are you listening to me?" The general's forceful voice jolted him.

"Yes, sir. Of course."

"Then answer my question."

Dobnik fought the fog in his mind. "Uh . . . you want to know about the drop."

He took the general's silence as confirmation he'd guessed correctly. "I delivered the documents yesterday evening."

"Everything go as planned?"

"Yes."

If the responses led Frantz to conclude that he'd personally delivered the papers to Sylvia during last night's performance, so much the better. No need to enlighten the general about the slight modifications to the original plan.

"You would inform me of any difficulties, wouldn't you, Colonel?"

"Of course, sir." Dobnik had no qualms about lying to the general.

"Good."

While Frantz pulled the center desk drawer open, Dobnik noticed a document stamped top secret on the corner of the desk. Taming his curiosity for the moment, he returned his attention to the general.

Frantz slid a thick envelope across the desk. "Take a look at these."

Curious whether he held the second drop, Dobnik folded back the unsealed flap and removed a yellow folder. His eyes fell on the name printed on the file label, Joachim Walter. The name sounded familiar, but he couldn't place it. He looked at Frantz, whose raised eyebrows meant he expected him to know.

"I've seen the name before." Speculating that the documents besmirched a West German official's reputation, Dobnik gambled, "He's in the West German government." He managed to keep his inflection flat so Frantz wouldn't realize he was guessing.

"You should know this person. He is an ardent supporter of the West German government's effort for unification. From what our agents report, he is an energetic and accomplished diplomat, and hell-bent on bringing about one Germany."

Dobnik recalled having read reports on Walter, a career diplomat and member of the inner circle of trusted advisors to Foreign Minister Hans-Dietrich Genscher, who himself was reputed to be a sterling diplomat and skilled negotiator. Not what the communist East German government wanted to see in the westerly neighbor at a time when it was striving to prevent unification, which it equated with annexation by the West.

"Colonel, I don't need to remind you of what we talked about yesterday. I doubt the West Germans will be able to overcome the distrust of the British, French and Soviets, who have good reason to fear a united Germany."

Dobnik knew their opposition was based not only on Germany's Nazi past but on economics as well. After the war, West Germany experienced such a robust recovery that it had been dubbed the "German economic miracle." Seeing themselves surpassed by the loser of the war had to generate resentment in the European World War II victors.

Again, the general interrupted Dobnik's thoughts. "But the way things stand now, we can't afford to rely on the Europeans to stop the West Germans. I'd like to give them added ammunition to help squelch the notion of one Germany, something that'll reinforce the world's mistrust of German intentions. The Allies can then insist on keeping Germany divided without appearing small or vengeful." Frantz pointed at the folder in Dobnik's hand. "Do you think these materials will do the job?"

The dossier detailed Joachim Walter's career, the first page containing basic personal data. A black-and-white photograph showed a broad face with pug nose, on which rested dark-rimmed glasses over inquisitive, piercing eyes. A high forehead expanded into a receding hairline of sparse gray strands. Dobnik noted in amazement the listed birth date of March 7, 1920, wondering why at age sixty-nine the man hadn't retired. Either he loved his work, or he still needed to prove something.

Frantz got up and strode to the window. Though he sensed the general's impatience, Dobnik took a few seconds to glance at the top secret document on the desk. He gasped.

Frantz turned around. "Did you say something?"

"Just clearing my throat. Sorry, sir."

Realizing he was under close scrutiny, Dobnik feigned concentration on the material in the folder in his hand. Yet, while he flipped through pages detailing Walter's education and work history, his real focus was on memorizing code words he'd recognized in the upside-down document. He paid enough attention to what he was reading to register that Walter had been a member of the Hitler Youth and an SS officer, disturbing but not uncommon in the backgrounds of West German government officials. Thinking this might be the information on which Frantz intended to rely to scuttle unification, Dobnik tried to find a delicate way to tell him it wouldn't do, when he came upon an intelligence report.

The memorandum, addressed to then Stasi Chief Erich Mielke, bore the date of November 15, 1989—two weeks ago. It recounted Joachim Walter's Nazi past. Dobnik's eyes were drawn to a disturbing statement. Walter was suspected of participation in atrocities against Jews toward the end of the war, but no firm proof had yet been uncovered. Dobnik felt this information also fell far short of what would be needed to stop West Germany's quest for unification. In truth, a number of former Nazis now held government positions, somehow having escaped close scrutiny. One had even been appointed chief of the Office for the Protection of the Constitution before exposure of his strong allegiance with the Nazis forced him to resign.

The general's voice brought Dobnik back. "Have you come upon the memo to Mielke yet?"

"Just now."

"Take a good look."

With Frantz still at the window, Dobnik scanned the document on the desk for a few more seconds. Had the general left it there thinking Dobnik could not possibly read it, or had he simply forgotten about it? Dobnik cut off his mind chatter and returned his attention to the folder in his hand. An intelligence summary on Walter's recent activities piqued Dobnik's interest. The report documented several meetings in the West German Foreign Ministry during the summer and fall of 1989. The foreign minister attended about half the time. When he did not, Walter chaired.

Colonel Dobnik marked his place with his thumb as he contemplated what this could mean: a former Nazi pushing for unification and chairing high-profile foreign ministry meetings. This could lead to something. He read on.

The first meeting focused on the political climate in East Germany, with different opinions expressed about the likelihood of a popular uprising against the regime, and if it occurred, how to respond. To his astonishment, Dobnik realized this discussion had taken place six weeks prior to the first mass demonstration in Leipzig. The West Germans must have had excellent intelligence to anticipate so well the events that were to come.

"Well?" Frantz asked.

"I'm still on the spy's report."

"Go on then."

Dobnik read how the inner circle of advisors to the foreign minister grappled with issues like the probability of the demonstrations continuing and if they did, whether they might be crushed by Soviet or East German military forces. There were strong disagreements about whether an attempt should be made to fuel popular discontent with the communist government. Walter argued fervently to employ every possible means to bring down the regime, even though he didn't offer any plan for responding to the communists' potential use of force.

A movement in his peripheral vision told Dobnik the general had started to pace, but he kept on reading.

Meeting discussions changed from whether the communists would be toppled, to when. Then the focus shifted how best to accomplish unification, with Walter as the most forceful advocate for a united Germany at the earliest possible time. Walter's tone reportedly differed on this point, depending upon who attended the meetings. In the presence of the foreign minister, he argued in favor of a proactive approach to influencing events in East Germany. In the minister's absence, Walter lapsed into rhetoric about how to defeat the communists and why a united Germany would once again be strong.

Frantz ceased pacing and resumed his seat behind the desk. Dobnik refocused on the report.

During the last meeting held a few days after the fall of the Wall, Walter gloated that Germany would become the economic powerhouse of Europe and finally avenge its humiliating defeat by the Allies. The report did not say whether anyone challenged his extreme views.

Dobnik exhaled and turned his attention on Frantz. "I believe this dossier provides the ammunition you're looking for. With Walter's Nazi past, those outrageous statements should set off alarm bells from Paris to London to Washington to Moscow."

"Exactly," the general said in a smug tone.

"Is this a forgery?"

"Not entirely. We do have a mole in the West German Foreign Ministry, and most of what's in that file actually did happen. We just added a few crucial embellishments. It's more credible that way, don't you think?"

"Very clever." Dobnik tried to discern who the Stasi mole might be. He thought he detected a flaw in Frantz's plan. "How is our passing this to the West Germans going to stop unification? Won't they just destroy it?"

"Good question. I'll make sure the Western Allies know about it too. You can imagine what would happen if the West Germans were caught trying to cover it up. More evidence of Nazis taking hold once again."

Dobnik considered how that might explain Schlechter's visit to the general's office yesterday. Perhaps things were on the up and up after all. But was he prepared to stake his life on it?

Before he completed the thought, Frantz's urgent voice boomed, "You do realize how important it is for you to get this envelope into the hands of the West Germans?"

"Yes. I will make sure it ends up there." Along with a few other things from my stash, he thought.

"You're making the delivery Wednesday evening at the opera house?"

"Yes."

"When exactly?"

The general's question raised his suspicions anew. Why did he want to know the exact time?

"I'll take them to Frau Mazzoni's dressing room at the end of the opera, if that's okay with you." Lying came so easily to him these days.

"What time will that be?"

"Around ten thirty."

"Do you know when the diva will pass them on to Schmidt?"

"No, not really. She is scheduled to check out of her hotel Thursday morning and fly back to Stuttgart. I believe Schmidt is in West Berlin, and I assume she'll give him the papers Thursday morning before going to the airport."

Frantz seemed troubled. "So, you really don't know the details."

"No, I don't," Dobnik admitted. "She might get rid of them on Wednesday evening right after the opera rather than keep them overnight."

"That would be the smart thing to do."

Frantz's insistent questions strengthened Dobnik's belief that the general planned to betray him. Perhaps he wanted to catch Sylvia with the documents. Exposing her as a West German spy would not only be good propaganda, but could provide Frantz with a credible method to plant the Walter file with the Allies.

"Very well. Proceed as planned." The general stood.

Resisting the temptation to sneak one more look at the document on the desk, Dobnik rose with the general and headed toward the door.

Frantz called out, "If you decide to change anything, anything at all, be sure and let me know immediately. Is that understood?"

"Yes, sir." With that, Dobnik took his leave. On the walk back to his office, his prior suspicions of Frantz became certainty. Satisfied with generalities on the first drop, the general seemed entirely too concerned with the details of the second.

Dobnik paced in front of the closed elevator door, fighting his growing impatience. He was anxious to return to his office and record the information gleaned from the secret document while it was still fresh. How fortunate that he had noticed it. Yet professional experience had taught him to mistrust such coincidence.

Chapter Twenty-Two

"Did everything go well last night?" Sylvia raised her cup.

Chewing a bite from a roll layered with butter and strawberry marmalade, Rolf held up a hand. Typical of German hotels, the price of a room at the Drei Sachsen included a continental breakfast, consisting not only of bread, butter, preserves, and croissants, but sausage and cheese as well. Rolf had passed up the latter, since he did not have the stomach in the morning for the kind of hearty fare he considered better suited to lunch or dinner.

He swallowed the last of the roll and glanced across the table squeezed between two hard vinyl benches. The shiny brown seats were so slick he had to plant his feet against the table leg to keep from sliding off. He noticed how attractive Sylvia looked with her long black hair swept up into a deep red clip.

"Well, are you going to tell me?" She seemed more amused than impatient.

"Sorry."

He scanned the breakfast room as he considered how to respond. The windowless restaurant on the hotel's ground floor, illuminated by fluorescent lights hanging from a low ceiling with only every other fixture turned on, created an oppressive mood rather than a cheery breakfast ambience. After a short night's sleep, Sylvia and Rolf had just made it to breakfast before the end of service at nine. Only a few guests remained, out of earshot.

"The materials are stashed in lockbox No. 87 in the Bahnhof am Zoo. The West Berlin taxi driver from last night will be here at ten this morning. I'll make copies before I deliver the stuff to Schmidt. Are you coming along?"

Sylvia studied him. "What time is the meeting with Schmidt?"

"Noon at Tiergarten Park."

"So we should be back by early afternoon."

"When we're through with Schmidt, I need to call my secretary, but that shouldn't take long." He paused, wondering why she wanted to return so soon. "I thought it might be more fun to spend the day in West Berlin than in this dreary place. Do you need to be back for something in particular?"

Before he could scrutinize her face for clues, she turned to signal the dour-faced waitress. Sylvia waited for the corpulent woman to amble over to their booth, refill her coffee cup, and leave.

"As long as we're back by four, I'll be okay."

Noting she had evaded his question, he glanced at his watch, swung his legs outside the bench, and stood. "Not to rush you, but the taxi will be here in fifteen minutes."

She nodded, set her half-empty cup on the laminated table top, and slid from her seat.

When they entered the lobby fifteen minutes later, Rolf saw the dark-blue Mercedes idling out front. "He's here already. Let's go."

Sylvia climbed in before he could grasp the door handle. As she moved across the seat to make room for him, she said, "Watch your head."

Ducking in an exaggerated motion, Rolf retorted, "Very funny," and pulled the door shut. "You won't let me crack my skull in peace, will you?"

Cab driver Schlosser's stoic face did not show any reaction when Rolf asked him to return to the train station they had left only eight hours ago. In heavy weekday morning traffic, the drive took twice as long. Sylvia remained in the taxi while Rolf repeated last night's watchful procedure in approaching the locker area. Not detecting anything suspicious, he retrieved the music score, put it in the canvas shopping bag Sylvia had produced from her luggage, and hurried back to the car.

He set the bag on the rear seat between them. He leaned forward, intending to give the driver the address to the copy shop he had located yesterday, but stopped himself. Perhaps he was becoming paranoid, but he did not want this man to know where they were going. He might catch on that he would be copying something he had stowed in the train station after smuggling it out of East Berlin. While it would be convenient to have the taxi available for their various errands, there would be plenty of time to accomplish them on foot or by taking the S-Bahn or a bus.

The driver looked at him in the rearview mirror. "Where to?"

"Take us to the Ku'damm." Remembering West Berlin's main shopping street stretched for quite a distance, he added, "I'll tell you where to drop us."

Sylvia peeked inside the bag as the taxi pulled out into traffic. Rolf watched the buildings and crowded sidewalks along the Ku'damm intent on finding the copy shop. After a few minutes, he recognized the area where he had strolled the day before and asked the driver to pull over. Once again, he gave a generous tip. When he saw that Sylvia had a firm grip on the bag, he exited the cab and waited for Sylvia to follow. Before closing the door, he leaned back inside the taxi.

"Does the Underground or the S-Bahn run between West and East Berlin now?"

Schlosser turned around. "The S-Bahn does. They can tell you at the station."

"Thanks. I may need another ride tomorrow."

"You've got my card."

Rolf closed the car door and joined Sylvia on the sidewalk as the Mercedes drove away. He peered down the boulevard trying to locate the shop, but a sea of pedestrians obstructed his view of shop windows and signs. Sylvia moved away from the curb toward the display window of a clothing store. Rolf noted with satisfaction she had a tight hold on the shopping bag. She'd put her left arm through the handles, which rode on her shoulder, and she pressed the bottom of the bag against her body. With her free hand, she unbuttoned her overcoat. An early morning cloud cover had broken up. As he felt the warmth of the late morning sun, he also opened his coat then joined her in front of the store window.

Hoping his sense of orientation wouldn't fail him, Rolf set out in a westerly direction. They fell in with the crowd moving along the sidewalk. Most pedestrians proceeded in an orderly fashion by walking on the right side, but a few dashed in and out of the moving mass of people, intent on arriving at their destination as soon as possible. Rolf marched ahead of Sylvia, guarding against anyone bumping into her. She understood and stayed close behind. Just as he began to doubt that he'd struck out in the right direction, they came upon a window through which several copy machines were visible. He entered the recessed doorway and opened a glass door to let Sylvia pass.

Judging from the shiny linoleum floor that reflected bright fluorescent ceiling lights and the half-dozen late-model copiers, the store had opened recently. Only one of the machines was in use. A middle-aged man dressed in casual clothes stood behind the counter, motioning them toward the closest machine. Sylvia asked if they could make their copies on the machine in the far corner. Good thinking, Rolf thought, once more appreciating her quick mind.

Rolf's earlier worries about having to ask for assistance subsided when he saw that the copiers appeared similar to those at Stein & Weston. Sylvia had already removed the papers from the *Carmen* score without taking the book itself out of the shopping bag. She unfolded the sheets, flattened them on a nearby white table surface, and started counting.

"Twenty-nine pages," she said while putting the stack face up into the document feeder. "Or do you want to use the glass? We're less likely to get a jam that way."

He hesitated. "No. It's too slow. The sooner we're done the better."

She pressed the start button. The machine sprang into action, swallowing the pages in quick succession, shooting a green light beam back and forth below the document glass, and spitting copies onto a side tray, all in less than a minute.

Sylvia counted the copies. "Twenty-nine pages and all legible." She slid the papers down the side of the bag sitting on the floor, careful not to wrinkle them.

Rolf reached into the feeder, and then stopped to look at her. "Did you want a set for yourself?"

"No. From what I saw last night, there's nothing there that relates to me."

He removed the pages, counted them and then returned the sheaf to her. She refolded the papers and replaced them inside the *Carmen* score. When he returned to the counter to pay, he spotted envelopes of various sizes on display and bought one. On the way to the front door, he motioned Sylvia to stop at a table propped against the side wall.

"Let me have the copies."

After inserting all twenty-nine pages into the envelope, he spread the metal clasp to secure the flap and handed the package back to her.

She dropped it into the bag. "I suppose you've decided what to do with these while we deliver the originals to Schmidt."

He nodded and exited the store, beckoning her to follow him to the curb, where he hailed a taxi. Within a few minutes they were back at the Zoo train station. Sylvia again waited in the car while he stored the copies. He had kept the key to locker No. 87 to ensure he'd have a place to stash the anticipated drop of Stasi documents on Wednesday. Things were crowded in Germany, and one could never count on finding an empty locker. With his third trip to the station in half a day, he felt like a regular at the place. Yet they couldn't take the chance of keeping the copies with them any longer than necessary—not in their East Berlin hotel and certainly not when meeting up with Schmidt.

The taxi dropped them at Tiergarten Park a few minutes before their noon appointment. Rolf struck up a brisk pace on the footpath at the park's east entrance. Sylvia kept up. She'd refused his offer to carry the bag.

"Keep your eyes open for a circle of benches surrounding a children's playground. It's supposed to be fairly close."

"Well, we could always jog, but something tells me Schmidt will wait if we're a bit late." After a few strides, she pointed straight ahead. "There."

Indeed, the trees on both sides of the path receded about a hundred meters ahead, making room for a wide sandy area. Rolf spotted the circle of benches facing a playground, just as Schmidt had described. A blond-haired boy in brown corduroys screamed for his mother's attention before he hurled himself down the multi-colored slide. A pig-tailed girl on a swing stretched her legs to the sky, her plaid skirt flipping up each time she swung forward. She entreated a young woman to push her ever higher. With each increase in the arc of the swing, her excited shrieks grew louder.

Rolf refocused his attention on the dozen or so wooden benches that lined the circular path before it narrowed on the other side and continued its westerly journey through the park. The benches were occupied mostly by older men and women soaking up the sun. A few were throwing crumbs to blackbirds, sparrows and gray-brown squirrels.

"Where is he?" Sylvia sounded impatient.

"He said to look for him on the seventh bench. We just passed number four."

"That may be him over there," she said without pointing.

Rolf scanned three benches ahead. His eyes fell on a broad-framed man in a business suit, who seemed engrossed in feeding the birds and squirrels. The green hat drawn over the man's forehead reminded Rolf of those he'd seen in Bavaria. This bench sat far enough from the playground that the children's noises were muted.

"Beautiful morning. May we join you?" Rolf asked in a casual tone.

"Sure," Schmidt replied as he picked up a gray raincoat lying by his side, exposing a beat-up, dark-brown leather briefcase with a flap closure and a dull, silvery metal lock. Government issue and definitely not silver, Rolf concluded.

They settled at his side. Schmidt reached into a small paper bag he held between his knees and tossed out the rest of the bread crumbs, causing a momentary scramble by birds and squirrels.

"How are things?" He looked straight ahead as if directing his question toward the birds.

Rolf waited. When Sylvia remained quiet, he responded, "So far so good."

He didn't see any need to bother Schmidt with details of the Stasi officer's unusual delivery methods.

"I see you brought me a present."

This time Schmidt turned his head slightly toward Sylvia. He moved the briefcase off his lap and nestled it against the shopping bag on the bench at her side. With an efficient motion he released the lock and peeled back the briefcase flap. Sylvia's transfer of the score book from bag to briefcase happened so fast that Rolf would have missed it entirely, if he hadn't been expecting it.

Schmidt closed the case without examining its contents. "How did the performance go yesterday?"

"The director has some strange ideas, but the audience seemed to like it all right."

Sylvia's matter-of-fact intonation surprised Rolf. He was tempted to add his own commentary but didn't. In all likelihood, Schmidt did not really care.

"Your second performance is Wednesday evening?"

"Yes," she replied.

"You expect another present then?"

Rolf interjected, "As far as we know."

A brisk breeze whistled through the bare tree branches above them. Schmidt looked up as if he were savoring the moment.

"Your flight back to Stuttgart is Thursday afternoon at four thirty. Put the next delivery in a locker at the Tegel airport." Schmidt looked around before he reached into his coat pocket. "Locker No. 53. It is close to where you need to check in for your Air France flight."

He pressed a key onto Rolf's palm. "Return this key to me no later than three thirty at the restaurant in the main terminal. I'll be there from two o'clock on in case you're early . . . or there is a snag."

Rolf slipped the key into his overcoat pocket, careful not to jingle it against the other one.

Schmidt added, "And if you run into a problem before then, I want to hear about it immediately. You know where I'm staying."

"Speaking of problems," said Sylvia, "have you determined who shot the terrorist who attacked me?"

"Not yet."

"And what about the immunity I asked for?"

"It's in the works." Schmidt's lightning response meant he had anticipated the question. "I wrote up a justification, which I gave to my boss yesterday. It has to be approved by the head of the agency."

"Any chance you'll have it to trade me for the materials on Thursday?"

He shook his head. "Frau Mazzoni. A trade is not part of the deal. You're to deliver the documents as you've agreed. I'll do what I can to get you your letter, but I've made no promises, as you well know."

Sylvia retreated. "Well, knowing the very deliberate speed of German bureaucracy, I want to be sure I'll have something in hand before I'm past my prime."

"You'll have your answer within a few weeks, I can assure you of that." Schmidt's tone signaled he considered the subject closed. "Well, if there is nothing else, good luck tomorrow evening."

Briefcase in hand and coat draped over his arm, Schmidt rose and strode off toward the west end of the park. When he was out of sight, Rolf glanced at his watch and then at Sylvia.

"Do you have time for lunch, or do you need to head back to the hotel?"

"I'm okay for lunch."

She folded the empty shopping bag and stood. During the five-minute hike to the park exit, neither spoke. The city traffic noises brought Rolf back to the task at hand:

find a lunch spot with nearby public telephones. German restaurants tended to have a single telephone in the hallway next to the restrooms—not conducive to carrying on a private, uninterrupted conversation.

When Sylvia pointed to an Italian eatery across the street, he shook his head. "Let's look for a hotel restaurant. I need to call my secretary at one."

They reached a compromise on the third hotel they entered. Sylvia approved of the menu, a strange combination of German, French and Italian dishes, and Rolf liked the phone booths in the lobby. The hostess insisted on taking their coats to hang them on the circular coat stand at the front of the restaurant, but not before Rolf transferred the lockbox keys into the jeans pocket where he kept the room key.

From their table by a window, they could observe the busy street life. West Berlin's restlessness reminded him of New York City. Nervous energy charged the streets of both cities.

The restaurant was only half full. He hoped the prices were the reason, not the quality of food. The lasagna proved delicious. Sylvia found her linguini in cream sauce satisfactory for a restaurant in Germany, though not anything close to the real stuff she'd be able to get in Milan. As the hands of the wall clock approached one, he pushed back his half-full plate, hoping his stay in Germany wouldn't be so long that he'd get used to its oversize restaurant servings. Sylvia had stopped eating some time ago.

She must have caught his quick glance at the clock. "Some urgent business at your office?"

He considered leveling with her for a moment but decided against it. He could always tell her later if Betty found out something. If she didn't, it would be just as well he hadn't bothered Sylvia with unfounded speculations.

"No. Just checking in. This shouldn't take long."

Rolf got up from the table and strode toward the exit, leaving the waiter to assume he planned to visit the restroom across the lobby. He headed that way, but stopped when he reached the three phone booths located between the restrooms. He chose the booth on the left because he could see the restaurant door from there, though he wasn't sure why that might matter.

Betty's voice sounded in his ear in less than a minute. "You're right on time. It's seven here."

"Listen, Betty, I've not had any brainstorm how you might manage to have a look at Stein's file, and even if I did, it was a bad idea. I can't ask you to jeopardize your job by—"

"Hold on, counselor. You may not have a plan, but I do."

"As I said, Betty, I can't really ask—"

"How about listening to what I propose before you decide?"

"All right, let's hear what you've dreamed up."

Her deep breaths told him she was collecting her thoughts. "You know the cute young secretary, Peggy Malone."

"The breakfast junk-food eater?"

"Stupid question, I know. No attractive woman ever escapes your eyes."

"What's the point, Mrs. Crandall?"

"You're not losing your sense of humor over there, are you? Don't let the serious German temperament rub off on you."

"Okay, Betty. I do notice the good-looking ladies. So, are you going to tell me how that is going to get us a peek at the senior partner's file?"

"Well, I had lunch with Peggy yesterday. You know she is dating the building's security chief, Ray Fielding."

Where was she headed with this? "Go on."

191

"Mighty impatient, aren't we? Do you need to be somewhere?"

"Actually, yes. Speaking of attractive women, I left the one I'm responsible for over here at the restaurant and need to get back pretty soon."

"Aha, thought so. I'll make it short. Peggy let it slip that her boyfriend plans to have one of his silly fire drills at nine tomorrow morning. As you know, everyone is under strict orders to leave their offices the moment the siren sounds. No cleaning up, putting stuff away, or taking anything."

Rolf began to have an inkling of what she had in mind. "You think you could sneak into Stein's office then. What will that accomplish? You can bet he keeps the file in his safe when he's not working on it."

"That's where you come in, Rolf. You need to make sure he's working on your file at nine o'clock tomorrow."

Rolf chuckled. "Betty, you are devious. Brilliant, but devious."

"To survive marriage to an abusive alcoholic, you've got to be both."

"I didn't know you—"

"Never mind. Forget I said that."

"I'd like to talk to you about that sometime." Hard to believe her past included an alcoholic husband. When she didn't respond, he changed the subject. "How are you going to get into his office? What if he and his secretary lock their doors when the sirens start blasting?"

"They're not supposed to lock out the security personnel." After a short pause, she continued, "So, I need to know whether you want to go ahead with this."

Rolf fell silent, debating whether he could ask her to take such a risk.

"Rolf, don't worry about me. You can always hire me when you open your own office in Timbuktu. I don't think you're going to be at Stein & Weston forever."

"Is it that obvious?"

"Only to someone who knows you as well as I do."
After a brief pause, she continued, "You just worry about
making sure he has that file sitting on his desk at nine
o'clock, and I'll take care of the rest. Is it a go?"

"Okay, Betty. Let's do it. I'll think of a reason for him
to need the file when I call him."

"All right. Finally, a little excitement in my life. Things
have been pretty boring at the office since you've been
gone."

"Betty, please be careful. I'd never forgive myself if
something happened to you."

From the corner of his eye Rolf noticed two clean-cut
men in their thirties scanning the lobby. He averted his
face. When he turned back to see if they were watching
him, he saw them disappear through the restaurant door.
Something about their demeanor disturbed him.

Betty's voice interjected, helping to shake off paranoid
thoughts. "Yeah, yeah. Nothing's going to happen to me.
Remember, nine o'clock sharp tomorrow."

When she hung up, Rolf depressed the receiver and
dialed another number.

"Hello." Stein's baritone came on.

"This is Rolf."

"Hi. How is it going?"

"The first delivery has taken place, and I have copies for
you."

"Excellent. Can you tell what it is?"

"Not really. There was no time to look at it."

"Is it in a safe place?"

"Yes, I think so."

"Rolf, I want you to fax the documents as soon as
possible to a secure number I'm going to give you. Take
this down."

"Just a minute."

He fumbled for his notebook and pen before he realized
they were in the inside breast pocket of his overcoat back in

the restaurant. Then his eyes fell on a handy pad and pencil, courtesy of the hotel.

"Go ahead."

Rolf recorded the number Stein gave him, tore off the top sheet of the note pad, and stuck it in his pocket. When he noticed the imprint the pen had made on the blank pages, he removed several and pocketed them as well. "It'll probably be tomorrow before I can fax."

"Why is that?"

He noted the sharp tone in Stein's question.

"The materials are safely stored, and it'll take me a while to retrieve them and find a place with a fax machine. Certainly not in East Berlin." He chose not to tell Stein about the lockbox. To cut off any potential objection, Rolf continued, "Something has come up about the second delivery that worries me."

"Oh? What is that?"

"I can't say right now. May I call you back tomorrow morning at the office a little before nine?"

"Okay. Call me at the first number I gave you. I'll be in my office. Can't say I like the sound of this."

"Well, it's probably nothing, but it's better to be suspicious than to miss something."

"Talk to you tomorrow morning."

He barely heard the click, his attention drawn to the two men in raincoats at the other side of the lobby with a woman between them. Rolf stopped breathing. Though he couldn't see her face, he knew it was Sylvia. They exited the restaurant and hurried out the front door. Rolf dropped the receiver and left it swinging back and forth on its coiled metal cord, banging against the booth. He pushed the phone booth door open so hard it sprung back and pinned him for a second. Another forceful push and he was free.

He sprinted across the lobby. The distance to the hotel exit was less than thirty meters, yet it seemed to take him forever to reach it. Once outside, he peered up and down the street. Nothing but street traffic and pedestrians strolling along. He ran down the sidewalk to the left but saw only unknown faces. Perhaps they had gone the other way. He turned around and dashed in the opposite direction. Again only strangers.

Why had he left her alone? He'd failed miserably in his assignment to keep her safe. There was nothing to do but to go back to the restaurant and find out if anyone had observed anything. But even as he reentered the hotel, he knew he'd not find any answers there. Sylvia had vanished.

Chapter Twenty-Three

Brigadier General Holger Frantz turned away from his office window to receive his second visitor on this Tuesday morning.

"General, you called for me?"

Schlechter appeared eager. Pleased, Frantz nodded and motioned toward a chair.

"Major, have the Brits been tipped off about the document drop this week?"

"Yes, sir. Per your order, our double agent planted the information yesterday."

"Any word how it was received?"

"Our man reports frantic activity at Whitehall. He doesn't know particulars but thinks a couple of MI5 agents have been dispatched to Berlin."

"Good work."

Frantz strolled from the window to his desk and sat. He reassumed the pained expression that had served him well just yesterday when he'd alerted Schlechter about a possible Stasi traitor.

"I'm sorry to have to inform you that I've come across more evidence that one of our own is selling top secrets to the West Germans." He paused for effect. "I suspect the traitor is Colonel Dobnik."

Schlechter's lips curled, and he snarled. "I'll take care of that son of a bitch."

"Not yet, Major. I will give the go-ahead should that become necessary. I want to catch him red-handed, do you understand?"

The major's broad shoulders slumped. "Whatever you wish, General."

"Good. I know I can count on you to do exactly as I say."

"Yes, sir."

Frantz leaned forward, propping his elbows on the desk top. "Major, it is important that you listen very carefully to what I'm about to tell you. I don't want anything to go wrong on this assignment. Is that clear?"

"Of course, sir."

"Have you ever been to the opera?" Frantz asked in an amused tone, quite certain he knew the answer.

"No, sir, I haven't."

"Well, you and I are going to the Staatsoper tomorrow evening. I believe Dobnik plans to pass on documents to the opera singer I mentioned yesterday."

He reached into a side desk drawer, retrieved a small photograph, and slid it across the desk. Without a word, Schlechter stood and bent over the desk to study it.

"This is Sylvia Mazzoni," the general explained. "Unfortunately, that's the only picture of her I could find. I know we have a file on her, but it's nowhere to be found. When you leave here, I want you to go to the records department and find out what happened to it. Also look for Horst Kreuzer's record. He was her boyfriend and a terrorist with the Red Army Faction. We trained him. She turned him in to the police. He died in a West German prison in the fall of 1977 about the same time that several RAF leaders were found dead in Stammheim Prison. The authorities claimed they committed suicide after the botched hijacking of a Lufthansa airliner failed to free them. Anyway, see if Kreuzer's file contains information about her."

"I will, sir."

Frantz redeposited the photograph in the desk drawer. "As you saw, this snapshot shows her in casual dress. She won't look anything like that tomorrow."

"What am I supposed to do at this opera?"

"Relax, Major. Attending an opera won't kill you. I don't expect you to become an opera buff, but you'll need to know a few things about this particular opera so you can do your job."

In a strange way, he delighted in Schlechter's impatience, evidenced by nervous body shifts that produced more creaking sounds from the black leather chair. Frantz picked up a writing tablet by the phone and tossed it across the desk. Schlechter jumped out of his chair and blocked its fall with his hand.

"Major, I suggest you take notes." He waited while Schlechter pulled a pen from a coat pocket. "The name of the opera is *Carmen*. It is in French with German titles projected above the stage. Sylvia Mazzoni is a supporting character named Micaëla. Look for a dark-haired woman in black leather pants and a lace-up bodice."

When the major's pen stopped moving, Frantz continued. "Write down these times. She'll be on stage twice during the first act. Close to the beginning, she interacts with soldiers for about five minutes and then leaves. Toward the middle she reappears and sings a duet with the tenor. That lasts about twelve minutes. The first act goes on for another fourteen minutes after Micaëla has left the stage."

He paused, waiting for Schlechter to finish writing. "Are you with me so far?"

"Yes, sir."

"Then let's go on. There will be twenty-minute intermissions after the first and second acts. Mazzoni returns to the action in the middle of the third act. She'll leave at the end of that act. The fourth act follows without a break and lasts twenty minutes. Still following?"

"Yes."

"Good. That means there will be about two hours in the middle of the performance when Mazzoni won't be on stage. And she'll be off stage during the twenty- minute fourth act until she returns for the final curtain calls."

Once again he waited for the major's scribbling to cease.

"The opera starts at seven thirty and ends at ten fifty. Mazzoni will be off stage from eight till a little after ten and again between ten thirty and ten fifty. Why are these times important, Major?"

He did not give the officer a chance to respond.

"Because your job is to keep an eye on Sylvia Mazzoni, especially while she's off stage. Your seat is next to an exit. Every time she disappears, you need to leave the auditorium and work your way back stage. Try not to draw attention to yourself. Operagoers hate people leaving during a performance."

Schlechter furrowed his brow. "What's the layout of the backstage area?"

Frantz opened the same desk drawer as before, this time pulling out a long cardboard tube.

"Here are the blueprints of the entire opera house. I've also made arrangements for you to tour the building. Werner Braun, the assistant director, will be awaiting you at the artists' entrance at two this afternoon."

He pointed the roll at Schlechter to underscore the importance of his next words. "By curtain time tomorrow, I expect you to know every nook and cranny in that place. Understand?"

"Yes, sir. You can count on that." Schlechter hesitated. "General, what about when she's in her dressing room?"

199

"Stay in the hallway. Make sure she doesn't notice you. Clear so far?"

"Yes."

"Then it's time I filled you in on what I think will happen tomorrow. I believe she'll be receiving Colonel Dobnik in her dressing room after the final curtain calls."

He waited until Schlechter met his eyes before asking him, "What time will that be?"

The major looked at his notes and after a moment answered, "A few minutes after ten fifty?"

"That's right." Schlechter appeared to be on top of things. "Wait a minute or two after Dobnik enters her room and then go in and arrest both of them. He may be carrying a pistol, so be careful. I prefer that you make the arrest alone, but if you need help, there'll be a man in the stage doorman's office. I'll also have men posted at all building exits. As soon as they're in custody and you've got the documents, call me on my beeper. I'll be in the foyer. Keep them in the dressing room until I get there."

Frantz caught his breath. "Any questions?"

"If you expect the drop to happen at the end, why track her in between?"

"I like to cover all contingencies."

He didn't have any reason to suspect Dobnik had been lying, but he'd be ready just in case.

Schlechter tore off a couple of notepad pages, folded them and together with his pen stuck them in his pocket. After placing the writing tablet back on the desk, he picked up the cardboard tube propped against his chair and stood.

"Major, don't let Mazzoni out of your sight. And report back to me whether you found anything on her in the archives."

"Yes, sir."

Frantz watched Schlechter march out of his office. The meeting couldn't have gone better. His thoughts turned to events after the arrests. The prospect of parading the forged

Walter report in front of Western reporters brought a smug smile to his face. He'd be the hero who saved the German Democratic Republic from annexation to the West. His political future looked bright indeed.

Chapter Twenty-Four

Should she tell Rolf about the Stasi agent's note asking her to meet him this afternoon? Sylvia had been chewing on that question ever since Rolf left to make his phone call. She pulled the piece of paper out of her jeans pocket, as if studying it anew would yield the answer. The words "for old times' sake" could only mean they'd met during their student years. Schmidt's hunch had been right. He'd probably been one of Horst Kreuzer's friends with whom he'd plotted over countless beers against West Germany's capitalist society and political establishment. Would she recognize him?

She didn't relish the idea of meeting a communist spy by herself. Common sense told her it would be smart to have Rolf along, and yet something made her hesitate. What if the Stasi had a file on her? Of course! That's why this agent selected her as recipient of the documents: he'd seen her file. The room felt smaller all of a sudden, and her breath grew shallow. How many more times could she be blackmailed?

Stuffing the note back in her pocket, Sylvia concluded she'd have to risk going it alone. If such a file did exist, she needed to learn of it without Rolf. She couldn't count on him not telling Schmidt or Stein. Her mind made up, she peered toward the restaurant entrance. Rolf should be returning any time now. She didn't pay any attention to the two young men in raincoats coming through the door until she saw them glance her way. They were looking for someone else, she told herself, but then realized all the tables behind her were empty. They approached her table.

"Frau Mazzoni?" the shorter of the two, with ruddy complexion and curly red hair, stated more than asked.

"Yes?" She noticed that his companion kept his eyes on the door.

"We need to talk to you in private. I suggest you come along before your friend returns."

"Who are you?"

The door watcher turned toward her and said in a raspy voice, "We're here to keep you out of an East German prison cell."

Recognizing their accents, she blurted out, "You're British," then, "Why should I go with you?"

The tall one returned his attention to the entrance as the redhead spoke, "Because you probably don't want your companion to hear what we have to say."

He kept his right hand in his coat pocket. She detected a slight bulge. Was he cradling a gun?

"We just want to talk to you," he assured her.

His companion chimed in, "Well, are we going?"

These were civilized English, she told herself. Better find out what they've got.

"Okay, but let me write a note."

"No time for that . . . and not a good idea."

He was right. What would she tell Rolf anyway? Went with two strangers, don't know where, what they want, or when I'll be back. This is crazy, she told herself, you have no idea who these guys are. But what if she didn't go? Would she let fear keep her from learning what they knew?

Her life and Rolf's could depend on what they told her, to say nothing of her career. She had to take the risk. Determined, she snatched her coat on the way out and hurried across the lobby between the two men. As they exited the hotel, a midnight blue limousine drove up. The shorter man ushered her in and climbed beside her while his partner sprinted around to the other side. He'd barely slammed his door when the car sped away.

The driver did not turn around. She studied the back of his head through the glass partition. He appeared to be a regular chauffeur—cap, uniform, and all. Sylvia returned her attention to the men on either side of her.

"Where are you taking me?" she asked the smaller man on her right.

"On a short city tour while we talk. I hope that's agreeable."

"For a couple of strangers barging in on me and threatening me during lunch, you do have manners, I must say." She heard the sarcasm in her voice. "So, what's this all about?"

"Frau Mazzoni, we know you're not in East Berlin just to sing," the redhead stated with emphasis.

"What are you talking about? And you still haven't told me who you are."

"I'm afraid our accents gave us away." The man on her left turned toward her. "I'm Dennis Kingsley and the gentleman on your right is Peter Ross."

His partner interjected, "We're with British Intelligence. That's all you need to know."

They were trying to keep her off balance with their one-two punch.

Kingsley interrupted her thoughts. "No need to pretend, Frau Mazzoni. We know some Stasi documents will change hands this week. We also know you're working for Schmidt."

The car turned off the Kurfürstendamm. Steel, glass, and neon transitioned to post-World War II housing. Gray, walk-up, five-story apartment buildings dominated. Small trees and shrubs grew in tiny cracks in the asphalt, as if trying to hide the cold bleakness of a city still waiting to emerge from the darkness of World War II.

"Where are we going?" She wanted to know, and she needed time to think.

"None of your concern. We'll drive around as long as it takes to persuade you that it's in your best interest to cooperate with us."

Kingsley must be the dealmaker, she decided. He hung in the background but spoke at crucial moments and with authority. Perhaps he didn't even carry a gun. At least, she hadn't noticed a telltale bulge in his coat pocket.

"How do you know about the Stasi papers?"

Kingsley responded, confirming her gut feeling he was the senior of the two. "The point is, we do. And we have reason to think you and your American friend are being set up to be arrested as Western spies and left to languish in an East German prison cell."

Sylvia's stomach tightened. Blood rushed to her head. She drew several deep breaths. Get yourself under control. You need to hear what they have to say. "Who is setting us up?"

"I wish we knew," Kingsley replied.

"So what leads you to suspect a trap?" she asked, while searching her mind for clues as to whether it might be Schmidt or someone else.

Kingsley studied her. "Frau Mazzoni. You don't know the contents of the documents, do you?"

"No. Do you?"

"Yes. Damning facts about a top West German official. We're talking career-ending and probably sabotaging reunification."

Ross glanced at her as if to underscore his partner's revelation. Sylvia regarded him and then turned toward Kingsley. "You want to make sure this information sees the light of day, and you think the West Germans will bury anything that might threaten reunification."

Ross turned away to resume his sightseeing, but not before she caught a look in his eyes signaling she'd hit a nerve. Neither one of them responded.

Sylvia pressed her advantage. "I'm still waiting to hear about this supposed frame-up and how you plan to save me from jail."

She heard a sharp exhale to her left. It sounded like a sigh, and she wondered whether this represented theatrics on Kingsley's part. After a moment, he said in a firm voice, "Look, Frau Mazzoni. We don't usually divulge this kind of detail."

"In that case, drop me off at this corner." She pointed ahead. "You haven't told me anything that would make me believe you. You're bluffing, trying to scare me."

Kingsley put up his hand. "All right, here is what I can tell you. The agent who informed us about the drop . . ." Kingsley cleared his raspy throat, ". . . We don't trust him. He's supposed to be spying for us, but we suspect he is a double agent working for the East Germans."

"What are you saying?"

"Someone from the Stasi planted this information."

Sylvia stared at him. "So the whole thing could be false. Perhaps there won't even be a drop."

"Oh yes. There will be a drop, and you're the intended recipient."

"But how did you find out about me? Did this agent of yours mention my name?"

"No, he didn't. We learned of your assignment from other sources."

"Like who?"

"That I won't tell you." Kingsley kept a stony expression.

She recalled the conversation with Schmidt in her hotel room the night of the attack. He'd never said how many people knew of her mission—probably several at his agency and perhaps even a few at the other German intelligence services. A British mole could be anywhere. Ross leaned forward, interrupting her train of thought. When he slid open a tiny window in the center of the glass partition, Sylvia caught sight of the border crossing on Potsdamer Platz.

Ross instructed the chauffeur, "Keep us in West Berlin for a while longer."

The driver nodded without taking his focus off the road. The methodical clicking of the turn signal interrupted the quiet of the passenger compartment, evoking in Sylvia the sense of a countdown. Ross shut the glass door, cutting off the sound. As the car slowed to negotiate a right-hand turn, Sylvia decided she'd had enough.

"So far I haven't heard anything that would persuade me to get involved with you lovely chaps."

Kingsley looked past her. "Tell her, Ross."

"When we dug into the background of your . . . uh . . . friend, Horst Kreuzer, we discovered something very interesting. Do you know where he was during the last week of March in 1977?"

Sylvia held her breath. She shook her head.

"As you well know, he was in East Berlin. We have proof. But he didn't just stay in East Berlin. We believe he spent a few days at Briesen. Have you heard of that?"

She felt cold. Again, she shook her head.

"It's a top secret Stasi base. We think he received weapons training there."

When Ross stopped, Kingsley spoke. "Frau Mazzoni, you were with him on that trip, weren't you?"

Both men were staring at her. She felt trapped but managed a defiant, "What makes you think so?"

Ross responded, "We know he crossed the border on Sunday, March 27, accompanied by a dark-haired female. He did not attend classes that week. Not unusual for him since he spent more time in beer taverns than in lecture halls. You, on the other hand, hardly ever cut classes. You did Monday and Tuesday of that week."

Kingsley interjected, "You should know that we did not receive this information from West German intelligence sources. Apparently, they don't know about your East German escapade. As far as we're concerned, they don't ever need to learn of it . . ."

"As long as I do what you say," she finished the sentence for him. "Well, I've got news for you. I don't know anything about Horst training with the Stasi. I spent three days with him at a small hotel outside East Berlin and then came back. He told me he needed to visit some friends. I didn't believe him, of course, but I didn't really want to know what he was doing. I didn't break any laws. You've got nothing to hold over me."

Sylvia stared out the window, noticing gray apartment buildings with a few shops and restaurants and taverns sprinkled in-between. She did not recognize this residential neighborhood.

Kingsley's soothing tone brought her back. "Hear us out. I think we can come to a mutually satisfactory arrangement."

She swiped an errant strand of hair out of her face. "What do you propose?"

"You deliver the papers to Schmidt, but not before you've given us copies."

The ever-increasing copy requests struck her as ironic. Yet if Rolf copied for Stein, why shouldn't she for the Brits? She had done nothing illegal, but the idea of her East Berlin trip becoming public chilled her.

"I'll see what I can do."

"You need to be a bit more specific than that." Ross's voice reflected amusement. "You expect to receive the documents tomorrow evening at the opera house?"

"As far as I know."

"Move that up if possible. There's a strong likelihood the Stasi plans to arrest you and your companion and the traitor . . . if that's what he is."

Sylvia thought of the note in her pocket proclaiming unexpected difficulties. Perhaps the defector had become aware of the setup. She'd have a chance to find out later that afternoon, but these two didn't need to know about that.

"If I can, I will. How do I get in touch?"

Kingsley handed her a card containing a phone number. "Call as soon as you know when the drop will take place. We'll instruct you on copying."

Sylvia tucked the card next to the note in her pocket. Ross reopened the glass door and told the chauffeur to drive into the eastern sector. They remained silent as the car crossed the border without being stopped by the Volkspolizei. Once in East Berlin, Ross repeatedly turned his head, shooting watchful glances out the rear window. When the Drei Sachsen came into view up the street, he instructed the driver to pull over.

"We'll let you off here," Kingsley said.

Ross opened the door and exited. When Sylvia started to follow, Kingsley touched her arm.

"Frau Mazzoni. Just to be clear. What we've told you comes from intelligence we've gathered about Kreuzer. We can safeguard its references to you, but we can't control what the Stasi might do with whatever information they possess."

Sylvia stepped out and tripped on the high curb. Ross caught her elbow and steadied her. Then he climbed back in the car and shut the door as the limousine pulled away.

She walked toward the hotel in a daze. With each step she became more convinced that the Stasi did have a file on her. She tried to tell herself the contents might well prove she had nothing to do with Kreuzer's activities. Yet the Stasi was not known for its benevolence. If a file existed, it likely contained incriminating data, true or not. No one would believe her protestations of innocence.

She thought of Norwegian diva Kirsten Flagstad, the greatest Wagnerian soprano of all time. Where others strained, she had soared and floated with seeming ease along Wagner's difficult notes, as if the composer had written them specifically for her. But then, that was the very essence of genius: making exceedingly difficult things appear simple. Nevertheless, after the war she'd been shunned by American opera companies because of her husband's business dealings with Nazi Germany until the Metropolitan Opera, amid much controversy, finally accepted her back. Sylvia could only imagine what effect exposure of her East Berlin trip would have on her budding career. She had to find a way to lay her hands on that Stasi file, and soon. Perhaps she could strike a deal with the defector she would meet in a few hours.

With that thought she hastened her stride, only to come to a dead stop the moment she spotted Rolf in front of the Drei Sachsen. Oh my God! What was she going to say to him?

Chapter Twenty-Five

Colonel Heinz Dobnik had just returned from his meeting with Frantz when his executive assistant, Lieutenant Traude Schreuter, walked into his office. Though not unattractive, her bleached-blonde hair pulled severely back underscored stern facial features and made her look older than her thirty-eight years. She tended to complain, mostly about her husband who didn't help with their two young children. Dobnik noted her exasperated look but did not ask what was wrong.

"Colonel, that counterintelligence project you wanted me to work on today—I'm afraid it'll have to wait. Do you know why?" She didn't wait for a response. "Because I am to get Mielke's signature on some documents having to do with his retirement, if that's the right term to describe what happened to him. As if I had nothing better to do than run errands."

"Well, you know how . . ." Dobnik's sentence trailed off when he recognized the opportunity this presented.

He'd been trying to think of a way to meet with deposed Stasi chief Erich Mielke without drawing attention to himself. A visit by a former subordinate to his villa in

211

Wandlitz without official business would raise suspicions. While Mielke had not been placed under house arrest after he left office two weeks ago, he was surely under surveillance. "Wait a minute. He lives in Wandlitz. I'm going there this afternoon anyway. Why don't I take those papers off your hands?"

She hesitated. "General Rittmeister's secretary gave them to me with his orders to deliver them."

"I'm sure there'll be no trouble. I'll bring you the signed copies in the morning. The general won't care who handled it as long as it gets done." He winked. "I won't tell him I was the errand boy if you won't."

"I suppose you're right. I certainly appreciate this."

"It's not really out of my way. Why don't you bring them now since I'll probably leave right after lunch?" He tried not to sound too eager, but he wanted to get the papers before she had second thoughts. She nodded and left.

Before he even had time to plan his afternoon, she returned and handed him a large white envelope. "Mielke knows to expect someone from headquarters this afternoon."

"I'll have these for you in the morning," Dobnik reassured her. "See you then."

Lieutenant Schreuter took the hint and departed.

Dobnik laid the envelope on his desk, going over in his mind all he needed to accomplish the rest of this Tuesday. He worked backwards from four o'clock— the time to meet Sylvia Mazzoni, if she showed. Since Mielke's home had probably been bugged after his dismissal from the Stasi, he would have to devise a way to talk to him somewhere else. That meant he'd need to allow at least an hour for the visit. A glance at the wall clock caused him to bolt out of this chair—almost eleven. He was halfway to the door, coat draped over his arm, when he remembered the envelope, rushed back to snatch it off the desk, and hurried into the outer office. His secretary stopped typing.

"Frau Ammer, I'm going for an early lunch and won't be back for the rest of the day," he told her, knowing full well there'd be no time for lunch.

She nodded.

He exited the building onto Normannenstraße and rushed down the sidewalk to a nearby hotel to find a taxi. Taking the underground back to his apartment would cost precious time he couldn't afford to waste. Ten minutes later, thanks to light East Berlin traffic, he stood in front of Building "D." Waiting until the cab's taillights disappeared around the corner, he entered the garage, pleased to find everything in place.

With the suitcase safely stored in the trunk, he willed himself to think positive thoughts while turning the ignition key. The Trabant hadn't been started in several weeks, and Dobnik held his breath during the three tries it took before the starter caught. Grateful to hear the Trabant's engine turn over at last, he exhaled and backed the car out. The neighborhood street was as deserted as it had been yesterday. He left the motor running while closing and locking the garage door, then climbed behind the wheel again and drove off.

He headed north out of the city. After a short drive on the autobahn, he exited onto a scenic highway winding its way through patches of forest. Usually by the time he reached this stretch he managed to relax, leaving office and city stress behind. Not today, with his mind churning over what to do first. As much as he wanted to get the visit with Mielke out of the way, he needed to hide the suitcase. Within a few minutes he reached the outskirts of Wandlitz where his cottage was located. None of his neighbors were there on this weekday in November. Relieved, he pulled up in front of his small cottage at the end of a narrow lane, and retrieved the suitcase from the trunk to carry it inside.

A quick perusal of the house assured him that things were the way he'd left them on his visit during the last warm weekend in September. He laid the case on top of the kitchen table and walked to the opposite end of the living area to push back heavy curtains, exposing a glass door. Then he pulled a nylon cord on the wall next to the door. Heavy outside shutters lifted with a loud squeal, flooding the room with daylight. Dobnik allowed himself a quick look at the idyllic setting beyond the patio: a sizable garden of grass, apple trees and bushes, shielded from the neighbors on two sides by man-high hedges. A chain link fence bordered the property to the rear.

He opened the door, crossed the small patio and strode toward a tool shed in the corner of the yard. Dobnik dialed the combination on the padlock and stooped to step through the door into the corrugated sheet metal structure. The opening admitted enough light for him to find what he needed. Within seconds he tossed a green plastic sheet, working gloves, a pickax, and a shovel onto the lawn, removed his uniform coat, and dragged the tools next to a cluster of lilac bushes in the nearest corner. He walked around the bushes until he saw a flat space where he could dig. In spite of their scraggly winter appearance, he could have sworn he smelled for a moment the springtime fragrance of the lilacs' white and purple flowers. For late November the soil was surprisingly pliable. Working with a shovel and pickax, he soon broke out in a sweat. After what seemed like an endless period of time, he had unearthed half a meter of soil—deep enough.

He carried the plastic sheet into the house and spread it on the floor by the kitchen table. A glance at his watch confirmed he was running short on time. He opened the suitcase and shuffled through files and papers, selecting documents that would convince Schmidt and Sylvia of the value of what he had to offer.

His eyes fell on a file he felt certain would induce the West Germans to accede to his demands. He laid it on the table and rummaged through the baggage, searching for the two files he might need in the next few days, if all went according to plan. When he located them, he started to take them out as well but changed his mind. The safe hiding place here would be worth the inconvenience of having to make another trip. Satisfied, he shut the case, scrambled the combination lock, and wrapped the luggage in the plastic sheet on the floor. After several more minutes of efficient labor the suitcase was securely buried among the lilacs and the tools were replaced in the shed. Dobnik dabbed at the pearls of sweat on his forehead with a bathroom towel before locking up.

Two kilometers separated the town of Wandlitz and the forest settlement called Waldsiedlung Wandlitz where Mielke and other top party functionaries lived. Dobnik had been inside the closely guarded compound only a few times. He knew it contained twenty-one homes, luxurious by East German standards, a clubhouse with an indoor swimming pool, tennis courts, two bunkers, a broadcast station and several installations for the approximately 650 employees who looked after every wish of the government officials and their families. The public had no access to the compound. A two-meter-high wall and 140 Stasi guards spread over twenty-one posts saw to that. Dobnik had seen a fiscal report indicating that it cost close to six million West Marks a year to supply the Waldsiedlung with western consumer goods unavailable to the general public in East Germany. George Orwell's sarcastic allusion to communist societies in *Animal Farm*—that all were created equal, but some were more equal than others—rang all too true for Dobnik these days. He could imagine the outcry sure to come once the population discovered the lifestyle of these government comrades after the demise of the communist regime.

Dobnik stopped his ruminations when he spotted the guarded entrance to the compound. He unclenched his lower jaw as he eased the Trabant up to the crossbar and tried not to think of the file hidden in the trunk. Although the guardsmen didn't know him personally, his uniform, identification, and the fact they knew Mielke expected someone from headquarters, made for a smooth pass. Just to make sure he wouldn't stray, the young guard reminded him that Mielke lived in House 14.

"Colonel Dobnik." Mielke's gruff voice greeted him soon after he'd rung the door bell. "Headquarters didn't tell me they were sending you with my retirement papers. You must have more important matters to attend to."

The general stared at him with suspicion. Folds of sagging flesh and jowls bulging as if they held a wad of chewing tobacco gave him the appearance of a pit bull ready to tear flesh, provoked or not. Dobnik found it odd that neither of the two domestics that came with each house had answered the door. Perhaps Mielke had fallen so far out of favor that his servants had been taken away.

"Good to see you, General. We miss you at headquarters. The place is not the same without you."

Never mind that his first two statements were lies. The third one certainly was true, though not in the way Mielke would understand it. The man whom citizens and Stasi officers alike had feared the most could no longer terrorize them.

"Come in, Colonel."

He followed the general into the downstairs living room and accepted his invitation to sit at the table. While some referred to the houses in the Waldsiedlung as villas—and perhaps they were by East German standards—Dobnik found them to be relatively plain.

Without a word, he handed Mielke the envelope. The deposed Stasi chief removed a thin stack of papers and pulled a pen from his shirt pocket.

"Are the signature places marked?" he demanded.

Dobnik had not looked at the documents. "I don't know, General."

Mielke rifled through the pages and then dropped them in exasperation on the table. "Of course not. Organization and discipline obviously have become lax at headquarters."

We don't need the kind of discipline you have in mind, Dobnik thought. But he said, "Let me find the signature places, unless you want to read everything first before you sign."

"No. What's the use? I don't have many options these days, do I?"

Clearly, Comrade Mielke was feeling sorry for himself, a sentiment he'd never wasted on the many he'd ordered killed or thrown into prison during his thirty-two-year reign of terror as Stasi chief.

The general signed each page Dobnik extracted from the pile. With the ritual over, the colonel reinserted the originals in the envelope and left a stapled set of unsigned copies on the table.

"Too bad you didn't come a bit earlier. You could have joined me for a gourmet luncheon at the clubhouse. My wife's in the city today."

Did Mielke really have a magnanimous side? Dobnik doubted it.

"Thank you, sir. That's very thoughtful of you. I'm sorry I had to miss it. General, I have some time until my next appointment. You wouldn't be interested in a little after-lunch stroll, would you?"

"I suppose a little exercise would be good for the digestion."

Dobnik was relieved he didn't need to spell out that he wanted a chance to talk without being overheard. A workaholic who'd been stripped of his office, Mielke was probably bored these days. He would relish the company, even if it came in the form of a former subordinate. A chill permeated the air, punctuated by an occasional breeze from the nearby woods.

Mielke struck up a relaxed pace, but then stopped, staring at Dobnik's pant leg. "Colonel, what have you done to your uniform?"

Dobnik saw to his dismay that he'd missed his soiled cuff during the hasty cleanup after digging.

"Oh . . . I'm sorry. I had to make a stop at a nursery and must have gotten some dirt on me."

He stopped to flick the dried dirt off the cuff. Mielke had slowed so that Dobnik could catch up to him.

"Colonel, you've been one of our best officers and hardest workers. How is morale holding up?"

Dobnik knew he had to be careful in responding. For all he knew, Mielke still had a pipeline to top management and would report any negative comments. Feigned compliments were always safe.

"As you can imagine, your retirement was a blow to the troops. But I think everyone is pulling together now that we're facing attacks by troublemakers no doubt working for the West Germans."

The general snorted. "Those fascist capitalists will never succeed in annexing our great state."

That was the opening Dobnik had been waiting for. "Operation Independence will see to that, won't it?"

Mielke raised his thin, pointed eyebrows. "What is that?"

"You know, the disinformation we're feeding the West Germans to scuttle unification. I thought it had been ordered by you."

"I don't know anything about it. But it sounds like a good idea. Anything to put the capitalist swine in their place."

They had circled the clubhouse and were walking back toward Mielke's house. Once there, Dobnik said his goodbye, citing an appointment in the city. As the guards waved him through, he drove toward Berlin with mixed emotions. In a way he felt relief that his suspicions had been confirmed—Frantz had lied to him about Mielke knowing about the document plant. Nor, as he'd learned during the birthday party yesterday, had the current chief, Major General Rittmeister, been briefed about Operation Independence. That meant whatever Frantz's plans might be, he'd kept them from the Stasi chiefs.

Dobnik reached his decision. He needed to implement the fallback position for which he had so carefully laid the groundwork by copying Stasi documents and insisting on Sylvia Mazzoni as the courier.

At the same time, he sensed impending danger. Frantz and Schlechter were formidable opponents. What if Sylvia didn't show? He told himself she would, but just in case she didn't, he knew he had the means to compel her. His thoughts turned to the buried suitcase and the file that bore the label *Sylvia Mazzoni*.

Peter Bernhardt

Chapter Twenty-Six

Rolf pushed open the door of the restaurant and scanned the dining room. The server who had waited on him and Sylvia was in the process of taking orders at a table in the back. Desperate to find out what he could about Sylvia, Rolf rushed over and grabbed the man's elbow. Startled, the waiter pulled away, but when he recognized Rolf excused himself from the table and beckoned Rolf to front where he presented him with the check. Rolf bombarded him with questions but he would not answer until after Rolf handed him a twenty mark note.

Only then did he acknowledge that he'd observed two men in raincoats approach Sylvia's table. No, he did not overhear their conversation, and no, he did not perceive anything threatening in the men's demeanor. They acted rather like acquaintances who happened to bump into her. Yes, he found it odd that they left after only a minute or so, but she went with them voluntarily, as far as he could tell.

Rolf looked around the table, lifted the tablecloth and searched the floor and both benches, on the off chance she might have left a note. Nothing. Retrieving his coat, he noticed hers was gone. After paying the bill, he trudged out

220

of the hotel and wandered aimlessly along the sidewalk. He didn't know how long he'd been walking when he passed a typical Berlin neighborhood bar. A cast iron sign protruded from the wall above the Kneipe's entrance, displaying the round profile of a beer-drinking, jolly-looking fellow above the name *Zum Gemütlichen Emil*. The door opened and a young couple, engaged in animated conversation, brushed past him. When the door swung back, Rolf glimpsed a cozy atmosphere and heard laughter, beckoning him inside. He moved away.

But a drink would steady his nerves and clear his head. Just one, that's all. Although he had no recollection of turning back toward the Kneipe, he felt the cold door handle in his hand. In that instant, his AA program kicked in. Don't listen to that voice. It's lying to you again. You know you can't take that first drink. The bearded bartender and an old man with a beat-up hat drawn onto his face were staring at him. Shocked, Rolf let go of the handle and jerked back, causing the door to swing back and forth like an agitated pendulum.

He turned and glanced up and down the street, taking the first few hesitant steps, which gained speed and purpose as he began to get his bearings. Despite the chilly afternoon, he felt beads of sweat on his upper lip. How easy it would have been to lose his sobriety. His relief gave way to renewed concern for Sylvia.

A sign drew him toward the far corner of the next major intersection and down the stairs to the underground. Logic dictated he should return to the hotel. What else could he do? He saw no point in wandering Berlin's vast street network to search for Sylvia without even an inkling of where to begin. Since he'd never made the trip from West to East Berlin by public transportation, he needed to pay attention, which took his mind off Sylvia's disappearance. Once seated in the train, questions bombarded his mind.

Was Sylvia in danger, or was the waiter's supposition correct that she knew the men and went with them willingly? If so, why hadn't she left a note? From his phone booth, Rolf had not detected any sign of force, but that didn't mean there hadn't been any. It could have been subtle, like a gun held against her from a coat pocket. If she'd been coerced, she was at the mercy of faceless men he had no chance of finding. If she hadn't, he had to consider that she might be working for someone else. He didn't know which of the two possibilities troubled him more.

Feelings of guilt and blame assaulted him. She had disappeared on his watch. Schmidt and Stein would not understand. Should he call them? No, not yet. His questions to the Drei Sachsen desk clerk, whether Frau Mazzoni was in and whether he had any messages, netted the expected neins. The woman assured him she'd call him as soon as Frau Mazzoni returned. If she found his insistent questions odd, she hid it well.

In his room he threw his coat on the bed cover and went to the window. For a while he watched the pedestrians and cars along Unter den Linden. Then the thought entered his mind that her room might hold a clue to her whereabouts. Wondering whether she'd locked her side of the connecting door, he depressed the handle. The door opened.

He slipped into her suite, gliding from room to room as his eyes swept across surfaces of polished furniture. Nothing caught his attention. The tidy bed told him the maid had been here. He opened the nightstand drawer but stopped halfway. What was he doing? Had he not learned anything during the twelve years since he'd spied on her and Kreuzer? Granted, he found himself in a different situation than when he'd been a jealous student. Today, Sylvia's life could be at stake, or perhaps his, if she was playing a double game. Nonetheless, rifling through her personal things went too far—at least for now. If she were still missing this evening, he'd return and conduct a thorough search, then call Schmidt and Stein. He drew the connecting door shut behind him and looked around as if to make sure no one had caught him.

Suffocated by the room's atmosphere, he retrieved his coat and strode into the hallway, tramping down the seven flights of stairs instead of taking the elevator. The exertion felt good. Before he left the hotel, he told the woman behind the counter he'd be right outside in case she heard from Frau Mazzoni. Her nod of acknowledgment did not reassure him.

Pacing the sidewalk, he almost wished he still smoked. Then he saw her, standing on the sidewalk. He blinked, not trusting his eyes. She noticed him looking at her, and the frown on her face disappeared as she ran toward him.

He took her by the shoulders. "Sylvia. Are you all right?"

"Yes, I'm okay."

He embraced her and she did not resist. He knew their relationship had changed.

"Rolf, let's walk."

He let go of her and fell in beside her in a slow-paced stroll, hoping she wanted to tell him what had happened. She appeared deep in thought, perhaps searching for the right words.

"Rolf, there are a couple things you should know about. Will you give me your word that what I'm about to tell you stays between us?"

"Of course."

His response had been so quick that she turned and scrutinized his face. "This is crucial. I need to be sure you're committed to keep this absolutely to yourself."

The pedestrian signal at the intersection turned green and Sylvia plunged into the crowd crossing the street. Rolf followed on her heels. As they stepped up on the opposite curb, he touched her elbow and said, "You have my word."

"Good. Two British agents wanted to talk to me. I thought it best to go with them. Sorry if I worried you, but there was no time to leave a note."

Rolf wondered whether their haste had anything to do with his expected return from the hotel phone booth, but held his tongue. He asked instead, "Where did they take you?"

"They drove me around the city to tell me we're being set up to be arrested as spies."

His pulse quickened. "By whom?"

"The Stasi."

"How do they know?"

"They suspect the documents are Stasi plants."

"And what leads them to believe that?"

She hesitated. "One of their sources."

Rolf exhaled, calming himself. "Well, I'm not an expert on intelligence agents, but I bet they didn't share this with you out of the goodness of their hearts. What do they want you to do?"

"Guess what? Another set of copies—for them."

"I'll be damned! Do you have any idea what they're looking for?"

"Intelligence that might foil unification." She glanced at her wristwatch. "I should be able to find out in a couple of hours."

He caught a touch of secrecy in her demeanor. While he thought about it, she suggested, "Let's stop here."

He'd been too preoccupied to pay attention to his surroundings. They had walked all the way to the Staatsoper. She reached into her jeans pocket, pulled out a crumpled piece of paper, and handed it to him.

"This is what Mozart added to the drop last night."

Rolf unfolded the note and read.

"Sylvia. Unexpected difficulties. Future performance in doubt. Critical that we meet Tuesday afternoon at four, corner Charlottenstraße and Unter den Linden by Humboldt University (for old times' sake). Come alone!"

He stared at her in amazement. Then he studied the message once more, hoping a second, slower reading might yield better understanding. It didn't.

"What does it mean?"

"I've had some time to think about it. It seems to confirm the British agents' story."

"What about the 'old times' sake' comment? Do you know him?"

"I never went to Humboldt here in East Berlin. Maybe he is referring to the student days at Free University, which means he may have been one of Horst's friends."

Rolf did his best not to react to the mention of her former lover. "Are you going . . . alone?"

She took the note from him, slid it into her pocket, and started to head back.

"To be honest, I had planned on meeting him without telling you, until the British agents talked to me, that is." She turned and met his eyes. "I want you to come with me, Rolf. If there is only half the trouble ahead that I suspect there might be . . . I don't see how I could handle it by myself."

He was moved by the trust he saw in her eyes. He was dancing with the thought of a second chance. He swore to himself to never let her down again. Here was the opportunity to make the amends he'd hoped for. To think that he'd almost blown it by going into that bar less than an hour ago!

She broke off her gaze and picked up the pace. "Well, will you come?"

"Uh . . . yes, of course." In his eagerness to agree, he stumbled over the words. "But he emphasized that you were to be alone."

Sylvia responded over her shoulder. "I don't care. If the Brits are right about the setup . . ."

"Then we shouldn't meet him at all. We should tell Schmidt the deal is off."

"That's not an option for me. But I would understand if you thought it too risky."

"No, if you go, I will too. But is saving your opera career worth taking the risk of going to an East German prison? Schmidt may be bluffing. Just because your boyfriend was an RAF terrorist . . . I doubt that would keep you off the stage twelve years later."

"If that were the only obstacle, I'd take my chances with Schmidt's blackmail." She paused. "Rolf, I'm afraid the Stasi has a file on me. I have to know what's in it."

"But if Mozart is in on the setup—"

"The way I read his note, I don't think so. Why would he insist on meeting me early unless he was in some difficulty? Perhaps he's gotten wind of the trap and is desperate to flee."

"But if he's scared, he may not show when he sees two of us."

She looked at her watch. "It's an hour till four. Plenty of time to scout the terrain and work out how we'll give him extra company without scaring him off."

They were standing at the corner of Unter den Linden and Charlottenstraße, the meeting place specified in the message. If they could catch the Stasi spy unawares, they might obtain some answers to the mounting questions about this operation. Perhaps he'd shed some light on the suspected trap unless, of course, he was one of the trappers.

Chapter Twenty-Seven

Heinz Dobnik maneuvered the tiny Trabi into a tight parking place on a side street near Humboldt University. Watching students stream from the final afternoon lectures reminded him of the early seventies when he and Horst Kreuzer had spent their years at West Berlin's Free University, imbibing *Berliner Weiße* and arguing over politics. How different from the discipline imposed on these young East Germans. Despite the freedoms in the offing, Dobnik detected expressions of quiet resignation. Years of having been subjected to unrelenting party propaganda, years without a chance to express ideas outside the official line were not easily forgotten.

His thoughts turned to Sylvia. He'd met her on one of the few occasions Horst had brought her to their nightly gathering at the Kneipe Studentenkeller, a popular student bar. She likely would not remember him from among Horst Kreuzer's numerous pals. On the other hand, she might recognize him as Horst's older friend.

Like others before her, Sylvia had fallen for that scoundrel's enthusiasm, wit, and rugged good looks. Perhaps he was good in bed. Dobnik had always envied the way women flocked to Kreuzer, who had continually changed companions until he snagged Sylvia. She'd been too naïve to realize what she had gotten herself into, yet Dobnik couldn't help her. Any attempt to warn her would have been written off to jealousy, correctly so in large measure. He'd never been burdened with any illusions about the fairness of life—he'd not win her affection. In those days he had been a true believer in communism. Nothing would have kept him from absconding to East Germany—presumably not even Sylvia.

He approached Unter den Linden with Charlottenstraße to his right. Experience had taught him to check out a meeting place an hour or so early to make sure no surprises awaited him. After his visit with Mielke, he'd gone by his apartment to change into civilian clothes and pick up a briefcase for the files. The ill-fitting gray suit, white shirt and thin striped tie, along with the worn satchel made of imitation cordovan, should let him blend in with the East German bureaucrats who populated the streets during rush hour.

He grimaced when he realized today's tasks had left him with only twenty minutes to find a place for the drop and to scout the vicinity—not nearly enough time, but it would have to suffice. Sylvia posed only a minimal risk, though he couldn't be sure. Nothing new in that: there were few certainties in his life. Better to concentrate on the task at hand than to worry about matters beyond his control.

After walking several streets, he found a hiding place for the drop—not perfect by any means, but good enough, given the time constraints. He did not have to wait long before the side street emptied, allowing him to stash the files unobserved. That done, he hurried back to the meeting place and strained to peer down Unter den Linden in both directions for signs of anything out of the ordinary. Of necessity, today's reconnaissance had to be superficial.

Workers spewing out of offices crowded the sidewalks, and car traffic swelled to rush-hour proportions.

Having detected nothing unusual, Dobnik retreated into the recessed doorway of a shoe repair shop on Charlottenstraße. Under his shoes, the faded beige of the artificial tiles, warped in several spots, attested to Berlin's harsh winters. The store had locked its doors a few minutes before, following the unfathomable practice of small shopkeepers—closing just as people got off work. A few paces from the street corner, it would serve as a perfect observation post.

The final minutes before four were the slowest he'd ever experienced, each glance at his watch causing the time to slow further still. He watched the sun set, turning this into a typical dreary November late afternoon. The distant sound of low bells, chime by chime adding up to four, unnerved him. He checked the nearby building entrances and the pedestrians moving along the sidewalks.

Two minutes past the hour now and no sign of Sylvia. How long should he wait? He'd settled on fifteen minutes when he spotted her long black hair and tawny complexion that stood out from the pale Germans rushing past her.

She hesitated, as if lost, then stopped at the corner, casting nervous glances around her. Dobnik shifted his focus to his surroundings. A quick scan of the thinning crowd gave him some assurance that she was alone. He peered once more at the building entrances. She might have brought Rolf Keller, whom he would easily recognize. He'd have to rely on instinct for sensing government agents, whether from Schmidt's shop or his own, unless, of course, the Stasi man turned out to be Boris Schlechter. His heartbeat quickened when he realized he really was looking for Lieutenant General Frantz's thug.

Sylvia paced back and forth on the sidewalk, still glancing around. She could wait a few minutes. He scrutinized the area once more, then eased out of his hiding place and strode toward her. She turned. He could tell by her look that she did not recognize him.

"Sylvia. You don't remember me."

"No, I don't."

"I was a friend of Horst."

He held out his right hand as he looked into her dark eyes. She did not offer hers.

"You're Mozart. But what's your real name?"

If he wanted to make a deal, he'd have to tell her sooner or later. Still, he hesitated. "Heinz Dobnik. We met at the Studentenkeller, remember?"

She gave his hand a curt, two-finger shake. "I'm sorry. I really don't."

"Well, it doesn't matter," he said in a nonchalant tone so as to hide his disappointment. "I hope you liked the roses . . . and the present."

"Yes, thank you. They're fine, which is more than I can say about your method of delivery."

She had lost neither her directness nor her spark.

"I thought it best to take certain precautions, and that seemed like a safe hiding place." He made a sweeping motion with his hand. "We're much too exposed here. Let's take a little walk."

"Only if my friend comes along."

Alarmed, he swept his eyes in a circle but could not detect anyone watching them. "You brought someone? Who? I told you to come alone."

"I'm not walking off alone with you. He's an old friend. Shall I give him the signal, or do you want to tell me what you want right here?"

"What does Rolf Keller know about this operation?"

He knew he'd surprised her when he saw the sharp contraction of her face muscles.

"He knows everything I do, which is not a whole lot."

Dobnik surveyed the vicinity once more. "He's in that café across the street, isn't he? There is something I've got to say that you may not want him to hear. Sylvia, the . . ."

The crosswalk light turned green and the last few stragglers leaving nearby offices rushed across the street toward them. He waited for them to pass. A young man in a heavy overcoat, swinging an attaché case, a newspaper tucked under his arm, stopped as he reached their corner to watch the next traffic signal. He did not have the circumspect air of an agent.

Dobnik waited until the man crossed before picking up where he'd left off. "The Stasi opened a file on you when you came to East Berlin with Horst. I have the only copy in existence. It's yours if Schmidt deals."

"What lies are they spreading about me?"

"Lies or not . . . you'll never sing again after it hits the press. It may even interest a federal prosecutor."

"What do you want?"

Dobnik ignored the scorn in her voice. He waved toward the café. "If you insist on including Keller, I'd rather have him listen in on the rest than hang around here."

Sylvia mimicked his wave and within seconds a figure emerged from the café and darted through the traffic on Unter den Linden. As Rolf drew closer, Dobnik saw his eyebrows arch in recognition.

"Heinz Dobnik. I don't believe it."

"Rolf. It's been a while."

"You two know each other?" Sylvia stared from one to the other.

"Yeah. We had a class together and a few beers with Horst and friends," Rolf explained. "After a while I quit going to their parties. Their politics were a bit too radical for my taste."

"Fair enough." Dobnik made no attempt to hide his impatience. "Time to leave. We've been here way too long already."

He struck out north on Charlottenstraße, crossed over, and didn't slow until he entered the first side street running west. Motioning Sylvia and Rolf on, he scanned the area. No one was following.

Several quick strides brought him alongside Sylvia. Briefcase in right hand, he kept her and Rolf to the outside of the sidewalk. "Keep walking while I talk."

He selected a pace, neither slow nor fast, the way three friends on their way to a restaurant might walk.

"The second drop can't wait till tomorrow evening. I'm being set up."

"You're not the only one," Rolf interjected.

"I don't know anything about that, but it wouldn't surprise me." He turned to Sylvia. "I have two files for you."

He saw her glance at his briefcase. "Not with me, of course."

The thought occurred to him that Mielke's retirement papers might provide good cover should that become necessary.

"Listen carefully, both of you. The first file is a dossier on Joachim Walter."

He paused to see if the name registered. Apparently it did not.

"He's a top West German government official, a former Nazi. The information on his background is true, but the dossier has been doctored to make it appear that he harbors secret plans for a fascist German state after unification. The idea is to plant this disinformation with the World War II Allies. I don't need to tell you what that would do to the West Germans' unification plans."

They were halfway down the first block. Dobnik's sweep of the meager traffic and pedestrians still yielded nothing to arouse his suspicion, though the fading daylight made it difficult to see.

"Why are you telling us about the forgery?" Sylvia's suspicions were evident in her face and voice.

"If Schmidt suspects I'm feeding him fake papers, he won't deal with me."

"What about the second file?" Rolf asked.

"It's my gift to Schmidt from my personal stash, which is rather extensive. I'm talking a suitcase full. The second file contains documents from the Stasi department in charge of training terrorists like the RAF." Dobnik turned from Rolf to Sylvia. "You remember the RAF, don't you?" He continued before she could protest. "Schmidt must act fast. I don't have specifics, only a notion that something's likely to explode before long. I'd say the sooner he gets that file the better. It may already be too late."

She asked, "And where might we find these files?"

"Before I answer that, I want you to etch into your memory the details of the deal I want from Schmidt." He looked at Rolf. "Perhaps it's just as well you came along after all. Two memories are better than one."

The light at the intersection ahead turned green and Dobnik herded them to the other side. Gradually, the neighborhood was becoming more residential, but not any less depressing. Still no sign of any surveillance.

"Tell Schmidt the file on the terrorists is nothing compared to what I'll give him once I'm safely in Pullach."

Rolf and Sylvia seemed to recognize the name of the small town south of Munich, housing the headquarters of Schmidt's agency.

"I'll be able to get myself to West Berlin. But I want a contact there. Set it up no later than this Thursday evening. By the time your last performance is over, Sylvia, I won't be safe here. You've seen the pandemonium in the streets. People here think of the West as the promise of paradise." He could feel sarcasm creep into his voice. "Imagine how disappointed these fools will be when reality sinks in."

"So, why are you so anxious to get there?" Rolf asked.

"You might say I'll do better in the West, but I have no illusions."

Sylvia cut in. "Let's get back to business. Anything else for Schmidt?"

"I have enough years with the Stasi to be entitled to a decent pension if I stay."

"Even under its new name, the Stasi won't be around much longer," Rolf pointed out. "Former Stasi agents may be looking at jail time instead of a pension."

Dobnik returned Rolf's challenging gaze. "I'll grant you that. On the other hand, you know how democratic bureaucracies work. I'll bet you all the spooks they can't convict of some specific crime will end up on a government pension."

Rolf laughed in apparent appreciation of Dobnik's point.

"Be that as it may, Schmidt will be able to weigh the odds. We're wasting our breath arguing about it. I want a government pension equal to what a colonel leaving at full retirement age from the Federal Intelligence Service would receive. And I want a house, title free and clear, no rent or mortgage payment, preferably in southern Bavaria. Munich, Garmisch, Oberstdorf or Mittenwald would be nice—he'll get the idea."

"You're not asking much."

Dobnik paid scant attention to Sylvia's remark. "I have information that'll make it easy for Schmidt to sell his boss on the idea. In fact, I may be asking too little." He paused to lend weight to his next words. "Tell him I'm prepared to give you intelligence about a plan to assassinate a key government official."

"Who?" Rolf asked with urgency.

"No names before Schmidt agrees to my terms. Tell him this: if the Stasi plan succeeds, there will be no united Germany. You know how eager Chancellor Kohl is to make it happen."

A sedan whipped around the corner of the intersection ahead and sped toward them. Dobnik froze.

A taxi with a young male driver and female passenger whizzed by. Dobnik relaxed.   "Keep walking," he told Sylvia and Rolf. "Cabbies drive the same everywhere. I call it controlled recklessness." He shrugged as if to wipe the disturbance from his mind.

"If Schmidt is ready to deal, I will have another *Carmen* score for you. Meet me at five thirty tomorrow afternoon at Café Franken across from your hotel."

Sylvia shook her head. "I can't. I have to leave for the opera house then."

"I can take care of it," Rolf offered.

Dobnik hesitated. He preferred handing the materials to Sylvia, but he couldn't risk making the transfer at the opera house when Frantz was expecting it. "I suppose that's all right, since you're both working for the same outfit. Just make sure you have Schmidt's instructions concerning my safe passage."

They walked in silence toward the intersection from which the taxi had come. Dobnik turned left.

He addressed Sylvia. "Your suite has two windows overlooking Unter den Linden. If Schmidt accepts my terms, open the curtain on your west window at seven in the morning, but keep the one on the east side closed. Don't make any changes until eight. If both curtains are either open or closed, I'll know Schmidt is not interested. Do you understand, Sylvia?"

She responded with a perturbed, "Yes."

Rolf's impatient voice interjected. "Now that we've got all that straightened out, where is today's material?"

"Do you remember my instructions?"

When both nodded, Dobnik spoke in a low voice, forcing them to walk closer to him. "See the metal wastebasket on the lamp post straight ahead?"

They peered ahead and after a moment nodded once more.

"At its bottom you'll find today's drop." He looked up and down the street. "I suggest you slow down to let that couple on the other side get ahead of you. If no one else is around when you reach the spot, pull out the files. Otherwise take as many passes as you need to be certain no one sees you raiding the trashcan."

Rolf gave him a quizzical look. "A public wastebasket . . . isn't that a risky hiding place?"

"No more than some of the dead drops Stasi spies have used for years. These baskets won't be emptied until seven in the morning, and there aren't any bums here to dig through the garbage for food or cigarettes."

He turned from Rolf to Sylvia. "I've read where you successfully resisted our recruiting efforts." He watched Sylvia's puzzlement gradually turn to comprehension.

"I knew it! That guy with the East German accent who kept trying to get me to go out with him was a Stasi agent." She scoffed. "Not all women are so lonely as to fall for that Stasi Romeo routine."

"You'd be surprised what a great recruiting tool it's been." He paused to let his next statement sink in. "Make sure you get Schmidt to agree. There's no need for publicity."

Sylvia's expression told him she'd gotten the message, but Rolf looked perplexed. Dobnik pointed down the street. "After your pickup, walk in that direction and you'll come out on Unter den Linden a short distance from the Drei Sachsen. Until tomorrow then." He turned to walk back to the last intersection, then stopped.

"One more thing. If I'm not at the Café Franken by five thirty tomorrow, something has gone wrong. In that case go to Henkelstraße 97. That's near Alexanderplatz." He added a loud, "Auf Wiedersehen," for the benefit of the couple several meters down the opposite sidewalk, turned the corner and entered a small restaurant.

He'd have time for a beer before he checked to make sure they'd picked up the files. Funny, he hadn't planned on giving them a fallback position. Yet it had felt right to do so. If something happened to him, all his illicit copying would go for naught unless his comment gave Sylvia and Rolf a head start on getting to his document cache. Until that moment he hadn't fully acknowledged the extent of his disenchantment with the communist regime and how much he wanted the Stasi papers to end up in West Germany, no matter what. And the fact that Rolf and Sylvia would never use his information unless General Frantz betrayed him made Dobnik's sense of justification complete.

Since he'd given the tip about Henkelstraße 97, he needed to go there now. He dreaded the difficult task awaiting him, but there was no one else he could trust. She'd been so angry with him. Could he count on her to come through?

Chapter Twenty-Eight

As soon as the pedestrians on the opposite sidewalk were out of sight, Rolf dug below beer bottles, soft drink cans, paper bags, and crumpled-up newspapers. There were no greasy food wrappers, half-full containers, or smelly cigarette butts. German neatness even extended to public wastebasket deposits. Searching for the files, Rolf moved his hands in a circular motion. Just when he thought he'd picked the wrong basket, he felt two files below wadded-up newspapers. He grabbed the files along with the newspapers and stuck them under his overcoat while Sylvia kept an eye on the surroundings.

"Done like a real spook," Sylvia proclaimed as she took off in the direction Dobnik had indicated.

Her light banter surprised him, given the tension he felt in carrying secret papers in a country where individuals were arrested, tortured and killed for much less. But he understood that was her way of coping with the stressful situation.

"What did Dobnik mean by that comment about no publicity?" he asked.

She frowned. "He's threatening to turn my Stasi file over to the news media if I don't convince Schmidt to accede to his demands."

Rolf listened with mixed emotions. Concern for her gave way to suspicion about what past activities were so damaging Dobnik could use them against her. He waited to speak until a woman clutching a purse had hurried past them. "Any idea what's in that file?"

Sylvia fiddled with an errant strand of hair, taking her time to respond. "I don't know . . . other than that it apparently shows the Stasi recruiting efforts Dobnik alluded to."

"You actually had a Romeo hit on you?"

He'd heard of the Stasi employing young men to woo lonely West German women vacationing on Mediterranean beaches. After the romantic relationship blossomed into more than a mere holiday fling, the agent would ask his love interest to spy for him. The targeted women were often government secretaries with security clearance. The full extent to which these women infiltrated West German public institutions, the government and its intelligence services was known only to the Stasi. Rolf suspected hardly any segment of West German society remained free of Stasi moles. Sometimes the Stasi would pay a recruit to obtain the training necessary to qualify for a sensitive government position. He shook his head, unable to fathom what they would want with an opera singer. Perhaps she'd make an attractive carrier once she was established and doing a lot of international travel.

Sylvia interrupted his thoughts, surprising him as he'd almost forgotten his question. "Between semesters at the Stuttgart Opera School I used to work at my mom's hostel in Milan. During my last summer break she insisted I go for a long weekend to the beach on the Riviera, saying I was stressed out and needed to relax. At the beach I got into a conversation with a German tourist. He was good-looking and smooth. We ended up eating dinner together at a beach restaurant. I couldn't put my finger on it, but something about him bothered me. He seemed too nice to be real."

"But you didn't suspect he was a Stasi Romeo."

"No. I only saw him that one time. He was way too insistent. Can you imagine, the next morning he had flowers delivered to my hotel room with a note asking me out again? And he left several messages. After the debacle with Horst, I'd made up my mind never to be blindsided again. Call it paranoia or a sixth sense, something about him gave me the creeps. I didn't return his calls and checked out of the hotel the following morning to drive back to Milan. Much to my mother's consternation."

"For him to approach you, he must have been familiar with your background. The Stasi targeted mainly German women who could infiltrate West German society, and you don't exactly look German. It would have appeared for all the world that you were enjoying a swim on your native Italian beach."

"Eew." She shuddered. "It gives me chills to think they were so close to me, and I had no idea."

They walked the last few meters to Unter den Linden in silence. Upon reaching the boulevard, Rolf stopped.

Sylvia pointed to the left. "The hotel is that way."

"Yes, I know. But we can't go back there with these papers. And you need to get an answer from Schmidt this evening, remember? First we need to copy . . . oh crap! It's past six. The copy shop is closed till morning."

They stood at the corner, looking at each other in dismay.

After a moment, Sylvia spoke. "Schmidt doesn't know about today's delivery. How about if we stash it in the train station and then go see him to get his response for Dobnik?" Before Rolf could point out the fallacy in her reasoning, she caught it herself. "No, that won't work. Without today's materials Schmidt won't have enough incentive to agree to Dobnik's terms." She stared at Rolf. "Looks like we're at an impasse. I need Schmidt's response by seven in the morning. If we hand the papers over this evening you won't be able to get copies made, but to be convinced that Dobnik is worth what he is asking, Schmidt needs to see them tonight."

As she finished her lament, an idea came to him. He reached into his rear jeans pocket for his wallet and leafed through its plastic divider until he found the card the journalist had given him on the plane.

"Sylvia, help me flag a taxi. You stay here and I'll try over there."

Before she could ask any questions he crossed against a red light and waited in the center of the street for several cars to pass. With rush hour winding down, he wondered what their chances were of getting a cab on a street corner. He kept his eyes on the traffic to his left and noticed Sylvia was doing likewise across the boulevard. Cars and buses rushed past him but no taxis. When one finally rumbled toward him, he raised his arm but dropped it as he spotted passengers. Two more cabs followed in quick succession, likewise occupied. He considered going back to the hotel to call for one when a movement caught his attention. Sylvia stood beside a stopped cab, waving at him. Rolf dashed across the street in front of an oncoming bus. The screeching brakes and the blaring horn rang in his ears as he hurled himself into the waiting taxi.

Looking at the journalist's card, he remembered Kent Ferguson telling him his office on Kantstraße was near Savigny Square. He instructed the driver, "Savignyplatz. How long a drive is it?"

Alert brown eyes studied Rolf through the rearview mirror. "You in a hurry?"

"Yes."

"Hang on."

The sharp acceleration surprised Rolf until he realized Sylvia not only had managed to catch a taxi, but one from West Berlin at that. He wasn't sure of the make of the car, only that it was too responsive for a Wartburg or Trabant.

"You have a plan?" Sylvia asked.

"Uh . . . yes. Sorry, there was no time to explain. I met a journalist on the flight from the States. We're going to his office. Reporters usually work late. Let's hope he does."

"To make copies?" She sounded doubtful. "Do you know anything about him?"

She was right, of course. Involving him carried a risk, but one he had to take.

"We're fresh out of options."

"As long as one of us is doing the copying . . ."

"Savignyplatz," the cabbie announced as he stopped next to a sidewalk bordering a small park, a green oasis of trees, shrubs and grass in the city center.

Rolf gave the cabbie a twenty mark bill and climbed out to join Sylvia on the park footpath. He caught the man's look of surprise at the generous tip. Then, as if to make sure his customer wouldn't change his mind, the driver pulled away fast and in no time his dark green sedan was part of the stream of traffic along Kantstraße.

"Do you see a number anywhere, Sylvia?"

"That hotel back there is 146. Are we looking for higher or lower?"

"Lower." Rolf strained to make out the next house number and then pointed west. "This way."

He touched Sylvia's elbow to encourage her along. She fell in with him at full speed. His quick strides dislodged the bundle of papers nestled against the small of his back, and he reached inside his overcoat to stuff them deeper down his jeans. In the middle of the next block past the square, he spotted huge black numbers matching those on Ferguson's card. They were affixed to gray cement above the revolving door of a steel-and-glass office tower. He motioned for Sylvia to enter the fast-turning door pushed by a man in a hurry to exit. Not wanting to get separated, Rolf stepped in behind her. The door frame hit him in the back, causing him to pitch forward. He braced himself by putting his hands on Sylvia's upper back. Her shoulders stiffened for a split second but then relaxed as she leaned back into his touch. Her scent triggered images from the past, smelling her fragrance, running his fingers along her soft skin, their bodies entwined. The intensity of the desire he felt alarmed him, and he pulled away as the revolving door spit them out into the lobby.

He kept his distance during the first few steps. Had Sylvia taken pleasure in their contact? He mustn't give in to those thoughts. They were too big a distraction. At least for now. They moved past a souvenir shop and a small bakery, both closed, toward a bank of elevators across the lobby. He noticed an occupied phone booth on the back wall but no directory. The heavy-set woman on the phone seemed in the middle of an intense conversation that had the look of lasting a while. If the building had any security officers, they were nowhere to be seen.

Thoughts of yanking the woman off the phone by asserting an emergency were flashing through his mind when he heard Sylvia hiss, "Psst. Over here."

She was looking at a wall on the side of the elevators. Sure enough, two glassed-in cases hung there, listing the tenants. The left one covered the letters A through L, and after sweeping down an endless list of lawyers, bearing designations of "Dr. jur." and "Prof.," he spotted Kent Ferguson's name. Curiously, the listing did not indicate the nature of his business. After a moment's reflection, Rolf shrugged it off as perhaps being not unusual for a freelance reporter.

"Suite 613," he read out.

They turned the corner in unison and after a short elevator ride were soon hustling down the narrow sixth-floor corridor. The carbon soles of his running shoes squeaked and Sylvia's leather boot heels clicked on the stark black-and-white linoleum floor. They almost ran past 613, so small was the name placard on the wall. The frosted glass on the upper part of the door shone with a yellow tint—a good omen.

Rolf knocked on the glass and listened. Not a sound. He depressed the handle, expecting to feel the resistance of a lock. To his surprise the door opened. He stumbled into a small reception area featuring two chairs in front of a metal desk, painted white, with a pullout that held an electric typewriter but no computer.

As Sylvia drew up beside him, a door off to the side opened and a surprised Kent Ferguson stared at them.

"I'm sorry, but we're closed."

Rolf could have sworn Ferguson still had on the rumpled white shirt he'd worn on the plane with the same necktie hanging off to one side.

"Rolf Keller. We met on the flight to Frankfurt."

Kent's face relaxed. "Of course. Sorry, I didn't recognize you."

He took in Sylvia's features with more than a disinterested glance. "Kent Ferguson."

"Sylvia Mazzoni." She introduced herself before Rolf could.

Still ogling Sylvia, Ferguson asked Rolf, "Did you bring me a gripping human interest story about unification?"

"I don't have anything for you right now, but I may in a few days."

Ferguson reluctantly switched his focus from Sylvia to Rolf, who held the reporter's gaze and said, "I've come to ask a favor."

Ferguson glanced at the ceiling as if looking for heavenly guidance on how to respond. By the time he spoke, the pause had been too long for him to sound sincere. "What can I do to help?"

"We need to copy some papers this evening, and the copy shops are already closed."

Rolf looked around. For the first time it occurred to him that the office might not even have a copier.

"Not a problem. I'll be happy to copy them for you." A curious expression spread over Ferguson's face. "Where are they?"

Rolf realized that he still had the packet stuck in his waistband.

As he tried to think of a graceful way to retrieve the documents, Sylvia piped up. "Actually, these are personal documents relating to my family's estate. Rolf is representing me." She paused. "You do know he's a lawyer?"

"Yes, he told me."

"We have an appointment in an hour for which we need two sets of copies." She gave Ferguson a conspiratorial look as if she were drawing him into her confidence. "You understand that we have to maintain attorney-client privilege."

It took all of Rolf's willpower not to walk over to her and kiss her. "Kent, if you'll show us where your copier is . . . we want to pay you, of course."

"You can pay me with an exclusive on that story of yours."

Rolf felt a pang of guilt for leading him on, but nodded.

"Come this way."

Ferguson led them through the side door into an office cluttered with newspapers, teletypes, reams of typing paper, and notepads. The splintered wood-veneer desk with its numerous scratches and dents and the sagging vinyl-covered chairs spoke of rentals. Ferguson walked over to a corner niche, housing a teletype and copier.

"It's ready to go. I'll be out front. Holler if you need help."

♫ ♫ ♫

"What kind of story do you have for this journalist?" Sylvia asked, as their taxi sped toward the Zoo train station.

"Good question." Rolf shrugged. "What we're doing certainly would make for interesting news, though Schmidt and Stein won't think so. But, you never know whose help we might need . . ."

He stopped himself to turn his attention to a more immediate problem—the black Opel three cars back.

"Driver. Change in plans," he shouted over the schmaltzy song playing on the car radio. "Take us to Flughafen Tegel."

As the cabbie nodded and pulled into the left turn lane, Rolf whispered to Sylvia, "We've got someone on our tail."

"How did they find us? Do you suppose your journalist friend—?"

"No telling. They could be Schmidt's people, the British or Stasi." The Red Army Faction popped into his mind as well, but he did not express the thought.

"What are we going to do with the copies? Don't you want to put them in the locker at the train station?"

He glanced over his shoulder at the Opel that had made the same left turn. "First we need to lose them."

"Do you think they know what we've got?"

"Since they're keeping their distance, I suppose they don't."

He raised his hand, letting her know he needed to think. After a few moments, he'd made up his mind.

"Sylvia, you remember where Schmidt's hotel is?" When she nodded, he laid out his plan.

♫ ♫ ♫

The taxi dropped them in front of Tegel Airport. Rolf made a show of paying the fare, noting in his peripheral vision that the Opel had stopped fifty meters behind.

He handed the driver two bills. "Remember, this is just a down payment."

The cabbie nodded and drove off. Rolf thought he detected someone getting out of the black sedan as he and Sylvia entered the hall.

"Don't turn around," he cautioned Sylvia. "I think there is only one following us."

Recalling Schmidt's detailed description, they had no trouble finding the lockers. He held in his hand a part of the newspaper that had been guarding Dobnik's documents in the back of his jeans. Schmidt's key opened box No. 53 without difficulty. Rolf deposited the newspaper into the empty locker, closed the door and withdrew the key. His movements were deliberate enough to let an onlooker observe what he was doing but fast enough to leave the impression he was trying to be circumspect.

"That was easy," he whispered to Sylvia. "Now for the hard part."

He hoped he was right that only one man from the black Opel had followed them into the terminal. If not, his plan probably wouldn't work. They walked past the Air France ticket counters to the restrooms. Rolf did not like the setup. The entrances to the men's and ladies' rooms were next to each other so they could easily be observed from one spot.

"Not here," he muttered. "Let's find something better."

Dodging travelers who scurried through the hall like ants, they came upon another set of bathrooms located on opposite sides about thirty meters apart. Not perfect, but probably the best they'd find. Sylvia stopped and raised her eyebrows.

"This will have to do," Rolf answered her unspoken question. "Remember to give me fifteen minutes."

She nodded.

He started to urge her to be careful, but when he saw that she was already at the door to the ladies' room, he swallowed the words. Although they had agreed they needed to split up, he didn't like the idea of Sylvia striking out on her own. No time for worrying about that now, he told himself as he hiked over to the men's room. When he reached the entrance, he glanced back down the hall and noticed a young man standing by a coffee bar on the other side of the ladies' room, watching its entry and surveying the hall. Rolf averted his eyes and withdrew into the men's room. He'd not seen anyone else loitering in the hall. With only one pursuer attempting to watch both restrooms, he liked his chances of being able to get away undetected.

The bathroom door swung back and forth from the constant flow of travelers coming and going. Rolf watched the men waiting for the urinals or stalls as well as the ones washing and drying their hands. There were several stocky fellows who might provide cover for slipping out. They were all still in line, however, and he couldn't afford to wait until they were done. An exchange between two men and a teenager who were drying their hands drew his attention. They were together. He eased over toward the door. When they left, he squeezed in among them. In so doing, he clipped the youngster's heels.

Rolf mumbled, "Entschuldigung."

He ignored their headshakes, thankful the three were turning in the direction he needed to take. Not having looked for the pursuer, he couldn't be certain whether he'd managed to leave unseen. He quickened his strides toward the building exit. Outside, the chaos of airport traffic greeted him. Slow-moving cars, vans and buses fought their way around vehicles dropping off passengers and luggage. Four or five taxis were parked along the curb, and incredibly, no travelers were waiting. That cinched his decision. He climbed into the cab at the front of the line.

After he'd told the driver his destination, Rolf asked him to stop at the curve ahead. The cabbie glanced at him in the rearview mirror, probably wondering about the strange request, but said nothing. He slowed as the road curved. Rolf held his breath. Would the other taxi be there? Then he saw the cab parked on the shoulder.

Rolf pointed. "Please stop over there."

When they were alongside the other car, he rolled down his window. The driver in the parked cab recognized him and waved. Rolf held up ten fingers and mouthed more than spoke, "Ten minutes."

The man nodded. Rolf rolled up the window and said to his driver, "Okay. Bahnhof Zoo . . . and make it quick."

♫ ♫ ♫

When studying a new role, warming up her voice, rushing to make a rehearsal on time, or singing, fifteen minutes passed in a flash, but not when having to linger in the ladies' room. She had hidden in a stall, because standing around or pacing might draw attention. This last quarter hour had been an eternity. Sylvia had always known that patience was not one of her virtues. Now, for the first time perhaps, she realized how truly impatient she could be. While she did not look forward to being followed again, she much preferred it to sitting around on this toilet. At long last, it was time to leave.

Sylvia actually hoped to see the pursuer. If she didn't, that meant he had followed Rolf, thereby jeopardizing their plan. As soon as she stepped into the hall, she noticed the young man by the coffee bar scanning the hall with nervous glances. He'd probably been worrying about their long restroom stops and whether they might have slipped away. With any luck, that was true in Rolf's case.

She struck up a purposeful pace on her way to the exit straight ahead. The cool evening air gave her an adrenalin rush. When she reached the curb, the last cab was pulling away, leaving only one couple waiting. She relaxed her shoulders. That probably meant Rolf had managed to catch a taxi here, a good sign.

Her next stop would tell. Sylvia strode along the sidewalk and glanced over her shoulder. She did not see anyone following her. Had she lost their pursuer, or was he keeping his distance? Her attention was drawn to the curve ahead, which their driver had described in great detail. It looked deserted. She wondered whether the cabbie had failed to keep his word or whether Rolf had taken that cab after all. If so, she'd have to turn back and catch one at the taxi stand. Then she noticed a flash of red taillights shrouded in rosy exhaust fumes. Her anxiety subsided when she recognized the vehicle parked on the shoulder, engine running. Sylvia burst into a full sprint to cover the last few meters. She tore open the rear door and flung herself inside the car. The driver stepped on the gas the instant she hit the seat.

She looked back. The young man stood near the spot where the taxi had been a moment ago. Then he turned and ran back toward the terminal. By the time he'd reach his companion at the far entrance, she'd be long gone.

"Where to, Miss?"

The driver's question cut short her state of elation at having gotten away. She gasped a few ragged breaths before responding, "Hotel Ludwigsburg, bitte."

As she settled into the seat, she admitted to herself for the first time that Rolf's presence had helped her forget the danger they were in, but now alone in the taxi the realization came crashing back. Images of the attack in the park flooded her mind. So many questions demanded answers. Once more, she speculated about who might have killed her attacker and why—the Stasi, Schmidt or his people, the Red Army Faction, or British Intelligence? How could she hope to extricate herself when she didn't even know the source of the danger?

Her thoughts returned to Rolf. The self-assurance she sensed in him nowadays gave her the belief that they would come out of this episode alive. She reflected how much he'd grown since their student liaison. Gone were the days of overt display of admiration. In a way she missed that. Yet, paradoxically, she knew at some level that his maturity was the reason she felt safe in his company.

"Hotel Ludwigsburg coming up."

The driver's mention of Schmidt's hotel made her wonder whether Rolf would be there already. She hoped so.

♫ ♫ ♫

Dieter Schmidt swished the pale golden liquid before lifting the bulbous glass to inhale the strong cognac aroma and take a sip. The burning sensation traveled down to his stomach, relieving most of the fullness he felt after a heavy German dinner in the hotel restaurant. Armchairs and sofas placed around small glass tables, interspersed with planters of live greenery, provided a relaxing atmosphere in the lobby bar.

Far from relaxed, Schmidt thought about Mozart's first drop. Bauman had called him just before dinner and confirmed that the documents contained an exact description of the coordinates of NATO Poseidon missile sites in West Germany. Undoubtedly, the Stasi had passed this top secret information on to the Soviets, enabling them to reposition their rockets to neutralize the Poseidon warheads.

Schmidt shook his head in disgust. The Americans had become leery of their German NATO partner after repeated security breaches by Stasi moles within the German Military Intelligence Division.

Peter Bernhardt

Schmidt's thoughts returned to the Stasi officer. The first delivery proved they were dealing with someone of the highest security clearance. What would he bring to the opera on Wednesday night, and why hadn't he made contact to spell out specific demands for his repatriation in the West? Schmidt had no illusions that he'd just want immunity from prosecution. Unless Mozart was a fool, which he doubted, he likely knew that odds of prosecution in the West were slim. Bauman had given Schmidt a free hand to make any deal as long as there was nothing illegal about it. He'd even said to call him if there were questionable aspects involved. In other words, negotiate the best deal possible, but make a deal.

Schmidt sat in a remote corner far from the business crowd in the lobby bar. He raised his cognac glass again but held it suspended for a moment, then set it down abruptly on the side table.

Sylvia Mazzoni had just entered the lobby. She gazed toward the reception desk but did not approach. Something was wrong. If she had come to see him, why did she not check on his room number and call him? Although he was curious over what she was waiting for, he realized she'd spot him sooner or later. He rose and ambled toward her, raising his arm to get her attention. It would look like two friends meeting at a designated time and place. When she saw him, he thought he detected apprehension, but so fleeting he couldn't be certain.

"Is something wrong?" He motioned her to join him in the lobby bar.

"I'm not sure." Her equivocation had an edgy tone.

He watched her slow her breath before she added, "We've got to talk to you."

"Rolf?"

"He's on his way . . . I hope." Nervousness crept into her voice.

"Please sit. Would you like a drink?"

Sylvia sat. She appeared so preoccupied that he wasn't sure she'd heard him.

"Uh . . . a drink? Yes. A glass of red wine would be nice."

After the waitress had taken the order, Schmidt asked, "Why are you and Rolf coming separately?"

"A car followed us. We split up."

Schmidt sat up. "Did they follow you here?"

"No. I lost them."

"What is it you need to talk to me about? Have you heard from—?"

The waitress set a glass of dark red wine between them and walked off.

"That's why we . . . why I'm here." Sylvia glanced toward the entrance, no doubt anxious for Rolf to arrive. Then she turned back to Schmidt. "Do you know Mozart's real name?"

"No."

"Heinz Dobnik. He was one of Horst Kreuzer's friends. Apparently we met during those days, though I don't remember him."

"Did you have contact with him today?"

"Yes. We—"

Schmidt held up his hand. "Excuse me. There's Rolf."

Sylvia whirled around while he got up and moved toward the front door. Rolf saw him but continued to look until he spotted Sylvia. He rushed over. Although they were restrained, Schmidt felt the genuine relief emanating from both. He had the distinct impression their relationship had grown beyond mere cooperation, perhaps to more than they themselves realized.

When they were seated, Sylvia spoke. "I was just about to tell Herr Schmidt about our meeting with Dobnik this afternoon."

"He met with you?" Schmidt looked from Sylvia to Rolf. "Both of you?"

They nodded.

"Tell me every detail."

Sylvia related the encounter while Rolf added a detail or clarified a point here and there. Revelation of the forged dossier startled Schmidt to a degree he wouldn't have thought possible at this stage of his professional life. Therefore, he almost missed subtle clues. Looks were exchanged, innocuous to an untrained eye but not to Schmidt's. They were not telling him everything. Over the years he'd seen too many people holding back details, sometimes because they considered them unimportant, at other times because they did not want him to know. He usually could tell when the picture was incomplete.

Sylvia had taken off her overcoat but Rolf hadn't. He knew why when Rolf told him where he was hiding today's drop. Rolf made a move to produce the papers, but Schmidt stopped him.

"Not here. When we're done, walk up a flight of stairs with me."

Rolf nodded.

Schmidt probed. "Is there anything else you need to tell me?"

"Dobnik seems to think terrorists may be getting ready to strike," responded Sylvia. "He said to tell you to act fast."

Schmidt picked up on the urgency in her voice, as if she were transmitting it from Dobnik to him. After a while, Schmidt asked, "You've told me everything?"

"Of course," Rolf answered.

"Are you sure?" Schmidt studied Sylvia.

"Yes."

The responses had been too quick. But for now, he'd have to accept them. He turned his thoughts to Dobnik's demands and what he had promised to deliver. This was better than he could have hoped.

He addressed Sylvia. "Give him the sign with your curtains tomorrow morning that he's got himself a deal."

"You accept his terms before having seen today's delivery?" Sylvia asked in surprise.

"We've seen enough in the first . . ." Schmidt stopped himself. There was no need to make them aware of the invaluable information yesterday's drop had netted.

"What about the contact he wants in West Berlin?" Rolf interjected.

"Just a moment."

Schmidt rose and walked over to the concierge's desk, ripped a sheet off a notepad, picked up a pen, and wrote a phone number on the paper before sealing it in one of the envelopes he lifted from the stack on the desk. He handed the envelope to Rolf, who stuck it in his overcoat pocket.

Schmidt looked at both. "That is for Dobnik's eyes only."

When they nodded, he continued. "If you want to finish your wine, Frau Mazzoni, Herr Keller and I will climb a few stairs. He'll return shortly."

He spotted the waitress at the bar and authorized the charge to his room. They found the staircase empty. The time it took for Rolf to reach inside his overcoat, feel for something in the small of his back, and finally produce two brown folders tested Schmidt's patience. He refrained from snatching the precious contraband, waiting instead for Rolf to hand it to him. Without a word he turned and climbed the stairs. The adrenaline rush from anticipating what might be in this drop was so strong that he found it difficult not to take two steps at a time.

♫ ♫ ♫

In the rear seat of yet another taxi, this one headed to Drei Sachsen to end an eventful day, Sylvia turned to Rolf. "I was sure glad when I saw you left that taxi for me."

"There was no line at the taxi stand. I couldn't believe it."

"Everything go okay at the train station?"

"Yes. No problems."

He hesitated.

"What is it?" she asked.

He moved close to her and whispered in her ear so she could hear over the music streaming from the radio. "I'll tell you later."

They rode the rest of the way in silence. Rolf instructed the driver to drop them a short distance from the hotel. Unter den Linden was busier than he would have expected at this late hour. The pedestrians coming toward them were dressed in suits and ties and evening dresses. The opera must have just let out.

"It's now later." He enjoyed Sylvia's momentary playful tone before she turned serious. "Did you get a chance to look at the papers?"

"I skimmed them in the taxi. I hope the information on the terrorists is specific enough so they can be stopped before they kill again."

When she didn't react, he changed the subject. "I knew you weren't going to tell Schmidt about the British agents and your Stasi file. But you surprised me. You didn't divulge Dobnik's plan to make his delivery before the opera tomorrow instead of afterward."

"I'm not sure why I didn't." She let a group of operagoers enter the Drei Sachsen ahead of them. "I suppose the fewer people who know about the earlier time the better. When it comes right down to it, there's no need for anyone but the three of us to know."

"And the same goes for Dobnik's Henkelstraße tip, I suppose," Rolf said as he opened the door.

She walked into the lobby without responding. Perhaps she was wondering whom they might encounter at that address. For his part, he hoped they'd never have to find out.

Chapter Twenty-Nine

Frantz hesitated when he saw the flimsy legs of the blue-upholstered chair to which Major General Rittmeister pointed. The chair's metal arms pinched his sides as he lowered his bulk onto the seat. He looked around the huge office dominated by cheap imitation teak—the parquet floor, a desk with credenza, a long conference table surrounded by a dozen chairs and a small round table. The sameness of hue made the office appear as if nothing exciting could ever happen here.

Frantz knew better. Erich Mielke had ruled with utter ruthlessness in this office. With the exception of Party Chief Erich Honecker, everyone had been afraid of Mielke. His tirades were legendary, and a few had been directed at Frantz. The humiliations were still so fresh that Frantz could hardly believe Mielke was gone for good and his desk now belonged to Major General Rittmeister. He looked nothing like his predecessor—tall and lanky instead of short and chubby. Nor did he have Mielke's predatory expression or mean spiritedness. Nevertheless, Frantz kept up his guard, anxious about the reason for having been summoned to the chief's office this Wednesday morning.

Rittmeister leaned forward. "Holger, we have a serious problem."

The familiarity took Frantz aback. Rittmeister had been a department head like Frantz before he was tapped as the new chief. Frantz had thought the three years of seniority he had on Rittmeister would land him the top job. If calling him by his first name was an attempt to soothe Frantz's resentment for being passed over, it wouldn't work.

"We've had a security breach. The West now knows we possess the coordinates to the NATO warheads."

Frantz feigned surprise. "Really?"

"You know what that means. Another traitor, probably looking to defect. We have seven officers with a top security clearance. Only they would have had access to this information."

The general picked up a piece of paper and handed it across the desk to Frantz. "Here is the list. You'll notice you and I are on it. You're not planning to visit the capitalists any time soon, are you?"

Although he realized Rittmeister was half kidding, the question shook Frantz. "No, not ever."

"I didn't think so. Do you have any inkling who of those other five might be?"

Frantz scanned the names. Dobnik was among them—good.

"No, I don't. But I will investigate each one immediately."

"Do. Run down what they've been doing these last few months. Any changes in routines, spending habits . . . the usual. And, we want to listen in on them, if we're not already."

"Yes, of course."

"And, Holger, we have no time. I need to know the traitor's name by this afternoon. There is supposed to be another drop this evening. We need to arrest him before then."

Frantz was stunned. How had the chief learned of the planned drop, and did he know about the opera setup?

"You'd best be going. There's no time to lose."

Frantz pushed himself up. Major General Rittmeister's voice followed him to the door. "Have the name for me before this evening."

By the time he'd reached his own office, Frantz had made up his mind. Dobnik had to be exposed—after he was eliminated. He shuddered at the possibility of Dobnik being arrested and interrogated. Whether willingly or under torture, there was no doubt he would finger him. This called for a slight adjustment in timing. Instead of waiting until after tonight's performance, he'd have to be liquidated immediately.

Frantz would have to find another way to get the forgeries to the West. He depressed the intercom button. "Frau Engler. Send up Major Schlechter right away."

Chapter Thirty

Approaching the end of a brisk ten-minute walk from his hotel to the Federal Intelligence Service's Berlin office, Schmidt stopped at a street booth and ordered a bratwurst. After indulging in the hotel's plentiful breakfast buffet this morning, he did not have much of an appetite for lunch. As he bit into the leathery sausage skin, careful not to spurt juice on his coat, a distant church bell chimed once. Sixteen hours had passed since he'd transmitted Dobnik's papers to Bauman—enough time for him to have tracked down the terrorists identified in the latest drop. That information had certainly removed any doubts about the defector's ability to deliver top secrets.

Schmidt finished off the bratwurst with a couple of big bites, wiped mustard off his lips, and dropped his crumpled paper napkin atop the grease pooled in the cardboard dish. He took a last swig of beer from a tall plastic cup and tossed the remains into a metal trash can.

Eager to learn what Bauman had accomplished, Schmidt took advantage of a momentary lull in traffic to cross to the opposite sidewalk. He entered a high rise and headed for a bank of elevators. He walked to the far door, the only one with a keypad, and looked around. No one was behind him. He entered the combination, wondering how much it had cost the agency to have this elevator restricted to allow access to its office only. It must have been stationed at the lobby level since its door opened the instant he punched in the last number. The conveyance catapulted him to the top floor in under a minute. During the car's rapid acceleration and deceleration, he felt the bratwurst lying heavy in his stomach.

Schmidt stepped out and approached an unmarked steel door opposite the elevator and punched in numbers on another keypad. When he heard a click, he pushed on the door and entered. The secretary had not yet returned from lunch. Nor did he hear any sounds coming from the other offices. He maneuvered his way around a metal desk and an artificial plant and entered the first office on the right, reserved for visiting agents. No decorator had ever set foot in here. The white walls were bare, and the furniture consisted of a worn veneer desk and one vinyl-covered chair. Not that the sparse furnishings bothered Schmidt. The room had everything he needed: a secure phone and fax and a high-speed copier.

He sat in the hard chair, picked up the beige phone and dialed.

Bauman answered on the third ring. "Dieter?"

"Yes, it's me," Schmidt acknowledged.

"I can only talk for a minute. We managed to track three terrorists to a train station. There was a shootout. Two of them dead, the other wounded."

"That was fast work."

Bauman did not acknowledge the praise. "We've got a problem."

"What is it?"

"There is something in the works, but the punk isn't talking. I could use you here. You might be able to get to him." Before Schmidt could respond, Bauman said, "I know. You need to stay there. Our analysts think the RAF is planning an assassination, but they can't pin down the target or the date."

"I told you what Mozart said. Something might explode real soon."

"Damn! I wish we had more to go on."

Schmidt felt Bauman's frustration creep through the line. Yet, he needed to protect Dobnik as much as possible. "Karl—"

"Just a minute, Dieter."

Schmidt heard a female voice and Bauman's, now sounding distant, "Tell him to hold for a minute." Then his baritone came back at full strength. "Dieter, make it quick. I've got to take another call."

Schmidt fought resentment welling up in him. He couldn't afford the luxury of letting his feelings get in the way. "Karl, is there any chance of keeping the shooting out of today's news? Mozart's employer could catch on where we got the information to track down these terrorists. Might not be good for his health."

"You expect him after tonight's performance?"

"Yes. If we could delay the news till this evening?" Even as he asked, Schmidt realized how unlikely that was.

"It's probably too late. You know how sensationalist the media is these days." Schmidt could visualize Bauman's disapproving head shake. "If I were you, I'd go on the assumption that news of the shooting will be all over TV and radio. I can already see the headlines in the evening papers."

Schmidt wasn't ready to give up yet. "But there's no need to tell the media right away that we're dealing with the Red Army Faction . . . at least not until after man and merchandise have arrived."

After a momentary silence Bauman spoke. "I'll see what can be done. But it may be out of my hands. Since the train station is not far from Cologne, we were told to use that office to handle the arrests. As you can see, they botched it—two dead terrorists. They may have already let the RAF angle slip." His tone had shifted from impatience to disgust.

Schmidt remembered their conversation of last Saturday morning. "So much for keeping the Constitution Protection Office out of it."

Sensing he'd gotten all he could expect, Schmidt was attempting to say goodbye when Bauman interrupted.

"Listen, Dieter. I'm working on this end to foil whatever these terrorists are planning. You need to make absolutely certain that Mozart makes it. If what he brings is anywhere close to what he's promised . . ." His voice trailed off for a moment, then reemerged as a command. "Do whatever it takes to get his suitcase. Do you hear me?"

"Yes, sir." They'd been working together long enough for mutual respect to have grown into friendship. But neither lost sight of the fact that Bauman was the boss.

"Good. And keep me current."

Bauman cut the connection. Schmidt stared at the bare office wall, reflecting on the words 'whatever it takes.' Translation: don't worry about legalities too much, and the documents come before the people. Images of Sylvia and Rolf popped into his mind, but he suppressed them. Bauman was right. He had to get the Stasi files. Schmidt broke off his stare and rushed out of the still-empty office.

There was nothing like a brisk walk to focus his mind. As he strode by his hotel, he mulled over whether to attend this evening's performance. He had not planned to, but now he reconsidered. News of the shooting would be out, and with the Cologne bunch in the picture, he'd have to assume the worst—the Stasi could catch on to Dobnik's treachery before this evening. His mind made up, Schmidt turned and headed back to the office he'd just left. This time he hoped to find the secretary. Arrangements had to be made.

Chapter Thirty-One

Harry Stein closed the file he'd been reviewing and looked up. What he saw did not improve his mood—rain sheeting off the huge window panes of his corner office. Wind gusts whipped around downtown Washington buildings on this miserable Wednesday morning. He rose from his chair and walked through an open doorway into a side room that featured a full kitchen, a bar and, around a corner, a side table holding a copier and fax.

Yesterday, Stein had made this trek more times than he cared to remember, each time returning to his desk empty-handed. This was the third time he'd checked this morning, and the obstinate fax still hadn't made a beep. Over the course of Tuesday afternoon Stein's disappointment had grown into angry resentment. Staring at the silent machine once more, he became furious with Rolf. Why hadn't he faxed the documents as he'd been told? This was not the conduct of an associate who wanted to make partner.

As he poured his third cup of coffee, his legal mind kicked in. Don't judge before you know all the facts. There may be good reasons for the delay. All the same, he intended to grill Rolf on those reasons and his explanation had better be good. Back at his desk, he glanced at the antique clock standing against the opposite wall. Seven minutes to nine. The call should come through any time now.

He drummed his fingers on top of the only file lying on the desk. When he became aware that he'd been shifting the folder around the surface without looking at it, he stopped the nervous habit. His fingers traced the letters "ARM" printed on the white label in the center of the file jacket. He'd had a feeling from the start that this matter might be trouble but he'd been unable to turn it down. Even now, when it looked as if the problems might be worse than anticipated, he felt he'd done the right thing in accepting the client. Still, doubts nagged at him.

He straightened up in his chair, startled by the phone even though he'd been waiting for the call. The staccato rings signaled long-distance. He picked up the receiver and answered. It was Rolf.

"Where are those papers you were supposed to fax me?"

"Sorry, I've been too busy keeping up with what's been happening over here. We've had another delivery and one more to come this . . . uh . . . evening."

Stein wondered about the hesitation. "This evening at the opera?"

"That's the plan. I'll fax you what we have so far in about an hour."

"Do that." As he spoke, Stein's mind latched onto an inconsistency. "Didn't you tell me yesterday there was something about the second delivery that worried you and that's why you needed to call me this morning?"

He heard Rolf breathing. Had he caught him in a lie?

"I thought we'd only have two deliveries, the second one being this evening. After our phone conversation yesterday, I found out about a meeting that afternoon. That's when the second drop was made."

"You and Sylvia met him?"

Stein listened with astonishment as Rolf related details of the meeting with the Stasi officer. Although he seemed far from finished, Rolf paused and then said, "Let me change the subject for a moment. I'm on a short time frame and want to make sure we discuss what I called about. Can you fill me in on some details about this assignment?"

Stein found Rolf's interruption odd but asked nevertheless, "Such as?"

"Would you check the file on this matter to verify something?"

"I know what's in my file. What information do you need?" The line went silent. Stein wondered whether his response had been too gruff.

"When were you first contacted about this matter?" Rolf sounded uncertain in his question.

"Late October. Why do you ask?"

"There is something peculiar about the time sequence. I'm sorry to trouble you sir, but I really need to know the exact date, if you have it."

"Well, I don't have all the dates memorized, but I've got the file right here. Let me—"

A deafening siren sounded from the hall. "Wouldn't you know it? We're having a fire alarm. I need to leave. Can you call me back in half an hour?"

"I don't have that much time, unless the fax can wait till tomorrow."

"No. You send that fax today. I'm sure this is just a drill. I'll be back in fifteen minutes. Call me then."

He disconnected and picked up the file. Then he saw the closed safe. Should he take the time to open it? No. Everybody had to leave the building. The file would be all right. He slipped the folder into the center desk drawer and marched out into his secretary's office. Mildred had left already and, following proper procedure, had thrown the deadbolt on the door to the hallway. Satisfied, he turned and rushed through the kitchen and side office until he reached another door. He unlatched the lock and stepped out, careful to shut the door but leave it unlocked. During fire alarms the security guards had to have access to all rooms. For Stein's office that meant the secretary's door would be locked, but not the side door. In theory, no one but building security should be aware of the true function of the unmarked door on a sidewall of the twelfth-floor corridor.

The empty hallway told him he was one of the last to leave. Nevertheless, he took the time to check the conference room. He found it just as it should be—empty and the door unlocked. Entering the staircase, he pondered the strange phone conversation. Something didn't make sense, but he couldn't quite grasp what it was.

♫ ♫ ♫

Mesmerized, Betty Crandall stared at the wall clock as it approached nine o'clock. The conference room's inner window ran along the twelfth-floor hallway. Even though she knew the one-way glass did not permit anyone in the hall to see inside, she stayed in the shadows of the unlit room. Since Rolf's call she'd been checking the firm's schedule continually to ascertain whether anyone had reserved the room for this morning. No one had. There were other places she could have chosen to bide her time until the alarm chased everyone from the office, but this had been her first choice because Stein and his secretary had to pass here on their way out.

The clock's hand jerked forward to nine o'clock. Betty held her breath, bracing for the sirens, but all remained quiet. She shrugged. Nothing was on time anymore, not even fire alarms. Had she gotten the time wrong, or had the drill been called off? Her doubt still hung in the room when the alarm sounded. The closed conference room muffled the noise, so it was not as shrill as she remembered. The first few employees were ambling down the hall, by all appearances unconcerned. These alarms invariably turned out to be drills instead of real emergencies, and no one would expect it to be different this time.

Betty didn't have to wait long before spotting Stein's secretary among a group of lawyers and secretaries heading toward the stairway. After a few minutes the steady stream of departing employees slowed to a trickle. When only a few stragglers strode by now and then, Betty became concerned. Where was Stein? Did he not follow the firm's strict evacuation procedures he had implemented?

Then she saw him coming down the hallway. Halfway past the conference room, he stopped and looked in her direction. What was he doing? Her heart raced when she realized he was turning back and heading straight for the door. Had he spotted her somehow? She ran to the coat closet at the far wall, jerked open the door, dove inside, and slid the door closed to within a tiny crack. The sound of the fire alarm filled the room, telling her that the door to the hallway stood ajar. Conquering her fear, she positioned one eye on the narrow slit. She saw Stein with a hand on the door knob, peering into the room as if to make sure no one had been left behind. Cold fear gripped her when she saw her folder lying on the telephone stand by the window. Stein must not have seen it though, because he retreated and drew the door closed, muffling the sound of the sirens again. After a few seconds she left the closet and rushed to the window. The corridor looked deserted. Calmer now, she realized he'd checked to see whether the conference room was unlocked for possible access by emergency personnel.

She would rather have waited another minute or two before venturing out, but she could not waste a second. Fire drills usually lasted no more than fifteen to twenty minutes. Folder in hand, she eased open the door and peered in both directions. Not a person in sight. When she reached

Mildred Reed's office door, she produced a pair of skin-colored latex gloves from her folder and slipped them on. She turned the doorknob and pushed. The door didn't budge. In disbelief she pushed again with the same result. How could it be locked when the procedures required all offices to be accessible during an emergency?

She let go of the knob and backed away until she bumped into the opposite hallway wall. Contemplating how to explain her failure to Rolf and how disappointed he'd be made her lean harder against the wall. Then she remembered a rumor that Stein's office had a second exit. Of course! An added layer of privacy for Stein, and the security people could get access that way during an emergency. She pushed herself off the wall. If there were such a door, where could it be? For the first time she noticed the corridors running along the sidewalls of Mildred's office. She strode to the one behind her. Shelves on both walls stuffed with law books left a narrow passageway that dead-ended in a wall after about fifteen feet. Stein's office, she surmised. No door anywhere. She hurried to the other end to find a similar walkway with shelves of more law books. About to retreat, she became aware of a gap between the shelves at the very end. Moving closer, she spotted an unmarked door. She turned the knob, and the door swung inward.

To her relief she did not find herself in a janitor's closet but in a small office. As she locked the door, she noticed that past the copier and fax the room made a right-angle turn. The closed door reduced the nerve-racking alarm to a tolerable level once again. A few strides carried her to the corner, from where she glimpsed a full-blown kitchen and a spacious suite beyond. She recognized Stein's office by its furnishings and layout despite not having seen it from this viewpoint before.

She swept through the room, moving from the desk to the sofa to the round table by the window. There were no files in sight. Her heart sank as she considered the possible reason for Stein's late departure, and she wondered if he had taken the time to lock the file in the wall safe. There was nothing to do but check the desk drawers, provided they were not locked like the safe. Neither of the right hand drawers was. Legal pads, pens and pencils were strewn in the top drawer, while the bottom contained hanging folders in alphabetical order. She leafed through the twenty-plus files, unsure of what to look for.

As she straightened up to examine the center drawer, a noise loud enough to carry over the sirens startled her. It sounded like someone was rapping at the side door. She rushed through the side office, and upon reaching the door, put her ear against the wood. The sirens were the only sound. She was about to conclude she'd imagined things when she heard a key scratching in the lock. Someone from security. She froze, paralyzed by fear.

Snap out of it, she admonished herself. On instinct, she leaned against the door trying to prevent the key holder from entering, then realized the futility of her action. Even if she could hold the door, she'd be discovered. Her mind raced. Should she try to find a hiding place or sneak out the front door? She began to retreat when there was a sharp clack—metal hitting metal. The key had stopped turning, apparently stuck. An angry male voice yelled an expletive over the alarm. She heard retreating footsteps, though she couldn't be sure with the alarm still going.

Betty steadied herself against the table and dabbed with her sleeve at the pearls of perspiration on her forehead. The alarm had been going for about ten minutes. She could count on only a few more. Either the drill would be over or the person from security would be back with the proper key. She ran back to the desk and yanked open the center drawer. Her eyes fell on a file sliding toward the back. She pulled it out and laid it on the desk surface. It was labeled "ARM."

She opened the folder. Papers were fastened to each
side. Where to start? The left column contained
correspondence interspersed with handwritten notes. On the
right side were international drafts drawn on First Security
Credit Union, Washington, D.C., and made payable to a
numbered account at Banca Comunale, Milan. The draft on
top in the amount of five hundred dollars was dated
December 1, 1985. Betty flipped through the stack. The
first draft on the bottom bore a date of April 14, 1970 and
was in the amount of one hundred dollars. She tried to
detect a pattern. During the early seventies payment
amounts tended to vary and were generally smaller than
later on, and they were often two or three months apart.
Later transactions increased in frequency and amount and
by the eighties appeared to have settled on a regular
monthly payment of five hundred dollars.

Betty leafed through the correspondence on the left side.
Most of the letters informed a Mr. Anthony Fabrini of
Alexandria, Virginia, that pursuant to his request a certain
amount had been transmitted to the bank in Milan on the
dates indicated. Stein addressed the recipient as Tony and
signed as Harry. Fabrini apparently was more friend than
client. As a long-standing client of Stein, his name should
be in the firm's client base. It was not. She was certain,
because the responsibility for keeping the list current had
been hers for the last fifteen years.

She had not seen anything that would have explained the
letters "ARM" on the file jacket, and she wasn't at all
certain this file related in any way to Rolf's current
assignment. But it was all she had. She decided to copy as
much as she could. Something startled her. After a moment,
she realized it was the absence of sound. The alarm had
stopped. The fire drill was over, and the employees would
be back in minutes. Frantic, she dashed with the file to the
copier in the side office. In the time remaining, the best she

could do would be to copy a few representative pages that might give Rolf enough information.

To her great relief, the copy machine was on. She copied a few letters, some handwritten notes and several of the bank drafts, not taking the time to remove them from the folder but simply pressing them onto the platen glass. She ran to the desk, tossed the file in the center drawer, slipped the dozen or so copies into the folder she had brought and rushed to the side door. She unlocked the door and opened it, ready to exit until she heard approaching footsteps—heavy enough to be a man's.

Betty shut the door and hurried through the kitchen into Stein's office. Sure enough, the side door opened. She darted into the secretary's office, praying Mildred wasn't back yet. No sign of her. Betty unlocked the door and went out to the hall. As she drew the door closed, she realized she could not leave it the way she'd found it—locked. There was nothing to be done about it. Perhaps Mildred would think she'd forgotten to lock her door, a fact she surely would not want her boss to know. Betty slipped off the gloves, stuck them among the loose papers in her folder and headed for the stairs that should now be empty.

♫ ♫ ♫

As he'd suspected, the alarm had been just another fire drill. Yet, having implemented the firm's emergency procedures, Stein was loath to object, even when the drill came at an inopportune time. He dumped the cold coffee from his cup into the kitchen sink, poured a fresh one, and returned to his desk. The file was still in the center drawer, though he didn't remember throwing it there in the skewed position he now found it. Nor did he recall the pages being bent so that the folder did not lay perfectly flat. Had someone messed with the papers in his absence, or was he getting paranoid? He turned his attention to the time. The clock showed twenty minutes after nine. The drill had taken longer than he'd thought. Had Rolf called back already?

"Ray Fielding is here to see you, sir." Mildred's voice startled him. He'd not heard her return.

Stein looked at his secretary and motioned for her to close the door. After she did, he asked, "Did he say what he wants? I'm expecting an important phone call."

It was not unusual for the building security chief to check in after a drill to get some feedback and review the procedures. But not immediately afterward.

"He just said he needed to see you right away."

"Okay. Send him in."

Stein had never liked the overeager attitude and subservient demeanor of the prematurely balding man who now walked into his office. His smile seemed forced. The belly protruding over his belt spoke of overindulgence in food and drink—beer, not wine, Stein thought.

"Sorry to bother you, sir, but I need to check with you about an irregularity during the drill."

The contemptuous way he spit out the word "irregularity" further cemented Stein's disdain for this rule-bound minion. "I'm expecting a phone call any minute. What is it?"

"Sorry, sir. I thought you ought to know that one of my men found both of your doors locked during the drill."

"Are you sure? I checked both doors when I left. My secretary's was locked, but not the side door. I made sure of that."

Fielding fidgeted. Stein had not offered him a seat. "He says he turned the knob and found the door locked. Then he tried to get in with his key, but he didn't have the right one with him."

Stein became concerned. The door locked after he had made sure to leave it unlocked, the file in a different position and appearance than he'd left it—he was not paranoid after all. Someone had entered his office and rummaged through that file. Yet the last thing he wanted was for this bumbling security man to know about it. So he did what every sharp litigator does when he has a weak case: attack and divert.

"You mean to tell me your guards don't carry the right keys with them in an emergency?"

The diversionary tactic worked. Fielding fidgeted even more.

"I'll make sure they do, sir. Sorry for the interruption."

Stein nodded while the man withdrew. The clock now showed twenty-five after nine, and it was clear that Rolf would not call back. Too agitated to sit, Stein got up and walked out to his secretary's office.

"Mildred. Did you notice anything unusual during the fire drill?"

Her look told him that she had something to confess.

"What is it, Mildred?"

"Well, sir. I thought I locked my door when I left, but I found it unlocked when I came back."

He could tell she thought she might have forgotten to lock it. "You're right, it was locked. I checked it before I left. You're sure it was unlocked when you returned?"

"I'm positive, sir."

"Don't worry about it, Mildred. I'll handle this . . . and Mildred, it's very important that you not mention this to anyone, not even Ray Fielding and his crew. Is that clear?"

"Yes, sir."

He turned to walk back into his office, a terrible suspicion forming in his mind. He stopped. "Mildred. Have Fielding come back to my office."

She nodded and picked up the phone.

Within a few minutes the security chief slunk into Stein's office, seemingly worried about being reamed out once more—vulnerability Stein could exploit.

"Ray. When did you decide to schedule this fire drill?"

Fielding fidgeted again. "I believe I planned it two days ago."

"And who besides you knew about the day and time?"

Fielding looked down, studying a spot on the carpet in front of his feet. After a pause, he lifted his eyes and responded with a hesitant voice, "Well, I informed my security guards, of course . . ."

Stein could tell there was more he did not want to volunteer. "Who else did you tell?"

Fielding resumed his study of the carpet. "I may have let it slip to Mr. Brownwell's secretary."

"What's her name?"

"Peggy . . . Peggy Malone."

Even though he already knew the answer, Stein asked, "Do you see her socially?"

"Yes, sir. We go out now and then."

Stein was aware they had started dating soon after Malone had come on board. He'd been amazed that an attractive woman like her would date a man of Fielding's ilk, but wrote it off to low self-esteem, and perhaps being on the rebound after a nasty divorce.

Looking at the pathetic figure Fielding cut, staring at the floor, Stein almost felt sorry for him. But he knew the day he felt sorry for a witness whose credibility he had destroyed on cross-examination would be the day to get out of the courtroom. He would definitely not allow that sentiment with Fielding in front of him.

"Did you tell anyone else?"

"No, sir."

The way he answered satisfied Stein that he was not holding anything back. "All right. You may go now." Although he was pretty sure Fielding wouldn't blab any of this to a soul, he added, "And not a word about this to anyone."

"Not on my life, sir."

After he was gone, the full impact hit Stein. It seemed that Peggy Malone or someone whom she might have told about the drill had used the opportunity to sneak into his office and peruse his file. What disturbed him the most was the realization that Rolf's phone call for additional information may well have been a pretense to make it possible. Stein played with a pencil, contemplating what to do about Rolf's deceit. He decided that could wait. For now the pressing questions were who had invaded his office and how much information had that person gleaned?

He depressed the intercom. "Mildred, send Peggy Malone to my office immediately."

Peter Bernhardt

Chapter Thirty-Two

Boris Schlechter regarded the open door into General Frantz's outer office. He took a deep breath and entered. The severe woman stationed at the desk studied him for a single heartbeat. She spoke above the rapid clickety-clack of her electric typewriter. "The general is expecting you."

Schlechter did not appreciate her accusatory tone, as if she were implying he should have made it up from his office in less time than the few minutes it had taken. Being the bearer of bad news to Frantz made him edgy. So he simply nodded and knocked at the door on the other side of her desk. At a faint "Herein" he opened the door and entered.

The general stood by the window looking out. Without turning around he barked, "Close the door and take a seat."

Schlechter obeyed the gruff command. As soon as he'd lowered himself into a chair, Frantz moved to his desk and sat. He picked up his glasses from the desk top and slid them onto his nose. For a long moment Frantz scrutinized him, apparently trying to read what news he held. All kinds of justifications ran through Schlechter's mind, but he

278

remained silent. He knew not to speak until the general asked him a question.

Frantz moved his gaze from Schlechter's face to his empty hands. "The Mazzoni File?"

Schlechter cleared his dry throat. "It's missing. I searched all the folders filed under 'M.' I also looked under 'S' in case someone misfiled it under her first name. Nothing."

"Did you check the index cards?"

"I did. No card."

Frantz stabbed a finger at Schlechter. "I'm sure we have a file on her."

To Schlechter's relief the general seemed more disappointed than angry.

"You're right, General. At one time at least we had a Mazzoni File."

Frantz stared at him. "Explain yourself."

Schlechter relished having the general's full attention and waited a moment before he responded. "I checked the register in the records department. Based on what you told me yesterday, I pored over Colonel Dobnik's checkout record during the last several weeks. He visited the department twice as often as anyone else, always signed out two files, which he returned two or three days later when he checked out another two."

"That son of a bitch!" Frantz pounded his desk. "I've suspected him all along."

The general's outrage seemed feigned, though Schlechter couldn't pinpoint what made him think so.

"You have a list of the files he signed out?"

Schlechter reached into his breast pocket and handed the general three sheets of handwritten notes. He wondered whether Frantz would detect that most of the files Dobnik had reviewed concerned matters outside his responsibilities. It had taken a bit of digging on his part to find that out, but Frantz, as Dobnik's superior, should spot it right away. Would he ask about it? If he didn't, Schlechter would not volunteer the information. It did not pay to advertise that he knew more than Frantz wanted him to.

The general tossed the sheets onto the desk top. Schlechter couldn't tell whether he had noticed anything out of the ordinary.

"Good work, Major. But that doesn't solve the mystery about the missing Mazzoni File. It's not on this list." Frantz removed his glasses. "What makes you so sure that the file exists?"

"Because the register shows that your secretary checked it out last February and returned it a few days later."

"I knew it!" Frantz slammed his fist on the desk again. "Dobnik must have smuggled it out. That leaves no doubt. He is the traitor."

Schlechter did not for a second believe that the general had reached his conclusion on the basis of this scant evidence alone. He must have had the goods on Dobnik already—certainly more than he'd let on yesterday when he said he suspected him.

Frantz put his glasses back on. He fixed his eyes on Schlechter. "Change in plans. We can no longer afford to wait and catch him at the opera this evening. Take care of him before then. Understand?"

Though he didn't see how the new information he'd given the general required that Dobnik be executed instead of arrested, he replied, "Yes, sir."

Still watching him, Frantz said, "Make sure you find out where he keeps the documents he's smuggling to the West. You know how to get him to talk."

"Yes." Schlechter considered the methods that would be required to break a professional of Dobnik's caliber.

"There's no time to waste. Get on with it!" Frantz's command cut short Schlechter's thoughts. "Report back to me as soon as it's done. And we're still going to the opera this evening. I'll have new instructions for you when you get back."

In the hallway Schlechter checked his watch. Half an hour till lunch time. With any luck, Dobnik would not choose this day to deviate from his habit of going out to lunch alone. Doing the job at Stasi headquarters was out of the question. By the time he arrived at his office, Schlechter had mulled over various options and concluded that he'd have to follow him and wait for an opportunity to catch him alone. With the door locked, he took out his East German Makarov pistol. Counting eight cartridges in the magazine, he snapped it back into place with a click and returned the weapon to his shoulder holster. He should only need one bullet, but it was best to have a fully loaded gun, just in case. Before leaving, he retrieved a silencer from his locked desk and slipped it into his overcoat pocket.

In the elevator to the lobby, Schlechter puzzled over how to shadow Dobnik unnoticed. Tailing a professional normally required several agents passing off the subject from one to another. For obvious reasons, Frantz did not want anyone else involved. This wasn't the first time he'd taken care of the general's dirty business, but with the changes sweeping the country it might well be the last. The first few times had been hard, but it was either follow Frantz's orders or go back to prison. To his surprise, killing had become easier over time, and now the prospect of knocking off Dobnik actually gave him a rush. He nodded to the guards as he exited the building, crossed over to a parking area on the other side of Normannenstraße, and turned east. He ducked behind a delivery van and peered toward the entrance of Stasi headquarters— about the right distance for spotting Dobnik without being obvious.

Schlechter put on his black leather wool-lined gloves and pulled his gray overcoat tight to ward off the cold east wind. Luckily, he could keep his back to it while watching the entrance. His eyes swept across the dreary gray exterior of the Stasi building, noticing how it blended with the lighter gray of the low-hanging overcast sky, creating an oppressive mood—appropriate for a day of death.

Schlechter watched the steady stream of Stasi employees leaving for lunch. After several minutes, the lunch crowd had dissipated. He grew worried that he might have missed Dobnik when he spotted him. He likewise wore a gray overcoat. Their profession had taught them to blend in.

To his surprise Dobnik did not set out toward any of his favorite lunch spots, but came toward him. Schlechter hid behind the van, which blocked his view of Dobnik. More important, the traitor could not see him either. Quick footsteps warned of a man in a hurry. Schlechter let him get well ahead before following, ready to duck behind a parked car if necessary.

He would probably turn at the next corner and have lunch at Freier Genosse, a restaurant frequented by Stasi employees due to its proximity and hearty German fare. Schlechter's mouth gaped when Dobnik crossed the intersection instead. Whatever he was up to, it appeared this would not be an ordinary lunch day. Dobnik crossed Normannenstraße in the middle of the block. As he did, he peered down both sidewalks behind him. By the time Schlechter realized that parked cars were no longer giving him cover, it was too late to dive between them, lest his sudden movement draw Dobnik's attention. He swore under his breath. There was nothing to do but keep up his moderate pace. He looked straight ahead, not directly at Dobnik, yet close enough to monitor his movements by peripheral vision. To his relief Dobnik's methodical scan of the sidewalk did not stop as it swept his area.

Dobnik continued down the sidewalk. As soon as he saw the underground station on the next block, Schlechter increased his pace to shorten the distance to his target. As he'd suspected, Dobnik hurried down the stairs. He did not look around. Having to follow at a safe distance, Schlechter could only hope the train would not pull up the moment Dobnik reached the platform. Schlechter passed up the first staircase to take one at the other end. As he descended, he spotted the gray overcoat at the other end of the station.

Schlechter leaned against the nearest post, which displayed the timetable for the two trains running on this track. One of the first tasks Frantz had assigned him upon his transfer from prison to the Stasi was to learn everything he could about the private lives of his fellow employees. Knowing where Dobnik lived, he was ready when the train to Alexanderplatz rolled into the station. Yet Dobnik appeared uninterested in boarding, looking instead up and down the platform. Then, just as the doors started to close, he sprang into the car. Schlechter had expected no less from the professional he knew Dobnik to be and dashed from behind his post in time to beat the closing car doors at his end of the train. The sudden movement might give him away, but he had no alternative. Besides, he felt sure he'd made it inside while Dobnik himself was still in the process of boarding.

Had Dobnik noticed him, or was he simply taking precautions? Whichever it was, there must be something he wanted to accomplish unobserved. Schlechter could not see Dobnik. He had to rely on leaning out the door at every stop, ready to exit the car in an instant. No one in a gray overcoat had left the train at any of the previous stops. Alexanderplatz was next. Schlechter decided to take a chance. If he waited to get off after Dobnik, he'd be spotted. As soon as his door opened, he leapt out and moved into the crowd waiting to board. If he'd miscalculated and Dobnik remained on the train, he still might be able to get back on.

Schlechter sensed the doors were about to close and moved toward them, but then he saw the overcoat down the platform. He retreated and mingled with the passengers heading for the exit. He pushed his way forward through the mass of people and saw Dobnik climbing the stairs. When Schlechter emerged from the station, Dobnik was across the square, entering the street that led to his apartment. Schlechter hesitated. Since Dobnik seemed to be going home, Schlechter could go one block over, dart up the parallel street and beat him there. That would minimize the risk of being seen, which would be much greater if he followed him up the same street. But what if the traitor did not in fact go home? Could he take that chance? Schlechter reached the other side of the square, still undecided as he watched Dobnik stride down the street.

♫ ♫ ♫

Wednesday morning at the office dragged for Heinz Dobnik. The day's early start had taken him to Café Franken, where he was in the middle of breakfast when the curtain on Sylvia's west window opened. He paused, crusty roll in midair, oblivious to the blob of strawberry marmalade dripping onto the tablecloth, holding his breath to see if the east window curtain would be drawn back as well. A second gooey trickle coated his fingers, causing him to drop the roll onto his plate without taking his eyes off the hotel across Unter den Linden. The east curtain remained closed. He relaxed with an audible exhalation.

He could finally see the payoff for the months he'd been copying and stashing documents to secure his survival, but he had no illusions about the remaining obstacles. Lifting his cup, he considered what lay ahead this Wednesday. His unsteady movement caused hot coffee to spill onto the saucer from where it splattered the red stain already on the tablecloth. He sensed a presence, and with a shrug of embarrassment looked into the amused eyes of the white-haired waitress who had approached his table unnoticed.

"Check, please," he muttered with as much dignity as he could muster. She didn't say a word as she hurried away.

Between paying the bill and finishing his coffee, Dobnik periodically peered at Sylvia's windows. When at fifteen minutes past seven the curtains had remained unchanged, he left the café to begin his day at the office. Nervous energy plagued him all morning while he pondered what he must accomplish by evening. As much as he wanted to get started, he decided that leaving the office before the lunch hour might arouse suspicion.

When his secretary left promptly at noon, Dobnik reminded her that he'd be gone the rest of the day. He wanted to follow her out the door but thought better of it. Most Stasi employees went to lunch on the dot, and he did not want to run into colleagues who might invite him to join them. At seven past twelve he slipped on his gray overcoat and rushed past the elevator to the staircase. His body, flooded with adrenaline, craved the action of running down the stairs, and he was less likely to encounter other employees that way.

As Dobnik entered Normannenstraße, the downside of leaving after the rush became apparent—he'd be a lot easier to track. If he hurried, he might catch the twelve-fifteen train to Alexanderplatz. After the first intersection he jaywalked through light traffic to the north sidewalk. During the crossover he surveyed the street and both sidewalks behind him. Pedestrians were clutching at their overcoats and hunching their shoulders against the stiff eastern breeze. He saw no evidence of a pursuer, but that didn't mean there wasn't one. Turning his chafed face into the wind, he quickened his stride toward the underground entrance.

He reached the platform about a minute before his train was scheduled to arrive. Prudence called for him to pass it up, take the next one to a different destination, and switch trains several times. However, he did not have the luxury of time if he wanted to make it to Wandlitz and return to Café Franken with the documents he'd promised Schmidt by five thirty. So he did the next best thing. He hung back as his train pulled into the station, as if boarding were the last thing on his mind. Looking up and down the platform, he waited until the doors were about to close, then leaped inside the car.

Although he had seen nothing suspicious in the station, when the train stopped at Alexanderplatz, he remained on board until the last possible second. As soon as he hit the platform, he looked down the row of cars. No one jumped off. If someone were following him, he either was clever or he'd lost him. Dobnik made for the exit, taking two steps at a time up to the square, which he raced across to enter the street leading to his garage, hoping he'd moved fast enough to lose any pursuer.

He walked by his garage without so much as a glance and headed to his apartment building around the corner. Not that he needed to go home for anything. Rather, he decided he could afford the time for one last maneuver to flush out anyone who was still shadowing him. Once inside his apartment, he stood by the window, still in his overcoat. The streets were deserted, as they had been during his Monday afternoon surveillance. After a few moments, failing to notice anything out of the ordinary, he locked up. He decided to take the stairs going down.

Dobnik peeked out from the building's entrance and saw someone in a gray overcoat disappear around the corner at the other end of the street. Although it was in the opposite direction of where he needed to go, he ran to the corner and looked up and down the street. Not a soul in sight. He retraced his steps and headed toward the garage. It was high time to start up the Trabant and drive to Wandlitz. Key in hand, he approached Garage D. Before unlocking the door, he peered in both directions. In quick succession he pushed the key into the lock, turned the handle, and pulled the wooden door up.

He reached for the wall switch but decided the garage was light enough. As soon as he was behind the Trabant's steering wheel, he rolled down the window on the driver's door. As he inserted the key in the ignition, the light in the garage appeared to dim. The rear view mirror showed the garage door was halfway closed. Had he not opened it all the way? A movement along the wall caught his eye. He turned and through the open car window stared into the cold eyes of Boris Schlechter. His mouth went dry at the sight of the gun barrel, centimeters from his nose.

♫ ♫ ♫

Waiting in the staircase, Schlechter began to regret his gamble of running straight to the apartment building. Just when he was sure he'd made a mistake, he heard the front door open and quick footsteps. A peek through the slit in the staircase door showed him Dobnik's back disappearing into the elevator. When he heard the motor gain speed, he left his hiding place. The light above the elevator door illuminated 3 and kept on going higher until it came to rest on 8, Dobnik's floor.

Should he go up? He'd prefer to deal with him somewhere else. Besides, it might prove useful to see what Dobnik was up to before confronting him. He decided to give him fifteen minutes. If he wasn't back by then, he'd pay him a visit. The elevator remained on the eighth floor.

Not more than a few minutes had passed when he heard footsteps echoing down the staircase. The son of a bitch was coming down the stairs, leaving him no place to hide. Schlechter ran out the front door and took a chance that Dobnik would not be heading back to the office. He decided to cover the garage, where he knew Dobnik kept his car.

He rushed down to the far corner so he could approach from the opposite direction he expected Dobnik to take.

Peter Bernhardt

When he turned the third corner onto the street fronting the row of garages, he saw a raised door. He sprinted to the opening, pulled the gun from his coat pocket, and with the silencer in place, stepped inside the garage and tugged the door halfway shut behind him.

Gun drawn, he approached the driver's door of the gray sedan. Schlechter relished the surprise and fear he saw in Dobnik's eyes. This could be easier than he'd imagined. "Put both hands on the steering wheel and then get out slowly! I'll get the door for you. You know the drill."

When he saw Dobnik's arms move forward, he switched the gun to his left hand and stepped closer to the driver's door to reach for the handle with his free hand. As soon as he did, he realized his mistake. The door flew open, crashing into his body. As he staggered backward, he got one foot on the car door and pushed it shut. On instinct, he squeezed the trigger, but too late—the bullet ricocheted off the ceiling. Schlechter rebounded off the wall and regained his footing.

He glimpsed Dobnik scrambling out the passenger door. Schlechter ran to the garage door and pulled it down, enveloping the room in darkness. He ran his fingers along the wall where he'd seen the light switch. Just as he touched it, the sound of a shattering light bulb reverberated through the darkness, followed by a clang as the metal object Dobnik must have thrown hit the wall behind him. Schlechter ignored the glass fragments glancing off his cheek. He turned the light switch, knowing it to be a futile act.

In the quiet darkness he listened for Dobnik's breathing sounds, but heard only his own ragged breath. Both his hands hurt, especially the right one holding the revolver. Yet he held the advantage. If Dobnik had a gun, he would have drawn it instead of smashing the light bulb. It was time to increase his odds. He bent down and raised the

288

garage door to admit daylight, but not enough for Dobnik to squeeze through. Still, he could not see the other man.

He was sliding around the back of the Trabant when its engine started, and the gear box emitted a grating noise. Schlechter aimed the gun through the rear windshield at the back of Dobnik's head and fired just as the car lurched back. He jumped off to the side, the rear bumper grazing his legs. The engine choked and the Trabant settled a few centimeters from the garage door. Schlechter moved to the driver's door and tore it open. Dobnik's body slumped against the steering wheel, blood oozing from his skull. Taking latex gloves from his coat pocket, Schlechter slipped them on before pushing Dobnik off the wheel and back into the seat. His eyes were fixed. There was no pulse.

Schlechter swore. Gone was any chance to get information about what arrangements Dobnik had made with the West, what secret papers he'd passed and what else he had planned to deliver and, most important, where he had kept the pilfered documents. General Frantz would not be happy.

Chapter Thirty-Three

"Good morning, Peggy. Please have a seat."

Watching the slender brunette dart to the nearest chair conjured up in Stein the image of a scared mouse, reinforcing his earlier assessment that low self-esteem might explain her dating Ray Fielding. Her eyes met his for only an instant before they shifted from floor to ceiling and then all around the office.

"I bet you wonder why I called you here."

A timid nod was her only response.

"It's nothing serious. I just wanted to ask you a few questions about the fire alarm." His soothing voice achieved the desired effect. She appeared to relax a bit.

"Did you have any trouble leaving the building on time?"

She looked at him, apparently gaining confidence. "No, sir."

Stein phrased his next question in a nonchalant manner, as if her answer wouldn't matter all that much to him. "It makes it easier when you know it's only a drill, doesn't it?"

"That's for sure."

As soon as the words escaped her lips, her jaw dropped and she gaped at him, realizing she'd said something she wished she hadn't. As a litigator, Stein had seen that expression on the face of many a witness. Now he needed to reassure her so he could extract the information he was after. "It's all right. Ray told me he gave you a heads-up about the alarm."

Her shoulders slumped.

"You did nothing wrong, Peggy." Stein watched resignation turn to relief. He stood, walked around the desk and took the visitor chair next to her. "I'd like you to tell me who you told about the drill."

He'd said it without a hint of blame or accusation. Nevertheless, she cast her eyes down. Patience, he told himself. The wall clock's ticking punctuated the silence.

Staring straight ahead, she said in a low voice, "I don't remember who all I mentioned it to." She took a deep breath and continued with a voice gaining in strength. "I probably told most of the secretaries on the eighth floor." She laughed nervously. "A lot of them think these alarms are kind of silly."

"I suppose they are," Stein replied while contemplating how he could narrow the field. He leaned across the desk, picked up a writing tablet and pencil and placed them on the pullout in front of her. "I want you to write down the name of every secretary whom you might have told about the drill."

After looking at him for a moment as if to gauge whether he was serious, she leaned forward, picked up the pencil and scribbled. Stein waited. Each time she looked up, he encouraged her with a nod and smile. Finally, she put down the pencil. She made no move to hand him the tablet until he held out his hand.

After a quick perusal, he asked, "Aside from these seven, you didn't mention it to anyone?"

"I've put down everyone I might have told. There is no one else."

Satisfied he'd gotten out of her what he could, Stein stood. "Very well. You may go now. Will you promise me to keep this to yourself?"

"Of course, sir."

As he watched her hurry out the door, he wondered whether she'd keep her promise. She might for a while, but eventually the temptation to gossip would be too great. All he needed was a few hours to interrogate the seven secretaries on the list. He suspected he would get his answer from the one he meant to grill first: Rolf's secretary.

Stein pushed the button on the intercom. "Mildred, have Betty Crandall come up at once."

♫ ♫ ♫

Even though wind and rain were no longer pounding his office window and occasional slivers of sun broke through the clouds, Stein's mood had not improved since the morning. On the contrary, he had grown more and more frustrated. It was now lunch time and he'd interviewed all of the secretaries on Peggy Malone's list except one. No one had seen Betty Crandall all morning. Her coat and purse were gone. After the last secretary left his office, Stein reviewed what he'd learned. Three recalled Peggy telling them about the drill, one had heard about it but couldn't remember the source, and two denied any prior knowledge. Stein's thorough probing had not turned up anything suspicious. None of them had been defensive, as if hiding something or protecting someone. Nor did any of them appear to have the nerve to pull a raid on his office.

He shoved his chair back so hard it smashed into the credenza behind him. The one person he wanted to talk to the most had disappeared. He was not used to having his wishes foiled, or even delayed, but stewing about it here would only frustrate him further. He marched into Mildred's office.

"I'm going downstairs for a quick bite. As soon as you locate her, call me there. I'll be back in twenty."

Without waiting for an acknowledgment, Stein walked out the door.

♬ ♬ ♬

Betty reached her eighth-floor cubicle before her colleagues returned from the drill. She opened the briefcase on her desk, laid the folder in her hand atop the file in the case, closed the lid and scrambled the combination lock. She could still feel adrenaline pumping through her veins after the narrow escape from Stein's office. With efficient movements she slid her coat off its hanger, put it on, retrieved her purse, and snatched up the briefcase on her way out. She again opted for the stairs. The elevators would be full of employees coming back to work.

She walked a few blocks east on K Street until she was out of sight of Stein & Weston's building before she hailed a cab. The bearded driver, Pakistani or Indian she guessed, nodded when she specified the federal courthouse in Alexandria. As the rattling old Chevy weaved in and out of traffic, Betty slowed her breathing. There was plenty of time to accomplish what was needed and be back at the office by the end of the lunch hour.

Rolf had left several projects for her to work on while he was gone. One of them had been the summary judgment motion and brief in her attaché case. He had just finished dictating it last Friday and asked her to run off signature pages, which he signed on his way out the door. She shook her head, considering the trust that took on his part. If she messed up, he could face sanctions, something which the federal judge presiding over this particular case was not shy in imposing. She had finished the brief Monday, let it sit overnight, reviewed it yesterday, and had planned on filing it then. For a reason she could not name, she had decided to wait until today's filing deadline. Now she was glad for the cover it would provide.

As the taxi turned onto George Washington Memorial Parkway, she opened the briefcase, took out the folder on top and leafed through the dozen or so pages she had managed to copy in Stein's office. To give Rolf a full report, she needed to memorize as much as possible of the contents. She looked up as they sped past National Airport, then resumed her study. As they entered Alexandria she replaced the folder in the briefcase. The driver dropped her in front of the courthouse. She did not enter the federal building but walked a few blocks to her bank. Within minutes she had deposited the folder containing the copies from Stein's file in her safety deposit box and was back on her way to the courthouse.

The filing of the motion and brief took longer than usual, thanks to an inexperienced deputy clerk. She had brown shoulder-length hair with puffy bangs in front. It looked silly to Betty, but that was the style so many young women seemed to prefer these days. The clerk had not yet mastered the routine of checking the docket sheet for unpaid fees and file-stamping the originals and all twelve copies Betty had brought. A new hire, Betty concluded. Still, upon leaving the building, she discovered that if she didn't take too long for lunch, she might have time for a little research in the public library on the way back to the office. The letters in the file to Anthony Fabrini had piqued her curiosity, and Rolf undoubtedly would appreciate any information she could gather on Stein's secret client.

♫ ♫ ♫

While Betty Crandall had never been his secretary, Stein had heard enough from the other partners over the years about her feistiness to realize she was no meek lamb like some he'd interviewed this morning. As he watched Betty lower her lanky figure into the chair in front of his desk, Stein decided to dispense with social convention and put her on the defensive from the start.

"Did you find what you were looking for this morning?"

She flinched, but held his stare. "I don't understand what you're asking, sir." Her steady voice surprised him.

He'd failed to rattle her, so he backed off for now. "What did you do during the fire alarm?"

Without hesitation she looked him in the eye. "I left the building, of course."

"You knew it was only a drill, didn't you?"

"Yes, sir. Peggy Malone told me."

"Where have you been all morning?"

"I filed a motion for summary judgment for Ro . . . Mr. Keller in the Eastern District in Alexandria."

"You filed it yourself?"

"Yes, Mr. Stein." He could tell she'd caught his tone of incredulity when she volunteered, "It's in the environmental case Mr. Keller is defending, and it was due today."

"When did you leave the office?"

"As soon as the alarm went off I took the papers and left. It seemed like a good use of time while the drill was going on."

Stein could see he was getting nowhere. Could she be telling the truth?

"You didn't leave word with anyone where you were going?"

"No, sir." She assumed a contrite expression. "I probably should have, but with my boss gone . . . I'm so used to telling Mr. Keller. It never occurred to me to notify someone else." She paused. "Sorry, I should have."

Stein enjoyed this less and less. She'd make a darn good witness under cross-examination.

"You filed a motion with a brief, I assume."

She nodded.

"How long was the brief?"

"About fifteen pages, as I recall."

"And Mr. Keller gave it to you to type last week?"

"Yes, on Friday, just before he left."

"Now Betty, from what I hear, you're a very fast typist. So you probably had it done early in the week."

She met his gaze. "I completed the proofreading yesterday."

"Any reason you couldn't use a law clerk or a courier and file it yesterday?"

"Mr. Keller told me to file it personally."

Stein detected no sign of defensiveness or evasion.

"When did he tell you that?"

"He called me yesterday to check on the motion. I was glad he did since I had a couple of questions, and I didn't know how to get hold of him. He had me make a few changes and asked me to file it myself this morning."

She had an answer for everything. His litigator instinct told him it all sounded too neat, too perfect, but he had nothing concrete with which to dispute her account.

"Do you know where he was calling from?"

"He mentioned something about West Berlin."

"Did he know about the fire drill?"

She raised her eyebrows as if to signal surprise. "I don't know why he would."

"You didn't tell him about it?"

"There was no reason to, him being over there."

That was the first evasion he'd noticed. She'd probably told him, or she would have simply said no. Stein had learned when not to pursue a matter. At this point, any further probing would net an outright denial.

"What time did he call you?"

"He caught me at home Tuesday morning just before I was leaving for the office."

"What else did you all discuss?"

She hesitated and glanced at him with an offended expression. "He wanted me to call his daughter for him. Apparently, he'd been unable to reach her from over there. He said something about the time difference making it difficult to catch her."

Time for a little psychology, he thought. "Betty, you're wondering why I'm prying into your phone conversation. It is crucial that you tell me every detail. Mr. Keller is on a very delicate mission. He may be in danger. I need to know everything you talked about." He paused for effect. "You would not want anything to happen to him because you've withheld vital information from me, would you?"

"Of course not. If there were anything else, I would tell you." She seemed sincere.

"Yes, I'm sure you would, Betty."

He rose and she followed suit.

"If anything else occurs to you, be sure to let me know immediately."

"Yes, sir."

As he watched her stride out of his office, Stein had the feeling she'd not told all she knew. Other than the one evasion, he could not point to anything in particular to fortify his intuition. From all reports, her loyalty to Rolf knew no bounds. The question was, did it extend to spying and lying for him?

Chapter Thirty-Four

Frantz scowled. "Are you telling me you didn't find out where Dobnik kept his hoard?"

Schlechter regretted his decision to report the bad news to the general early rather than wait until the opera. He knew that excuses and justifications would enrage Frantz even more, so he nodded with the slightest movement he could manage. A stronger nod might be taken as insolence or even as justifying his failed actions. Nor was it advisable to meet the general's stare.

He lowered his eyes. "I searched his car and the garage. Nothing. I even turned his apartment upside down. No files."

Frantz slung his glasses onto the desk. "How do you propose to recover those files before they fall into the wrong hands? Tell me that!" He looked ready to explode.

"I will find his stash. His ex-wife might know something . . . or his daughter. I'll go talk to them right now, if you wish."

After a quick glance at the wall behind Schlechter, Frantz waved his hand. "No, there's not enough time. You can do that tomorrow . . . if it's still necessary."

He smirked as he pulled a folder from a drawer. He shoved it at Schlechter across the expansive desk surface. "As soon as Sylvia Mazzoni appears in the third act, go to her dressing room and find a good hiding place for this. Remember, she's on stage for the last half of the third act, but not the fourth. You'll have about twenty minutes."

Schlechter picked up the file. He thought he knew where this was going. "And I arrest her when she returns."

Frantz raised his index finger. "You'll do no such thing. Just watch from the hallway as she arrives and then leaves again to take her bows at the end of the opera. It seems she has a traveling companion who's a West German spy like her. Expect him to come to her dressing room after the final curtain calls. They'll be waiting for Dobnik to make the drop." He dropped his finger and sneered. "Little will they know that the papers are already in the room."

It was Schlechter's turn to smirk. "I'll wait till I can catch both of them in her room, find the contraband and arrest them."

"Yes, but don't attempt the arrest by yourself. Take along the officer stationed by the stage entrance. The rest of the plan stays the way I outlined yesterday. Buzz me as soon as you have them in custody. Is that clear?"

"Yes, sir."

"And not a word to anyone about this!"

Holding Frantz's gaze, Schlechter supplied the appropriate response. "Certainly not, General."

The corners of the general's mouth turned upward. "I imagine you'll find a way to persuade the diva and her friend to sing—a sweeter melody to my ears than that French bourgeois crap coming from the stage." He laughed at his cleverness. "Perhaps Dobnik told them about his cache. If not, you visit his ex-wife and the daughter tomorrow, and search every place this traitor ever set foot in." Frantz dismissed him with a wave of his hand. "See you at seven at the opera."

Schlechter was halfway to the door when he heard, "And Major . . ."

He turned. "General?"

"Don't foul it up this time!"

Two mean eyes impaled him. He felt himself cringe and barely managed to suppress an outright shudder. There was no mistaking Frantz's meaning.

Chapter Thirty-Five

During the past ten minutes Rolf must have glanced at his watch half a dozen times and scanned Unter den Linden from his window table at Café Franken. The boulevard didn't have enough light to afford him a clear view. There were many dark corners and alleyways from where the Stasi officer might be watching to make sure Rolf had come alone.

He walked to the counter, not to survey the varied assortment of pastries in the glass case, but to check his wristwatch against the establishment's wall clock. It was now a quarter till six, fifteen minutes past the appointed time, and Dobnik had not shown. Rolf could no longer deny his anxiety that something had gone wrong. Back at his table, he poured the last of the coffee from the floral porcelain carafe into his cup of the same pattern. He had planned on ordering a slice of the fresh apple strudel as soon as Dobnik arrived—not the sumptuous-looking Schwarzwälder Kirschtorte, whose kirsch-liqueur-soaked chocolate layers would threaten his sobriety. He recalled hearing of more than one instance when an alcoholic's craving for drink had been triggered by something equally

301

innocuous. It was certainly a moot point now. Worry about Dobnik had erased all desire for pastry.

Rolf sipped the coffee, postponing his moment of decision. A few minutes later he gave up. He drained the last drop, paid the bill, and strode out into the evening cold. When one last look up and down Unter den Linden did not yield any sign of the Stasi officer, he struck up a brisk pace toward the Staatsoper. The guard at the stage entrance eyed him with suspicion but let him pass, as did the dressing assistant after checking with Frau Mazzoni. To his dismay a middle-aged woman wearing a white plastic apron was in the midst of braiding Sylvia's long, dark strands.

"What are you doing here?" Uneasy surprise permeated Sylvia's question.

"Do you think you could interrupt your makeup for a moment?"

Sylvia's questioning glance in the mirror went from Rolf to the hairdresser.

"I'll be done in a minute." The woman's harsh voice matched her hard-etched face.

Rolf ignored her disapproving look and perched himself atop one of the stools in the back of the room. The wait seemed endless, but she finally packed up her gear and left.

"Problems?"

"Is there a radio in here?"

Sylvia gave him a quizzical look until she understood. "I have a tape player I sometimes use for inspiration. Would you like to hear Micaëla sung by one of my idols?"

Without waiting for an answer, she pushed the play button on the portable player sitting off to the side, and the creamy voice of Mirella Freni filled the room. Rolf came up behind Sylvia, reached past her and cranked up the volume.

He put his hands on her shoulder and spoke directly into her ear. "Mozart didn't show. Something's wrong. You can't perform tonight."

She winced under his intense grip. "You're hurting me. What's the matter?"

He removed his hands. "Let's go for a short walk."

She shut off the player. Without a word they left the dressing room. Sylvia told the assistant in the hallway, "I'll be back in five minutes."

Rolf could feel mistrustful eyes following them as they burst through the stage door and turned the corner. Sylvia had not brought her coat, so Rolf took off his and draped it around her shoulders against the chill night air. Her shivers stopped.

He erupted like a pent-up volcano. "Something's gone wrong. The Stasi must be on to Dobnik . . . and to you. We have to leave now. If you sing tonight, you'll never get out of here."

"What makes you so sure he didn't just change his mind?"

"Remember what he told us in case something should happen to him? He's been risking too much for freedom in the West to give up now. Something's wrong." Rolf became more and more convinced of the truth of what he was saying.

"But I can still perform. Without a drop the Stasi has nothing to hang on me . . . on us."

"What if this whole thing is a setup? Do you think for a minute the Stasi wouldn't find a way to plant materials on you during an arrest?" He grabbed her elbow, forcing her to slow her walk and face him. "Sylvia. Let's leave while we still can."

She looked deep into his eyes, unguarded for a moment, but then controlled again. "Rolf, I have to sing. Canceling a performance at the last minute like this . . ." She paused, searching for words. "I could kiss opera goodbye."

He squeezed her arm. "Sylvia, I implore you. Don't go on that stage! If you're sitting in an East German prison cell, your opera days are over for sure. There's no 'could' about it."

She shook her arm and he let go. They had walked full circle around the opera house and were returning to the stage entrance.

"Rolf, I understand if you want to leave. But I'm going to sing this evening. I've worked too hard and too long to quit now."

He stopped her again a few meters before the door. "I was hoping to persuade you, but I didn't really expect to. At least listen to what I propose."

They walked by the entrance and made one more pass around the building while he laid out his plan. With every word he sought to persuade not only her, but himself as well, that it might just work. He was unaware of how his nervous energy hastened the pace of his speech until she asked him several times to slow down and repeat a detail.

When they approached the stage door for the second time, he tugged at her elbow. "Sylvia, are you sure you won't call off the performance? I'd feel a lot better if we got out of here now."

During the brief moment before she looked away he caught the mist in her dark eyes. "Rolf, please don't think I'm ungrateful. I do appreciate your concern." Her warm voice toughened. "But I have to sing tonight, and that's the end of it."

She turned, handed him his coat, and before he realized what was happening, gave him a quick hug. He was too surprised to hold onto her.

"Besides, your plan will work to perfection," she whispered and moved toward the entrance.

Watching her disappear, he felt briefly like a blushing schoolboy, then like a fool for not having embraced her when he'd had the chance. These sentiments were immediately supplanted by thoughts of what lay ahead. For them to have a shot at a clear getaway, his entire focus had to be on setting the plan into motion.

Rolf fished his wallet out of his back pocket and leafed through the stack of business cards until he found the one he needed. As he strode to the front of the opera house in search of a public phone, he reviewed what he had told Sylvia, hoping she'd etched every detail into her mind. His plan had to work. He did not dare contemplate the alternative.

Chapter Thirty-Six

Schmidt handed one of his new fake business cards to the stage doorman. The Berlin office had worked wonders in producing them this afternoon, yet the man in the gray uniform seemed unimpressed and looked suspicious when Schmidt asked to see Frau Mazzoni.

"Is she expecting you?"

Schmidt hesitated. "Yes, I told her I'd be by." He smiled at the humorless face behind the window. "But you know artists. She may not remember."

Deadpan, the doorman slid the glass panel closed, centimeters from Schmidt's nose, walked over to the black phone on the side wall, and dialed. Schmidt shot a glance in the direction of a man standing by the entrance, which had the desired effect. The observer looked away. Schmidt nudged the pane back a fraction—less than a centimeter.

The man's voice carried through the tiny crack. "Frau Mazzoni . . . Herr Siegfried Nothung is here to see you."

After a moment, the doorman put down the phone, leaned over the shelf, and pulled the window pane halfway open. "She's busy." His voice carried a note of triumph—a petty bureaucrat getting a rare taste of power.

She apparently had not associated the alias with him, so Schmidt used his backup. "Tell her I've brought the release she's been waiting for."

He watched the man on the phone relay the message. The ensuing silence stretched for a long moment. Just when Schmidt concluded his clues had been missed, the doorman said, "As you wish."

He replaced the receiver, opened the panel, and pointed. "Turn right at the corner. Then take the first hallway to the left. Room 27 will be the last door on your right."

Schmidt turned the corner and entered a hallway lined with rooms. He passed by empty benches along the walls and stopped at the fourth door. Before he could knock, it flew open. If he hadn't just seen her in the skin-tight leather pants onstage, he might well not have recognized her.

"Herr Nothung. What a surprise. Come in."

He ignored the mocking tone and entered. As he scanned the room for listening devices, he felt her eyes following him. She walked to the first dressing table and turned on a tape player. A strong soprano voice began a tune that sounded familiar, and he realized he'd just heard Sylvia sing it in the first act. She settled in a chair in front of the dresser. After he sat in the chair next to hers, she spoke into his ear. "Siegfried Nothung. Very clever. Nothung is the sword in Wagner's opera *Siegfried*. But I didn't make the connection between Siegfried and schmidt—both forgers of steel—until the porter mentioned the release." She held out her hand. "You have the letter of immunity for me?"

He held her gaze. "No. That's the only thing I could think of to alert you to who I really was."

"Lying is part of your job, isn't it?"

She sounded contemptuous, but resigned. He couldn't blame her. "Sometimes it is necessary. I had to find a way to warn you. There was a shooting near Cologne today.

Several terrorists were killed. The story has been dominating the news. I'm afraid Mozart may be exposed."

"His documents were what led you to the terrorists?"

She was sharp. Schmidt nodded. "Have you heard from him today?"

"No."

He sensed the tension in her voice, but pressed on. "Any idea when he'll show?"

"As far as I know, sometime between now and the end of the performance."

Something in the way she'd said that struck him as odd. "Is that everything you know?"

"Yes."

Had she hesitated? He had an uneasy feeling. "And where is Mr. Keller?"

"I believe he's keeping an eye out for Mozart until I get off the stage." She paused and then leaned closer. "Isn't it dangerous for you to be here?"

"I had to take the chance. I'm counting on the Stasi being under such heavy scrutiny from the populace and the West that if they catch me they'll just tell me to leave." It was time to get to the real purpose of his visit. "You know how important it is that I receive the documents he's promised. As soon as you have them, I want you and Keller to get out of here. Don't stop for anything. Leave in your stage attire if you have to. Do you understand?" His urgency got her full attention.

Her eyes widened. "Do you think the Stasi is on to us?"

"We'd best assume that they are. Leave through the stage door. There'll be a white Mercedes passing by every few minutes. The driver knows to look for you. He'll bring you straight to my hotel." He looked at the door. "I wish Keller were here. Tell him about this as soon as you see him."

When she didn't respond, he continued. "Frau Mazzoni, if the man shows before the end of your performance, for

God's sake, take the documents and leave immediately. Don't even *think* about staying for your curtain call."

"Not to worry, Herr Schmidt, you'll have your stupid documents."

He did not react. "You know he's promised us a suitcase. If he has it with him, I want all three of you to catch that car. If he doesn't, tell him to go get it tonight and make his way to West Berlin. Make sure Keller gives him the envelope with the contact information."

Sylvia nodded, but she did not meet his gaze. Could he trust her to follow through? "Are you clear on this?" he pressed her.

"Yes." Her voice breathy with impatience, she was drumming her fingers on the dressing table.

He did not feel reassured, but it was clear she wouldn't be pushed further, so he turned off the tape player. "It's been a pleasure, Frau Mazzoni. I'm looking forward to your appearance in the third act." He rose and walked to the door.

"Thank you, Herr Nothung. I'll see you after the performance."

He closed the door and hoped her last statement would come true, never mind Bauman's admonition to do whatever it took to get Dobnik and his suitcase. By the time he'd passed the sentinel parked at the stage door and headed for the auditorium to catch the second act, Schmidt had almost convinced himself he could not afford the luxury of scruples at this late date. Yet no matter how many times he told himself to keep his focus on the documents—that they mattered most, that they held Germany's future—Mazzoni and Keller kept intruding. He had gotten them into this and he felt responsible.

♫ ♫ ♫

Just as General Frantz finished checking on his men, the house lights flickered, signaling the end of the twenty-minute intermission. Satisfied they had the foyer, its exits, and the stage door covered, he fell in with the hardy Teutonic theatergoers who were streaming back inside after having refreshed themselves in the frigid evening air. The two-way radio inside his coat pocket vibrated. He stopped, causing an elderly couple to stumble into him. Frantz ignored their apologies and moved off to the side, away from the main entrance. Out of earshot, he pushed the talk button. "Yes."

"Schlechter. Frau Mazzoni just had a visitor."

"Did you recognize him?"

"No."

"Describe him."

"One meter ninety, stocky, brown hair, mustache, late forties probably, charcoal pin-striped suit, western cut."

Frantz blurted, "That's Schmidt, Dobnik's contact. How long was he with her?"

"About five minutes."

"Where is he now?"

"I saw him head for the foyer."

"He's attending the performance. What audacity!"

"General, do you want to have him arrested?"

Frantz thought for a long moment. An arrest would gain him nothing. He could not take the chance of provoking an international incident without Rittmeister's or Honecker's express approval. And he did not want to have to answer a lot of questions about this elaborate opera house stakeout, at least not until after he had his prisoners.

"No. Just make sure the guard doesn't let him through the stage door should he come back. Keep your eye on Mazzoni and her friend Keller. You have his description."

"Yes, sir."

"The lights are flickering for the third time. I need to go. Remember, Mazzoni will be on stage from a few minutes after ten till about ten thirty, the end of the third act. You're all set for that?"

"Yes, General. Everything's ready."

Frantz cut the connection, slid the radio into his pocket, and rushed inside. The house lights dimmed as he settled into his aisle seat in the third row. Neither the applause for the conductor taking the podium nor the orchestral entr'acte preceding the second act reached his consciousness. Instead, his mind was occupied with possible reasons for Schmidt's presence. Irritation alternated with admiration for the Western spy's nerve. It was not until the curtain rose that he relaxed into his chair, contemplating the events to come. What he'd give to see Schmidt's face when he'd learn of his amateur surrogates' arrests!

♫ ♫ ♫

Sylvia eyed the braided Micaëla peering back at her out of the mirror above the dresser. The image of the innocent country girl did not square with the repeated lies she'd told Schmidt, and she'd accused *him* of deception. Rolf had insisted she not tell him about the failed rendezvous with Dobnik. So she hadn't, and that was that.

The house was well into its second intermission, a good time for her to begin her preparation for the third act, but as much as she tried, she could not focus. Although Rolf had been uncertain of the exact time, he thought he'd be back before she had to go on stage, but not to worry if he weren't. Easy for him to say. Stop fretting, she told herself, he'd be there by the time she got off stage at the end of the act. With that she started the process of deep breathing for relaxation. Whenever apprehension surfaced, she did not resist but acknowledged its presence, breathed into it and let it melt away.

Faint light reflected on the inside of her eyelids as if she were watching a classic black and white movie. Realizing the flickering house lights signaled the end of the intermission, Sylvia emerged from her meditative state. She sang a few scales, but to maintain spontaneity she resisted the temptation to rehearse any part of Micaëla's big third-act aria. Her voice was ready.

She lingered a few minutes until she had to accept that she wouldn't see Rolf before going on stage. When she opened the door, she bumped into the assistant director. Hair disheveled and red-faced, he gestured for her to follow him. They rushed toward the stage, his body language communicating his exasperation, but apparently he knew not to upset divas and held his tongue. When they arrived backstage, she heard Carmen and her sister gypsies sing the last few chords of the card trio, then launch into their playful musical scheme to flirt with the customs guards so the gypsy band could smuggle their goods past. Then she remembered that this hideous modern production, which probably had Bizet turning over in his grave, featured groupies seducing policemen so the gang members could push their drugs. Sylvia knew she had just three more minutes to slip into her role.

Despite excellent performances, the gypsies' number only drew faint applause from a reserved audience. She entered the stage with hesitating steps, a lost and frightened Micaëla looking for Don José. Sweeping her eyes across the audience, Sylvia was jolted out of her character. The red-haired British agent, Ross, and his tall companion, Kingsley, were in the front row. For the longest moment, movement, sound—everything—stopped. There were just the three of them, suspended in time.

The introductory notes to her aria pulled her back into consciousness. She forced her eyes onto the spot on the stage she needed to reach in the next few seconds. To the audience, her hesitation might have seemed in character with the frightened girl, but the agents would have seen that she'd recognized them. By choosing front row seats, they obviously wanted to be noticed. Had they learned about the drops Dobnik had already made and come for the copies she'd promised them?

The moment to begin her aria approached as she rushed into position. Her voice teacher's words sounded in her mind like a mantra. "Use adversity to give you strength." She poured every ounce of her fear into the opening phrase about finding the gang's hideout. As she paused and listened to the horns' wistful introduction of the melody, she felt the overwhelming intensity with which she had imbued her introductory lines—more gripping and real than she'd ever sung them before. Tapping into the power of her teacher's wisdom, she knew that Micaëla would indeed overcome her fear.

♫ ♫ ♫

The moment he saw Micaëla take the stage, Major Boris Schlechter left his seat in the rear of the center box and slid out the door. The other patrons did not seem to notice. Thanks to the blueprints Frantz had given him and the assistant director's tour yesterday, he knew his way around this building and found the unmarked door guarding the backstage passageway without difficulty. He emerged from the maze of corridors to the sound of horns. Poised to proceed to the dressing rooms, he stopped, mesmerized by a high female voice singing a haunting melody that touched him, though he couldn't understand a word. He'd have to disagree with Frantz's characterization of *Carmen* as French bourgeois crap.

A sudden thought about the general's warning not to screw up again shook Schlechter from his momentary trance. The twenty minutes Mazzoni would be on stage afforded him more time than he needed, but he'd better get started. The music faded as he rushed toward the rear stage exit and, by the time he turned the corner into the dressing room area, was only a memory. No assistants were loitering in the hallway. Good. The fewer eyes and explanations the better. In one continuous move he entered Sylvia's room, perused the still deserted hallway, and closed the door.

Schlechter scanned the room's sparse furnishings: two dressing tables, several stools of various heights, and two chairs. He was looking for a hiding place not so obvious that Mazzoni would stumble upon the stash when she returned, yet not so concealed that his finding it later with relative ease would arouse suspicion. He studied the dressers. Various bottles on the surface of the one closest to him and clothes hanging on the rod at its side indicated it was in use, while the table in the back of the room looked untouched.

He pulled open the shallow center drawer of the near dresser. Its thin metal scraped on resistant rollers. Schlechter frowned at the contents: pencils and pens in several colors, a box of face powder, makeup brushes, rouge, several small packets of tissue, and other odds and ends. This would not do. The top side drawer wasn't much better, containing more tissues, a braided hairpiece, a writing tablet, and in the back a stack of some kind of papers. Exasperated, he yanked the handle of the bottom drawer. The sight of a shawl and socks lying on top of a pair of women-sized sports shoes did not please him. Mazzoni had stashed part of her street wardrobe here, the rest hanging on the clothes rod.

Undecided, he shut the drawer and surveyed the room once more, confirming what he already knew. There was no other place to hide the contraband. Reluctantly, he reopened the top side drawer and slid the folder among the papers in the back. Not perfect but maybe good enough to prevent its discovery until he burst in for the arrest, he told himself as he closed the drawer.

The hallway was still empty when Schlechter eased out the door. The whole operation had taken less than ten minutes. He could see no good reason why he shouldn't listen to the rest of the act and follow Mazzoni back to the dressing area when she came off the stage. As he approached the backstage, he was surprised by the hullabaloo that greeted him. Instead of a lone female singing a beautiful melody, an array of male and female voices sounded from the stage, apparently engaged in an argument or fight of some sort. After a chorus he thought he detected Mazzoni singing as if she were beseeching someone. He listened, entranced.

It was a shame she would not sing on a stage again for a very long time, if ever. The restrained applause, signaling the end of the act, tore him from his reverie. He had a job to do. Schlechter retreated to the side from where he could watch Mazzoni leave the stage and follow her. Not much longer now, and he'd get to deal with her up close.

♫ ♫ ♫

Rolf sat on the sofa in Sylvia's hotel suite staring at the two suitcases, registering for the first time that his was bigger than Sylvia's. For an opera singer she traveled light. Then he remembered that opera houses provided all of her performance garb. Having packed their belongings in a hurry, he had checked all nooks and crannies to ensure he'd not overlooked anything and resisted the urge to walk through the rooms again.

A knock made him jump to his feet and race to the peephole. After a quick glance, he pulled back the door. Bernd Schlosser entered. Rolf remembered the herringbone chauffeur's cap and gray beard sprawling over a full-cheeked face. He'd not seen him outside his cab before and had not realized what a short, round figure he cut. He'd assumed the man would be taller.

"Sorry I'm late. Traffic's a mess in the western sector this evening."

"I'm glad you made it." Rolf pointed at the cases. "Do you think you can carry both of those?"

"No problem." Schlosser picked up the bags. He showed no sign of curiosity about his able-bodied passenger's failure to lift a finger to carry at least one.

"Would you take those straight to the car?" Rolf asked. "I'll be there in a few minutes."

Without a word, Schlosser carried the suitcases through the open door. There was really nothing left for Rolf to do other than delay his trek through the lobby to minimize the chances of the desk clerk's connecting him with the cabbie carrying the cases. They were not skipping out on the bill, since Schmidt presumably had arranged for payment when he reserved the rooms, and the longer everyone thought they would spend another night here, the better.

He took his time walking down the five flights of stairs to give Schlosser plenty of lead. Walking across the lobby, he avoided looking toward the front desk. Peripheral vision failed to detect any human movement. He held back his pace on his way to the front door, not wanting to appear in a rush. His heart sank when he saw the empty driveway. Where was the taxi? He pushed through the door and relaxed when he spotted the dark-blue Mercedes across the lot.

He crossed the parking lot, laughing at himself while remembering he'd told Schlosser to park away from the entrance. This sneaking around East Berlin brought more tension than a jury trial. He climbed into the back. Before Rolf could ask, the cabbie volunteered, "The two suitcases are in the trunk. Where to?"

"Head for West Berlin." When the taxi was moving, he added, "I need your advice. Do you know of a car rental place open at this hour?"

"Hmm . . . it's seven thirty. There is one near Bahnhof Zoo where I took you the other day. It should be open at least till eight."

"Can you get me there before then?"

The driver nodded. They made good time until they crossed the border and hit the heavy traffic Schlosser had complained about earlier. Rolf tried to pay attention to the busy street life, but his thoughts ran to the Staatsoper where Sylvia would be singing in the first act about now. He wondered how long this escapade would take and whether he'd make it back in time to see her before she had to go on stage in the third act. When the Zoo Station came into view, Rolf looked on both sides of the street for a car rental agency, but saw the Europcar sign only when the cabbie pulled into its lot.

The agency was open and had cars available. Although he had no idea how long he'd need the vehicle, Rolf answered the clerk's questions as if there were no doubt about his plans. With trepidation he used the credit card Stein's secretary, Mildred, had given him. He'd sort it out later with Stein. After all, he wouldn't be here if it weren't for this crazy assignment. Rolf realized the credit charge made him easier to trace, but he wouldn't be any less so if he used his personal credit card. He wished he'd brought cash of his own, as Stein had not arranged for much currency—probably by design, Rolf now realized with chagrin.

The Opel he drove out of the lot twenty minutes later was white, the only color available. The clerk couldn't understand why he'd wanted a boring gray. Rolf almost asked for a hotel recommendation but thought better of it. If he were traced to this rental place, it would be better if they looked for him at the hotel he had given—the one where Schmidt was staying.

It took him an hour to find a small hotel near the Zoo Station that looked shabby enough not to bother with formalities. The desk clerk acted as if it were the most natural thing to rent two rooms to a single male carrying two suitcases. He did not ask for identity papers, but demanded payment up front. Rolf paid with Mildred's card before seeing the rooms. He opened the door to the first, then went next door. Though small, the rooms were clean and certainly adequate for one short night.

It was nine twenty when he steered his rental car out of the hotel lot. The third act would start in thirty minutes or so. If he hurried, he might just make it before then. He had not counted on the one-way street outside the hotel leading away from the opera house. It spat him out onto a busy four-lane artery, and he was lost in less than a kilometer. He pulled into a gas station to ask directions, thinking that would be faster than studying the map the rental agency had provided.

The man behind the counter looked at him as if he'd never heard of East Berlin and was too busy with a line of customers to pay any attention, even if he had. Frustrated, Rolf returned to the car and, after several minutes of studying the map and glancing at the street sign, he pinpointed his location. He'd driven five kilometers in the wrong direction. Keep your cool, he told himself. At least now he knew where he was and how to get to Unter den Linden. He gave up making it to the Staatsoper during intermission. The important thing was to get there before the third act was over. She'd be worried, but she'd just have to trust him.

He reached the opera house without getting lost again and couldn't believe his luck when he saw an empty parking space in front of the theater. Someone unimpressed with *Carmen* must have left during the second intermission. After a moment's thought, he opted for the main entrance rather than the stage door. He'd rather not have the porter keep track of his comings and goings. This late into the performance there was no longer a ticket check—though he had one if needed—so he entered the deserted lobby. The closed auditorium doors told him the third act was underway. He headed straight for the unmarked door his guide had shown him the other day and, holding his breath, depressed the handle. It was unlocked, just as the woman had said.

Rolf was tempted to reach for the sketch in his breast pocket, but he found that he remembered every detail of the underground pathways. When he emerged backstage, he thought he could hear Sylvia singing, but he did not stop to listen. He rounded the corner to the dressing area and stopped. The door to Sylvia's room was being opened. He retreated around the corner into the men's dressing area. On instinct he opened the first door. The room was empty. He entered but kept the door cracked and peeked out. There were only two ways to go from Sylvia's room—toward the outside stage door or through here to backstage. He was just telling himself it probably had been one of the dressing assistants when he saw a burly man pass by in the hallway leading toward the stage. Although he caught only a fleeting glimpse, he was sure it wasn't Dobnik. But neither was he a theater employee, judging by the way he'd scanned the hallway as if to make sure he'd remain undetected.

Rolf hurried to the corner and saw the figure disappear into the vast backstage area. He returned to the women's dressing area. From the empty hallway he slipped inside Sylvia's room. No one was there. He looked for signs that might explain the stealthy visit. If that man was not a theater employee, what had he been looking for? Could he have been a courier for Dobnik making the drop?

Rolf began a methodical search. There weren't too many places to hide things. He pulled on the top side drawer of the near desk. If the drawer hadn't stuck and scattered a pile of papers as it opened, he probably would have overlooked the beige folder among them. Bingo. It contained several sheets of paper, all marked top secret. Rolf rifled through them. They looked strangely familiar. His mouth gaped when he recognized the dossier on

Joachim Walter, the West German Foreign Ministry official. These papers were duplicates of parts of Dobnik's first drop, the one he'd said contained forgeries.

Rolf stared across the room, looking at nothing. This didn't make sense. Why would someone—the Stasi?—stash these here? Unless . . . yes, of course! It *did* make sense. Dobnik had been compromised and probably arrested. This was part of the setup. They'd use the folder as evidence to arrest Sylvia and him as Western spies.

The wall clock showed a few minutes before ten. Sylvia should be arriving soon. He held the folder, not knowing what to do with it. Putting it back where he'd found it was out of the question. Then an idea came to him. If he hurried, he could take care of it and be back by the time Sylvia arrived.

♫ ♫ ♫

As she dragged Don José off the stage to lukewarm audience response at the end of the third act, Micaëla reverted to Sylvia at once. Never mind that her mid-act aria had earned action-interrupting applause, she needed to get back to her dressing room. Surely Rolf was there by now. Behind the closed curtain the stagehands were changing the scenery to a bullring in Seville while the orchestra played the entr'acte. She let go of the tenor's arm and rushed off. Upon reaching her dressing room, she swung the door inward with so much force that it crashed against the wall. The sight of Rolf standing by her dresser brought a smile of relief to her face. He did not reciprocate. Despite his serious demeanor, she thought for a moment he might embrace her as he moved toward her. Instead, he whispered in her ear, "I've got all your things in this plastic sack. We have to leave now."

She gazed around the room. The clothes rod was empty. He'd seen her looking at the dresser. "Everything you had in the bottom drawer is in here." He swung the sack back and forth, as if that would somehow validate his words.

Sylvia nodded and spoke into Rolf's ear. "Schmidt was here. After we have the documents, he wants us to catch a car he has circling outside the stage exit. I didn't tell him that Dobnik moved up the time for the drop or that he's missing."

Rolf shook his head. "Let's stick with our plan."

He opened the door, but held her back until he had taken a precautionary look. Apparently satisfied, he motioned her on and closed the door. She pointed in the direction of the backstage. With a nod, Rolf charged ahead. As they passed the men's dressing rooms, she thought she detected movement out of the corner of her eye, but when she looked, she saw no one.

♫ ♫ ♫

Schlechter ducked around the corner as soon as he saw Mazzoni and her companion hustle down the hall. He listened for footsteps but could only hear the distant sound of a chorus. A quick look assured him the men's dressing area was empty. He crossed the corridor. When he reached the main hallway, he saw the pair entering the backstage area. She was still wearing her stage costume, as she would for the final curtain calls. But they were at least ten minutes early, and instead of stopping they turned left.

Alarmed, he reached for the two-way radio and called Frantz, hoping the general hadn't turned off his unit while watching the last act. No answer. He tried twice more with the same result. Swearing under this breath, Schlechter pondered his options. He decided he had to pursue them. If they knew about the underground passageway, they might escape. Even if his hunch proved wrong and they returned to the dressing rooms after the final curtain calls, he'd have several minutes to make it back to Mazzoni's room in time to arrest them.

Schlechter had not been paying attention to the music coming from the stage. But now two agitated voices, male and female, rising in a heated argument, diverted him momentarily from his concentration on the search. It sounded like something tragic was about to happen. His attention snapped back to his quarry.

When he reached the spot where he'd last seen the pair, Schlechter knew that whatever course of action he pursued, if it didn't work out Frantz would have his hide. If he were lucky, that meant no more than going back to prison. Looking to cover himself, he tried to reach the general one more time. Again, Frantz did not answer. Would this opera never end? Disgusted, Schlechter dropped the radio into his pocket.

He roamed the entire side stage. There was no sign of the diva or her friend. They must have gone into the passageway. He ran to the door, opened it, and started down the staircase. The sound from the stage grew faint as the door closed behind him. When he could no longer hear the music, he paused to listen for footsteps. He tensed when he heard someone approaching. A young man in gray uniform, probably a stagehand, came up the stairs.

Schlechter said, "Guten Abend."

The employee nodded. Before he could pass, Schlechter asked, "Did you see a couple just now? She has dark hair, braided."

The man stopped on the step below Schlechter and studied him for a long second before responding. "Yes, I just passed them in the hallway to the foyer."

Schlechter flew down the rest of the stairs and into the hall, not bothering to say thank you. Although Frantz had assured him there were Stasi guards posted at all exits, he did not want to take any chances. He thought he heard footsteps just before he reached a fork in the hallway. To the left was the door to the basement stairwell leading to the opera café. The right branch, where the stagehand had reported seeing the fugitives, went to the foyer. When Schlechter reached the corner, all was quiet. He turned to the left, opened the door into the basement stairwell, and moved to the top of the stairs from where he could see the narrow corridor below clear to the door of the café. There was no movement, no sound.

♫ ♫ ♫

"In here," Rolf pointed to the wardrobe shop. "I checked it out earlier. It's deserted.

"Aren't we in a hurry?" Sylvia asked as Rolf closed the door.

"Yes, but you need a disguise. There are guards at every exit."

Dim light from the hallway bulb outside the open doorway fell on half a dozen rows of tables, some with sewing machines. Mannequins stood around the room. Thousands of garments were hanging on racks that stretched along the entire rear wall. Masks, spears, knives, rifles, revolvers and countless tools and accouterments were spread out over the numerous open shelves covering the side walls. Sylvia couldn't imagine what the drawers lining the wall behind her might hold.

She followed Rolf to the rear wall. He seemed to be looking for something. He motioned her to stay behind the long rack of hanging clothes, and she watched him head for the men's clothing section. He returned with a black brimmed hat and a long coat.

"Is this large enough to hold your braids?"

She swept up her braids and stuffed them inside the large hat before putting it on her head.

He grunted approval. "I'll hold the coat while you look for flat-heeled shoes."

She found her size with relative ease among the shop's extensive shoe collection. When she returned with the new shoes on her feet, Rolf held out the gray coat to her.

"If you can pass for a man, we might be able to sneak out with the theater crowd."

She noticed the garment's broad cut—perfect for hiding her figure and the tight leather pants she was still wearing. Before she could slip it on, Rolf pulled her to the floor, putting his fingers to his lips. She peered out between the evening gowns hanging from the rack and saw a burly man standing at the entrance. Faint hallway light came in through the open door behind him. The backlighting lent him a ghostlike appearance.

♫ ♫ ♫

Schlechter retreated and took the hallway to the right. In the dim light from the sparse ceiling bulbs he had to squint to see ahead to the next corner. While contemplating which way to turn, he strode by the dark hallway windows of the costume shop. Recalling the footsteps he'd heard earlier, he stopped, then stepped to the door. He tried the handle. It gave. Schlechter opened the door. Intent on not making a sound, he tiptoed inside the huge rectangular room. In the faint light coming in from the hallway, he scanned the workshop, listening for the faintest sound. All he heard was his own breathing. Yet he felt the prickly sensation of a hunter who knows his prey is near. He crept along the center aisle, looking under tables as he went. A swishing sound interrupted the silence, startling him. Plastic garment bags along the rear wall swayed as if someone were moving between them. He drew the Makarov from its holster and advanced toward the spot.

♫ ♫ ♫

Sylvia felt Rolf's touch on her shoulder. He motioned for her to put on the coat. She struggled in her crouch to slip her second arm into the sleeve and inadvertently brushed against the plastic garment bags hanging in front of her. Just then the heater blower came on. She gasped. The man holding a pistol drew closer. Rolf pushed her along the wall, motioning for her to stay clear of the clothes. When they drew even with the next aisle, Rolf took her hand and, ducking low under the garments, pulled her into the passageway. He stooped to a crawl, and she followed him.

She heard muffled static from the back of the room and then a low voice. As much as she wanted to turn around, she did not, but kept on Rolf's heels. The front door stood partially open, but not enough to allow them to slip out. He widened the gap, and after they'd crawled through, returned it to its original position. As soon as they were in the hallway, he pulled her up and to her surprise turned to the right.

"Aren't we going to the foyer?"

"No, this way." His forceful whisper allowed no objection.

In a few seconds they came to a door. He pushed it open and pulled her inside to the top of a staircase leading to a basement.

Rolf pointed at the corridor below. "It's about thirty meters to the opera café. We'll go up to the foyer from there and mingle with the public." He started down the stairs, waving her on. "Let's go. The performance is over. We'd better hurry before the audience leaves."

♫ ♫ ♫

Using the pistol to part the garments, Schlechter scanned the entire area behind the clothes. Nothing. He relaxed, deciding that the rustling sound had been made by the heater blower stirring the air. A burst of static crackled in his pocket. Swearing to himself for not having turned the device on vibrator mode, he depressed the talk button.

"Schlechter," he answered in a low voice while turning down the reception volume.

"Did you call me?" Frantz's voice was barely audible.

"Yes. They left the dressing room. They're somewhere in the underground passage."

"Is that where you are?"

"Yes."

"Find them."

"Yes, sir."

"Flush them out. Call me as soon as you locate them."

Schlechter's response stuck in his throat when he sensed a change in the light. He whirled around, peering toward the front of the room, and detected a slow movement in the door.

"Son of a bitch—"

"Schlechter, what is it?" the general's voice rasped over the radio.

"Got to go, sir. I've spotted them."

With drawn pistol he was at the door and through it in a matter of seconds but still too late to catch a glimpse of the fugitives. How could they have gotten away so fast? They must have taken the path to the foyer, probably hoping to sneak out with the departing theater patrons. Schlechter ran in that direction. Even with sentinels stationed at the main exit, he wanted to be there to catch them. His freedom was at stake—perhaps even his life.

♫ ♫ ♫

Schmidt couldn't decide whether it was a good or bad omen. Carmen, Don José, and Escamillo had taken their bows. Micaëla should have been next up, but Sylvia didn't come out. Did that mean Dobnik had delivered the documents and she'd followed his instructions to catch the car to his West Berlin hotel? Just to be sure, he waited for the second round of curtain calls. When she still didn't show, he stood and, ignoring the stares he drew for his rudeness, pushed his way past applauding patrons to the aisle. He rushed to the main exit. Once outside, he walked around to the stage exit and waited. After he'd been there several minutes, he began to think they had indeed caught the car and were on their way to West Berlin. His heart sank when the white Mercedes came around the corner. He waved the driver over.

"You haven't seen them?"

"No."

Schmidt climbed into the front passenger seat. Even though he didn't hold out much hope, he told the driver to keep circling for another half hour.

♫ ♫ ♫

"Bloody hell! Where is she?" Ross jumped to his feet as soon as it became clear Sylvia Mazzoni was not coming out for the final curtain calls.

"Let's find her." Kingsley, the more pragmatic of the two Brits, headed for the exit.

♫ ♫ ♫

Frantz knew something was wrong when Mazzoni did not appear to take her bows at the end of the fourth act. Stuck in the crowd winding its way to the auditorium exits, he turned on his two-way radio. It beeped, indicating someone had been trying to reach him. He called Schlechter. The short conversation confirmed that the planned arrest in the dressing room would not happen. But there was no way they'd get out of here with all the guards he had posted at the exits and Schlechter on their trail.

♫ ♫ ♫

Rolf eased open the door leading into the opera café. Only every third light fixture glowed, and chairs were stacked on top of the dozen or so round tables. He wondered if they'd be able to access the exit to the foyer.

He turned to Sylvia. "Stay here and don't let this door close until you see me open the one over there."

A few quick steps brought him to the door across the room. It was not locked. He waved at Sylvia, and they were on their way up the circular staircase to the foyer. When they made the last turn, Rolf stopped to look and listen. Their timing seemed perfect. A throng of theatergoers streamed toward the main exit. Satisfied that Sylvia's hat and coat were in place, he motioned her to follow. At the top of the stairs he waited until she was by his side and then fell in with the pace of the crowd heading for the exit.

Two men on each side of the double doors were studying the departing patrons. Passing them, Rolf looked straight ahead and hoped Sylvia would do the same. In seconds that seemed to stretch into minutes, they were both outside. He led her to the parked rental car. As he pulled the Opel away from the curb, he took a deep breath.

Rolf slapped his palm against the steering wheel. "We made it! Now for a good night's sleep in West Berlin." When Sylvia didn't respond to his exuberant relief, he glanced over at her. "What's the matter, aren't you excited?"

She looked pensive. Finally, she said, "Rolf, we need to go to Henkelstraße 97 . . . now."

Although he'd heard her perfectly, he asked, "What? It's eleven o'clock. You're not serious!"

"Rolf, we must find out tonight what Dobnik wanted us to know, before the Stasi does. And the last place they'll be looking for us is in East Berlin."

"It's too dangerous. We barely made it out of the opera house."

"You know Dobnik has that file on me. I have to do everything I can to find it." She paused. "I have no right to ask you to do this. If you want us to go to West Berlin, I'll come back in the morning."

She was right. To have any chance of beating the Stasi to Dobnik's cache, they couldn't waste a second.

Chapter Thirty-Seven

"They've vanished," Schlechter admitted to Frantz, who was pacing in the foyer as the last patrons filed out the door. "We've searched the entire underground passageway. There is no sign of them anywhere."

Frantz stopped pacing and froze Schlechter with an icy snarl. "Major, I'm not interested in where they are not. I'm interested in where they are."

The general resumed his trek.

"They must have gone down the basement stairs to the café and somehow managed to sneak out the main entrance." Schlechter wanted to add that the general's Stasi guards had let them through, that it was their fault and not his, but thought better of it. The general was not in the mood for justifications.

Frantz's jaw muscle pulsed. "All right, if you're so smart that you've figured out how they got away, you can sure as hell figure out where they are. Does West Berlin perhaps sound right to you?"

Schlechter thought it wise not to respond.

"Go to her dressing room and get me the folder," Frantz barked.

"General, I've already checked. It's no longer where I hid it. I searched the entire room. It's gone."

"What! Are you telling me you've not only lost them but the file as well?"

Again Schlechter did not answer. It was not really a question.

"What a disaster!" The general stepped in front of Schlechter and stabbed his index finger into his chest. "Go talk to Dobnik's ex-wife and daughter. Find out where he kept his stash and get it."

"Yes, General. I'll get on it first thing in the morning."

"No, you get on it right now. It's only eleven. If you hurry, you might even catch them before they go to bed. Take the two officers at the main entrance with you. Go!"

At Frantz's command and wave of the hand, Schlechter turned on his heels and marched out of the opera house. Collecting the two guards stationed at the exit, he tried not to think that it was their fault Mazzoni and companion had slipped through the net. Instead, he needed to focus on whom to visit first—ex-wife or daughter.

♫ ♫ ♫

"There's a map in the glove box," Rolf told Sylvia, keeping his eye on the brisk opera traffic crossing Bebelplatz. "I know how to get to Alexanderplatz. It's just over a kilometer. But you'll have to find Henkelstraße for me."

Sylvia had opened the Berlin map before he finished the sentence. She looked in the street index and then folded it to a particular section. Karl-Liebknecht-Straße, on which he was now driving east, seemed to provide enough light for her.

"Found it," Sylvia declared, triumph in her voice. "It's on the other side of Alexanderplatz."

"East?"

"Yes."

Within a few minutes, Rolf drove the Opel through the square. Sylvia directed him through several turns onto a small side street lined with apartment buildings. They almost missed Henkelstraße 97, a white three-story house hidden among taller gray buildings. Rolf squeezed the Opel into a tiny spot a few cars past the entrance on the opposite side of the street.

He reached into the back seat for his overcoat. A minute later they stood at the entrance to Number 97. The dark brown wooden door featured an oblong frosted-glass window, beyond which lay darkness. He had not thought to bring his flashlight from the car, but a streetlamp a few meters away illuminated the building façade. Before he could study the nametags on the house wall, Sylvia whispered, "An Erika Dobnik lives on the top floor."

She held her index finger over the bell next to the name she'd just read, looking at him. He glanced up at the three windows on the top floor. They were dark, as were the apartments on the floors below. He nodded, and she pushed the button. A faint high-pitch bell sounded from above. All remained dark and quiet. Sylvia positioned her finger over the button again, but Rolf put up his hand. As he did, light reflected from the top floor corner window. Then a lamp above the entrance came on, blinding Rolf. He stepped back and peered up as he heard a window open.

A female voice called down, "Who is it?"

He shielded his eyes against the light, but could see only a silhouette leaning out of an upper-story window.

Sylvia shouted, "Frau Dobnik?"

After a pause, the woman asked, "What do you want?"

"Heinz Dobnik sent us."

Rolf heard the window close. Then a buzzer sounded at the front door. He pushed the door inward and held it for Sylvia to enter. They climbed the well-lit staircase. A woman, not yet twenty in Rolf's estimation, clutched a pink dressing gown as she stood in a half-open door at the top of the stairs. Her short, blonde hair was disheveled. They'd probably gotten her out of bed. Sylvia introduced herself, then Rolf.

The woman motioned for them to enter while she threw nervous glances down the stairs before following them in and closing the door. She pointed to a vinyl-covered brown sofa that stood along the wall opposite the window. Rolf felt the thin carpet under his soles, a far cry from the lush carpeting in Stein's office. For an East German apartment, the living room was quite spacious, accommodating, in addition to the coach, a small table and four chairs in the center, a television and radio on one wall, and two easy chairs on the other. All the furniture looked flimsy and cheap, reminding him of college rental furniture in the United States. He saw no evidence that anyone else lived with her, and wondered how a young, single woman had come by living quarters considered luxurious by East German standards. Being the daughter of a Stasi officer might have something to do with it. He sat next to Sylvia on the worn couch surface.

"You're his daughter?" Sylvia asked, mirroring his assumption.

She nodded, taking a seat in the easy chair next to the sofa.

Rolf asked, "Should we listen to some music?"

"No, it's not necessary. My father always sweeps . . ." Her demeanor darkened, and now in the living room light Rolf noticed her puffy eyes. "He swept this apartment for bugs when he came by yesterday evening. I think it's safe for us to talk."

"Your father was here last night?" Rolf asked.

"Yes."

"Have you seen him since? He was supposed to meet me this afternoon but didn't show."

Erika Dobnik looked down. "He's dead."

333

Sylvia gasped. After a long silence she said, "I'm so sorry."

Rolf wanted to comfort her, but couldn't think of anything to say that wouldn't sound hollow.

Without looking up, Dobnik's daughter spoke in a matter-of-fact tone. "He was found this afternoon in his garage, slumped over the steering wheel of his car. He'd been shot in the back of the head." She sounded like an automaton. Rolf guessed she'd long since cried herself out of all emotion.

"Is there anything we can do?" Rolf heard himself ask, though he had no idea what that might be.

Erika continued, as if she hadn't heard his question. "The police came by this afternoon. They said it was a robbery gone bad, but I don't believe them. I know it has to do with his job."

"Do you mind if we ask you some questions about that?"

Sylvia looked at Rolf in disbelief, probably thinking him incredibly insensitive.

Erika must have caught the gesture. "It's all right. My father gave me specific instructions. He told me to expect you if something should happen to him." She took a deep breath. "We were estranged for several years. I blamed him for my parents' divorce. I was a teenager, and I judged him."

Rolf thought of his seven-year-old daughter, Ashley, who'd shown signs of blaming him for divorcing her mother.

"But lately I came to realize it was not that simple." She took another deep breath. "I'm babbling on about family matters that don't concern you. My father told me he was going on an assignment and might not see me for a long time. I suspected there was more to it, but did not pry. He obviously wanted to protect me by not telling me what he was really up to."

She stood. "When he came by last night, he asked me to do a favor for him." Without further explanation, she walked through a door into another room.

Rolf and Sylvia remained sitting. She clutched her overcoat tighter. He surmised it was not only the cold apartment but also the news about Dobnik that made her shiver. Neither spoke.

Erika returned carrying a small box, which she handed to Rolf. "He left this for you."

Rolf looked at the combination padlock. Before he could ask, she said, "The number is 3-9-7-1, my parents' wedding date." She hesitated and then explained. "My father wanted to join the communist cause after he graduated from Free University. He came to East Berlin where he met my mother. She was several months pregnant with me when they married."

Rolf had only been half listening while he dialed the numbers. He pulled open the lock and lifted the lid. The box held a map, a chart, two photographs, and a key. Erika motioned them to the table where Rolf could spread out the map. As he laid it across the surface, he saw that it showed Berlin and its surroundings.

Erika leaned over the map. "Are you familiar with Wandlitz?"

"I've heard of it. The compound for the party bosses is there."

She pointed to a suburb north of the city. "This is the Waldsiedlung Wandlitz, where Honecker and the big shots live. You don't want to go near there. It's still heavily guarded by the Stasi." She moved her finger in a northwesterly direction. "Here is the town of Wandlitz, about two kilometers from the Forest Settlement. That's where my father's cottage is."

Rolf noticed the red mark to which she was pointing. "It's about a thirty-minute drive on the autobahn. The highway route is more direct, but it takes a little longer. On the other hand, the autobahn goes right by the Forest Settlement, so your chances of running into Stasi security are much higher. The address of the cottage is Feldweg 35. It's the last one on that street."

She reached into the box Rolf had set on the table and pulled out the key, the drawing, and the two photos. "This is the key to the cottage. He said you'd figure out what the drawing meant."

"Who are the men in the photos?" Sylvia asked.

"Two Stasi officers. The older one is Brigadier General Holger Frantz. He is . . . he was my father's boss. The younger man is Major Boris Schlechter. My father wanted me to tell you to look out for these two. He suspected Frantz was setting him up and Schlechter is his henchman." She hesitated. "I believe Schlechter murdered my father."

Rolf studied the pictures for a few seconds before passing them to Sylvia. He recognized the younger man as the one who'd come out of Sylvia's room and followed them into the costume shop. The beefy face and cold eyes staring out of deep sockets were not easily forgotten.

As if she'd read his thoughts, Erika said, "I expect they'll pay me a visit in the morning."

"So we should drive to Wandlitz now," Rolf proposed.

"It's too difficult to find your way in the dark. But be sure you get there at daybreak. You'll need the combination I gave you for this lock, 3-9-7-1."

Remembering that Europeans put day ahead of month in listing dates, he asked, "Your parents' wedding day was the third day of September, 1971?"

"That's it."

He noticed Sylvia silently repeating the numbers to herself. Then she looked at Dobnik's daughter. "What are you going to tell the Stasi?"

"My father warned me they would question me. He didn't want me to know any details. He said to tell them ·about his cottage in Wandlitz, since they probably already know about it. That's why you must go there first thing in the morning, before the Stasi shows up."

She put everything back in the box. Rolf replaced the lock, and they took their cue to leave. As they walked to the door, Sylvia said, "I don't know how we can thank you. Is there anything we can do for you?"

Erika regarded her for a long moment. "Just make sure that whatever my father wanted to accomplish gets done."

Rolf assured her, "We'll do our best."

He gave Sylvia a nudge, but she wasn't finished. "Will you be all right with the Stasi?"

"I think so," replied Erika. "I can tell them only what my father said to me. The Stasi won't be around much longer, you know . . . and the same goes for the party bosses."

"I hope you're right," Sylvia said as she followed Rolf out the door.

The Opel's engine cranked a few times before it started in the cold night air. As he maneuvered the car along Henkelstraße, Rolf noticed it was half an hour before midnight. He stepped on the gas.

"In a hurry to get to the hotel?"

"In a hurry, yes, but we're not going to the hotel."

She jerked her head toward him. "You mean . . . you've heard what Erika said. It's too difficult in the dark."

"Sylvia, if we want that suitcase and your file, we can't wait till tomorrow. You can bet the Stasi won't."

♫ ♫ ♫

Trying to suppress his frustration, Schlechter consoled himself that the visit with Dobnik's ex-wife hadn't been a total waste of time. She hadn't learned of his death and Schlechter did not enlighten her. Still bitter about the divorce, she was more likely to rat on him as long as she thought he was among the living. After quizzing her for half an hour, he was satisfied she knew nothing of

Dobnik's clandestine activities. He must have started the illicit copying of Stasi documents after the divorce. At least she'd confirmed the daughter's current address and told him how to get there. She also mentioned a cottage Dobnik had acquired after the divorce. The daughter would know where it was.

"Do either of you know where Henkelstraße is?" he asked as he got into the backseat of the Wartburg.

He drew blank stares from the lieutenant behind the wheel and the captain sitting next to him. "All right, head for Alexanderplatz, and I'll direct you from there."

The driver was moving too slow to suit him. "What are you waiting for? I haven't got all night. Step on it!"

"Yes, Major."

A few minutes after midnight, Schlechter rang the doorbell of Erika Dobnik. He was surprised to see light shining from the windows of her top-floor apartment. She buzzed him in after he identified himself. He left the lieutenant in the car and the captain inside the front entrance. There was no need for them to learn the details of this operation.

She made him show his identification. Although he'd never met her, he could have sworn she knew who he was. Her eyes were red, probably from crying. She must know about her father's death. He couldn't decide whether the way she looked at him, which she did only now and then, signaled fear or hatred, or a mixture of the two.

"Frau Dobnik, you know about your father's death?"

"Yes."

"I'm going to have to ask you some questions about him." Without giving her a chance to protest, he started right in. "When's the last time you saw him?"

"He came by yesterday evening."

So far so good, he thought. She seemed forthright.

"What was the purpose of his visit?"

"He told me he was leaving on a foreign assignment and wouldn't see me for a while. So he came to say goodbye."

Schlechter suppressed a smirk as he considered the idea that absconding with Stasi secrets to the West German intelligence service could be called "a foreign assignment."

"Have you kept in regular contact with him since your parents' divorce?"

"No, I was angry with him at first. But during the last few months we've been seeing each other occasionally.

"Did he ever tell you about his job?"

"I know he worked for the Stasi, but he never told me what he did."

"Did you notice any change in his behavior after he began visiting you?"

"Major, why are you asking me all these questions about my father?" The mistrust in her voice and eyes was palpable.

"We're trying to find out who killed him."

Though he had lied with ease, he sensed her disbelief.

"What else can I help you with?" she asked in a way that did not invite further questions.

Unperturbed, Schlechter probed further. "Where is your father's cottage?"

She did not appear surprised by the question. "In Wandlitz, at Feldweg 35."

"You've been to it?"

"Yes, I visited him there a few times this summer."

"When did he acquire it?"

"Last spring. I don't know if he owned it or rented it."

"Did you ever stay overnight?"

"No, I went on a Saturday or Sunday and always came back to the city at the end of the day."

"Did you ever observe anything unusual there?'

"What do you mean?"

"Did your father ever have something with him he seemed secretive about?"

She looked at him with a quizzical expression, as if she still didn't understand what he was asking. His instinct told him she was feigning ignorance.

"Can you be more specific?"

"For instance, did he have papers he kept you from seeing?"

"Not that I can recall."

"Did he have any locked storage there?"

"Not that I know of."

"Were there any areas in the cabin or yard you weren't permitted to enter?"

"No."

"Did he have any kind of workspace there?"

"There's a shed in the yard, but not really a workspace."

"Ever catch him putting something away when you arrived?"

"No."

"Did he ever ask you to keep anything for him?"

"Never."

"You can give me directions to the Wandlitz cottage?"

While she wrote them down, Schlechter reviewed the interrogation in his mind. She'd appeared straightforward, yet there was something in her demeanor that gave him pause. An interrogation at Stasi headquarters might be in order. But not tonight. He needed to get to Wandlitz. Since he'd not found anything in Dobnik's garage and apartment, the stash was probably hidden in that cottage.

At half past midnight he was back in the car. He told the driver to head for Wandlitz and not to worry about speed limits. They should be there by one o'clock.

♫ ♫ ♫

Sylvia opened the box's combination lock and took out the map and drawing. She scanned the Opel's interior for a moment. This basic model rental car did not have individual lights for driver and passenger, but only one bulb in the center of the ceiling for the entire interior.

"You have a flashlight in the car?"

"It's in the glove box, under the owner's manual."

Sylvia moved the light beam around the map on her lap. She was still engrossed in her study when he approached Alexanderplatz. "Do I go back onto Karl-Liebknecht-Straße?"

"Yes, but in the opposite direction. Turn right and drive north. It'll run into Prenzlauer Allee."

He'd been driving north heading out of the city for a few minutes when Sylvia looked up. "We have a decision to make. Do we take the autobahn or the highway?"

"This time of night the highway may be just as quick, and I think we ought to give the Stasi security forces at the Forest Settlement a wide berth."

"Okay, then stay on B109 all the way through Basdorf to Wandlitz."

He had no trouble locating B109 and following it into Wandlitz. The traffic was so sparse they entered the southern outskirts of the town at only a few minutes after midnight. After passing Basdorf, Sylvia had returned the Berlin map to the glove box and had studied Dobnik's chart. When they turned onto the dark country roads, he had to stop a few times and ask her to shine the flashlight on street signs so they didn't miss a turn.

Finally they were rolling down Feldweg, a small country lane. Rolf cut the headlights as he remembered Erika saying that Dobnik's cottage was all the way at the end. The cabins along the lane were dark. Weekend retreats for city dwellers, Rolf surmised, and probably not occupied during the week, especially in late November. He stopped in front of the last building, which looked like all the others—small, one-story, gray mortar exterior with two small windows facing the street.

Sylvia reached for the car's door handle. "Not yet," Rolf told her. "I don't like this. There is only one way out of here. Does Dobnik's drawing show parallel streets?"

She took the paper down from the sun visor where she'd stored it, and after fiddling with the flashlight for a moment, announced, "There is a street along the houses in the back of these. Go back down Feldweg, turn left onto Tannenstraße and make an immediate left onto . . ." She squinted. "It's called Waldpfad."

He put the Opel in first gear, and driving without headlights, turned around at the end of the lane. Lining Waldpfad were cottages identical to those they'd seen along Feldweg, and likewise dark. The lane dead-ended at the edge of a forest with a hiking trail taking off into the woods. Hence the name Forest Path. Rolf turned the car around so it faced out. Although the cottage across from Dobnik's looked deserted, they retraced on foot the route they had just driven rather than cutting through the back yard and climbing over the fence. The walk took less than two minutes.

The door to Dobnik's cottage opened after two turns of the key, the type of secure lock Germans preferred. Although the windows had shutters and curtains, they did not turn on any lights for fear they would be visible from the outside. Instead they sat at the kitchen table and studied the back side of Dobnik's paper by flashlight. It seemed easy enough. To locate the buried suitcase, they had only to look for disturbed soil among lilac bushes.

"What about tools for digging?" Rolf asked.

Sylvia pointed to the drawing. "There is a shed." As she spoke, the flashlight began to flicker. "The batteries are going."

He took the light out of her hand and shook it, causing it to become brighter for a second. Then it dimmed again. "Better get started." He went to the patio door, drew back the curtains, and after a momentary search located the nylon cord that lifted the outside shutters.

"Let me have the light back for a minute." She walked over and took it out of his hand before he could protest. As he opened the glass door, he heard her rummaging through drawers. The next minute she stood behind him, a flashlight in each hand. "I couldn't imagine him not keeping one of these."

He took the weaker light from her and walked across the lawn to a metal shed. As he'd expected, a combination lock hung from its door. He dialed Dobnik's wedding date, and the lock sprung open. In Sylvia's strong light beam he saw the pickax and shovel they'd need. "See if you can locate the spot by the lilacs marked on Dobnik's drawing. I'll bring these."

She backed out of the tool shed. When he emerged carrying both tools, he saw her standing a few meters away, shining light upon some fresh looking dirt. This might be easier than he had thought. His delight was short-lived. There'd been a freezing rain since Dobnik had buried his loot, and the ground was rock solid. The digging became very hard work after the initial few centimeters of top soil. Rolf started out swinging the pickax with his overcoat on, but soon discarded the garment.

While Sylvia used the shovel to remove the soil he'd loosened, he rested from the strenuous labor. The recovery periods grew longer. Being in shape for running did not equate with the ability to do the physical labor of a ditch digger, he realized. He almost lost his grip when the ax hit a rock. Sylvia insisted on trying her hand while he rested. As he licked a blister on his right hand, she disappeared into the shed and returned with a pair of work gloves. "They're men's size."

Rolf glanced at his watch. One o'clock. They must have been digging for over thirty minutes and had only a few centimeters to show for it. It was during Sylvia's turn that they heard a thump.

"Stop!" He picked up the shovel and scraped off the dirt she'd just loosened. A green plastic cover became visible. He ran the shovel along the edges and felt the outline of what had to be a suitcase. As he scraped off more dirt, a handle came into view. He pulled upward, but the object didn't budge. Without a word, he took the pickax from Sylvia and cut around the edges. The earth gave way more easily than before, and after a few minutes' work, he'd loosened the soil enough to pull out a case in a plastic cover. It was so heavy he almost asked Sylvia to help him, but managed once he had it halfway out of the hole.

He set the load on the lawn, stripped off the cover, exposing a gray molded plastic suitcase with a single combination lock. Sylvia took the pickax and hacked away at the dirt in the hole.

"What are you doing?"

"Just making sure there isn't more than one."

"You're always thinking, aren't you?"

"Looks like one is all we get," she replied, ignoring his compliment.

"All right, let's cover up this hole, put everything back, and get out of here." No sooner had he finished the sentence than they heard engine noise coming down the lane in front. Headlights reflected off walls and illuminated tree branches, the light beam spreading out into the side yards between the cottages. Rolf and Sylvia stood transfixed as the noise grew louder, then abruptly stopped in front of Dobnik's cottage.

Sylvia looked at him in horror. "The Stasi?"

Rolf did not respond, but turned off his flashlight, and listened into the darkness. When he heard a car door close, he pointed to the back fence. "This way."

He dropped the shovel, slipped on his overcoat, grabbed the suitcase, and ran after Sylvia who was already at the fence. It was head high. Sylvia jumped down to the other side as he arrived. His attempt at scaling the fence was another matter altogether. He heard car doors slamming followed by heavy footsteps and rapping on a door— Dobnik's front door, no doubt.

"Come *on* Rolf," Sylvia whispered.

Holding the case in his right hand, he tried to get a toehold half way up the chain link, gripping the top of the fence to boost himself over. All seemed to go well until his shoe slipped, causing him to fall back onto the grass.

"The suitcase first." Sylvia's urgency had turned to desperation. They heard a noise at the side of Dobnik's cottage that sounded like someone climbing into the back yard.

Rolf heaved the case up to the top of the fence, and with all his strength pushed it over. Sylvia looked as if she were going to catch it, but thought better of it and moved out of the way. It landed at her side with a thud. Rolf could now see reflections from flashlights inside the cottage and along the side yard.

He flung himself at the fence and pulled his body over the top so forcefully that he lost control, tumbling onto the grass on the other side. He felt a dull pain in his left hand and wrist. Only jammed, he told himself. As he jumped to his feet, he saw Sylvia carrying the heavy load toward Waldpfad and their car. By the time he caught up with her, there were shouts behind them. Rolf understood just enough to realize their pursuers had discovered the hole and the discarded cover.

♫ ♫ ♫

When the driver turned off the engine and cut the lights, Schlechter looked toward Dobnik's dark cottage. Then he saw a faint light beam toward the rear of the building. He tore open the rear door, jumped out, and in his excitement slammed it shut.

"There is someone there. Lieutenant, try the side. Captain, come with me."

The light went out as he ran toward the front door. His comrades were as careless as he had been in slamming the car doors. Having announced their presence this way, there was no longer any point in being quiet. He rapped on the door, and as an afterthought depressed the handle. The door opened. The captain was now at his side. They both got out their flashlights and stepped into the dark cottage. Their light beams bounced around the living room and the adjacent kitchen. They quickly examined the bedroom and bath.

Returning to the living area, Schlechter noticed the patio door curtain had been drawn and the glass door stood ajar by a few centimeters. He slid the door open. As he and the captain rushed across the patio and onto the lawn, the lieutenant came running from the side yard. All three shone their beams across the grass, first noticing a tool shed and then an uprooted bush. As they moved closer, they spotted the open hole.

"Son of a bitch!" shouted Schlechter.

"Someone uncovered the treasure," the lieutenant volunteered, irony in his voice.

"Shut up!" Schlechter was seething. He pointed his flashlight beam around the back yard and into adjoining yards. His underlings did the same. There was nothing to see but cottages and yards.

♫ ♫ ♫

Rolf's heart stopped when another fence rose before them, separating them from the street and their car.

"There is a gate," Sylvia whispered.

Though locked, it was so low that they had no trouble climbing over it as they passed the case between them. They were at the car in a few seconds. Rolf searched for the keys in his coat pocket, then remembered he'd put them in his left trouser pocket. With shaking fingers he fumbled around the keyhole until he managed to insert the key and open the driver's door, then hesitated. If they were stopped, they'd be safer with the case in the trunk. But he couldn't afford the extra time. He unlatched the rear door lock, opened the door, and tossed the case onto the backseat. Sylvia jumped in. He eased the Opel down the lane, praying the Stasi hadn't thought of patrolling this area.

"Can we avoid going back the way we came?"

"Yes, turn left." Sylvia pointed ahead. "We'll be off Dobnik's drawing, but we'll find our way somehow."

Approaching Tannenstraße, he looked to the right, and to his relief did not see any vehicles. Keeping the headlights off and driving in second gear to keep engine noise down, he eased around the corner to the left and shifted up to third gear. The engine strained, groaning at the low torque, but just when Rolf thought it might stall, it pulled through.

♫ ♫ ♫

Schlechter hissed, "Sshh!" He thought he'd heard a vehicle behind the cabins on the opposite row. "Get in the car!"

Back in the Trabant, Schlechter ordered the driver to speed down Feldweg, turn left and left again into the parallel lane. The street where he'd heard a car only moments ago was now deserted. Resigned, he had the lieutenant turn around and stop at the corner of Tannenstraße.

"Turn off the lights and motor."

After the driver complied, Schlechter rolled down his window and looked and listened into the dark, eerily quiet countryside. He sat motionless, his head spinning with speculations about who had stolen the cache. Was there someone in cahoots with Dobnik who had gotten wind of his death and decided to abscond with the documents? Or had Dobnik made a deal with the West German intelligence service, telling them where to find his hoard? Finally, he thought of the remotest of all the possibilities: the amateurs, the opera singer and her friend. Well, whoever they were, they'd gotten away for now.

The Forest Settlement Wandlitz, with 140 Stasi security personnel guaranteeing the safety of party functionaries, was only two kilometers southeast. He regretted not having requested reinforcements from them to cut off all escape routes. It was too late now.

"Drive back to the cottage," he instructed the driver. All they could do tonight was to turn Dobnik's place upside down in the hope of finding something. But even as he entered the building once more, he knew the intruders had made off with the only thing that mattered to General Frantz. He ordered the two men to search the place while he wondered what he'd say to the general in the morning.

♫ ♫ ♫

"We're off the map now," Sylvia told Rolf. "Turn right the next chance you get. As long as we can keep going in that direction and then turn back to the right again, we should be able to find our way to the south end of Wandlitz. I can get us back from there."

The first turn came up fast, but he had to drive over a kilometer before he could turn right again. After he did, Rolf stopped the car on the dark country road to lock the suitcase in the trunk. Back behind the wheel, he switched on the headlights. Beyond this point, they'd arouse more suspicion driving without them.

"That was a close call, the second one this evening." Rolf wiped his forehead although it was too cold for sweating.

Sylvia discarded the coat they'd taken from the opera wardrobe room and tossed it into the rear of the car. He could hear her shallow breathing, as she probably reflected on how close they'd come to capture.

"You scared me when you couldn't get over that fence." She looked straight ahead. "What are we going to do now?"

He looked at her profile, wanting to tell her they'd be going to the hotel in West Berlin he had booked for a good night's sleep. He now realized that was no longer an option. Even though the East German borders with the West were reported to be wide open within days of the fall of the Wall, they could not count on that. If their luck held, they might be able to slip across the border between East and West Germany tonight. By tomorrow it could be too late.

"Sylvia, an hour ago I would have said, let's get a good night's sleep. With what's happened, I believe we have to get out of Berlin and East Germany tonight."

She turned to face him. "We're not flying back to Stuttgart?"

"No, even if the Stasi aren't watching the airports yet, you can bet that Schmidt's people and the Brits are. I've got enough adrenalin coursing through my body to keep me awake driving all night, and you can sleep."

"What about our suitcases and the copies at the Zoo station?"

"We'll take care of that as soon as we're back in West Berlin. But first we need to find our way out of here."

Sylvia's sense of direction proved accurate, and after a few kilometers they drove into the south end of Wandlitz and from there onto the B109. After a thirty-minute drive on deserted highways, they approached the western part of

Berlin, where he no longer needed Sylvia's navigational help. He worried about the kind of inspection they might face at two in the morning when the border crossing was likely to be deserted. To his relief he saw several cars ahead of them as they approached the border station. Just when he thought they'd be waived through yet again, the young man in police uniform raised his palm indicating for them to stop.

Rolf fished his passport out of his breast coat pocket and took Sylvia's from her outstretched hand. He rolled down his window and started to hand over the passports when the guard nodded and then motioned them through. Apparently he'd recognized their nationality by the color of their passports and had no interest in examining them.

As soon as they were in West Berlin, Sylvia said, "You were nervous about that."

"You noticed. I thought for sure we'd be checked closely at this time of night."

"Lucky for us that all this excitement about the opening of the Wall keeps more people up till early morning."

After a lengthy silence, Sylvia asked, "Rolf, what was the deal with the dressing room? Why did we have to get out right then?"

"Because I saw the Stasi man, the young one in the photos Erika gave us, leave your room, and I found what he had hidden in your dresser. If you reach behind my seat you'll feel a folder."

Sylvia contorted her body, and with an exhalation turned back with the folder in her hand. She flipped through the pages illuminated by her flashlight. "I don't understand. This looks like the same stuff Dobnik left in my hotel room."

"It is." Rolf looked over at her. "Your British friends were right. Schlechter was setting you up. He planned on arresting you after the final curtain calls."

She slapped her forehead. "I get it. As far as the Stasi knew, we'd be waiting for Dobnik to deliver his final drop. That's why Dobnik moved up the time." She frowned. "But why did you put it in the car?"

"Why not? Anything was safer than leaving it in the dressing room."

Apparently satisfied, Sylvia turned around and looked out the window. "Nice neighborhood."

He parked in front of a run-down hotel. "Sorry, but this was the only place I could find close to the Zoo Station that was not likely to ask for our passports. I could tell you that it's clean, but that's a moot point, since we can't afford to spend the night. Let's collect our luggage and head for the West German border."

She got out of the car. While he locked the doors, Sylvia moved to the rear of the Opel and stood by the trunk. "I want to see what's in the suitcase we risked our lives for."

Feeling time pressure, he wanted to say no. On the other hand, they needed to know whether what they had was worth transporting to the West. He opened the trunk and lifted out the suitcase. "Okay, but just long enough to get an idea what we've got. We don't have much time."

Chapter Thirty-Eight

Sylvia rang the bell on the counter twice before a sleepy night clerk in a rumpled uniform shuffled in from a side door and handed her and Rolf their room keys. Apparently eager to resume the dozing they had interrupted, he mumbled, "Gute Nacht," and left.

They went to Rolf's room. He opened the combination lock on Dobnik's suitcase. Sylvia stared in amazement at the *Carmen* score, which looked identical to the one Dobnik had hidden in her nightgown. She leafed through its pages. They were all intact. Dobnik must have planned to use it for a later drop. Rolf picked up two folders on top of the pile of papers strewn loosely about. After a brief glance, he handed one to her and opened the other. Her heart raced when she read the label. Dobnik had been true to his word. She held in her hand the Stasi file bearing her name.

One look confirmed that the Stasi had kept tabs on her during all the years since she'd taken that ill-advised trip with Horst Kreuzer to East Berlin. There were references to Kreuzer's receiving training at the secret Stasi Base Briesen, just as the British agents had claimed. And her suitor at the Italian Riviera had indeed been a Stasi Romeo.

Her stomach tightened when she read comments tagging her as a prospect for recruitment as a Stasi spy. When her eyes fell on a statement that she seemed sympathetic to the communist cause, she hissed, "Those lying bastards!"

She looked up self-consciously. Rolf appeared not to have heard. Mouth wide open, he was engrossed in the folder he was holding. Sylvia shut her file. She'd seen enough. The Stasi had not only collected data on her comings and goings, but had added bogus prejudicial comments. She could not let this become public.

Finally, Rolf closed his file and asked if she wanted to return hers to the suitcase before he locked it. "I won't look at it," he assured her. She hesitated but then gave him the file, surprised at the trust she placed in him nowadays. After he replaced the folders and the score book, Rolf scrambled the combination lock and picked up his and Dobnik's suitcase. They stopped by her room for her to retrieve hers. This time they did not ring the bell, but dropped their room keys in a slot on the side of the counter.

With the suitcases safely stored in the trunk, Rolf maneuvered the Opel through quiet early morning streets. The heater was blowing cold, and Sylvia snuggled into her coat against the car's frigid interior.

"What do you want to do about the Brits?" Rolf asked, keeping his eyes on the road. "Do you want to tell them where to pick up their copies?"

"Yes, that might get them off my back, at least for a while. No need to tell them about the suitcase."

Rolf chuckled. "I suspect they'll find out about it soon enough, but we'll worry about that if and when it happens."

At two thirty in the morning, he found a parking place reasonably close to the Zoo train station. He backed into the space and applied the brake, but did not turn off the engine. He turned toward her. "I want you to sit in the driver's seat, keep the engine running with all the doors locked, and watch out for anyone approaching."

"You're expecting trouble?" She sensed an edge creeping into her voice.

"Let's just play it safe." He got out and motioned for her to climb over the gearshift. "If you see anything suspicious, drive away and keep circling around the station. I will look for you over there." He pointed toward the intersection on the station's southwest corner.

By the time she made it into the driver's seat and depressed the door locks, Rolf had disappeared into the building. She fought the impulse to lean back into the headrest, thinking a cup of coffee would be nice to overcome her fatigue. Every now and then, a person hurried in or out of the station, bundled up against the chilly morning air. Only two passed close enough to the Opel to make Sylvia tense up. During her vigilance she periodically thought Rolf was late in returning.

A policeman walked in front of her car, stopped and pointed toward the hood. She took a panicky breath. What did he want? Should she drive off? No, running from the police would not be smart. He pointed again, and she realized Rolf had left on the headlights. Anxious, she scanned the instrument panel, located the light switch, and turned it. The policeman nodded and walked off.

She took a deep breath to slow her pounding heart. Her pulse spiked again when she heard a rap at the driver's door window. It was Rolf. She unlocked the door and clambered over into the passenger seat. She was wondering why he was so slow in getting in, when she noticed he was balancing a tall white paper bag on top of several folders. He handed the bag to her, dropped the folders onto the rear seat, and closed and locked the door. She found the coffee aroma that pervaded the car's interior comforting.

"I'll take one of those coffees," he muttered as he drove out into the street. "I hope you like day-old croissants. The train station café didn't have a lot to choose from at this time of night."

She opened the drinking slot on the plastic lid on one of the paper cups and handed it to him. "Where are we going? Do you need me to navigate?"

"The autobahn to Hof. I could use some help until we pick up the signs." He slurped the hot coffee.

She set the bag on the floor mat and unfolded the city map. Between giving directions now and then, she sipped her coffee and munched on a croissant. Rolf asked her to hold his pastry, then without warning, pulled into a parking spot on the outskirts of West Berlin.

"What's the matter?"

"Nothing. I've read that within days after the Wall was opened, border controls on the routes to the West became quite lax, but just to be sure, I want to put these folders out of sight."

He withdrew the key from the ignition and took the folders. She could not see him behind the open trunk lid, but heard him fiddle with one of the suitcases. He'd stopped at the right time, since they came upon the East German border only a few minutes later. She held her breath as she looked for a border patrol, then exhaled as the lone guard waved them through. Rolf had been right. The border was essentially wide open.

On the autobahn toward Hof, he accelerated until the speedometer needle hovered at one hundred kilometers. Relaxing his foot on the gas pedal, he turned toward her. "We're on our way."

"You're keeping pretty close to the speed limit. Aren't we in a hurry?"

"On these designated routes to the West, the East Germans strictly enforce a hundred kilometers per hour speed limit. It's their way of collecting Western currency to help pump up their lagging economy. The last thing we need is to get stopped for speeding." He put the cup between his thighs. "I'll take that croissant now."

She peeled the waxed paper far enough back to expose the top of the buttery pastry before handing it to him. "Are we going back to Stuttgart? I am singing there tomorrow evening, you know."

"Hmm. I didn't realize your next performance was so soon." He chewed on a bite." I don't think it would be wise to head for Stuttgart right now. We may have a few people looking for us there. First, we must go through Dobnik's suitcase and assess what we have and what to do with it."

She did not like what she heard. "I'm not going to miss my Stuttgart engagement."

"I wouldn't let you miss it for anything. I know it means your future. Today I thought we'd drive to some place in Bavaria close enough to Schmidt's headquarters in Pullach to allow us to deliver the suitcase, if that's what we decide to do. But it shouldn't be too far from Stuttgart. Any suggestions?"

"Pullach is just south of Munich?"

"Yes."

"I know a comfortable guesthouse in Mittenwald. It's about an hour's drive from Munich and probably three from Stuttgart, and it's secluded." She thought for a moment. "What about the Brits?"

Rolf cracked a smile. "I left their copies in the Zoo station locker. Once we're in Bavaria, we've got a couple phone calls to make. You call the Brits, and I can't wait to find out who'll answer the phone at the number I found in the envelope Schmidt gave me for Dobnik."

It hadn't occurred to her that he'd open the envelope. Yet there was no reason not to once they learned of Dobnik's murder. She asked, "Did it have anything besides a phone number?"

"Yes, get this . . . a code phrase."

She chuckled. "This promises to be a little more fun than what we went through earlier tonight." She turned serious. "I feel torn about giving the copies to the British agents. If I don't, they could make good on their threat and publicize my . . ." She stopped, realizing she had not told Rolf about her East Berlin trip with Kreuzer. "My association with Kreuzer." She couldn't tell whether Rolf had caught the cover-up. "If I do give them the papers, they'll use the forged documents to derail unification."

"Not to worry." Rolf finished off the pastry with one big bite. He glanced at her for a second before returning his eyes to the autobahn. "I removed the pages that make Walter, the Foreign Ministry official, out to be a neo Nazi. I wouldn't like to see the British scuttle unification any more than you would."

On impulse, she squeezed his hand as it rested on the gearshift. When he looked at her in surprise, she abruptly withdrew her hand. Then she found the courage to say, "You know, Rolf, you've grown a lot."

After a long silence, he responded, "We both have."

She suppressed the urge to ask him to elaborate. Instead, she forced herself to think about what had to be done. "What do I tell the British agents?"

He handed her the butter-smeared food wrapper, empty now except for croissant flakes, and took a sip from his cup. "Tell them where to find the locker key."

"You hid it?"

He nodded. "It's in the Zoo station men's room. I'll give you the particulars before you make the call."

Tired, Sylvia leaned back into her seat. Despite the rough ride on the uneven concrete plates of the roadway, her eyelids began to droop thanks to the tires' monotonous humming, which grew ever fainter.

When she felt the car slowing, Sylvia realized she must have been dozing. Disoriented, she opened her eyes and saw flashing lights that illuminated a barrier across the roadway ahead. A guard stepped out of a small building, waiting for Rolf to roll down his window.

"Guten Morgen." Rolf sounded cheerful, as if he were well rested after a good night's sleep.

"What brings you out so early in the morning?" the young man in uniform asked. His tone was not unfriendly. Sylvia noticed the dashboard clock showed five thirty.

Rolf answered, "We need to be back at work today."

"You come from West Berlin?"

"Yes."

"What was the purpose of your trip?"

"Visiting relatives."

To Sylvia's surprise and relief, the guard neither asked to see their passports nor inspected the car's interior or trunk. "Have a safe trip." He went inside the building, and a few seconds later the barricade lifted.

Rolf eased the Opel past it and gradually accelerated. "Amazing how relaxed the border guards are now. I suppose they don't want to burn any bridges to the West, knowing they may be part of it before too long." When he reached cruising speed, he said, "But you can be sure if the Stasi had been looking for us, we would have had some trouble. Thank goodness we decided to leave tonight."

The first rest stop on the West German side appeared. Sylvia asked, "Where are we?"

"Near Hof." Rolf exited and stopped at a gas station. He opened the driver's door but turned back toward her. "Let's wait till later in the morning to make those phone calls. I'll gas up while you use the restroom, and you watch the car while I go."

She wanted to protest that she didn't really need to use the facilities. Her expression must have betrayed her thoughts, as he quickly added, "I don't want to stop again till breakfast."

He was right, but did he have to be so authoritarian about it? Groggy from her nap, she mumbled, "Yes, sir," as she pushed herself out of the passenger seat and made off toward the restaurant and gift shop.

When they were ready to leave, Sylvia offered to drive, but he refused. He obviously was in the mood for pushing ahead and drove for three hours straight. A little after eight thirty he turned into a rest stop south of Munich. He circled the parking lot until he found a spot that seemed to satisfy, probably because it would be visible through the restaurant's windows, Sylvia surmised.

They found a table that afforded them a view of the Opel. The restaurant looked like many others she'd seen along the German autobahns, featuring functional tables and chairs, not too comfortable, but adequate, windows facing the highway, and offering a plain continental breakfast or a buffet. They opted for the breakfast buffet, which would be quick. Rolf told her to go ahead while he went to the entry hall in search of a public phone.

The selection of waffles, omelets, egg dishes, sausages, and breads was surprising, but the fruit offerings were skimpy, as could be expected during the winter season in Germany. By the time Rolf reappeared, she had finished what might qualify as the biggest breakfast of her life. Her last full meal dated back to yesterday's lunch, and the narrow escapes last night had taken enormous amounts of energy. Rolf sat down with a plate overflowing with food, apparently as hungry as she'd been.

She could not read his expression. Without saying a word, he dug in. Despite her curiosity, she waited until he'd taken several big bites. "What did you find out?"

Rolf swallowed and answered, "A male voice answered the phone under 'First Class Travel.' I followed the spiel on Schmidt's note, and after he was satisfied that I must be Dobnik, he simply asked how many suitcases I had. When I said one, he responded 'three' and hung up. According to Schmidt's sheet, that means he'll be waiting at three o'clock at the Zoo by the polar bear exhibit."

"I don't understand. That doesn't tell us anything."

"At first, I thought the same thing. But then I remembered . . . I've heard that voice before."

"Not Schmidt, I gather."

"No, none other than our good friend, Kent Ferguson. Apparently, he's more than a journalist."

"I had a funny feeling about him. Remember, we picked up a tail after leaving his office. He's tied in with Schmidt or Stein somehow."

Rolf nodded. "It was no coincidence that he sat next to me on the flight over. In any case, we can assume Schmidt knows we copied Dobnik's second drop."

"I didn't pick up any clues that he knew when we delivered the papers to him at his hotel Tuesday evening."

"Don't forget, he's a professional who's been in this business for a very long time. I imagine he's learned to conceal weightier secrets than that." Rolf pushed back his empty plate. "He may not have learned about our visit to Ferguson until later. I'm sure he knows now and is looking for us."

"Are we running from him?"

"Him and the Brits." He hesitated. "And the Stasi too. Once they realize we've got Dobnik's copies and your original file, you can bet they'll pursue us no matter where we go." He looked at her. "Now would be a good time for you to call the Brits. I'll pay and watch the car while you do. The phones are next to the rest rooms." He bent forward and told her where he'd hidden the locker key.

After a quick visit to the ladies' room, she dialed the phone number on the card the agents had given her. A raspy male voice answered without identifying himself.

She took a guess. "Mr. Kingsley?"

Without confirming her identification, he replied, "That was quite a disappearing act you pulled last night. Did you get the idea from the von Trapp family in *The Sound of Music*?"

"We did what we had to do to get out of there. Your copies are in locker eighty-seven in the Zoo train station."

The sharp intake of breath told her she'd caught him off guard, if only for a moment.

"And the key?"

"Men's room, third stall, taped to the back of the toilet bowl."

"Have you given us copies of everything?"

She didn't want to answer that and needed to terminate the conversation. They'd be tracing the phone call to pinpoint her location.

"I've got to go."

"Wait. Where are you?"

She hung up and hurried back into the restaurant.

Rolf rose when he saw her. "Time to get going."

"What about Schmidt?"

"I'll call him after we've had a chance to review the contents of the suitcase in detail. From what I saw, we may have a great bargaining chip to get you your immunity letter."

"Why is that?"

He unlocked the passenger door. "I can't be sure, but the papers I looked at this morning hinted at a covert operation aimed at assassinating a higher-up in the West German government. It appears the Stasi is desperate to prevent unification."

Sylvia settled into her seat as he drove toward the autobahn access road. "That would go hand in hand with the disinformation they're spreading about the foreign ministry official, Walter."

"Exactly." Rolf spoke with emphasis while shifting through the gears.

She thought a little. "You know, I want that assurance against future blackmail. But I don't know that I want it at the cost of causing someone's murder or scuttling unification."

Rolf eased off the gas pedal at 130 kilometers per hour and glanced at her. "I think we can get your immunity assurance *and* give Schmidt the documents in time to foil the murder."

As they sped toward Mittenwald, Sylvia fervently hoped he was right.

Chapter Thirty-Nine

Everything seemed to be in order when Alfred Herrhausen exited his heavily guarded Bad Homburg residence and climbed into the backseat of the waiting company car. His chauffeur drove the armored Mercedes along residential streets on the way to the Deutsche Bank office in Frankfurt. As usual he was escorted by bodyguards in two vehicles, one in front and one behind the Mercedes. The chairman of the board of one of the most powerful banks in the world wondered how much longer he'd have to endure this special protection by the Federal Criminal Investigation Office. As a director of Daimler-Benz and personal economic advisor to Federal Chancellor Helmut Kohl, he was high on the list of potential terrorist targets.

Could these measures really protect him against the Red Army Faction? He thought of Federal Attorney General Siegfried Buback, Dresdner Bank Chairman Jürgen Pronto, Employers Association President Hanns-Martin Schleyer, and Siemens Manager Karl-Heinz Beckurts, who had all been assassinated despite tight security. And NATO Commander Alexander Haig and US General Frederick

Kroesen had barely escaped attempts on their lives. He shook his head. There was no point on dwelling on it. He was in a position to influence not only Chancellor Kohl's plans for unification of Germany, but also global economic policy, implementing his vision to forgive large amounts of debts owed by third-world nations. Yet he wondered whether the position of power he had attained at age fifty-nine was worth the risk to his life and to the safety of his family.

The dashboard clock showed a few minutes after eight thirty on this gray morning. He reminded himself of the date, November 30. In a few days he'd be in New York to deliver a speech. For a moment he thought of pulling out the pages containing his remarks from his briefcase, but decided against it. Instead he looked out on his usual route through Bad Homburg. He noticed a few meters ahead on the sidewalk a bicycle leaning against a post with a school bag on its rear luggage rack. Strange, to find a school bicycle parked on this road.

As the Mercedes passed by, there was a loud hissing sound, then a deafening explosion, a blinding fireball of searing heat, the car door caving in, metal scraps flying, pain in his upper thigh, spreading, so excruciating that he welcomed the darkness.

♫ ♫ ♫

Dieter Schmidt stepped out of the hot shower. He'd tossed in bed most of the night worrying about what had happened at the Staatsoper. No sign of Dobnik, Sylvia or Rolf and no suitcase. All he could do was to have the Berlin office check the usual things—West Berlin hotels, train stations, airports, rental car agencies, credit card charges. Unless he got a break, it might take a long time to track them. He was in the middle of drying off when the phone rang. Wrapping the bath towel around his waist, he walked to the bedside stand. He noticed it was a few minutes after nine. That had to be his boss, Karl Bauman, wanting to know if he'd gotten Dobnik's documents.

He sat on the bed and lifted the receiver. "Hallo."

"There's been another assassination." He recognized Bauman's voice.

"Who?"

"Alfred Herrhausen, Deutsche Bank Chief, about a kilometer from his home in Bad Homburg, on his way to the office this morning."

"Terrorists?"

"All signs point that way. I'm told it may have been a TNT bomb activated when Herrhausen's Mercedes interrupted a light beam."

Schmidt exhaled. "I guess Mozart's documents didn't point to this plot."

"No, only to the terrorists we hunted down in the train station yesterday."

"Herrhausen was under special protection, wasn't he?"

"A lot of good that did."

"How did they do it?"

"This was precision work by professionals. It required split-second timing to overcome the car's special armor plating, and they had to account for the bodyguards' lead vehicle."

After listening to Bauman take a few deep breaths, Schmidt responded. "Those are Stasi methods." As soon as he said it, he wished he hadn't.

Sure enough, Bauman followed up. "Looks like the Red Army Faction, and we suspect they've received Stasi training. Do you have the latest documents? They might help us track down these terrorists."

"No, something went wrong last night. I'm working on finding out what."

"Just what I wanted to hear." Schmidt could hear the frustration, bordering on disgust, in Bauman's voice. "You know what's at stake. Call me as soon as you have news."

Before Schmidt could respond, the line went dead. He dressed in a hurry. He had all of East Germany in which to locate Dobnik's suitcase, assuming it was even still there.

Chapter Forty

Brigadier General Frantz turned off the radio on his credenza. The nine o'clock morning news had brought a pleasant development: the successful assassination of the Deutsche Bank Chief Alfred Herrhausen only half an hour ago. Training Red Army Faction members at the Stasi Base Briesen had paid off. The West German terrorist organization was still viable three weeks after the fall of the Wall, raising doubts about the peaceful future of a large German state. That and the forged Walter dossier might be sufficient to scare the Western Allies away from unification.

His mood darkened as he wondered whether Dobnik had actually delivered the dossier to the opera singer. While contemplating what could have happened to those documents and others Dobnik had, his thoughts turned to why he hadn't heard from Schlechter. Hopefully, that meant he was busy tracking down Dobnik's cache. Although aware of the irony that the man he'd intended to frame as a traitor turned out to be one, he did not find it amusing.

The intercom buzzed. "Yes?"

"Major Schlechter is here," announced his secretary.

"Send him in."

The major seemed uneasy, which did not bode well. Frantz confronted him as he approached his desk. "You didn't find Dobnik's hiding place."

Schlechter made eye contact. "General, we did, but someone beat us to it."

"What! Who?"

"I'm not sure."

"Damn! I'm running out of patience, Major." Frantz shot up from his chair and began pacing. "You don't get the information out of Dobnik, you let the singer and her companion get away." He stopped and glared at Schlechter. "And now you bungled the job recovering the traitor's cache. Sie Dummkopf! You're just asking to go back to prison."

Schlechter remained silent, standing in front of the desk. Having vented the worst of his anger, Frantz returned to his chair.

"All right, what happened?"

After the major finished his report, Frantz shook his head in frustration. "I don't believe this. Why didn't you get there in time? Did it not occur to you to request reinforcements from the Forest Settlement Stasi guards to cut off all exit routes?"

Schlechter stared straight ahead, not responding. Frantz continued, "You've thought about who could have dug up the cache?"

"Yes, General." Schlechter made eye contact again. "Either Dobnik had an accomplice, or the Federal Intelligence Service knew about his cottage."

Frantz perceived Schlechter's hesitation. "Go on, Major. Who else?"

"Well, this may be far-fetched—"

"Get on with it, spit it out!"

"What if Dobnik told Mazzoni where to find the stash, and she and her companion went there from the opera house?"

Schlechter looked uncertain, as if his speculation were preposterous. At first Frantz thought it was. "A couple of amateurs running scared—not likely." But the more he thought about it, the less remote the idea seemed. "It might just be possible, Major. The intelligence I have doesn't point to the existence of an accomplice. The traitor acted alone. And I can't believe he'd give away his bargaining chip to the West Germans. That leaves us with Mazzoni and her friend."

Deep in thought, Frantz got out of his chair and walked over to the window. The gray November morning matched his dismal mood. He took a deep breath and reached a decision. "I'll investigate to see if there is any evidence of a collaborator. You track down Mazzoni and her friend. I'll alert the borders, but I suspect they'll fly out of Tegel Airport rather than drive. Whether they're still in West Berlin or in West Germany, they should leave a trail."

"Your orders, General? Do I pursue them to the West?"

Frantz liked Schlechter's eagerness. "Yes. See my secretary for a West German passport." Frantz fixed his eyes on the major. "Do whatever is necessary to secure the stolen records. Understood?"

"What do you want me to do with the two spies?"

"I leave that entirely up to you. Just don't return without the documents."

While dismissing Schlechter, Frantz already thought ahead what he'd have to do about him. If things didn't turn out as planned, or even if they did, he couldn't very well afford to keep around the sole witness to his actions. But there would be time to work that out later. Right now he needed to take care of the business at hand.

He depressed the intercom button. "Frau Engler, I have a dictation."

By the time she walked into his office, Frantz had finished mentally composing the wording of the wire to be sent to the borders.

♫ ♫ ♫

Fifteen minutes later Frantz's secretary burst into his office. "General, we've just heard from the guard at the Hof border. A couple fitting the description you wired came through at five thirty this morning."

"*Verdammte Scheiße*!" Frantz slammed his fist on the desk. "What were they driving?"

"A white Opel sedan."

"Did the guard give any other details?"

"No, sir."

"Okay. Get Schlechter on the phone."

She retreated to her desk and a few moments later put Schlechter through to him. "Major, they crossed over the border at Hof early this morning. I have a hunch they might be going to the Federal Intelligence Service headquarters in Pullach. Get on the next flight to Munich, rent a car there, and drive to Pullach. You must intercept them before they can make delivery to Schmidt."

"Yes, sir."

"And call me as soon as you get there."

Frantz hung up the phone. He was not looking forward to the long wait.

Chapter Forty-One

Gasthof Bergblick looked like the typical Bavarian guesthouse: a wood-façade two-story building with a steep-pitched roof, green-shuttered windows, and small balconies with now empty window boxes. Having seen the bright geraniums that adorned houses in southern Germany from spring until fall, Rolf had no trouble visualizing how cheery this guesthouse would appear during flower season. Even now at the end of November, it had a cozy atmosphere. True to its name, it looked out over the German Alps and, standing at the dead end of a sleepy residential street, was secluded as Sylvia had promised.

Rolf parked in the walled courtyard, turned off the engine, and looked at Sylvia. "Do you think we can get rooms this early—before checkout time?"

"It should be a bit slow right now. The fall hikers are long gone, and the skiers have not arrived yet."

They got out of the car. He locked the Opel and followed her up the few steps to the front door that featured a beveled glass inlay etched with mountain peaks. The door swung inward as Sylvia depressed the ornately curled brass handle, admitting them to a spacious room that seemed to serve as a combination reception area, restaurant and bar. Light streaming in through numerous windows lent the wood-paneled walls and bar a rich luster providing a warm ambiance.

From behind a far door faint kitchen noises intruded upon the quietness of the room. Sylvia sounded a soft bell on the reception counter. Within seconds the kitchen door swung open and a short, red-haired woman, dressed in a traditional dirndl, strode into the room. Rolf watched the expression on her freckled face change from serious to welcoming when she noticed them.

"Grüß Gott."

"Grüß Gott, Frau Greindl. Perhaps you'll remember me. I'm Sylvia Mazzoni. I've stayed with you a few times before."

The innkeeper's face brightened. "Of course, welcome back, Frau Mazzoni."

"Do you have any rooms available?"

Rolf detected a slight hesitation and an air of uncertainty in the hostess's demeanor. After a quick glance at him, she answered Sylvia. "All I have right now is a one-bedroom suite."

Sylvia didn't miss a beat. "That'll be just fine. Frau Greindl, I'd like you to meet my fiancé Rolf Keller."

The woman wiped her palms on a red-and-white checkered apron adorning the bulging front of her dirndl before offering Rolf her right hand. Her damp sausage-like fingers and the rough-textured skin were those of a woman used to household chores.

She smiled at him. "Congratulations. When is the wedding?"

He stared at her, feeling himself blush.

Sylvia came to the rescue. "Thank you, Frau Greindl. We haven't set a date yet."

He wondered whether her answer would convince a Bavarian Catholic innkeeper to rent them the room.

Although thinning, the smile remained on her face—a good sign.

"I have a very nice suite for you with a mountain view. It's ready now." As if to explain its availability, she added, "A last-minute cancellation."

"Wonderful," exclaimed Sylvia while filling out the registration form. After a moment she looked up. "Frau Greindl, we're not sure whether we're staying one night or two. Is it all right if we let you know in the morning?"

"Of course. Just leave that part blank."

Rolf wondered how much that nice suite with a view would cost but neither of the two women raised the subject.

"It's up the stairs and to your right." She laid a large key attached to a round wooden block onto the counter top. The number seven, written in the German manner with a central horizontal line, was carved into the blond wood.

After declining Frau Greindl's offer to have her husband help with luggage and agreeing to eat lunch at her establishment, they made off to the car. When they returned with the suitcases, Rolf looked for an elevator. Seeing none, he carried Dobnik's heavy case and his own up the narrow polished wood staircase. Sylvia followed with hers. Once he reached the second floor, he put down his load and let her pass. She turned right, as Frau Greindl had instructed, and inserted the key into the door at the end of the hallway.

By the time he got there, Sylvia had disappeared inside. The living room featured a sofa, a coffee table and two chairs at a small round table in the corner. While he set the cases down on the parquet floor next to Sylvia's, he felt a cold draft. Through a partially open glass door he saw Sylvia on the balcony and stepped out to join her along the balustrade. They admired in silence the clouds swirling around the top of the Karwendel mountain range. Every now and then, the dense cover parted for a few moments to afford them a quick glimpse of the towering peaks.

A sudden breeze swept across the balcony. Rolf noticed Sylvia shivering and took off his coat to drape it over her shoulders. Not detecting any resistance, he maintained his light touch, likening his hands to the layers of clouds hugging the peaks. He hoped that the bond of trust he'd felt growing during the past several days was real. Yet he could not repress a nagging doubt that there was something in her past she'd kept from him.

The spell broken by his negative thoughts, he dropped his hands. "We need to go through the suitcase."

"Yes. The spy stuff. Of course."

He heard the touch of sarcasm and wanted to see her face, but she kept looking out toward the mountains. Arms hanging awkwardly at his sides, he turned and went inside. She must somehow have sensed his mistrust. He heaved Dobnik's case onto the corner table and spun the lock dials so fast that he overshot the combination. When he finally got the numbers aligned, he yanked the case open, spilling papers onto the table and the floor. Staring at the mess, he dropped the suitcase in disgust onto the table surface. The loud clunk startled him. He tried to control his irritation. How he could use a drink! No sooner had the thought popped into his head than he recalled AA's warnings that frustration brought on crazy thinking. Why *was* he so frustrated? Was he feeling guilty about not keeping in touch with Stein or ditching Schmidt? Probably the real reason was simply that he'd been acting like a jerk toward Sylvia. She seemed open to putting their relationship on a new footing, while he was stuck in the past.

As he bent over to pick up the papers strewn across the floor, he heard Sylvia behind him. "Need help?"

Their eyes met. In hers he saw teasing rather than mocking.

"Matter of fact, I do."

To help him regain his composure, he busied himself by dumping all of the documents onto the table surface. "I'll look through these and indicate what each relates to. See if you can organize them . . ."

Sylvia's wide-eyed stare stopped him in mid-sentence. "What's the matter?"

She pointed to the suitcase. He turned it around and saw what had startled her: his rough handling had dislodged part of a side panel. He pulled on the loose panel and it opened up, revealing a hidden compartment.

When he started to reach into it, she exclaimed, "Wait! It could be a bomb."

Rolf took a closer look. "No, it's a gun."

He carefully dislodged the weapon from its close-fitted hiding place. A few moments later he held a pistol and a fully loaded magazine in his hand. The front of the grip bore the stencil mark *Ernst Thaelmann Mod. M.*

Rolf whistled. "It's an East German Makarov pistol."

He inserted the magazine into the grip, flipped down the safety, and held the pistol out to Sylvia. "I don't expect we'll have to use this. But just in case, do you know how to shoot one of these?"

"Release the safety, aim and pull the trigger," she recited, deadpan, without taking the gun.

He looked at her in surprise.

"I took a gun safety course several years ago, and . . . Horst used to play around with guns."

Rolf appreciated her honesty, but even after all these years the mention of her former boyfriend still bothered him. In as nonchalant a manner as he could manage he laid the weapon aside and pulled up a chair. "Let's get started on sorting these papers."

Sitting across the table from each other, they spread out the papers between them and soon had several piles going. As far as Rolf could comprehend, the subjects included information about West German government, intelligence and military offices, intelligence on East German citizens, and East German training bases. His preliminary perusal gave Rolf the impression that there was evidence that foreign terrorists, including the Red Army Faction, had been trained at secret Stasi bases. There were also several sheets identifying terrorists and their whereabouts in the West.

At the bottom of the original pile he found two separate folders. They must have been on top before he upended the suitcase. One was Sylvia's file, which he handed to her. He opened the second one. It contained a single sheet of handwritten notes. They appeared written in haste, and Rolf strained to make out the words. To help, he started to read out loud.

"'Brigadier General Frantz, Head of Counterintelligence, summoned me to his office on Tuesday morning, November 28, 1989, to give me instructions about passing on Stasi documents to the West German Federal Intelligence Service. He named the project "Operation Independence" and assured me that it had been authorized by former Stasi Chief Mielke and that the current Chief General Rittmeister had been fully briefed on it. I discovered that Rittmeister knows nothing about this operation, and I suspect neither does Mielke.'"

Rolf's eyes fell on the first line of the second paragraph, but he paused when he felt Sylvia's touch.

"Does it say anything about my being the carrier?"

He held her intense gaze. "Not unless it's in the next paragraph, but that seems to be about a different subject."

"Go on!"

Feeling her impatience, Rolf started to read faster.

"'I noticed a document with a top secret stamp lying on the corner of Frantz's desk. Each time the general's attention was elsewhere, I tried to read the upside-down document. It was a memorandum from General Rittmeister and had five names on the distribution list. Under the subject line I saw what looked like "Operation Eradication." I managed three looks. The words I could make out seemed to relate to a plan to eradicate a foreign vegetable. There was mention of a December meeting (I could not read the date). During my last glance, I saw a reference to churches but could not make out the rest of the phrase.'"

"What on earth is he talking about?" Sylvia's puzzled question caused Rolf to look up once more.

He shrugged. "There is more."

Without waiting for her to urge him on, he read the rest.

"'Based on the code terms I recognized, I believe there is a plot afoot by the Stasi leadership, but without more to go on, I can only guess that it is directed against West Germany, perhaps an assassination (eradication) to prevent unification.'

"'I have made these notes on this 28th of November, 1989.'

"'Colonel Heinz Dobnik.'"

"That's the assassination plot Dobnik was hinting at, his bargaining chip with Schmidt." Sylvia let go of Rolf's arm. "Rolf, we have to get this to Schmidt."

Deep in thought, he looked out toward the mountains before facing Sylvia. "I suppose we do . . . but not before he agrees to your terms."

"You mean—"

"Your immunity letter, you'd better believe it."

"Rolf, I want that letter more than anything, but we can't withhold Dobnik's notes. There's too much at stake. Something big is going to happen sometime in December . . . and tomorrow is the first."

"Agreed. But Schmidt can't be sure we care a whit about Germany's future, so we'll try a bluff. He'll come around when I tell him of the documents about the terrorists and the assassination plot." His eyes fell on the eight stacks Sylvia had arranged. "Could you check whether Frau Greindl has some file folders we could fit these into? If not, rubber bands might do."

While Sylvia went downstairs, Rolf checked out the rest of the suite. A large bed, framed by dark wooden posts at the corners, took up most of the bedroom. Images of his liaison with Sylvia during college days flooded his memory. He would not go there, but it took a real effort to refocus. To divert himself he continued his tour. The tiny bathroom was typical of old German guesthouses. It had a free-standing sink with no space to put things, and a bathtub with a handheld shower for use while bathing but not as a shower, since there was neither a wall hook nor a shower curtain. He smiled. His years in the States had caused him to forget some of the conditions under which he'd grown up.

Sylvia returned with folders and rubber bands. It took several large folders, rubber banded together, to contain each of the taller stacks. After a few minutes they had everything back in the suitcase, organized for the first time, Rolf suspected. He could only imagine how nerve wracking it must have been for Dobnik to risk his life copying and hiding those documents. Organizing them would have been the last thing on his mind.

He returned the Makarov to its secret compartment and waited for Sylvia to add her file before closing the case. She watched him scramble the lock. "It smelled heavenly in the kitchen. She's prepared Schweinelendchen mit Preißelbeeren und Knödeln."

"Light fare," he quipped, locking the door behind them. Despite the ample breakfast, he felt very hungry all of a sudden. Bavarian cuisine was famous for its pork delicacies. He couldn't remember the last time he'd eaten pork loin served with cranberries and Bavarian dumplings.

Judging by the bustling restaurant and bar, Frau Greindl's cooking attracted a sizable local following. She seated them at a table for two in the corner. Whether due to the fresh mountain air, the excitement of uncovering Dobnik's secrets, or the uncertainties facing them, Sylvia and he had huge appetites and devoured everything Frau Greindl served up. Perhaps the incomparable Bavarian way of preparing pork was to blame. Meals were typically accompanied by a huge glass of Bavarian beer and followed by a shot of schnapps to help digest the fatty fare, and it took several firm refusals for Frau Greindl to accept the fact that they weren't going to adhere to the custom. He saw her shaking her head as she retreated into the kitchen, probably mumbling something to herself about those Americans and Italians.

He pushed his plate back. "Sylvia, I don't mean to be presumptuous. If you'd rather call Schmidt yourself—"

"Rolf, don't be silly. I want you to call him, but I'd like to listen in."

They went back to the room and Rolf dialed the number Schmidt had told him to call in case of an emergency. He recognized the gruff voice that answered on the second ring.

"Hallo."

"Rolf Keller." He heard Schmidt's sharp intake of breath.

"Where in the hell are you?"

"Do you have the letter from your boss for Sylvia? We've got something to trade you'll be very interested in."

"Can you be more specific?"

"It's everything that was promised."

"So Mozart came through?"

"Well, we . . ." Not knowing how to tell Schmidt about Dobnik, Rolf hesitated. "We managed to get the merchandise, but Mozart won't be able to join us."

"Is that a temporary or permanent condition?"

"I'm afraid it's permanent."

"Sorry to hear that."

The genuine concern in Schmidt's voice startled Rolf for a moment. Did Schmidt really care about Dobnik's fate, or was he merely disappointed that the Stasi officer couldn't be debriefed in the West?

Rolf refocused on what he needed to accomplish. "What about the letter?"

"I'm still in Berlin. But I can be back at headquarters this afternoon and get the letter then. Are you anywhere close to either place?"

"Headquarters suits us fine. Can I call you there at this number?"

"Yes. I'll be there by six."

Rolf was about to hang up when he saw Sylvia raise a finger. "Ask about government conferences," she whispered.

He nodded and spoke into the phone, "Are there any conferences or meetings in December of high-level government officials?"

Schmidt's surprise permeated the momentary silence. "I don't know. Why do you ask?"

"Could you have the answer for me when I call you later? It's something we've come across. It could be very important. And be sure to have Sylvia's letter."

"Wait. Don't hang up yet." Schmidt's forceful voice stopped Rolf's finger from depressing the hook. "The Deutsche Bank chief, Alfred Herrhausen, was murdered this morning. It has all the hallmarks of a Red Army Faction operation. Wherever you are, be very careful. The sooner you get me those documents the better for her and you."

Rolf's stomach tightened. He wanted to ask for details but realized he couldn't afford to prolong the discussion if he didn't want Schmidt to trace the number. He said, "We'll keep that in mind," and cut the connection.

While he pondered whether to tell Sylvia about Schmidt's warning, she walked out of the bedroom. He followed her into the living room. She opened the suitcase on the table and took out a file—her personal file, no doubt.

As she settled on the sofa, he decided to keep to himself the disturbing news about the banker's assassination, at least for now. Instead, he turned his attention to the file in Sylvia's hands and the burning questions it raised in his mind. Did its contents brand Sylvia as a terrorist sympathizer? How could he find out?

Chapter Forty-Two

Schmidt slammed down the phone. The call probably had been too short to allow a successful trace. He now cursed his idea of bringing in this expatriate lawyer as a watchdog for Sylvia. There was no one to blame but himself. Leave it to a sharp Washington lawyer to press his advantage. Schmidt hadn't made much headway in moving the Federal Intelligence Service bureaucracy to act on Sylvia's immunity letter. It was time to get blunt with the higher-ups. He had to make them understand they must give Sylvia what she wanted.

He stomped out of the visitors' office and down the hall to the secretary's desk. The plump woman interrupted her typing to look at him.

"Frau Wesendorf. Book me on the next flight out of Tegel to Munich and order a taxi to take me from my hotel to the airport."

"Yes, Herr Schmidt."

"Any word on the trace?"

She shook her head. Just then the phone rang and she answered it. She scribbled on her notepad and hung up.

"Did they trace the call?"

"Not all the way. They couldn't get the last digit of the area code."

"Crap!"

He ignored her disapproving look, stepped around her desk, and read her notes. "0882 is the part they traced?"

"Yes."

He fought his irritation for having to drag the information out of her. "And could they tell where that is?"

"It's in Upper Bavaria." Her quick response told him she'd caught his impatience.

Pencil still in hand, she circled a number on the page. "There are seventy-seven communities that share these area code numbers. The tracer mentioned five major towns." She squinted to read her notes. "Garmisch-Partenkirchen, Oberammergau, Mittenwald, Oberau, and Krün. He promised to have the complete list to me shortly."

"So the call could have come from any of these seventy-seven communities." He turned to leave. "I don't have time to wait for the list. Fax it to my Pullach office. And leave word at the hotel about the flight and what time the taxi will arrive."

The ringing of the phone interrupted. She nodded to him while she answered it. Schmidt was about to open the door when she stopped him with a sharp tone.

"Herr Schmidt. Wait just a moment."

"Who is it?"

"Mr. Stein is returning your call." She held out the receiver. "Do you want to take it here?"

Schmidt hesitated. He'd have more privacy in the visitors' office, but he had a plane to catch. He took the phone from her.

"Hello Mr. Stein."

"Mr. Schmidt?"

"Yes. I'm sorry to be so abrupt, but I need to catch a flight. Any luck?"

"Yes. We traced several charges to the firm's credit card issued to Mr. Keller. Yesterday evening he rented a car at a Europcar store near the Zoo Station. It's a white Opel—"

"Just a minute. Let me get something to write with." Schmidt gestured to Frau Wesendorf for her notepad and pencil. "Okay. Go on."

"A white Opel, license plate number B-54798."

"What are the other charges?"

"Two rooms at a Hotel Greinke, also near the Zoo Station. And the last one is from this morning at a . . . Raststätte Höhenrain, if that's how you pronounce it."

Stein mangled the German so badly that it took Schmidt a few seconds to compute the name.

"Did you get that?" Stein asked.

"Yes. It's a rest stop on Autobahn A95, near the Starnberger See."

"My German geography is not the best—"

Stifling his impatience, Schmidt replied, "It's a lake south of Munich and north of Garmisch-Partenkirchen. But you didn't give me the date on the hotel charge."

"Uh . . . November 29, last night about an hour after the car rental."

"If they spent the night at a hotel in Berlin, how'd they get to Upper Bavaria by this morning?"

"They must have left in the middle of the night. When the clerk checked their rooms early in the morning, he found the beds untouched."

Eager to end the conversation, Schmidt said, "Thank you, Mr. Stein."

"Call me as soon as you've located them."

"Of course."

Schmidt handed the receiver back to the secretary. He tore off the top two sheets of the notepad containing the notes. Half way out the door, he reminded her, "Don't forget to fax that list to me in Pullach."

She nodded. His mind on hurrying back to the hotel, packing, and fitting in a call to Bauman, he charged out of the office. The wait for the elevator seemed interminable. When it finally arrived and he was about to step in, he heard a soft click behind him as if a door were being carefully closed. Blocking the elevator door with one hand, he pivoted around and just caught the distinctive black and gray pattern of Frau Wesendorf's dress disappearing around the corner. Why was she not on the phone calling the airlines? Don't get paranoid, he admonished himself, and entered the elevator. Even Wesendorf needed bathroom breaks.

Despite the slow elevator and having to dodge pedestrians crowding the sidewalks, he made it to his hotel in less than ten minutes. He was surprised to learn that the secretary had not yet left a message about the flight and taxi. He knew there was a mid-afternoon Air France flight to Munich and it would not be full on a Thursday. She should have been able to make the arrangements by now. Suppressing the thought she might have hit a snag, Schmidt asked for his bill and requested to be notified immediately when Frau Wesendorf called.

In the middle of packing, he received word that he was on a three-thirty Air France flight. A taxi would pick him up in fifteen minutes, at two o'clock. For Berlin traffic, that was cutting things pretty close. He tossed the rest of his clothes into the suitcase. Being a meticulous person, he always did a final walkthrough before checking out of hotels. Not today.

He also broke his rule of always calling Bauman from a secure phone. When his boss answered, Schmidt spoke with urgency. "Karl, I've only got a minute. I'm catching a plane and will be back at the office by six. Frau Wesendorf will be faxing a list of towns. They called me an hour ago from one of them."

"I understand."

Schmidt felt relieved he didn't need to say Sylvia and Rolf's names. "Look for a white Opel, B-54798. I have a hunch they'll be at one of the larger towns."

"Can you tell me what's going on?"

"I'm expecting a call at my office at six. I need to have the letter I drafted signed by then. Can you get that done?"

Bauman whistled. "I'd say that's nearly impossible."

"Look, Karl. This is really big. I've *got* to have that letter."

"Okay. The chief hasn't turned it down yet, but he's inclined to. Give me something that'll convince him to change his mind."

"Tell him Mozart is dead, but his creations live on. I've got a chance to lay my hands on some of his most important ones, but not without the letter."

After an audible breath, Bauman responded. "I'll try, but without more to go on, don't get your hopes up."

Schmidt checked his watch. "I have a taxi waiting downstairs. There's one more thing. Can you get a list of any meetings in December to be attended by high-ranking government officials?"

"What level are we talking about?"

"Someone whose demise could derail unification." His watch showing a minute after two o'clock, Schmidt added, "I'm late. See you around six."

Sitting in the cab a few minutes later, he wondered whether Bauman could deliver on even one of the three things he needed. He reflected on his early years as an agent when the Federal Intelligence Service was small and flexible. As it had grown over the years, the sluggishness typical of bureaucracies had taken hold. Schmidt's mood darkened as he weighed his odds of ever being able to lay eyes on the contents of Dobnik's suitcase.

Chapter Forty-Three

When the phone rang, General Frantz glanced at the clock on his office wall. Ten after one. He hoped that was Schlechter.

But when he answered, he heard an excited female voice, which he recognized as Brigitte Wesendorf's. "I only have a minute, General. It took me a while to get to a pay phone."

"What is it?"

"They're in Upper Bavaria. That's south of—"

"I know where that is." He did not disguise his impatience. "Go on."

"Uh . . . yes, General."

Frantz wrote down the partial area code, the make of the car and license plate and the charge card information she passed on.

"Great work, Comrade."

Barely registering her thank you as he hung up the phone, Frantz reviewed the data. What his mole in the Federal Intelligence Service Berlin office just delivered made worthwhile the enormous efforts the Stasi had expended in recruiting and placing her.

He resisted the temptation of further self-congratulation and depressed the intercom. "Frau Engler, I need you in here."

When his secretary entered a few seconds later, he tore a sheet from his notepad and held it out to her. "These are the first four numbers of an area code. Find out immediately which towns in Upper Bavaria share this area code. There should be seventy-seven of them. Give this the highest priority."

"Yes, sir." She took the piece of paper and rushed out of the office.

She was one of the most capable and efficient secretaries at Stasi headquarters. That's why she was working for him. But would she be able to get the information in time to give Schlechter a head start on recovering Dobnik's cache? And once they had the list of towns, how would they be able to zero in on the one where Mazzoni and her companion were hiding?

Frantz grew impatient. He should have heard from Schlechter by now. The general went over the phone conversation with Wesendorf one more time. Something she'd said had triggered a hint of recognition in his mind, perhaps a memory of something. He'd been too busy writing to focus on it and now it was gone. Whatever it might be, it felt important. But the more he tried to think of it, the fainter the concept became. The ring of the phone rescued him from his increasing frustration.

This time it was Schlechter. "General, I've just arrived in Pullach and am checking in per your orders."

Frantz asked, "Any leads yet?"

Schlechter began in a hesitant voice, "Well—"

"Never mind. I've got your leads for you. Take this down." After relaying the information to the major, he couldn't resist adding, "I'm glad I decided to send you to Pullach on a hunch. Your quarry is in Upper Bavaria just south of there. I should have a list of all the towns shortly."

"Do you want me to wait here in Pullach until then, sir?"

Frantz hadn't considered the issue. What were the towns Brigitte Wesendorf had mentioned, and did it make any sense to send Schlechter to one of them at random? As he started to recall some of the names, he spoke them into the phone. "Major, some of the larger towns in the region are Garmisch-Partenkirchen, Oberammergau, Mittenwald, and . . ."

Wait! There it was. Of course, as soon as he said Mittenwald the memory flooded back. Sylvia Mazzoni had vacationed there numerous times with her mother. He had read it in the Mazzoni File that was now missing. The file listed the guesthouse at which they usually stayed, but he couldn't remember the name.

"Major, are you there?"

"Yes, sir."

"Drive to Mittenwald immediately. Mazzoni has stayed there several times in a guesthouse. It's all in her missing file. Check all inns and guesthouses. If you don't find them there, canvass the hotels. Do you follow?"

"Yes, General."

"And call me when you get there. I may recall the name of the place by then."

Frantz cut the connection. He leaned back, resisting the urge to rack his brain to come up with the name, for he knew the harder he tried to think of it, the less likely he would. When he realized that he had given Schlechter a head start, he began to relax. Unless the Federal Intelligence Service's file on Mazzoni was as thorough as the Stasi's, which he doubted, Schmidt's agents would have to canvass all seventy-seven communities in hopes of finding Mazzoni and her companion. Sure, Mittenwald as one of the premier tourist destinations would be high on their list, but they couldn't afford to concentrate all of their efforts there. The more he thought about it, the more he liked Schlechter's chances of recovering the Stasi documents before the West Germans got even close.

His thoughts turned to what Dobnik's suitcase might contain. Without question, the traitor would have been able to copy highly sensitive material revealing the identity and whereabouts of Red Army Faction terrorists and their having been trained by the Stasi. And the cover of scores of Stasi moles embedded in all levels of West German society might be blown. The defector probably had managed to get his hands on that kind of secret information as well.

Then the scariest thought came to him. He squirmed as he considered the odds that Dobnik might have somehow gotten wind of the plot underway to deal a mortal blow to West Germany's ambitions about unification. Frantz shook his head, reassuring himself. Dobnik had not been among the select group of Stasi higher-ups whom Chief Rittmeister had kept informed of the plan. Nonetheless, he had to consider the possibility, however remote, that the top secret memorandum could alert the West Germans to the secret plot. That made it all the more imperative for Schlechter to succeed. Failure would not only jeopardize Frantz's political ambitions but put him in prison or even the morgue.

Chapter Forty-Four

Brigitte Wesendorf listened to the coins drop as she pushed open the phone booth's folding door, but then pulled back her hand to let it close again. She couldn't shake the thought that this was her big opportunity, since she might never again have access to information as valuable as what she'd passed on to General Frantz a moment ago. The Federal Intelligence Service paid her a meager salary, and she didn't expect much, if anything, from the Stasi. She was not stupid. Clearly, the Stasi's days were numbered.

Still, it was a weighty decision. Once she sold secrets to British agents, there would be no going back. She opened her purse, and after a quick search retrieved a piece of paper, on which she'd scribbled a phone number. If someone had walked up just then to use the phone, she might have changed her mind. But no one did, so she picked up the receiver, inserted two coins, and dialed.

When she heard the British-accented "Hallo," Wesendorf asked, "Do you like divas?"

After a moment, the male voice responded, "Yes, very much so."

"And how much is that?"

"Our offer still stands."

Instinct told her the British would pay more than the two thousand marks they'd previously promised. The information she possessed was worth more. "Make the first number a five, and I'll tell you where you can find one and what she's got."

The line went silent. She pictured Kingsley struggling to make a decision. Would he have the authority to pay her five thousand marks? Then he spoke, "Agreed, if your information is good."

"Oh, I have no doubt you'll be satisfied."

"Can you be at the Romanisches Café in half an hour?"

She checked her watch. Breitscheidplatz was fifteen minutes away, and she had to make Schmidt's travel arrangements first. "No. I'll see you there at two."

"Don't come inside. Just stroll by. We'll find you." A sharp click punctuated the end of the sentence.

♫ ♫ ♫

Stein pulled his Lincoln into the side parking lot of Ristorante Divertimento, one of the many ethnic restaurants in Washington's Adams Morgan district, and Anthony Fabrini's favorite. He insisted on meeting there for a meal or drinks whenever they needed to talk in private.

A young, attractive hostess approached. "Your party is already seated."

Stein waved off her offer to accompany him. "Thank you. I'll find him."

Fabrini was a man of habit and would be at his usual table. As Stein approached the rear of the dimly lit dining room, he saw his friend's gray hair, thick and combed straight back. He wore a dark blue double-breasted business suit, quite unlike Stein's charcoal pin-stripe.

"Don't get up," said Stein, as he shook Fabrini's hand. "Sorry I'm late. It's been a hectic morning."

"That's quite all right." Fabrini lifted the bottle on the table and held it over the wine glass in front of Stein with a questioning look. Stein nodded.

"I hope you don't mind my selecting the wine." He poured the Valpolicella. "I suppose that's the prerogative of the one who arrives first."

Stein marveled at his friend's composure. He must be dying to hear the latest about the German project. Yet here he was making small talk.

"I'm hungry. Let's order and then I want to hear all about what's going on in Berlin." Fabrini's hand gesture brought a dark-haired fortyish waiter to their table.

After listening to a recitation of the lunch specials, Stein ordered spinach-filled handmade pocket pasta in a white cream sauce and Fabrini selected veal scaloppini. When they were alone, Fabrini broke off a piece of the hot, crusty bread, dunked it in the olive oil on his plate, and took several bites, which he chased with a sip of red wine.

He set down his glass. "So, how are things in Germany?"

"Rolf and Sylvia smuggled the Stasi papers out of East Germany. They're somewhere in southern Bavaria. Schmidt's people are working on locating them."

"Why didn't they give the documents to Schmidt as they were supposed to?"

"You mean after making our copy?"

"Yes, of course."

Stein let his irritation show. "Good question. And another one is why Rolf hasn't faxed me the copies he's supposedly made."

Fabrini studied him. "Sounds like Rolf Keller won't make partner at your shop."

"We're not partial to renegades at Stein & Weston."

"Are they in any danger?"

393

"As long as they have the papers, I believe they are."

"You don't think the Stasi . . ."

Stein nodded. "The Stasi and . . . you've heard about the murder of the Deutsche Bank chairman this morning. They suspect the Red Army Faction."

"Working with the Stasi?"

"It's possible."

After a grave silence, Stein steeled himself to break more unpleasant news to his friend. "Tony, there is something else I need to tell you."

"Oh?" Fabrini raised his bushy eyebrows.

"I suspect Rolf's secretary got a look at your file."

"What! How did that happen?"

Stein related yesterday's events around the fire drill. Fabrini hung onto every word and did not interrupt.

"You ought to make him partner. If your suspicion that he and his secretary planned this proves correct . . ." Fabrini paused. "I tell you, he's one smart son of a bitch."

"Too smart for his own good. I'm sorry, Tony. I know how much you wanted that file to remain private. But, if it was his secretary in my office during the drill, I disturbed her coming back early and she may not have had much time to get a good look or . . ."

"Make copies." Fabrini finished the sentence for him. "Can you put the squeeze on this secretary and find out what she might have told her boss?"

"Yes, I plan on doing that. But she's a tough cookie, and my sense is she'd do anything to protect Rolf."

"So convince her you need to know in order to save his life."

Stein nodded slowly. "I've already planted a seed. It might just work."

As the server wheeled a cart toward their table, Fabrini looked Stein in the eye. "Do what you have to."

♫ ♫ ♫

Although they had no reason to suspect that Dieter Schmidt knew them, both Peter Ross and Dennis Kingsley were careful not to look toward him as they moved down the center aisle to the rear of the aircraft. As soon as they took their seats, the crew closed the door and the Air France plane began its one-hour flight from Berlin to Munich. Brigitte Wesendorf's information had indeed been worth what they paid her. Kingsley was sure their boss at Whitehall would agree. Still, to locate Mazzoni and Keller, much legwork awaited them once they reached southern Bavaria.

Since there were too many tourist class passengers close by to discuss business with Ross, Kingsley turned his attention instead to consoling himself that they knew as much as Schmidt about the fugitives' whereabouts—if Wesendorf had been straight with them. Hopefully, headquarters would have the list of towns ready by the time they landed. According to their informant, the Stasi papers contained evidence incriminating a top West German official, which could prove useful in the British government's efforts to thwart reunification. If he and Ross didn't find Mazzoni before Schmidt's people did, that information would disappear forever. At least at this point they had an equal chance.

But the Stasi—not the West Germans—posed the greatest threat to the British agents' quest to get hold of the documents. By now the Stasi must be aware that the opera singer and the American lawyer had smuggled Dobnik's cache out of East Germany and would be giving chase. He and Ross had to reach Mazzoni and Keller first. Those two amateurs almost certainly had no inkling of the utter ruthlessness of the Stasi killers pursuing them.

Chapter Forty-Five

"Didn't you say you needed to call your secretary?"

Rolf caught the annoyance in Sylvia's eyes as she looked up from the file she'd been reading for some time. He realized he must have been pacing.

"Sorry, if I'm bothering you. I am worried about Betty, but I've been waiting to call so I won't wake her up."

He checked his watch. One-fifteen in the afternoon in Germany translated into a quarter past seven in the morning in Washington. Betty should be up by now and getting ready to go to the office.

Sylvia reached for the notepad by the phone, tore off a sheet, and inserted it in her file. She yawned. "Rolf, I'm worn out from last night. I'm going to catch some sleep while we're waiting to call Schmidt."

File in hand, she walked toward the bedroom. "I'll finish reading this later. If I'm not up by five thirty, would you wake me?"

"Sure."

She pointed to the living room sofa. "You got less sleep than I did. Aren't you going to take a nap?"

"I'd like to, but first I need to call Betty, and after that I'm going to get rid of the Opel. If someone is trying to find us, they've probably traced the credit card charge to the car by now. And while I'm at it, I'll store Dobnik's papers in a locker at the train station."

"Good idea."

"I suppose you want to hang onto your file?"

"Definitely."

"I thought so." He studied her. "You're okay with my leaving for a couple of hours, aren't you?"

"Yes," a firm reply, apparently to convince herself as well as him. "But be sure to lock the door when you leave." She halfway closed the bedroom door behind her.

Rolf moved toward the phone on the coffee table but then stopped. Why risk calling Betty from the room when he could be at the train station in a few minutes and use a public phone?

A little over ten minutes later, having parked the Opel on a side street, Rolf carried the gray suitcase into the train station. The lockboxes were straight ahead. He felt himself grow tense as he considered the possibility that he might not find one large enough to hold Dobnik's suitcase. His apprehension proved justified. After several attempts to squeeze the case at different angles into the largest box available, he realized it was hopeless. What now? He looked around. No one seemed to have noticed his struggle. There was only one thing to do. He opened the case, took out the folders—careful not to dislodge the rubber bands that held them together—and placed them in the locker. His eyes fell on the side panel compartment holding the pistol. Should he put it with the files? In spite of Schmidt's admonition against carrying a weapon, Rolf decided to follow his instinct to keep it, and shut the case quickly before he changed his mind.

Breathing easier, he locked the box and withdrew the key. The coins he had deposited dropped with a series of clunks. After scanning the lobby once more, he carried the suitcase, empty now except for the Makarov, to the row of telephones lining the wall next to the lockers. He selected a phone at the far end, away from the few that were in use.

After dialing a string of numbers for his international phone card and then Betty's home number, he listened to the clicks as the signal made its journey of several thousand miles. She answered after the first ring.

"Good to hear your voice, Betty."

"I figured that had to be you, counselor. How are you doing?"

"Well, I've had some adventures. The telling will have to wait until another time."

"You're not the only one. We'll swap stories when you get back. Any idea when that might be?"

"Shouldn't be too much longer. The job is almost done." As he spoke the words, he felt a strange sense of regret.

Betty's voice interjected, "You want to hear what I found?"

"You actually did it?"

"Of course, what did you think?"

"Betty, you're the greatest."

"Hold your praise till you hear what I've got. I'm not sure it will be of much help."

He was tempted to ask her how she managed to get into Stein's office, but that too would have to wait, since he could hardly contain his excitement. He simply said, "Shoot."

"When I got into his office during the fire drill, I found one file in his center desk drawer. It was labeled 'ARM.'"

Rolf pulled a pen from his shirt pocket and his notebook from a coat pocket. "Betty, is that in all caps?"

"Yes."

"With periods between the letters?"

"No, no periods. Do you know what it means?"

"No, I don't. But go on."

398

"The client appears to be Anthony Fabrini. Have you heard of him?"

"No."

"Not surprising. He is not listed in the firm's client list."

Rolf wrote down everything Betty told him about the correspondence between Stein and Fabrini and the dates and amounts of the international drafts she had seen and copied. There had to be some connection to his assignment, unless Stein had put the pertinent file back in the safe before leaving for the fire drill. When Betty related the friendly and informal tone of the correspondence between Stein and Fabrini, Rolf recalled Stein's insistence that no one else in the firm was to know about this assignment. A secret client, perhaps a friend of Stein's, and money sent to a bank account in Milan since the seventies—he could not fathom what the link to his mission might be.

Betty's voice interrupted his thoughts. "After I filed your summary judgment motion yesterday, I stopped by the public library and did a little research on Mr. Fabrini. In the limited time I had, I only found one newspaper story. It was about his making partner in an Alexandria law firm."

"What year was that?"

"Wait a minute. I need to look at my notes." He heard the soft thud of the phone being put down. Betty was back after a few seconds. "The newspaper is from April 9, 1970. He was named partner as of April 1 of that year."

"What kind of practice does he have?"

"Corporate law. That might explain why he's not in the papers like the criminal trial lawyers."

"Any personal information about him?"

"Married, two sons, received an honorable discharge from the Army in the early fifties after he returned from European duty," Betty recited in a matter-of-fact tone.

Rolf glanced at his notes. "Betty, you did say the first draft to the Milan bank was dated April 14, 1970?"

"That's right."

Rolf scratched his forehead. "Hmm. Right after he made law partner. Coincidence?"

"You're the lawyer-turned-sleuth, Rolf."

He reviewed his notes with her one more time to ensure he'd written everything down correctly.

When he got ready to sign off, she asked abruptly, "Are you in danger there?"

Not knowing how to answer her, he hesitated. There was no point in worrying her, but he didn't want to lie either. "Well, we had a close call last night, but I think we're in the clear now."

"You're out of East Germany?"

"Yes."

"Glad to hear it. I don't suppose you want to tell me where I can call you?"

He considered it for a moment. "No, Betty. I think it's better that you don't know. Stein may put some pressure on you."

"Tell me about it."

"You mean he already has?"

"He had me in his office for a twenty-minute grilling after the fire drill. But not to worry. I can handle him."

"As well as you handle me?" He enjoyed her laugh, but then turned more serious. "Really, Betty, watch your back. I'd better go."

"You be careful too. I'm counting on you to make it back here and give me a job in that law firm you'll be starting."

He could hear the concern beneath her kidding. "You can count on that. The Germans have a saying, 'Unkraut verdirbt nicht'—'weeds don't spoil.' You won't get rid of me easily."

"Call me if you need anything else."

"I will."

He replaced the phone, picked up the weightless suitcase, and left the terminal. Quick strides brought him to the Opel. He drove around the corner to the Europcar outlet, which he had spotted earlier. Within minutes he entered the store and handed the rental contract to the male clerk behind the counter.

"Returning a car, sir?"

"Yes, but I need another one."

The clerk looked at him puzzled, then examined the papers. "Sir, you're supposed to return this car to Berlin. There will be a substantial drop-off charge if you turn it in here."

Rolf thought about the AA twelve-step program. It prescribed rigorous honesty in all things in order to maintain sobriety, but he convinced himself this was a necessary exception. "You don't understand. I'm returning the Opel because I don't think it's safe. There's something wrong with the brakes."

The man studied him and Rolf waited to be quizzed in detail about the defective brakes, but then the employee's expression relaxed. "Oh, I see. Of course we'll give you another vehicle. Do you want the same model?"

"If you have it in a different color."

Apparently other customers had rented cars by color previously as the clerk showed no surprise at the request. He thumbed through a stack of papers in front of him. "Would you prefer gray or red?"

"Gray. You don't need to fill out a new contract, do you?"

"No, I'll just make the changes on this one."

Rolf tried not to show the relief he felt. There would be no new credit card charge that could be traced.

By the time he walked into their suite at Gasthof Bergblick it was close to three o'clock. He laid the suitcase on the coffee table and tiptoed to the bedroom door. Sylvia was lying on her back on the bed covers, fully clothed and breathing rhythmically. Rolf turned around, set the alarm on his runner's watch and, after shedding his coat, opened out the sleeper sofa. With a small pillow propped under his head and his long legs extending several centimeters over the end, he dozed off in seconds.

♫ ♫ ♫

The rapid beeps of his watch alarm roused him. He saw Sylvia at the table, reading her file once more. He got up and closed the sofa.

She turned. "How did it go? You couldn't find a place for the suitcase?" She pointed toward the case lying on the table.

"It's empty except for the gun. I stashed the folders in a locker at the train station. The case wouldn't fit. And we have a new car. We should be safe for a while longer from anyone tracking us."

She nodded. Realizing the time, he picked up the phone. Sylvia lowered her file.

Upon hearing Schmidt's baritone, Rolf asked, "Do you have the letter?"

"Not yet. The boss is out, but he agreed to sign it. I'll have it by late morning."

While Rolf was considering his options, Schmidt spoke again, "So you've got the deal you wanted. Tell me where you are and I'll come for the merchandise."

"Not so fast. What time exactly will you have the signed document?"

"Nine o'clock."

"So you could fax it to me then?"

There was a slight hesitation. "Yes, I suppose. What number?"

"I'll call you at nine and tell you. We can agree on a meeting place then."

"Herr Keller, I give you my solemn word that Sylvia will get that document. As long as you have Mozart's belongings, both of you are in grave danger. You must turn them over to me now. Remember what happened to the banker this morning."

The urgency in Schmidt's tone gave Rolf pause. Was he bluffing, or were they in real danger? It was tempting to get rid of the Stasi files. But could he trust Schmidt?

"What do you say?" Schmidt's forceful question interrupted.

Rolf realized he needed to terminate the conversation lest they'd be able to trace the number. "No, I'll call you at nine. What about the high-level meeting I asked you about?"

"We're still working on that."

"Give it the highest priority. Talk to you at nine."

Rolf hung up and saw Sylvia's questioning look. "I'll fill you in over dinner."

The dining room was deserted. When Germans went out to eat, it was usually for lunch. In the evenings, they typically had cold cuts at home. Sylvia and Rolf ordered a cheese and sausage plate to share. Frau Greindl brought the wine list. When Rolf saw Sylvia hesitate, he insisted she order some for herself. She studied him, searching for evidence of sincerity, and ordered a glass of red wine. Rolf settled for mineral water.

First he told her of the arrangements with Schmidt.

"How are we going to get access to a fax machine?"

"I was hoping Frau Greindl could help us with that. Will you ask her?"

She nodded. Then she mused, "Here's an idea. My mom has a fax in her hotel. Why don't we have him fax it there, and then I can call her to confirm."

He shook his head. "Let's try Frau Greindl first. We'll be standing right with her so she won't be tempted to read it, and I'd prefer not to get your mom involved, except as a last resort."

"Of course, you're right."

When the innkeeper brought their food, Sylvia asked her.

"Certainly, Frau Mazzoni. Have your friend fax the papers here." She wrote a seven digit number on the beer coaster under Sylvia's wine glass.

When she was gone, Sylvia whispered, "Is that all right?"

Rolf thought for a moment. "It's not ideal. Schmidt will know where we are. But since we're leaving right after the fax, I suppose it'll have to do. Better than involving your mom and having to call to Milan to confirm."

They ate in silence. Then Sylvia asked, "Learn anything interesting from your secretary?"

"Yes, you could say that."

When he had finished telling her, she wanted to know more about Stein's mysterious client Fabrini and the money transfers.

He shrugged. "I have no idea who he is or what to make of it."

"And what does 'ARM' stand for?"

"Here are the possibilities that came to my mind. A person's arm? It's the same word in English and German. Or in English it could refer to arms or weapons or someone arming himself."

"And in German the word also means 'poor,'" Sylvia added.

"I hadn't thought of that. But I can't see a connection between any of those and this assignment, can you?"

She shook her head. "It could be either an acronym or initials."

"More likely an acronym, since initials usually have periods." Rolf swallowed the last bite of his dark crusty bread, spread with butter and German Camembert. "But Stein could have deliberately left them off to be confusing."

Sylvia took a sip of wine. "Acronym or initials of what? An organization?"

"Like RAF stands for Red Army Faction or Royal Air Force, depending on what country you're in." The instant the words left his lips, he regretted them. "I'm sorry. That just came out. I didn't mean to remind you—"

"It's all right, Rolf." She sought his eyes. "When we get back to the room, I want you to read my file. I know you've been wondering about what's in it."

He raised his hand. "You don't have to do that."

"I know, but it's important to me that you see it. There are some lies in there about me, but also things that unfortunately are true. I'd rather you know about them than keep imagining what they might be."

Unable to speak, he held her gaze and saw the trust. Well, their relationship was definitely on a new footing. He felt his pulse quicken.

As if reading his mind, she touched his hand. "Rolf, don't misunderstand. I'm still attracted to you, and I've noticed signs that you feel the same. But this is absolutely the wrong time to think of taking it further."

He swallowed and then spoke reluctantly. "I guess I agree. But I make no promises about when we get through this . . ." He didn't know how to finish the sentence, so he didn't.

"Yes, after this is over . . ." Her voice trailed off too, but what Rolf mostly heard was the yes.

When they got back to the room, Sylvia handed him her file.

"Are you sure about this?"

"Positive. Just so you know, the statements that I was sympathetic to the communist cause are total fabrication."

He settled on the sofa and leafed through the file. The sheer volume of information the Stasi had gathered on her was amazing. He felt self-conscious and skipped a lot of personal information. All he really needed to know was whether she had been part of the RAF and how much she knew about Kreuzer's activities. When he got to her East

Berlin trip with Kreuzer he slowed down. Then he reread it. So this was the damaging information. He stared at the wall.

Sylvia came out of the bedroom wearing silky light-blue pajamas. "You've come across my East Berlin trip, I see."

He nodded.

"Horst left for a few days. I suspected he had some business with the East German government. Whatever he was involved in, I certainly didn't want to know about it. That's the truth, Rolf. But if this were publicized, I don't think I'd be singing on any opera stages, even small ones."

He put the file aside, moved towards her, and wrapped an arm around her. "I believe you, Sylvia. We all make mistakes, and God knows I've made my share. Let's burn this file. Frau Greindl wouldn't mind us feeding her fireplace in the morning."

"Burning it is." She sounded relieved as she kissed him on the cheek, then moved away. "If you're through with the file now, I'll take it."

He handed it to her and then went to the bathroom to get ready for his night on the sleeper sofa. When he passed through the bedroom, she turned off the lamp. "Leave the door halfway open, please. Good night."

Rolf tossed for a long time thinking about Sylvia in the next room. Common sense told him they were doing the right thing in not sleeping together, but that didn't make it any easier.

♫ ♫ ♫

In the bedroom Sylvia had a hard time finding sleep as well, but for a different reason. Something was nagging at her. Her mind replayed her conversation with Rolf this evening, but nothing jumped out. Then she thought about the contents of her file. Again nothing clicked.

She knew she must be overlooking something. Whether that "something" was obvious or obscure, it would not come to her. She fought her growing frustration, realizing it was keeping her awake. Thoughts and dreams about the matter and its source intermingled as she drifted in and out of sleep all night.

At the first light of dawn Sylvia bolted straight up in bed. She turned on the bedside lamp and reached for the file on the nightstand. Frantic, she flipped its pages until she found what she was looking for. She stared at the page. How could she have missed something so obvious?

Sylvia snatched the paper from the file. She flung the covers aside and ran into the next room.

"Rolf! Rolf, wake up!"

Waving the page in front of his half-opened eyes, she cried, "We've got to get out of here now. The Stasi know about the times my mother and I stayed in this place. They know exactly where to find us."

Chapter Forty-Six

"When did you last speak with Mr. Keller?"

Harry Stein hit Betty with the question before she even had a chance to take a seat. She lowered herself slowly into one of the visitor's chairs, deciding how to respond. On the off chance the senior partner knew about this morning's phone call, she said, "He called me at home this morning." She could tell Stein wanted more.

"What did he call about?"

"Let's see." She wrinkled her face into what she hoped portrayed a thinking expression. "He wanted to know if I called his daughter for him, as he'd asked."

"And what did you tell him?"

"That Ashley missed him and wanted to know when he would come home."

"What else did you talk about?" Stein's skeptical expression told her he did not believe her.

"He said to tell her he'd be home soon."

Stein raised his hands in exasperation. "Betty, I've told you before that Mr. Keller is in grave danger. Don't make me pull every word out of you. The tiniest detail could be important . . . could save his life."

He seemed sincere in his concern, but Betty had been around trial lawyers long enough to know she couldn't trust their outward expressions. And Stein was known to be one hell of a litigator.

"You know where he is, don't you Betty?"

"No, sir, I don't."

"Betty, if something happens to him and I find out you knew where he was but didn't tell me . . ." His look communicated more than if he had completed his threat.

"I'm sorry, sir. I'd tell you if I knew." Rolf had been smart to keep his whereabouts a secret, which made it that much easier for her to sound convincing. And recalling Rolf's repeated admonition that a good witness only answers the question asked, she did not volunteer that he was no longer in East Germany.

"Why did he call you at home and not at the office?"

"I guess it's because he called about personal matters, or maybe it had to do with the time difference."

Stein stood. "You may go now. You will let me know the instant you hear from Mr. Keller again."

"Certainly, sir." She hurried out of the office, as if she could leave the lie behind that way. She would do no such thing. Something didn't add up. If Rolf needed Stein's help, he knew how to contact him. The fact that he hadn't could only mean he didn't trust the boss. Perhaps what she'd told him about the ARM file had confirmed his suspicions about Stein and the German mission. In any case, no matter the pressure or threats, she would reveal nothing, unless Rolf instructed her otherwise.

Upon reaching her office, she sat in her chair and stared at the wall. Stein could be telling the truth about the dangers facing Rolf, but there was nothing she could do about it. Though she recognized the futility of worrying, she couldn't stop. In her twenty-years at Stein & Weston, she'd never worked for an attorney who treated her with the respect Rolf had. She couldn't imagine being secretary to another lawyer. He simply had to return safely.

Chapter Forty-Seven

Rolf rubbed his eyes and shook his head to clear it. "What are you saying, Sylvia?"

She stabbed her finger at the page. "Here . . . and here." She shuddered. "I can't believe how much the Stasi knows about my personal life. To keep track of where Anna and I vacationed . . ." She looked at him with an expression of incredulity that took on a hint of panic. "Rolf, we need to go. Now!"

He sat up. "Let's think this through. We don't know when Dobnik stole this file. He could have had it for months."

"Are you saying that those Stasi officers in the pictures Dobnik's daughter gave us—"

Brigadier General Holger Frantz and Major Boris Schlechter," Rolf interjected.

"Are you saying they might not have seen this file?"

"That's right, and even if they had, would they have noticed a tiny detail like that and recall it after so many weeks or months?"

"But if one of them read it and remembered . . . we can't take that chance."

Her reasoning and forceful manner convinced him. "Okay. Let's get moving."

As they packed up, Rolf's eyes fell on Dobnik's suitcase. With Sylvia in the other room, he opened it and took the pistol from its hidden compartment. After checking that the magazine was loaded and the safety on, he considered putting it in his overcoat. Even though he'd played the devil's advocate by giving Sylvia various reasons why the Stasi might not know their whereabouts, it was best to be prepared. Not wanting to carry a gun on his person, however, he decided to return it to the suitcase side panel for now.

Less than half an hour later, they carted their belongings downstairs. Kitchen noises signaled that someone besides them was up early. Sylvia rang the counter bell, and Frau Greindl appeared in a matter of seconds. She looked puzzled when she spotted their bags. "You're leaving this early?"

"Yes, we've got a full day ahead of us," Sylvia responded.

While the innkeeper wrote out the bill, Rolf asked, "Do you know what time the copy shop across from the train station opens?"

Frau Greindl gave him the ticket. "Probably at seven-thirty or eight. I have a machine here if you need just a few copies."

He handed her his credit card. "Thank you, but we have a whole stack."

As they left, Sylvia reminded her of the fax she was expecting. "We'll be back a few minutes before nine."

♫ ♫ ♫

When Schlechter answered the phone, General Frantz barked, "Are you still in bed?"

"I'm just getting up, sir."

"How many inns did you check after you called me yesterday?"

"Nine, sir."

"How many are left?"

"Just a moment, sir." Schlechter fumbled on the nightstand for the list he'd gotten from the Mittenwald tourist office. He turned on the lamp and scanned the listings. "Close to thirty, General."

"Major, I remembered something about the guesthouse where Mazzoni stayed in the past. Its name has something to do with a view or mountains. Do you have a directory?"

"Yes."

"See if any of the names fit those criteria. Read out any you think might."

Schlechter went down the list. "Pension Alpen, Gasthof Karwendel, Hotel Alpenrot, Pension Bergblick—"

"Bergblick. That's it!" Frantz shouted in Schlechter's ear. "Go there now. And report back to me."

The line went dead. Schlechter leapt out of bed and threw on his clothes, not bothering to shower. At eight thirty sharp, he parked the dark blue Ford Taunus he'd rented in West Berlin in front of Pension Bergblick.

The plump woman behind the reception desk studied him. "Coming for breakfast or to rent a room, sir?"

He pasted a charming smile on his face. "Good morning. I'm Franz Xavier. I'm supposed to meet a couple of friends for breakfast here. I believe they're staying with you: Sylvia Mazzoni and Rolf Keller."

Schlechter saw fleeting recognition cross the innkeeper's face. "They just checked out. But they didn't say anything about expecting a friend." She paused. "Hmm, perhaps that's why . . ." She stopped herself as if remembering not to blab a secret.

Schlechter looked at her without saying anything. She struck him as the kind of person who could not endure a silence very long without volunteering additional information. As he'd expected, she spoke up. "Well, it's just that they are coming back to receive a fax in about half an hour."

"Thank you for telling me, Frau . . ."

"Greindl."

"While I wait, start me with some coffee, black."

"Certainly." She pointed toward the dining area and walked off.

Schlechter chose a table in the back of the room. He patted his chest. The Makarov sat securely in its holster.

♫ ♫ ♫

Sylvia and Rolf ate a standup breakfast of buttered *Brezeln* and strong German coffee at the train station kiosk. Afterward they moved Dobnik's cache from the locker to the suitcase and crossed the street. They had to wait only a few minutes until the copy shop opened promptly at seven thirty. Copying over a thousand pages was no small task. They divided the files between them to run two sets of copies, one for Stein and one for the Brits. Utilizing four copiers simultaneously, they managed to finish the job in a little over an hour. They returned Schmidt's stash to the suitcase and put the other sets in four boxes they purchased at the shop.

Sylvia asked the owner, "Do you have a shredder?"

"It's kaput," he replied.

Rolf recalled they had not had time this morning to burn her file in Frau Greindl's fireplace, as they had planned last night. He put the copy charge of over two hundred marks on his credit card and told Sylvia, "We'll destroy it later."

They had fifteen minutes to put the Brits' set into a train station locker and make it back to Bergblick to call Schmidt about the fax. Rolf started to pick up the case and two of the boxes when he felt Sylvia tugging at his arm. She pointed toward an area behind the counter. While he tried to see what was there, she asked the shop owner, "Sir, is that fax machine for public use?"

"Of course. The charge is one mark per page for sending or receiving a fax."

"Do you have a phone we may use?"

"There is a pay phone behind you."

Before either of them could ask, the owner handed Sylvia a card. "Here is the store fax number."

Although it was not quite nine o'clock, Rolf decided now was the time to call Schmidt. He had the letter. Within a minute or two after Rolf hung up, the fax machine awoke from its slumber and spit out a one-page document. Sylvia took it from the owner, read it, and handed it to Rolf. "You're the lawyer. You tell me if it's okay."

A quick reading showed the document, signed by the President of the Federal Intelligence Service, was straightforward. "It looks all right. Of course, as an American lawyer, I don't know how binding it is under German law."

Sylvia folded the paper and stuck it in an overcoat pocket. She nodded and Rolf went back to the phone. Schmidt answered on the first ring.

"You'll have the original for us when we give you what we've got?"

"Yes," replied Schmidt. "Can you be at my office by eleven?"

"I think so. What about the information on high-level meetings?"

A sigh came over the line. "There are meetings all over Germany today. The Interior Department heads are meeting in Hamburg; the Foreign Ministry has a retreat in Berlin; several high-level cabinet members are meeting in Bonn; the Economics Minister is attending a function in Düsseldorf; and Chancellor Kohl is scheduled to give a speech to the Bavarian Chamber of Commerce in Garmisch-Partenkirchen."

Rolf was considering the information when Schmidt spoke again. "Why don't you tell me what you've come across that hints at an assassination plot."

"Over the phone?"

"Yes. If something that important is in the works, I need to get on it right now."

Rolf related what he recalled from Dobnik's memorandum. Sylvia, standing next to him, chimed in every now and then, adding a detail he'd forgotten. When he'd finished, there was a considerable pause. "Well, nothing rings a bell. I'll have my people working on it while you're on your way here. See you at eleven."

Rolf replaced the phone and turned to leave, but Sylvia stopped him. "We need to call Frau Greindl and tell her we won't be stopping by."

He fished in his pockets for more coins and handed several to her. While she leafed through the phone book for the number of Pension Bergblick and then dialed, Rolf's attention was drawn to the local news that blared from a television set behind the counter. The newscaster reported that Chancellor Kohl was expected to outline his plan for Germany's unification in a speech to the Bavarian Chamber of Commerce conference this afternoon.

Rolf turned away. He had to focus on what remained to be done to finish their mission: put the set of copies for the British agents in a locker at the train station and drive to Pullach. After that, they'd be done with all this and could finally head to Stuttgart for Sylvia to sing and him to enjoy another marvelous performance of *Carmen*.

Just then Sylvia called out his name. The wall phone was dangling from its metal cord. She stared at him in horror. He rushed over and hung up the phone. "What's the matter?"

"Frau Greindl said a Franz Xavier is waiting for us at the inn. He told her he's a friend and is supposed to meet us there."

"Did she describe him?"

"She started to, but the line went dead. Something's happened to her. We must go back there."

"No, we can't. It's too dangerous. I'll take care of stashing the Brits' copies in a locker. While I do that, you call the police from here. But don't give your name. Just tell them to check on Pension Bergblick and hang up." He handed her the car keys. "Then carry Stein's copies to the car. Hide them in the side panels in the trunk, start the engine, and keep the windows up and the doors locked till you see me. And give me the Brits' phone number. I'll call them for you."

He'd spoken so fast, he wasn't sure she'd understood until she handed him a card with a phone number. "See you at the car in a few minutes."

Suitcase in one hand and two boxes under his arm, he hurried out the door while Sylvia picked up the phone.

♫ ♫ ♫

When the phone rang, Schlechter left his table and moved through the empty dining room to the reception desk. The innkeeper took the call on the other side of a partition. He stepped around the counter and entered a room set up as an office. Frau Greindl had her back to him. When he heard her say "Franz Xavier," he moved behind her, reached over her shoulder, and depressed the hook.

She jerked around, shock on her face. "What do you think you're doing?"

"That was Frau Mazzoni, wasn't it?"

The innkeeper maintained a stubborn silence.

He gave up any pretense of friendliness. "Where is she?"

She glared at him. "You're no friend of theirs. And I'm not telling you . . ."

417

Her voice trailed off and her defiant glare turned to fear when he stuck the Makarov into her round middle.

"You tell me right now where she is or I'll blow a hole right through your belly."

"She . . . she called from the copy shop."

"Which is where?"

"Across from the train station."

"And she is not coming back here?"

Frau Greindl shook her head, and Schlechter ran for the door. Maybe he could catch them before they left.

♫ ♫ ♫

Shaken by the ordeal, Frau Greindl sank into the chair by the phone, wishing her husband were there. But she did not expect him back from town before lunch time. What about Sylvia and her fiancé? She had to warn them. With shaking fingers she flipped through the Mittenwald telephone directory until she found the number for the copy shop. It took her several tries before she managed to dial the correct numbers on the rotary dial. She was too late. According to the owner, a couple fitting her description had just left the store. Dejected, she hung up. If she'd acted more quickly, she might have been able to tip them off. She pondered whether to call the police or wait for her husband.

♫ ♫ ♫

Major Boris Schlechter swore under his breath when he saw the copy shop empty of people, except for a man behind the counter. He'd barely begun to describe Mazzoni and Keller when the man interrupted to tell him they'd been there but left a few minutes ago. Schlechter had the impression he was not the first to ask about them. Just as he started to follow up and find out who else was looking for

418

them, the man pointed behind him. "Why, I think that's the fellow you mean."

Schlechter whirled around and peered through the store glass front toward the train station. He caught a glimpse of Keller coming out of the station. When Schlechter ran out of the shop, he saw Keller heave a suitcase into the back of a gray Opel across the street and jump into the passenger seat. The car accelerated down the street, passing Schlechter's Ford parked along the curb. He sprinted to it and made a U-turn to follow them, narrowly avoiding a collision with an oncoming van. His breathing slowed when he caught sight of the Opel at the next traffic signal.

Schlechter's mind churned as he trailed several car lengths behind. That had to be Mazzoni at the wheel, and with luck the suitcase held Dobnik's cache. Now he just had to wait for a good opportunity to overtake them. Sooner or later, it would come. They were amateurs after all.

♫ ♫ ♫

Rolf worked methodically. In a few minutes' time, he had stored the boxes in a locker, taped the key to the rear of the toilet bowl in the third stall of the train station men's room, just like in Berlin, and called the number for the British agents. The only hitch was that he got an answering machine. Odd that they weren't manning the phone. Had they left Berlin, trying to track them down?

After a brief hesitation, he decided to leave a cryptic message. "You'll find the key for the final delivery in the same spot as the first one. The only thing that's different is the city: Mittenwald."

By the time they'd pick up the message and collect the documents, Sylvia and he would be long gone. Carrying Dobnik's suitcase, he hurried from the train station toward the Opel. Sylvia spotted him and leaned over to unlock the passenger door. He heaved the case into the back and climbed in the passenger seat. She stepped on the gas.

He took a deep breath. "You know how to get back to the autobahn toward Munich?"

She nodded while slowing for the traffic ahead that was just starting to move as the signal changed to green.

"Just think, Sylvia, in a few hours we'll be on our way to Stuttgart and this whole thing will be over." He hoped it was true.

She accelerated as they reached the outskirts of the city. "I'm ready to get back to singing, that's for sure. It'll seem like a vacation after this."

He fell silent, thinking about having to call Stein and receive instructions on when to return to Washington. Not eager to get an earful from his boss about neglecting to keep regular contact and failing to fax the first set of documents, Rolf decided to put off the call until later. Besides, from what Betty had said, the senior partner might very well suspect that the phone call before the fire drill had been a setup. Rolf harbored no illusions that bringing Stein's copies back to Washington would salvage his partnership. That did not seem important any longer.

The Opel hugged the sharp curve of the autobahn entrance. They should reach Pullach in less than an hour. While he watched the speedometer needle hover around 120 kilometers, his thoughts turned to the unanswered questions. No matter how he tried, he was no closer to discovering the connecting thread between Stein, Fabrini, the ARM file and this mission than when he'd spoken with Betty.

"Finding answers to any of the riddles?" Sylvia asked.

"I'm stumped on the ARM matter."

"What about Dobnik's memo? Did Schmidt give you any help?"

Rolf related the various meetings Schmidt had told him about. Sylvia shrugged. "Could be any one of them, and that's just today. We don't even know which day in December or what location. I guess, we'll let Schmidt and his professionals grind their teeth on that one."

"There's something else." Rolf sat up. "While you called Frau Greindl, I caught the end of a newscast on the TV in the copy shop. It was reporting on a major policy speech on German unification Chancellor Kohl is expected to give to the Bavarian Chamber of Commerce today."

"Hmm. If they could eliminate Kohl that would certainly put a damper on plans to unify the country. Did the news say where he will speak?"

"If they did, I missed it. But Schmidt said he'll be in Garmisch-Partenkirchen, the town we drove through earlier before getting on the autobahn."

The engine protested with a high-pitched whine when she downshifted to pass a long line of trucks. Steering the car back into the right hand lane, she asked, "What did Dobnik's memo mention about the meeting? Oh, I remember. Eradication of a foreign vegetable and a reference to churches."

Then it hit Rolf. "The last part of the name Partenkirchen is the 'churches,' and Kohl means cabbage!"

"But why foreign?"

"Well, foreign to Communist East Germany."

She stared at him. "But that means—"

"A plot to assassinate Chancellor Kohl while he gives a speech in Garmisch-Partenkirchen," Rolf finished the sentence for her.

"Did Schmidt or the news say anything about the time of the speech?"

"I believe it's this afternoon . . . Sylvia, take the next exit. This can't wait. By the time we get to Pullach it may be too late. We need to find a phone and call Schmidt now."

Sylvia switched to the passing lane and accelerated. Finally, a green sign spanning the two autobahn lanes

421

showed an exit to Murnau and Kochel am See. Rolf reached into the glove box for the map. Sylvia was already slowing and moving into the exit lane.

"Head for Murnau. It's only a few kilometers."

They drove the country road in silence. The first phone booth they passed in town was occupied. Rolf motioned her on. They'd either come across another public phone or the post office. A few moments later, they saw an empty phone booth next to a gas station. As soon as Sylvia pulled into the station, Rolf jumped out of the car. There was no need to talk. She'd fill up while he called Schmidt.

After the fifth ring a female voice answered, "Bundesnachrichtendienst."

Startled, Rolf asked, "Is this the number for Herr Schmidt?"

"Yes."

"I need to speak to him right away."

"He's not available. Would you like to leave a message?"

"Are you his secretary?"

"Yes."

Rolf put urgency into his words. "Listen, it is very important that I speak with him this instant."

"I'm sorry, sir, but that's not possible."

"Not possible," Rolf repeated the words to himself. "I'm supposed to meet him at eleven. Is he not there?"

"He's in a meeting and is not to be disturbed." The voice was firm.

Frustration boiled over. "You don't understand. If I don't talk to him now . . ." He realized it wouldn't matter what he said, the secretary on the other end wasn't going to budge. "Give him this message. The plot is going down this afternoon in Garmisch-Partenkirchen. We are driving there now and won't meet him at his office at eleven. You got that?"

"Yes, but what's your name?"

"He'll know. And crash that meeting to give him this message now or I guarantee you'll be without a job tomorrow."

Rolf banged the receiver onto the hook and pulled open the folding door, ready to return to the gas station. Then he noticed the Opel was next to the phone booth, its engine idling and Sylvia at the wheel. He got in.

When she started to drive off, Rolf touched her arm. "Sylvia, wait a minute. We need to discuss something."

She stopped on the other side of the garage out of the way of the pumps and kept the motor running. "What is it?"

"I couldn't get ahold of Schmidt, and I don't trust his secretary to deliver my message to him in time. If she doesn't . . . Sylvia, let's drive back to Garmisch. We have to warn Kohl's security people."

"It's after ten now. We'll miss the eleven o'clock meeting with Schmidt."

"I already told the secretary that. Besides, we'll be in Garmisch by then. I'll call him from there." He saw her doubtful expression. "Sylvia, we can get with Schmidt afterwards and still make it back to Stuttgart well before your performance."

Her eyes met his, and he held her gaze. With a shrug she engaged first gear and drove in the direction of the autobahn. "I don't know why I'm doing this. Playing the rescuer for a government that's been blackmailing me . . . threatening to ruin me."

He wanted to point out that it was not about the government, but about the chancellor's life, and the country's future, but he restrained himself. Sylvia knew all that. She just needed to vent her frustration.

♫ ♫ ♫

Dennis Kingsley slipped out of the phone booth and broke into a run down the sidewalk. Being in good shape, he covered the several hundred meters to the rental car in less than two minutes. The brown Mercedes was locked. He'd sent Ross to check this hotel while he called their Berlin phone number to pick up messages. Breathing hard, Kingsley had started toward the hotel entrance when Ross came out.

"They left our copies in a locker in the Mittenwald train station. The key is in the men's room." Kingsley checked his watch. "The message was recorded at ten after nine, twenty minutes ago."

Without a word, Ross started the engine. They were in Garmisch-Partenkirchen, less than twenty kilometers from Mittenwald. London had come through and given them the list of towns that matched Brigitte Wesendorf's partial area code. Since yesterday afternoon they'd been checking hotels and inns in the Zugspitz region, working their way toward Garmisch.

"Let's go. Maybe they're still in Mittenwald."

With the car already in gear, Ross let out the clutch and gave it gas. Kingsley kept his eyes on the left side of the road, looking for a white Opel. If Sylvia and Rolf were driving from Mittenwald to Pullach to meet Schmidt, they might be taking this highway through Garmisch on their way to the autobahn. But they could also take Highway B11 and connect to the autobahn further north. Ross's fast driving made it difficult to get a good look at the vehicles coming from the opposite direction. The only Opel he spotted was not white but gray.

They reached the Mittenwald train station in twenty minutes. Luckily, the third stall in the men's room was unoccupied. They retrieved the key and found the locker without difficulty.

"Wow, that's quite a load," exclaimed Ross, lifting the two boxes.

They carried them straight to the car and proceeded to leaf through the contents, which appeared to have been organized by subject. Their quick perusal yielded intelligence regarding Stasi spies in the West and Red Army Faction terrorists. But, as with the first set they'd received in Berlin, it did not contain anything approaching the type of damaging information that could be used to scuttle unification.

Kingsley set the document boxes on the floor behind the driver's seat and looked at his partner. "Either our source was misinformed or lying, or Sylvia is holding out on us."

Ross nodded. "I'd say we keep looking for her. Perhaps Brigitte Wesendorf has that additional information she promised us."

"Wait here. I'll check the answering machine again." Kingsley got out of the Mercedes and strode into the train station.

♫ ♫ ♫

Schlechter followed the gray Opel at a discreet distance. He assumed they were driving to Pullach to deliver Dobnik's papers to Schmidt, counting himself fortunate they hadn't done so previously. When the Opel exited the autobahn, his first thought was that he'd been detected. On the road to Murnau he kept wondering about their detour, but convinced himself they weren't aware of his presence since they were not taking any evasive action.

When the Opel drove into a gas station in Murnau, Schlechter was even more puzzled. They could have filled up along the autobahn. Then he saw Rolf enter a phone booth across the parking lot. Perhaps their meeting with Schmidt hadn't been arranged yet. Schlechter pulled in and parked behind a car along the curb, satisfied he was far enough back not to be noticed. While he watched the station attendant fill the Opel's tank, Schlechter decided this was not the right time to make his move. There were too many people around.

His concern grew when the Opel traveled through the filling station in his direction, but then stopped abruptly. What were they doing? After a few moments, the car entered the street and passed him. Once more he made a U-turn and followed. When they entered the autobahn heading south instead of north, he didn't know what to think. If they weren't going to Pullach, where in the devil were they headed? To Garmisch or back to Mittenwald? None of this made sense.

Schlechter refocused. He didn't need to worry about where they were going or why. Instead, his job was to stay on their tail and capture them and their loot as soon as possible. He considered and quickly rejected the idea of running them off the road. The brisk traffic made it too risky. Frantz would not be satisfied with anything less than the return of all of Dobnik's documents, and causing an attention-getting accident was not the way to accomplish that. The better plan was to wait for an opportunity. One was sure to turn up.

The Opel exited at Garmisch. Once in town, their behavior seemed stranger than ever. They drove around like lost tourists. After they had passed several hotels without stopping, Schlechter's puzzlement grew. Finally, they drove up to a large hotel. A doorman walked over to their car and leaned into the passenger side. He gestured and pointed as if giving directions. Thereafter their driving became more purposeful.

He followed them through several turns, past directional signs to Kongresshaus, a convention center. Did they know about this afternoon? Impossible, he told himself. But then again, even though he'd not been told about the plot, he'd managed to pick up snippets surreptitiously. Dobnik could have done the same. Schlechter's worries grew when they approached a square. A sign proclaimed it the Richard Strauss Platz. It was lined on three sides by shops and apartments. The convention center stood at the end, and a huge banner welcoming the Bavarian Chamber of Commerce hung above its entrance.

There were no pedestrians in the square, and only a few at a distance around its perimeter. The Opel slowly proceeded across the plaza, as if its occupants were surveying the surroundings. There were several policemen stationed at the main entrance to the convention center, which made Schlechter nervous. He relaxed when his quarry drove past the parking lot entrance on the side of the building. A sign declared it restricted to Chamber of Commerce meeting attendees.

Pursuing them into a side street that led away from the square, he saw to his amazement empty parking places along the curb. It apparently surprised Mazzoni as well, as she passed several before stopping. He'd hung back far enough to allow him to pull into the first open space at the same time, with three parked cars between them.

Frantz would be pleased if he not only recovered the documents but prevented any interference with the plans at the convention center, but he had to act now. Schlechter pulled out the Makarov and with practiced movements attached the silencer to the barrel. He exited the car and with quick strides moved toward the gray Opel.

Chapter Forty-Eight

Rolf began to question his memory. None of the larger Garmisch hotels showed any signs of hosting a convention. Finally, they learned from a doorman that the meeting was at the convention center. Following his precise directions, they arrived at the Richard Strauss Platz after a few minutes' drive.

Sylvia pointed to the banner hanging above the entrance of the building ahead. Red letters on white canvas welcomed the Bavarian Chamber of Commerce. "This is the place. What now?"

Police were stationed around the convention center. He also saw some milling around the plaza. "Looks like they're expecting an important visitor." He pointed to the right. "Take that street. I'd like to get an idea of the surroundings."

She drove up to the parking lot on one side of the convention center. "Don't we want to alert the police?"

"Soon, perhaps. Keep going. Let's find a place to park on the street and look around on foot."

"First we need to find out when the chancellor is expected. We may not have much time to explore." She turned down the next street and passed several empty spaces along the curb.

"Any of these is fine," he told her.

After they had parked, he turned to her. "Sylvia, we need more details. If we tell our crazy tale to the police they'll laugh at us, or detain us. Schmidt would know what we're talking about, but he isn't here."

"So what do you suggest?"

"There must be access from the park behind the convention center for deliveries. And there should be emergency exits from meeting halls into the park. Maybe we can figure out where the assassins are going to be."

She was reaching to turn off the ignition when the left rear door flew open. Rolf turned and stared into the barrel of a handgun. He caught his breath. The cold deep-set eyes and beefy face of the man holding the pistol left no doubt this was Stasi Major Boris Schlechter.

Sylvia gasped.

"Frau Mazzoni, put the car in gear and drive where I tell you. I know a secluded spot where we can talk undisturbed, and the three of us have much to discuss."

She was breathing hard but did not move.

Schlechter got in and slammed his door shut. "Now, or I'll blow his head off."

Rolf felt the cold metal of the pistol pressing against his face. "Do as he says," he told Sylvia.

She forced the gearshift against a half-depressed clutch pedal, producing a high-pitched grinding sound. Rolf cringed. She was on the edge of losing it, he knew. The car lurched forward into a near-stall before the engine pulled through.

"Relax. Do as I say and nothing will happen to you."

Rolf knew the smooth deep voice was lying. They'd both be dead unless they found a way to outmaneuver this professional killer. The pistol looked similar to the

Makarov in the suitcase, except that it had a silencer. Schlechter had probably used it to murder Dobnik.

Although he sensed the futility of bargaining, Rolf could think of no other option at the moment. He looked Schlechter in the eye. "Look, stop the car. You let Frau Mazzoni go, and I'll tell you where to find what you came for."

Schlechter sneered. "Nice try, Herr Keller. Your slick lawyer talk is not going to get you anywhere with me." He jerked his massive head in the direction of the rear cargo area. "I already know where you're keeping the papers you stole. The suitcase back there is the one you dug up in Wandlitz."

Rolf doubted that Schlechter had gotten a good look at the case during their escape in the dark from Dobnik's bungalow, but there was no point in denying what it held. Unless they found a way to disarm him, the Stasi agent would soon see the contents for himself.

"You're right. That case contains Dobnik's documents. Take it. You don't need to kidnap us—"

"Shut up! You'll get your chance to answer my questions later. Until then keep your mouth *shut*!"

After a silent drive that spanned several minutes, they reached the outskirts of Garmisch. Schlechter stared out the window, looking for something. Then came his sharp command from the rear, "Turn right at the next intersection."

Beyond a small settlement of fewer than a dozen houses, the edge of a forest came into view. Rolf realized the Stasi major must have noticed the woods while following them into town. A thick cloud cover oppressed the landscape, hanging so low it merged into the dark treetops of the woods ahead. He felt as if they were coming to the end of the world. Maybe they were. Rolf was very conscious of Sylvia's hands trembling on the wheel. He reached over and clasped one of them, his mouth set in a stubborn line.

After they'd passed the last house, they came upon a dirt road leading into the forest. Despite a sign depicting a tractor in silhouette, indicating it was restricted to local agricultural traffic, Schlechter motioned Sylvia onto it. She stepped on the brake instead.

"Go on. Surely your nice western car can handle a forest road." Schlechter obviously enjoyed his own sarcasm.

With hands still shaky, Sylvia turned the wheel and let the car creep onto the rough trail. She zigzagged around deep ruts and occasional puddles of half-melting snow. Now and then the car bottomed out, the scraping noise from dirt and rocks jolting Rolf. After a few hundred meters, spruces, pines and firs crowded out most of the sycamores and beech trees they'd passed at first.

Schlechter pointed to the left. "In there."

This time Sylvia did not hesitate, but steered the car onto a narrow trail leading into a small clearing. Rolf sensed her resignation as she dodged patches of snow on the shady side of the path.

"Stop, turn off the engine, and hand me the key!" Schlechter commanded. After she complied, he motioned with the gun toward the driver's door. "Get out very slowly, walk to the front of the car, and put your hands on the hood."

Rolf saw raw fear in Sylvia's eyes. They begged him to do something, but what? He felt so helpless. The thought that he'd once again fail Sylvia infuriated him. He would not give in to this Stasi hoodlum. Keep your head, he told himself. You *will* find a way.

The pistol swung toward him. "All right, your turn."

When Rolf got out, Schlechter followed him along the side of the car. Before he leaned forward on the hood, Rolf glanced around—grass and thick trees, that was it. No sign of human life.

"Looks like a good place for a private talk," the Stasi agent mocked. "But before we chat, I have a little job for you, Frau Mazzoni."

Out of the corner of his eye Rolf saw Schlechter pull something from his pocket. "Take this and tie Herr Keller's hands behind his back."

When Sylvia approached, Rolf raised up from the hood to keep his balance as he moved his arms backward. Her hands felt as cold as the nylon cord she was wrapping around his wrists. He tried to keep his hands apart a tiny bit, but Schlechter barked, "Hands together. Pull it tight. Make a double knot. Now go back to the other side."

Rolf felt rough hands tugging to test the tightness of the knot. Satisfied, Schlechter stepped back. "Frau Mazzoni, get the suitcases out of the back and bring them here."

Sylvia moved to the rear of the Opel and raised the rear door.

"Remember, your friend's life is in your hands." The gun barrel pressed against the back of Rolf's skull.

When she had laid the three suitcases on the ground, the Stasi major ordered her to step to the side of the car. Rolf watched him rifle through their clothes, then turn his attention to Dobnik's locked case. "What's the combination?"

"3-9-7-1," replied Sylvia. She seemed to have recovered somewhat. Her voice was almost calm.

Schlechter spun the lock and lifted the lid. Rolf held his breath, praying he would not discover the hidden compartment with the Makarov. Rolf turned his head toward Sylvia. When their eyes met, he moved his head and eyes toward Schlechter and Dobnik's case. Would she catch his meaning?

"These are all the files you took?"

Rolf replied before Sylvia could, "Yes. That's all of them."

"And you've not delivered anything to Schmidt?"

While Rolf considered how much this Stasi agent might know about Dobnik's deliveries and how to respond, Sylvia said, "Nothing since the first drop."

"Why not?"

Rolf answered, "We were on our way to meet him."

"Where?" Schlechter rose from the case and moved toward Rolf.

"His office."

"Don't lie to me." The pistol pressed into his neck once more. "He's in Pullach, and you were checking out hotels and the convention center in Garmisch? Explain that."

"We took a detour to try and prevent an assassination we think is planned at the convention center today."

"You got that from these documents?"

"Yes."

"I'm impressed. But you should have gone to Pullach when you had the chance instead of snooping around here."

"Who are the assassins and how are they going to do it?" Rolf asked, not expecting an answer, even if this Stasi agent knew the details of the plot. The longer he kept him talking, the better their chances for survival. Perhaps someone would stumble upon them—a slim chance in this remote place.

Schlechter pulled the gun back. "I ask the questions and you give the answers." He approached Sylvia. "Close the suitcase with the documents, but don't lock it. Put it back in the car. Leave the other two. You won't need them."

Rolf caught Sylvia's terrified look at his implication.

"What are you waiting for?"

She moved toward Dobnik's case. Rolf knew this was their last chance. "Wait. Hear me out, Major Schlechter."

"You know my name. Dobnik tipped you off."

"General Frantz won't be happy to see you return with this suitcase full of documents."

Even though the Stasi agent tried to control his reaction, Rolf could tell he'd caught him off guard.

"Why is that?"

"Because we copied everything. By the time you reach East Berlin, British Intelligence will have a duplicate set."

"You're bluffing. Give me one reason why I should believe you."

"You were at the Bergblick when Sylvia called there this morning." When Schlechter did not respond, Rolf continued, "You know that she called from a copy shop."

Rolf could see that his words had an impact. He had to shake the Stasi agent's confidence now. "When General Frantz learns that you failed to keep the documents out of the hands of Western agents . . . you know better than we what he'll do."

Schlechter spluttered, "You son of a bitch."

"Rolf, watch out!" Sylvia's warning and a swift movement behind him caused him to move to his right. Schlechter's blow glanced off the side of his head and the pistol struck his left shoulder, hard. He winced at the sharp pain. Through tears he forced himself to speak. "Schlechter, listen to me. We can make a deal."

The butt of the gun stopped in midair. "What kind of deal could you possibly offer me?"

"You can't go back to East Germany. Even if Frantz doesn't have you executed, you'll be arrested for murder once the communist government falls. And you know its days are numbered." While Rolf was speaking urgently, he sensed that Sylvia had moved closer to the suitcases. He had to keep Schlechter's attention. "If you help us prevent this assassination, you'll be a hero, and the West Germans might just overlook your past."

When there was no response, Rolf turned around, doing his best to ignore the pain the movement caused.

Schlechter's eyes were on Sylvia. "What do you think you're doing?"

She stood over Dobnik's case. "Getting ready to carry it to the car, as you told me."

Schlechter seemed unsure of what to do. Finally, he said, "All right, close it and put it in the Opel. And remember what happens to Herr Keller here if you try anything." He turned back. "As for you, smart lawyer, I wouldn't be so sure about what will happen in East Germany. Our communist state will be around for some time, especially if Kohl is assassinated. With him out of the picture, there's not going to be a unified Germany any time soon."

Sylvia carried the closed case toward the rear of the car and heaved it into the cargo area. Disappointment washed over Rolf. He'd failed to convince Schlechter, and Sylvia either hadn't caught his signal about the hidden pistol, or was too afraid to reach for it. They would die right here. His mind churned, still trying to think of a way out.

The Stasi major had just identified Kohl as the target. Rolf had not mentioned the chancellor's name. That proved Schlechter knew of the plot. Keep talking, he told himself. "Sooner or later there will be one Germany. You know that. Assassinating the chancellor may delay it, but it won't prevent it. Do you know what kind of information General Frantz has kept on you? Can you afford to have it fall into the hands of the Western authorities?"

Schlechter waved his pistol. "If you don't shut up on your own, I will do it for you."

Rolf knew he had him thinking. Perhaps they'd get out of this yet. Then, without warning, Schlechter ran to the rear of the Opel just as Sylvia's upper body emerged from the open cargo area.

♫ ♫ ♫

While bending forward to slide the case into the luggage compartment, Sylvia glanced through the side window. The Stasi agent was not looking her way. She'd understood Rolf's cue reminding her of the gun. Could she risk making a grab for it? Rolf's life was at stake. If she did nothing, Schlechter would kill them both in any event. There was no other option. With Schlechter's attention still on Rolf, she lifted the lid just enough to let her free hand reach the side panel compartment. She ripped it open and clutched at the pistol. When she straightened up, she saw the thug run toward her. She released the safety.

"Shoot!" Rolf shouted.

She fired at the figure coming around the car. Her ears rang from the shot as the recoil knocked her back. Schlechter cursed. She aimed again, but Schlechter had retreated behind the rear fender. She realized too late that he'd run back to Rolf.

"Drop your gun, or he dies."

She heard rage in the agent's voice and noticed a trickle of blood on his neck. The bullet must have just grazed him.

"Drop it now!"

Resigned, she lowered her arm and let the pistol fall to the ground. It was over.

"Come over here," Schlechter commanded.

She tried not to look at Rolf, but couldn't help herself. He nodded at her defeated expression, as if everything was going to be all right, but she knew she'd doomed them both.

Schlechter retrieved the pistol. "A Makarov," he declared in a matter-of-fact tone, as if he were a gun dealer lecturing an ignorant customer. "Dobnik left you this present." He stuck the pistol in his waistband and stared at her and then Rolf. "I should kill both of you right now. But perhaps I'll let you live, if you give me the answers I want."

He motioned for her to step to the other side of the hood. Then he turned to Rolf. "Tell me where you left the copies for the Brits."

When there was no answer, Schlechter said, "You want to play the hero? I'll tell you what. If you don't spill every last detail right now, I'll kill you both. But first, I will have a little fun with your girlfriend here in the grass." He sidled up to her, and before she knew what was happening, reached inside her open coat and began fondling her breasts. "I bet you've got a sweet pussy."

She jerked away in horror, banging her hip against the car's grill. Rolf started to charge Schlechter, but the pistol stopped him.

"Get back over there! If you don't talk right now, I'll tie you to a tree so you can watch the show. You can look away, but you can't block out her screams. Before I'm through with her, she'll beg me to kill her."

"You bastard!"

Rolf's guttural outburst scared Sylvia almost as much as the thought of how this monster would hurt her before he killed her.

"It's in a locker in the Mittenwald train station." Rolf spoke with resignation. "The key is in the men's room, third stall."

"When did you notify the British?"

"A few minutes after nine this morning."

"By telephone?"

"Yes."

"What's the number?"

"It's on a card. I think I gave it back to Sylvia."

Schlechter gave her an expectant look. She froze. Where had she stuck the damn thing? Then she remembered and pulled it out of her rear jeans pocket. The agent snatched it from her hand.

"That's a West Berlin area code. How many agents are you dealing with?"

"Two."

"Names?"

"Dennis Kingsley and Peter Ross," she replied.

Schlechter smirked. "You just lost your argument, counselor. Your British friends have a long way to come. I can beat them to the locker in Mittenwald."

"I wouldn't be so sure," Rolf said defiantly. "Kingsley told me that his partner Ross would be there in half an hour. That means he was in the area looking for Sylvia and me."

Sylvia held her breath. Would the agent buy the lie? If he thought he had any chance of beating the British to the stash, he'd dispose of her and Rolf and make a run for Mittenwald. His face bore a steely expression as he considered his options.

♫ ♫ ♫

This smart-mouthed lawyer had a point. If Frantz found out that British Intelligence had copies of Dobnik's documents . . . He didn't dare finish the thought. On top of that, the end of the communist regime *might* very well be near. And even if it managed to keep its grip on power, the reformist zealots would be calling for the arrests of the hard-line Stasi officers to ingratiate themselves with the people.

He told himself to ignore his doubts. Perhaps Keller was lying and the Brits were still in Berlin, a long way from Mittenwald. But could he take that risk? He realized these amateurs could not promise him anything, and there was no telling what Schmidt and his horde would do to him. But even if they didn't make him a deal he liked, whatever happened to him here might be preferable to his fate in East Berlin. Assuming he'd survive Frantz's wrath, would he be safe in a liberalized East Germany, let alone a unified Germany, if he killed these two?

Schlechter reached his decision. He'd take his chances on beating the British to the locker, and he'd bet on the communist regime's survival. He'd done the Stasi's bidding for too many years. He wouldn't know how to live any other way.

"Move over there, both of you!" He pointed the Makarov toward the huge trunk of the lone sycamore among the evergreens. The look that passed between them told him they knew it was over. Besides fear, he sensed the affection between these two. He'd never have a woman of Sylvia Mazzoni's caliber, unless by force. When they reached the tree, they started to turn to face him.

"Keep your backs to me. Maybe you'll be united in the next world like the lovers in your stupid opera plots." Schlechter aimed the Makarov at Rolf Keller's head.

♫ ♫ ♫

Rolf and Sylvia turned toward Schlechter, Rolf's mind spinning, still groping for some way out. Every muscle in his body was taut, ready for a last-ditch effort. Limbs extended in karate form, Rolf lunged desperately at the Stasi killer, hoping to catch him off guard. A sharp explosive sound pounded his ears.

♫ ♫ ♫

With his pistol pointing at Rolf, Schlechter froze at a rustling noise from behind. He glanced over his shoulder, looking for movement in the woods. Nothing. On instinct he spun back around and saw Rolf hurtling toward him. He squeezed the trigger. A shot sounded. His hand went limp. The Makarov tumbled to the ground. He felt as if his head were exploding. As he collapsed, everything around him went dim.

Someone bent over him. "How will they kill Kohl? Tell me!"

Schlechter attempted to clear his blurred vision. He tried to talk but could not make a sound through the blood in his throat. With a gigantic effort, he finally managed to say, "Bomb."

Someone shook him. "Who are the assassins?"

The buzzing in his ears swelled to a roar. Daylight faded. "Rot in . . ." He gave up the effort with a gasp. Stillness and darkness engulfed him.

♫ ♫ ♫

Rolf was struggling to his feet when Sylvia rushed to his side. "Are you all right?"

"Yes. Thank God." He stretched his arms behind him toward Sylvia. "Cut me loose, quick."

His hands free, he looked around but could not see anyone. He bent over the dying Stasi agent, imploring him to divulge details of the assassination plot. After Schlechter had drawn his last breath, Rolf stood and peered once more in the direction from which the fatal shot must have come. Now he could make out police uniforms moving toward them through the woods. Turning back, Rolf noticed Dobnik's pistol stuck in Schlechter's waistband. He pulled it out and slipped it into his own coat pocket, but left Schlechter's Makarov in the leaves where it had fallen.

Sylvia walked up. She looked with apprehension toward the trees.

"It's all right," he reassured her. "It's the police."

She wrapped her arms around his waist. With his good arm, he drew her to him and nuzzled his face into her thick curls. He felt her shudder. They held each other, motionless, and listened to the wind sighing in the pines. Rolf looked down on the lifeless body at his feet, blood oozing from temple and mouth. It was just a pile of flesh and clothing. The eyes that had been so menacing only moments ago were now glazed over, seeing nothing. How close he and Sylvia had come to being in Schlechter's place!

At the sound of approaching footsteps, Rolf looked up and saw Schmidt with two policemen, grim looks on their faces. One pointed a rifle at the body in the grass while the other checked for signs of life.

Rolf let go of Sylvia. "He's dead." Saying the words brought a strange sense of relief.

Schmidt turned away from the body. "Major Schlechter?"

Rolf nodded. "He confirmed that there would be an attempt on the chancellor's life this afternoon."

"I wish we'd caught him alive. But we could see he had a gun on you, and when our man had a clear shot at him, he took it. Did he say anything before he died?"

"All he said was 'bomb.' But he didn't answer my question about the assassins." Rolf turned, wincing at the pain in his shoulder. The events during the last few minutes had blocked it out. Now it had returned, full force.

Schmidt noticed. "Are you hurt?"

"Schlechter hit him on the shoulder with the butt of his gun," Sylvia interjected. "He was aiming for his head."

"Can you lift your arm?"

Rolf grimaced. "Yes, with pain."

"We'll take you to the hospital in Garmisch."

"Not until we do everything we can to stop the assassins." He looked at Sylvia. "I can't help you with the baggage or the driving."

Schmidt motioned for the two officers to carry the suitcases to the car. He asked Rolf, "Where are Dobnik's documents?"

"Gray suitcase in the car."

Schmidt lifted the case out of the cargo area and put it on the rear seat. "I'll look at this on the way." He instructed one of the officers, "Make arrangements to secure the scene."

"The detective and more officers are on their way."

Peter Bernhardt

Schmidt climbed in the back seat of the Opel and nodded to Sylvia. When they were back on the forest road, he asked, "You have the combination?"

Rolf gave it to him, and Schmidt wrote it in a notebook. Then he opened the case and glanced at the files. "Have you been through these?"

"Yes."

"Did you see anything about the assassination other than Dobnik's memo?"

"No," replied Rolf. "Most of it relates to terrorists and Stasi spies in the West."

"I'll have it analyzed later. Right now I've got more pressing problems."

He closed the case. Apparently he'd not noticed the empty side compartment.

Rolf could not contain himself any longer. "How did you find us?"

"One of the policemen at the convention center recognized Schlechter's car. We learned he had been dispatched to catch you and got a description of his rental car. Every policeman in Germany has been looking for him. We came too late to stop him from kidnapping you but were able to follow at a distance. Too distant. We lost you, until we heard a gunshot."

Thank God Sylvia had fired that pistol, Rolf thought. To Schmidt he said, "I guess your secretary interrupted your meeting?"

"Whatever you said to her got her attention. I've not seen her barge into my office quite like that before."

Rolf didn't respond, doing his best to keep a straight face, when Schmidt asked, "What do you make of Schlechter's tip about the bomb?"

"I don't trust it at all. But you can't afford to ignore it."

"Do you have my letter with you, Herr Schmidt?" Sylvia cut in.

He nodded and reached into a coat pocket.

She glanced at Rolf. "Would you look at it?"

He opened the envelope Schmidt handed him. "Looks like the faxed copy."

"Keep it for me for now." She stared straight ahead. "Rolf, I know you want to stay. But I'm really anxious to get back to Stuttgart. If I miss my performance, I may lose the two-year contract the company has offered me. Is there any reason I can't just go on after I drop you off at the Kongresshaus?"

"There is." Schmidt's firm voice resonated inside the vehicle. "You'll have plenty of time to make your performance. I need you here this afternoon. Your past associations and what you went through in East Berlin might trigger something that will identify the assassins."

After a few moments, a resigned Sylvia glanced in the rearview mirror. "Do you have any information about what happened to Frau Greindl? You know, the owner of the Gasthaus Bergblick."

"Oh, the police got an anonymous call about her. That must have been you. When they checked it out, they found she was distraught but otherwise fine. Apparently, Schlechter took off in a big hurry to catch you."

Rolf watched as Schmidt tried to squeeze the case behind the driver's seat. Then abruptly, he lifted it and reached underneath the seat. His hand emerged, holding a file. "Sylvia Mazzoni," he read.

Rolf saw Sylvia's panicked expression. "That's mine," she protested.

"It's a Stasi file. I need to review it. If it's yours, you'll get it back."

Rolf spoke up. "Herr Schmidt, Dobnik gave that file to Sylvia for her personal use. It's got nothing to do with the documents he left for you. Please give it to her now."

"Not until I've had a look. If it is as you say, I will return it promptly."

No one spoke the rest of the way. When they reached the convention center, Schmidt broke the silence. "Chancellor Kohl is supposed to arrive at two thirty, and we don't know who the assassins are or what they have planned. We tried to talk the chancellor out of appearing, but he would have none of it. That means we have a little over an hour to catch the bastards."

Schmidt directed Sylvia toward the parking lot. He showed his badge to the attendant, and they were waved through. When Sylvia turned off the engine, he said, "Wait for me here. I'll put these in my car first." He gripped the suitcase handle, and pinned the Mazzoni file under his arm.

He opened the rear door but did not move. Instead he looked at both of them. "I wish the chancellor weren't so stubborn. But now that we have confirmation of the plot to kill him . . . perhaps I can change his mind. At the very least, he's got to delay his appearance. We'll have to evacuate the convention center and search for a bomb. And if Schlechter lied and there isn't one, Lord knows what else we'll have to do in the little time we have."

Chapter Forty-Nine

"Just as we thought. No bomb." Schmidt shook his head. "Schlechter laughed all the way to hell."

"Any chance they could have missed it?" asked Rolf, still nursing his aching shoulder.

"There's always that chance, but these bomb squad officers are the best." His eyes swept the square, populated with curiosity seekers hoping to catch a glimpse of Chancellor Kohl. "I'd say Schlechter tried to throw us off track."

A nearby church bell struck eight notes of the Westminster chime, indicating the half hour. Sylvia checked her watch. Two thirty. "The chancellor is late."

"We've got another half hour. He refused to cancel but did agree to delay until three."

Rolf pointed to the building behind them. "Don't tell me he plans on using this front entrance."

"We asked him to use the safer park entrance, but he insisted on coming through the square." Schmidt shrugged. "He's a politician. There's no way he'd pass up the crowd and the television cameras."

Sylvia's thoughts turned again to this evening's performance. "Herr Schmidt, you say the police have checked the buildings surrounding the square and the park. They've not turned up anything. What can we do that they haven't done already?"

He met her gaze. "Probably nothing. But at this point I'm running out of options. If there is even the slightest chance that either of you could uncover something . . . I can't afford to let you go."

"I have to leave by three thirty to get to the opera house in time. At the very latest, I must be there an hour before the seven-thirty curtain. If I'm not, they'll replace me."

"Frau Mazzoni, if the assassins are here, they'll have made their attempt before then. If not, the chancellor will have finished his speech and be on his way to Bonn. In either case, you'll be able to leave in time."

"Do I have your word on that?"

A flicker of annoyance crossed Schmidt's face. "You do." He hesitated. "In fact, I can even have one of my men call the opera house and explain why you might be a little late."

She raised her hand. "Absolutely not. If management gets even a whiff of my involvement with your outfit, they'll start asking questions I may not be able to answer to their satisfaction. And since I have your word that I'll be out of here in an hour in any case, there's no reason to alert them to any of this."

In lieu of responding, Schmidt scanned the square once more. He fidgeted. "They could be anywhere. I wish I knew who to look for." He turned toward her and Rolf. "I want the two of you to walk through the crowd. If something strikes you, anything at all, no matter how insignificant it may seem, ask the nearest policeman to page me."

When Rolf started to move, Schmidt said, "Wait. After you've checked the square, walk around the perimeter, and if you don't see anything unusual there, go through the park."

Sylvia nodded and followed Rolf into the plaza. "Do you have any idea what he expects us to find?"

He slowed to let her catch up. "I think he's counting mostly on you, Sylvia."

"You mean . . ." She had to force herself to say the words. ". . . Red Army Faction terrorists?"

Rolf kept moving as he studied the people around them.

She spoke to his back, "It's been twelve years since Kreuzer. What makes him think I'd recognize any of these left-wing extremists?"

As soon as she'd asked the question, she realized how angry she was with Rolf. She expected Schmidt not to trust her, but Rolf? Did *he* think she still sympathized with the RAF? She jerked his arm. He winced. It was the injured one. "Sorry."

But her anger resurfaced. "You don't trust me. You think I'm still in league with Kreuzer's buddies."

He wheeled around, put his good arm on her shoulder, and looked steadily into her eyes. "Sylvia, if I didn't trust you, I wouldn't have come here with you. We would have dropped the goods in Pullach and been on our way to Stuttgart by now."

She broke away from his stare. "So why do you and Schmidt think I know these assassins?"

"It's a long shot. But the Stasi is not going to do the dirty work themselves. As we learned from Dobnik's documents, they train terrorists to do the killing. Just yesterday a prominent banker was murdered, probably by RAF terrorists. They're still active, and Schmidt's hoping you might recognize someone."

She felt herself flush. "When did you learn about this murder?"

He looked at the ground for an instant, then made eye contact. "Schmidt told me on the phone yesterday. I didn't want to worry you."

During the last few years, she'd told herself she'd made a clean break with her past. Then Schmidt used it to blackmail her. Now the possibility, no matter how remote, that she might run into an RAF terrorist she'd known twelve years ago chilled her. Images of sleepless nights during her final days with Horst Kreuzer flooded her mind. She shook her head to banish the horrific memories.

"Sylvia, are you okay?"

His concerned expression softened her anger. "I wish you'd told me. If the RAF killed someone else, I ought to have known about it." She charged ahead. "Let's not waste any more time."

They crisscrossed the cobblestone pavement of the Richard Strauss Platz, studying the people who were milling around. Not having detected anything out of the ordinary, they looked into shops and building lobbies bordering the square. Even if they had a way to gain access, there was no time to check inside apartments and offices. She hoped the police had done so.

Ten minutes were gone, and they'd made no progress. Sylvia walked toward the side of the convention center. "Let's try the park."

When she sensed that Rolf was not following her, she stopped and turned around. He was glancing back and forth along an imaginary line between the center's main entrance and a four-story building—one side painted green, the other pink—across the square. She moved toward him. "What are you doing?"

"Sylvia, would you stand right here for a minute?" Without waiting for a response, Rolf trotted off. She lost sight of him in the crowd. Then she spotted him across the way. He disappeared from her view intermittently, each time resurfacing in front of a different shop and looking her way. After several minutes of watching him wander the south end of the plaza, she saw him wave her over.

When she reached him, he pointed toward the spot she'd just left. "I figure that's where the chancellor's motorcade is going to stop. He'll have to walk about ten meters to the main entrance. No doubt he'll take time to shake hands and wave to the crowd."

"Less than thirty meters from here, an easy target for a good marksman," she guessed at his thoughts.

"With his big frame and at almost two meters tall, he'd be hard to miss. They don't call him 'the colossus' for nothing."

"Where would a shooter hide?"

"That's what I've been puzzling over for the last few minutes. The killer would need to be high enough to have a clear shot over the crowd. That means higher than ground level and a line of sight unobstructed by trees."

"That's what you were doing—locating houses suitable for getting a clear shot."

He nodded and pointed upward. "A top-floor window somewhere along here would be a perfect vantage point for a sharpshooter."

She glanced at the numerous apartments that occupied the upper three floors of the two-tone building. The ground floor housed retail outlets. Signs advertised a drug store, a photo shop, an optical business, and a book store.

Rolf was looking at the businesses as well. "I didn't spot anything unusual in any of these stores, but the two of us should take a closer look. Maybe you'll see something."

While she considered what she could possibly discover that he hadn't, Rolf touched her arm and led her across the street to the photo shop. The doorbell brought forth a middle-aged woman. Thin brown hair, perched high atop her head in a large bun, lent her a grandmotherly appearance.

"Grüß Gott. May I help you find something?"

After responding with the same southern German greeting, Rolf asked, "Are you the owner?"

She hesitated, as if deciding whether that was any of his business. "Yes, this is my shop."

"I'm curious whether a big event like today helps your sales."

Sylvia saw how few customers were in the store and thought for a moment the woman would laugh at the ridiculous sounding question. Rolf was obviously warming her up with small talk, getting ready to pump her for information.

If the store owner thought the question stupid, she didn't let on. "I wish that were true." She sighed. "I'm afraid most are curiosity seekers."

"Have you gotten any unusual requests during the last few days?"

The shopkeeper gave him a quizzical look. "Such as?"

"I don't mean to be nosy, but I assume you also own the apartments above the store."

"Yes, I do."

"And you don't have any vacancies?"

She shook her head. "I've had the same renters in all three apartments for years." She rubbed her chin. "Funny."

"What's that?" Rolf asked quickly.

Sylvia admired the way he spiked his lawyerly extraction of information with personal charm. The store owner responded, "Well, it's only that I haven't had any inquiries for months, and now I've had two in the same week."

"Someone else asked to rent from you?"

"Yes, a couple in their thirties, I'd say. I could tell they weren't married. But I didn't have a vacancy in any case."

"What day was this?"

"I believe the couple came in Monday." She gave him a sharp look. "You're asking a lot of questions."

Rolf smiled, attempting to diffuse her suspicion. "So what did you tell them?"

"I told them I had nothing available." She scratched her head. "But there is something I forgot until just now."

Sylvia was itching to jump in. Apparently sensing her impatience, Rolf brushed her arm, signaling her to hush. She held her tongue. Getting witnesses to talk was his profession.

Sure enough, the woman volunteered, "I sent the couple to the drugstore next door. The owner has a top-floor apartment he's been remodeling. I told them he was not advertising it yet, but it might be ready for occupancy."

Sylvia couldn't contain herself any longer. "Do you know if they rented it?"

"No, I don't."

"Maybe it's still available." She looked at Rolf. "Let's check it out."

Rolf faced the shopkeeper. "Thank you. You've been very helpful. Auf Wiedersehen."

He headed for the door. The doorbell drowned out the shopkeeper's goodbye.

As soon as they were outside, Rolf peered around the square. "Do you see a police officer?"

The only ones in sight stood near the convention center entrance clear across the plaza. If any were closer, they were hidden by the crowd.

"Where are all the policemen Schmidt was talking about?"

The sound from the church bell punctuated Rolf's frustrated outburst. This time it signaled a quarter before the hour. The chancellor would arrive in fifteen minutes. Just then Sylvia spotted a white flat-top police cap. She tugged on Rolf's good arm and pointed down the street. He broke into a run, and she fell in behind him.

By the time she reached the policewoman, Sylvia heard Rolf's excited ". . . above the drugstore, over there." He pointed behind them.

The officer scrutinized Rolf, apparently assessing whether she was dealing with a crazy man. When she saw Sylvia, her face brightened. "Ah, the opera singer and the American attorney we've been told about."

"There's no time to lose. Call Schmidt and have him meet us at the drugstore."

The woman reached for her walkie-talkie. Rolf did not wait to listen but motioned Sylvia on. Quick strides brought them to the drugstore's glass door. They rushed in. A plump, elderly woman was staring at an array of medicines and cosmetics piled on the countertop while a fiftyish man behind the counter rattled off the benefits of the salve in his hand.

Rolf tried to get his attention. "Excuse me—"

"You'll have to wait your turn, sir." His disapproving voice was underscored by little pallid eyes that impaled Rolf through round wire-rimmed glasses.

Rolf would not be deterred. "Are you the owner?"

The customer turned around to study them. Sylvia sensed a good-natured woman. The man sighed, getting ready to brush Rolf off once more. Before he could, the woman spoke. "It's all right, Herr Ratzinger. Go ahead and help these people. It'll give me a chance to look these over." She took the tube from his hand.

When the man came around the counter, Sylvia had to force herself not to stare. The difference in body type from the short, stout customer was striking. His gangly frame gave him an emaciated look.

"Yes, I'm the owner. Why do you ask?"

"You have an apartment available?"

"No, it's been rented."

"When did you rent it?"

The shop owner seemed to grow taller as he looked down on Rolf. "That's none of your business."

Rolf showed no signs of being intimidated. Sylvia imagined that the kind of haranguing he might have experienced in the courtrooms of autocratic judges had steeled him for dealing with the likes of this obstinate shopkeeper.

"Look, Herr Ratzinger, there's no time to explain. We need to know whether the tenants in your top-floor apartment are new."

"And I say it's none of your business. Now, I must ask you to leave my store." He glanced at Sylvia. "Both of you."

"Not until you answer my question."

Seemingly disturbed by the angry interchange, the customer left the counter, brushing past the two men and Sylvia. Before she reached the door it swung open and Schmidt with police officers in tow strode in. "What's going on?"

The shopkeeper pointed at Rolf. "This man is causing a disturbance. I want you to—"

Schmidt put up his hand, then turned to Rolf. "What did you find out?"

"We think he's just rented his fourth-floor apartment, but he won't answer my questions."

Schmidt glared at the shopkeeper. "When did you rent it out and to whom?"

"I don't see what concern it is—"

In one quick motion, Schmidt produced a badge from an inside pocket and stuck it in the man's face. "This is a matter of national security. Answer. Now!"

"Uh . . . a couple came in Monday. I wasn't going to lease the place until January, but they only needed it for a month, and they paid cash."

"You have a key here?"

"Yes, but—"

"Get it!" Schmidt barked. "If we don't make it up there in time, you're in deep trouble."

Gone was the man's obstinacy. Eager to comply now, he pulled open a drawer behind the counter and produced a small key. Schmidt took it. "What about the door to the stairwell?"

"It's the same key. Next door to the left of the store. There's only one apartment on the fourth floor. Don't wreck it. I just had it renovated."

Schmidt and his two policemen rushed off. Sylvia hesitated, but Rolf nudged her forward. They reached the entrance to the stairwell just in time to prevent the door from closing. Schmidt and the officers had already made the turn at the second-floor landing. Sylvia and Rolf ran after them. By the time they reached the top floor, Schmidt was holding the key in front of the apartment door lock. Out of breath from running up three flights of stairs, Rolf and Sylvia were panting. Schmidt turned around, put a finger to his lips, and motioned them to stay back.

Sylvia watched him insert the key in the lock and turn it with great care. For an instant she wondered what Rolf the lawyer might think of the legality of the entrance, but dismissed the thought. With only a few minutes until the chancellor's arrival, this was no time for legal niceties. Schmidt turned to look at the officers, weapons drawn, hugging the wall on either side of the door. They nodded. The key clicked inside the lock. Schmidt threw open the door. It smashed against the wall. The officers stormed inside. Schmidt followed them.

There was eerie silence for an instant. Then startled shouts and scuffling noises carried out into the hallway. Rolf and Sylvia edged closer to the door. She jumped back at the sound of a muffled shot that was answered by loud gunfire.

"Drop your weapons!"

The harsh command was followed by a thud, then another. All grew quiet once more.

"Watch out!" Schmidt's warning pierced the silence.

A man ran into the hallway. Sylvia watched in amazement as Rolf instantly pivoted, and using the escapee's momentum, pulled him over his hip, smashing his backside into the hallway wall. His body slid headfirst onto the floor. He groaned and then grew quiet. Blood trickled from a bullet wound on his arm.

Schmidt stood in the doorway, his mouth open. He looked from the semi-conscious assassin to Rolf. "You did learn something in your self-defense classes." Then he yelled, "Officer, out here."

One of the policemen came out, handcuffed and dragged the prisoner inside next to a woman sprawled face down on the brown carpet, her hands in cuffs behind her back. Schmidt walked over to the window and studied a rifle perched on a tripod. The barrel, with scope attached, pointed at the open window. After a minute, he turned around and spoke to the officers. "Lift up their faces."

When the policemen pulled them up by the hair, Schmidt asked Sylvia, "Do you recognize them?"

Spiked red hair contrasted with the pale complexion of a woman in her thirties. Sylvia braced against the hateful stare. The man next to her, who appeared to be of similar age, had regained full consciousness. From beneath black hair entangled in the policeman's grip, dark eyes in an acned face glared at her in defiance. He curled his lips and spat. "Pigs!"

Though she was out of range, Sylvia unconsciously stepped back. When she saw Schmidt looking at her, she shook her head.

He towered over the red hair. "You and your friend are going away for a long time. You can help yourself by talking. Are there more of you around?"

"Go to hell!"

"That's where *you're* going. A dark cell for the rest of your life—I'd call that hell."

Schmidt turned from her to the officers. "Get them to talk, and fast. I must know whether there are any others."

He motioned Rolf and Sylvia into the hallway. "Great work, you two. You may have saved the chancellor's life. I can't believe the police not finding out about this apartment rental. They could learn interrogation techniques from a lawyer like you, Herr Keller."

"Stop that! Spit it out!" came an angry command from inside.

Schmidt leaped into the apartment. He yelled, "Son of a bitch."

Sylvia peeked inside. The lifeless bodies of the assassins lay on the floor. One of the officers removed his fingers from the woman's throat and shrugged. "Cyanide."

"What a way to avoid interrogation!"

Sylvia got up her nerve and managed to say, "I need to leave for Stuttgart, now." In truth she wanted to escape the horrible scene as much as to start for the opera house.

Without turning around, Schmidt made an absentminded gesture shooing them out.

They were halfway to the third floor when his voice reverberated down the stairwell, "I want both of you to remain in Stuttgart until I catch up with you there tonight or tomorrow. And, Herr Keller, have that shoulder x-rayed."

A throng of curiosity seekers, alerted by the gunfire, greeted them when they left the building. Several policemen were coming toward them. Rolf pulled Sylvia to the side and headed in the direction of the parking lot. She strode alongside him, fighting an uneasy feeling. It was not until they reached the Opel that she admitted to herself what she felt—a sense that she should not leave, of business still unfinished. But surely they had done enough.

"What's wrong, Sylvia?"

"I don't know." She stopped and listened to the full Westminster chime, followed by three hourly rings of the church bell. "Rolf, this sounds crazy, but I think we ought to go back."

"What about your performance?"

"I can afford a few more minutes."

"Okay, but let's hurry. The chancellor's motorcade is entering the plaza."

They made it back to the Richard Strauss Platz in time to watch Chancellor Kohl exit a black Mercedes 600 limousine. As soon as he stepped onto the cobblestones, police clustered around him. Two men in gray suits got out of the second car and joined the chancellor, throwing watchful glances into the crowd. True to Rolf's prediction, Kohl reached past his escort to shake hands as he made his way slowly to the entrance of the convention center. Once there, he turned around and waved to the assembly of supporters, reporters, and television cameras.

Sylvia located the photo shop behind the crowd and let her eyes wander up to the top-story apartment. Its closed window gave her a sense of satisfaction and accomplishment. She felt Rolf's gaze and met his eyes.

He exclaimed, "We did it, Sylvia. He's safe now."

The chancellor turned to enter the building with the throng of uniformed police trailing him. Sylvia had counted to half a dozen when she did a double take. That woman in a green Bavarian police uniform at the chancellor's side looked familiar. Impossible, she told herself. She didn't know anyone with the local police.

Sylvia gasped. Rolf touched her arm. "What is it?"

She pointed. "That woman there . . ."

"In police uniform?"

"She's no policewoman. That's Monika Rau. She was one of Kreuzer's girlfriends."

Rolf shook her. "Are you sure?"

"It's her. Where's Schmidt?"

"He's among the police. Let's go."

Before they could take the first step, a male voice said, "Not so fast." Ross and Kingsley blocked their way. "You owe us a file, Frau Mazzoni. The one you neglected to include in your first drop."

"You're the British agents," Rolf blurted out.

"Yes, Herr Keller."

"For God's sake not now," Sylvia pleaded. "There is a terrorist disguised as a policewoman with the chancellor's entourage."

Ross started, "Nice try, Frau Mazzoni but—"

"Wait a minute," Kingsley interrupted. "How do you know?"

"She was one of Kreuzer's girlfriends. We must warn Schmidt."

Kingsley seemed convinced. "All right, but this had better not be a ruse."

When the four of them reached the convention center entrance, a guard stopped them. "Closed to the public."

"The chancellor's life is in danger," Rolf exclaimed. "Let us through. We need to warn him."

The burly doorman looked amused. "Don't you worry about him. He's plenty safe. The bodyguards and police surrounding him are practically tripping over each other."

"You don't understand," Sylvia yelled. "It's a terrorist in police uniform who'll kill him."

At first the guard looked annoyed, then regarded her with pity, no doubt thinking her to be just one more crackpot of the many he'd encountered in the line of duty. "Sorry. No admittance. Please step back."

She wanted to protest, but felt herself pulled back. Kingsley produced a badge and waved it in front of the man's face. "Herr Schmidt is expecting us."

"Schmidt?" He let loose a riotous laugh. "Ha, ha." He shook his head in disbelief. "You couldn't think of a better name than Schmidt?"

"He's with—"

The guard cut Kingsley off. "I don't care who he's with, if he even exists. Your fancy badge doesn't impress me. I told you no admittance."

Ross erupted. "Look here you—"

Kingsley took him by the arm and pulled him back toward the entrance. "We're not getting anywhere."

"This guy's a moron," Ross whispered. He pointed to a woman in her sixties sitting at the registration desk across the entryway. "Let's have her page Schmidt."

Rolf beat them to the desk. The receptionist listened politely to his request as skepticism crossed her face. "I'm sorry, but I can't interrupt the chancellor's party."

Kingsley stuck his badge in the woman's face. "This is a matter of national security. The chancellor is about to be murdered. Now pick up that microphone and page Herr Dieter Schmidt or I'll do it for you!"

With shaking voice and fingers, she announced, "Herr Schmidt, Dieter Schmidt, please come to the registration desk immediately."

"Once more," commanded Kingsley.

"Paging Herr Schmidt to the registration desk."

Sylvia looked toward the guard. He was watching but made no move to interfere.

Red-faced, Schmidt came running around the corner. His eyes lit up in surprise when he spotted them. "What's wrong? What are you doing here with these British spooks?"

Rolf answered, "There is an RAF terrorist with the chancellor in a Bavarian police uniform."

Schmidt looked at her for confirmation. She nodded. "A girlfriend of Kreuzer. Her name is Monika Rau."

Schmidt turned to the guard. "I'm protecting the chancellor." He showed his badge. "These people are with me."

The guard let them pass. Schmidt led them through the terracotta-tiled foyer. He slowed when they reached the first of several doors leading into the Festsaal Werdenfels. At the farthest entry, the figure of Chancellor Kohl towered above a squadron of officers and intelligence types.

"Which one is she?" Schmidt asked Sylvia. "Describe her."

"Dark hair, about my height, very skinny."

"Do you see her?"

They were now close enough for her to study the group. A policeman approached, but retreated when Schmidt waved him off. Sylvia hastily scanned the twenty or so people. Where was Monika? Had she imagined things? Then she spotted the woman near the chancellor. When Monika looked her way, Sylvia averted her eyes so as not to be noticed and whispered in Schmidt's ear, "She's on the chancellor's left."

He took one of the plainclothesmen by the arm and spoke quietly into his ear. Wondering whether Monika had a companion, Sylvia examined the green police uniforms once more. She knew that the RAF liked to use mixed gender teams, so she concentrated on the men. Then she caught Monika throwing nervous glances. This time Sylvia did not look away fast enough and Monika's pupils widened in recognition. The terrorist reached for her gun.

"Hold it!" the plainclothesman commanded, pressing the nose of a pistol into Monika's uniform jacket. "She's a terrorist. Arrest her!"

Two policemen rushed forward. One slapped her hand away from her holster and removed the pistol. The other pulled back her arms into handcuffs. While a policewoman frisked her, Sylvia caught a movement. A policeman drew his weapon. She had a memory flash of this dumpy-looking fellow drinking beer with Kreuzer in the Kneipe Studentenkeller. He'd had long hippy hair back then. Now it was cut short as befitted a policeman. That's why she hadn't recognized him earlier.

"Watch out!" she heard herself yell while diving for the chancellor. She flung herself against his massive body, causing the surprised chancellor to stagger. A shot whistled past her ear. Then several shots in succession rang out. The chancellor pulled her to the floor with him. As she went down she saw the terrorist stumble. Dark blood spots soaked through his uniform jacket. He fell forward, his face slamming into the tile floor.

The chancellor stood and pulled Sylvia up. Rolf was at her side. "Are you all right?"

Before she could respond, Rolf shouted, "Achtung!"

He sprinted past several policemen. During the commotion Monika Rau had managed to get loose and was running down the foyer. Despite handcuffed hands, she was moving fast. When Rolf caught up with her, he tackled her to the floor. Sylvia, along with Schmidt, ran toward them. Halfway there Sylvia observed Rolf jamming his hand into Monika's mouth just as she chomped down. Sylvia could see the pain in his eyes. What was he doing? The answer came when Schmidt grasped the woman's jaw and forced her mouth open. Rolf withdrew his bite-marked hand holding a capsule. Cyanide—just like the other two.

Monika glared at Sylvia. "Traitor bitch! You killed Horst. He trusted you."

The plainclothesman approached Schmidt. "The other one is dead."

As a policeman pulled Monika away, Rolf put his arm around Sylvia. "You had a difficult choice to make twelve years ago. But you did the right thing. Don't even think about feeling guilty."

She leaned against him, comforted by his touch and words. She didn't know how long she'd let herself indulge when she heard Schmidt's voice. "I told the chancellor the two of you saved his life today . . . not once, but twice.

He's going to deliver his speech now. But he wants to meet you."

Sylvia didn't know what to say, but Rolf did. "It'll have to wait. I've got to get this world-class soprano to the Stuttgart Opera."

Sylvia jumped. "What time is it?"

"Just past three thirty."

"Frau Mazzoni, before you go, we have a matter to settle with you," Kingsley said.

Schmidt turned toward him. "Mr. Dennis Kingsley, I believe. And Mr. Peter Ross."

If the British agents were surprised that the German agent knew them, they hid it well.

Schmidt continued, "I know what you're looking for. If you come with me to Pullach later, perhaps we can trade some information. Meanwhile, since you're here, you can make yourselves useful and guard against any further trouble coming the chancellor's way."

Sylvia's stomach clenched. Surely Schmidt wouldn't include her Stasi file in bargaining with them, or would he? Rolf tugged on her arm. "If we hurry, we can still make it."

Reluctantly, Sylvia pulled herself away and hurried after him.

Chapter Fifty

Schmidt entered the elevator at Federal Intelligence Service headquarters in Pullach. He exhaled, trying to relax. This had been a hell of a day, and at five o'clock it was a long way from over. He pushed the third-floor button and closed his eyes for the duration of the short ride. After the steel door retracted, he hurried down the hall and entered Bauman's outer office.

The secretary's typewriter was covered with a black vinyl hood as if it were a tropical bird requiring darkness for its rest. Schmidt noticed the door to Bauman's office stood ajar. Opening it slightly, he peeked inside and saw his boss sitting at his desk engrossed in a file. Sensing his presence, Bauman looked up, waved him in, and shut the folder.

Heaving a sigh, Schmidt flumped into an armchair. "What a day! The chancellor is fine, thanks to our two amateur spies."

"I can't believe it. Who would have guessed?"

"I'll fill you in later. I'm expecting the two British agents at any moment."

"Dennis Kingsley and Peter Ross?"

Schmidt nodded. "Are you okay with me sharing some information from Dobnik's files with them?"

Bauman studied him. "What's in it for us?"

"I'd like to find out what they're after. I suspect they are already familiar with most of what we have."

"What makes you think so?"

"They must have been tipped off somehow about Mazzoni and Keller to show up in Garmisch so fast. I suggest you keep an eye on that secretary in the Berlin office, Brigitte Wesendorf."

"You picture a mole everywhere, Dieter. But we'll see how she does on the lie detector."

Schmidt was debating whether to mention Mazzoni's Stasi file when the phone rang. Bauman looked at him as he spoke into the receiver, "Yes, he's here," and hung up. "Your secretary is working later than mine. The Brits are here." He stood. "Do whatever you think is best. Dobnik gave us some sensitive stuff, but nothing that's going to hurt us with the Allies—not even the Walter dossier, since we know it was doctored."

Schmidt stood. "Thanks, Karl. I'll call you later."

When he walked into his secretary's office, the British agents shot from their chairs, as if they'd been waiting for hours. Rather impatient, he noted. Neither of them expressed any interest in coffee, so he sent his secretary home for the day and invited them into his office. As they sat down, he asked, "How about some single-malt scotch? A day like today calls for something special, don't you think?"

Ross looked at Kingsley, who nodded after a brief hesitation. "I suppose it's technically after hours. And I could use a drink."

Schmidt opened a cabinet door behind him, took out a bottle and three glasses, and poured generous double shots. "I can offer water but no ice."

Ross hoisted one of the glasses. "There's no sense in spoiling a good whiskey." He gulped down half his drink while his more refined partner sipped.

Schmidt followed Kingsley's example. When the burning sensation reached his stomach, he looked from one to the other. "I'm curious how you gentlemen knew where to find Frau Mazzoni and Herr Keller. You had some help, maybe?"

He zeroed in on Ross as he asked the question and was rewarded with a split second drop of the agent's lower lip and widening pupils before his guard went up.

Kingsley cut in quickly, "We figured they'd be near the chancellor. Fortunately, we guessed right."

Not bad, thought Schmidt, and asked, "What did you want from Frau Mazzoni? Has she promised you something?"

Again, Kingsley was the one to respond, artfully ducking the question. "We understand that the Stasi defector's drops included intelligence casting serious doubt on the West German government's motives for unification. We need to see those documents."

Stalling for time, Schmidt sipped his whiskey. For them to zero in on the Walter dossier meant they were familiar with the contents of Dobnik's documents. Either Dobnik had played the Brits off against the West Germans or Mazzoni and Keller were double-crossing him. Perhaps he could catch Ross off guard again. Instead of responding, Schmidt asked, "What do you have on Frau Mazzoni that would make her tell you about the Stasi papers?"

This time Ross did not flinch. Kingsley answered, "We could ask you the same question, Herr Schmidt. Except we know your means of coercion: her past liaison with RAF terrorist Horst Kreuzer." His serious demeanor faded. "Look, we're not getting anywhere probing each other. How about showing us the papers that shed some light on West German intentions?"

Realizing he wasn't going to get any more information out of these two for the moment, Schmidt unlocked the top desk drawer, pulled out a folder, and dropped it on the desk. Maybe it would pave the way for later cooperation. "This is what you're looking for. It's a dossier on Joachim Walter. Ninety percent of it is accurate. We highlighted the portions the Stasi concocted. Go ahead and read."

He sat back and watched them pour over the document, sipping his scotch now and then and refilling all three glasses.

After several minutes, Kingsley fixed him with a stare. "Even if the highlighted parts are forgeries as you say, you've got an ex-Nazi wielding great influence in the West German Foreign Ministry. That's not going to sit well with our government. Or with the Soviets, French and Americans."

"Herr Walter retired yesterday," Schmidt replied, trying his best not to gloat. "As embarrassing as his past is to the West German government, I don't believe your prime minister will be able to use it to stop unification now, though I'm sure she'd like to."

Even self-possessed Kingsley couldn't disguise that Schmidt had hit a nerve. He picked up his glass and took a swallow. When he set it back down, he bore an expression of someone accepting that he'd been bested. "It seems you've thought of everything, Herr Schmidt. But I wouldn't be so sure that Walter's retirement solves Germany's problem. May we have a copy of this?" He touched the paper lying on the desk in front of him.

"This is your copy." While he spoke those words, Schmidt decided he'd try once more. "As I've shared my documents with you, I believe it's your turn to tell me what you've got for me."

"I'm afraid we don't have anything of value to you." Kingsley's tone signaled he'd recovered from his defensiveness.

"You may not have any documents, but it's clear to me that you know the contents of the Stasi papers we've got. You accused me of coercion. What did you use to force Mazzoni and Keller to give you copies?"

As hard as he tried, Schmidt could not read anything from the agents' stone-faced expressions. If they did have anything, they weren't going to give it up. For an instant he wondered whether he could use the Mazzoni Stasi file for bargaining with them but dismissed the thought. He needed to review it first. Had Dobnik indeed intended to give it to her, or had she confiscated it from the stash in the suitcase? If it were her file, did it hold anything valuable enough to let him overcome his qualms about breaking his word?

Kingsley's voice brought him back. "Nice try, Herr Schmidt. You know that we won't reveal our sources any more than you will yours. But thanks for the Walter dossier. We owe you one." He nodded to his partner. "We'd better be off."

After escorting them down to the lobby, Schmidt collected the Mazzoni file from his office and headed home. As soon as he arrived, he called Bauman on the secure line in his study to report on the events in Garmisch and the British agents' visit. He did not mention Mazzoni's file. Unless it contained evidence of her complicity with Kreuzer, the RAF, or the communists, which he simply had to pass on to his boss, Schmidt would not break his word.

Bauman said, "Great job, Dieter. The chancellor is alive, we've got leads on Stasi spies and terrorists in this country, and the Brits have nothing to derail unification. I'd say you can close this matter."

"You're probably right, Karl. I'll drive to Stuttgart in the morning to debrief Keller and Mazzoni. You know the chancellor wants to meet our two heroes. Who knows, he may even want to pin medals on them."

After hanging up, Schmidt pulled the Mazzoni file from his briefcase and began to read. The minute details the Stasi had collected about her activities amazed him. He whistled when he read how a Stasi Romeo had tried to recruit her at the Italian Riviera. She'd been too smart to fall for that. There were several entries characterizing her as a communist sympathizer and a potential candidate for Stasi informant. Schmidt stared at the bronze wallpaper of his study. Mazzoni had kept bad company, but a communist recruit and Stasi informant? He shook his head. It didn't ring true. These assertions were either embellishments by an agent trying to impress a superior or deliberately placed there much like the bogus statements in the Walter dossier.

He returned his attention to the file. When he finished reading, he leafed through it once more, this time judging its overall appearance. He held in his hand not a copy like the other files Dobnik had delivered, but an original Stasi file that he had somehow managed to smuggle through security. He'd probably used it to induce Mazzoni to go through with his scheme for defection. If so, this had been his present to her.

Clanking noises from the kitchen meant Ellen would call him to the dinner table at any moment. He peered through the bay window out into the night. What he saw caused him to flip the light switch. Heavy snowflakes reflected in the beams of the outdoor lights. His first thought was to leave extra time for the drive in the morning. Then he wondered how long it had been snowing. His watch showed a quarter past six. Keller and Mazzoni should be approaching Stuttgart about now, if they hadn't run into one of those mammoth traffic jams that afflicted German autobahns whenever the weather turned nasty.

He joined his wife at the kitchen table. She'd made one of his favorites—spaghetti with meat balls in marinara sauce. But the delicious meal did not allay his concern that this winter storm might somehow prevent Sylvia Mazzoni from reaching the Stuttgart opera hall in time.

Chapter Fifty-One

Rolf pointed to the illuminated green sign bridging the autobahn. "Exit to Ulm is coming up. From there it's only an hour to Stuttgart." He checked the dashboard clock. "I'll have you there by six thirty."

He said it as much to convince himself as to assure Sylvia. Just before dark, he'd noticed ominous looking clouds in the west. All they needed was to run into a winter storm. Keep pushing. You'll make it just fine, he kept telling himself. His concentration on the roads leading from Garmisch to the autobahn had been total, a fact not lost on Sylvia. She had not interrupted him once while he exceeded the highway speed limits and then pushed the Opel engine to its limits driving in the fast lane of the autobahn.

No sooner had they left Ulm behind than snowflakes began to swirl around the windshield. He turned on the wipers. Sylvia sat up straight. "I don't believe this."

"A few kilometers and we'll be down in the valley. I bet it's not snowing there," he said to assuage her worries.

"If we make it down the Drackensteiner Hang."

He knew she was referring to the steep downgrade where the autobahn dropped several hundred meters from the Alb plateau, the Swabian Mountains. This route had not seen many modernizations since its inauguration by the Nazis in the mid-1930s. Accidents were commonplace even in good weather. Snow made the driving downright treacherous.

"Let's hope it hasn't been snowing there for very long," he told her.

"Yes, a lot of those big trucks ignore the no passing signs, no matter what the weather." She flipped on the radio and turned the dial. "They broadcast local traffic conditions on Bavaria Radio 3."

Rolf could hardly stand the schmaltzy song emanating from the tinny-sounding speakers, and was relieved to hear the radio station's three-tone introductory signal for its traffic report. A female voice with a slight Bavarian accent announced various trouble spots on the regional autobahns and highways. Rolf slowed the car when he saw red brake lights ahead. Sure enough, the radio voice reported a ten-kilometer *stau* as a result of a jack-knifed truck on the Drackensteiner Hang. Before the end of the announcement, the traffic was already beginning to back up.

"Damn!" Rolf couldn't suppress his frustration. "A traffic jam ten kilometers long." He turned off the radio. "Get out the road map and look for the town of Merklingen." He pointed to a road sign. "The exit is five hundred meters ahead. See if we can take a detour from there."

He started to tell her to hurry but refrained when the cars ahead slowed even further, giving her plenty of time to consult the map before they'd reach the exit. And it was possible there would still be no way to circumvent the traffic jam. He downshifted into second gear and turned on the interior light. Watching her fiddle with the map, he told himself to be patient.

Finally, she said, "Take the next exit. We can bypass the traffic jam on local roads and get back on the autobahn on the other side of the Drackensteiner Hang." She squinted. "At Mühlhausen."

As she spoke, the cars ahead came to a complete standstill. Rolf stopped the Opel right next to the sign indicating they were one hundred meters from the exit. What a cruel tease to be stuck so close to the only potential escape route. Flashing lights reflected in the rearview mirror and sirens swelled from faint to ear-splitting as an ambulance followed by a police vehicle passed on the right shoulder.

He turned to Sylvia. "See if the shoulder is clear up ahead."

She rolled down her window and leaned out as the frigid winter air rushed in. "Looks open all the way to the exit." Shivering, she closed the window.

After a quick glance behind failed to reveal any other law enforcement cars approaching, he steered onto the road shoulder, telling himself this was one of those extraordinary situations that justified defying the strict prohibition against driving on that part of the autobahn. He glanced at Sylvia. "We're going to make it."

Her back was rigid as she stared straight ahead, not saying a word. All he could do now was to make sure they'd reach the exit and not get lost on the back roads. He didn't even want to contemplate what it would mean for her if she missed her performance.

As he headed for the exit, Sylvia said, "Rolf, we'll be passing through several towns before we get back on the autobahn. If you see a pay phone, stop. I have to call the opera house director and tell him I'm on my way. Otherwise, he'll get a substitute Micaëla."

♫ ♫ ♫

"Seven o'clock." Ignoring the no-stopping zone, Rolf brought the Opel to a halt on the busy street alongside the opera house's rear entrance. He looked at Sylvia. "You've got half an hour."

An irate driver who'd almost rear-ended them leaned on his horn, increasing the tension she felt despite her gratitude that they had managed to bypass the traffic jam. She slammed the passenger door, dodged four lanes of traffic, and darted across the broad sidewalk into the artists' entrance. Waving at the porter, she hurried down the hall to the dressing room. His eyebrows shot up in surprise when he recognized her. She shook it off. There was time for only one thing now: to get ready for her first act appearance.

Sylvia swung the dressing room door inward with such vigor that she lost her grip on the handle when confronted with the scene in front of her. The door crashed into the wall and caused three women to stare at her in bewilderment. The two standing next to the fortyish woman in the chair were wearing aprons. The makeup crew. Sylvia braced against the doorframe when she saw the sitting woman's braids. Although she knew the answer before she asked, Sylvia blurted out, "Who are you and what are you doing here?"

The stout woman swiveled her chair in Sylvia's direction. "That's what I'd like to ask you, young lady. As you can see, I'm getting ready for the performance."

"You're . . ." Sylvia couldn't make herself say it. "You're singing . . . Mica—"

"Yes, I'll be Micaëla half an hour from now. I'm Dagmar Breuning." She raised her eyebrows. "You're Sylvia Mazzoni. You covered for me last Saturday."

"And I'm covering tonight."

"Not according to the director. He sounded so frantic on the phone that I agreed to come in. Herr Meisinger just didn't feel he could wait any longer, and unless he tells me otherwise, I'll be singing tonight."

Sylvia stared at her, groping for words which wouldn't come. Finally, she stuttered, "But . . . but I couldn't help it. I did everything I could to get here . . . and I did."

"The decision was made by Herr Meisinger, and he alone can change it. You might still catch him in his office." Breuning turned her swivel chair away from Sylvia and faced the dressing table mirror once more. "And now, if you'll excuse me, I need to finish my makeup. There has to be a Micaëla ready when the curtain goes up. Really bad luck, Frau Mazzoni, but sometimes that's the way it goes."

The dressing assistants, who'd been eyeing Sylvia, turned their attention back to this evening's Micaëla. Like an automaton, Sylvia closed the door and trudged down the hallway to the director's office. When she turned the corner, she found him locking his door. "Herr Meisinger, wait. I'm here to perform."

The portly man in his sixties stuck his keys into a pocket of his gray suit trousers and peered at her through his horn-rimmed glasses in the stern manner of a school principal scolding a misbehaving pupil. "You're too late, Frau Mazzoni. I waited as long as I could. I had to scramble for a replacement as it is, and was lucky to convince Frau Breuning to give up her well-deserved night off. I'm certainly not going to send her home now that you've graced us at last with your presence. If this is your idea of how to become a diva, it won't fly here as long as I'm the director."

"But I called the stage manager from the road and told him I'd be here."

"Frau Mazzoni, you're not singing tonight."

Even though she sensed his mind was made up, Sylvia's plea poured out. "Please listen to me, Herr Meisinger. Today I was held at gunpoint and nearly killed. I was detained to help in an urgent matter of state, and because this engagement means so much to me, I still managed to break away in plenty of time to be here. I did my best. It was an accident on the autobahn and the bad weather that made me late, but I still have time to get ready and sing. And I will gladly pay Frau Breuning for her trouble. Please, you *must* let me go on!"

The director looked at her askance. "I'm not interested in hearing your excuses, Frau Mazzoni." He began to walk off, then stopped and turned around. "And our contract offer is withdrawn."

As she watched him disappear around the corner, tears came, slowly at first, then faster and faster until she sobbed uncontrollably. She beat her fist against his door—back to singing bit parts with provincial opera companies . . . and that only if Herr Meisinger didn't put out the word that she was too unreliable to be employed by them.

Minutes later, Sylvia pushed herself off the door. Yes, she mourned the loss of the opportunity to forge a meaningful career, after having come so close, but now what she began to feel was rage at the unfairness of it all. Even though she was not that tardy and had the best of reasons, opera management couldn't care less. Germany was awash with talented young sopranos. Why would they waste their precious time on someone like her who didn't keep appointments?

Images of her voice teacher and then her mother came up and resolve surged through her. They had taught her to pursue her goal with single-mindedness. To quit now would be to let them down, betray their trust. And she'd invested far too much to give up—not now, not ever. Wiping her face with her sleeve, she strode with determination toward the foyer, hoping to find Rolf at the box office.

Chapter Fifty-Two

In a hurry to make her two-thirty appointment, Sylvia traversed Stuttgart's Schlossplatz, wishing she hadn't answered the phone just before leaving the hotel. Ursula Sommer's words still rang in her ears. "I *told* you to sign the contract Stuttgart Opera offered you when you were in Berlin." Then the agent had the gall to fire her as a client. No great loss, Sylvia told herself while the clichéd image of rats jumping off a sinking ship flashed across her mind. She hoped it was not an omen.

She steeled herself against the chilly December wind, crossed the street, and entered her favorite café. But she was in no mood to enjoy the most delicious black forest cherry torte in Stuttgart or the café's cozy atmosphere the Germans called gemütlichkeit. She spotted Schmidt at a table for two in the far corner of the mostly empty establishment. The lunch crowd had left, and the afternoon kaffee-klatsch patrons who would occupy every seat in the place weren't due for another half hour. When he saw her, Schmidt rose, took her coat, and hung it on a nearby hook next to one she recognized as his.

"I'm so sorry about your missing last night's performance," he said before she even sat down.

"I didn't miss it. The director refused to let me go on even though I'd called the stage manager from a pay phone to tell him I'd be there in time. We made it by half an hour, but he had already called in the original soprano to sing."

Schmidt shook his head. "Unbelievable! Herr Keller told me about it when we met this morning before he went to get his shoulder x-rayed. He said to tell you he's got something to take care of and won't be back until very late."

She wondered whether Rolf was stashing Stein's copies somewhere, a fact he surely had kept from Schmidt. The waitress took Sylvia's order—coffee but no pastry—and left. Sylvia pointed to the briefcase lying next to Schmidt's half-full coffee cup. "My file?"

He folded back the unlocked leather flap and produced the folder she recognized instantly. "I suggest you burn or shred this right away." He pushed it across the table. "If anyone learns what's in it or even that it exists, you're not the only one who'll be in trouble."

She looked at him, not understanding. He continued. "I'm the only person at my agency who knows about this file. If they find out I've kept it to myself . . ."

Maybe he wasn't jumping off the ship after all. She squeezed his hand. "Thank you. There is a print and copy shop on Königstraße that has a shredder." Hopefully not broken like the one in the Mittenwald store, she thought to herself.

"Frau Mazzoni." His voice brought her back. "I wanted to meet with you to officially terminate your mission. I told Herr Keller the same thing this morning." He leaned forward. "But first there is something I must know. What did the British agents have on you?"

His question hung in the air when the waitress brought her coffee. Sylvia took her time to stir in cream and sugar, but her mind was racing. What did Schmidt know? When in doubt, play dumb, she told herself. "I don't know what you mean."

He studied her, his eyes full of skepticism. She held his gaze. Finally, he said, "Well, whatever it is, that's between you and them. I just hope for your sake, it's nothing that'll come back and bite you later."

"Speaking of potential hazards, what about giving me the file your agency has been keeping on me?" She didn't really expect a positive answer, but at the very least, it would get him off the subject of the Brits.

Schmidt chuckled. "You're persistent, I'll give you that. But, not a chance. The letter I gave you is all the protection you'll need to keep us off your back. And you'll be rid of me for good."

The waitress appeared. "Will there be anything else?"

Although she didn't have much of an appetite, Sylvia ordered a black forest cherry torte. Schmidt opted for plum kuchen with whipped cream.

Anger welled up as she replayed last night's events in her mind. Could she elicit Schmidt's help? She summoned her courage. "Since that opera bureaucrat works for the same government you do, I want to know if there is any chance you could put some pressure on him to renew my contract offer."

Schmidt put both hands around his cup and looked down.

Sinking ship, she thought, as she pressed him. "Well?"

"I wish I could help you, but I can't talk to him about your mission. You must understand—"

"No, I *don't* understand. First you force this crazy assignment on me, almost get Rolf and me killed, and then after we save your butt by keeping Kohl alive, you won't even consider using your influence to right this injustice. I'm talking about my career. If I don't get this contract . . ." She waited until he met her gaze before continuing, "Herr

Schmidt, I cannot let this opportunity slip away. In this business it only comes once. You must help me."

He leaned forward, looking her in the eye. "Frau Mazzoni, what they've done to you is unfair. Officially, I must tell you that there is nothing I can do."

"What about unofficially?" she asked with a glimmer of hope.

"I will do whatever unofficial checking I can, but that's all I can say."

Her shoulders sagged.

The pastries arrived and Schmidt dug in while Sylvia picked at hers and thought about his equivocal comments. After he'd finished his pie and coffee, Schmidt said, "You and Herr Keller have been heroic, and I expect you'll get a call from the chancellor's office."

Sylvia thought a little and then asked, "Do you have a pen in that briefcase?"

He gave her a curious look while producing a pen and pad. She wrote down Erika Dobnik's name and address and turned the tablet around so he could read it. "This is Colonel Dobnik's daughter. Without her help we wouldn't have gotten our hands on his papers. She's sure Schlechter killed her father on orders of General Frantz. I believe the West German government owes her a big debt."

Schmidt studied her and then slowly nodded. "I'll do what I can. You have my word on it." After a slight pause, he added, "And we know about Frantz. I expect he and Mielke will be arrested soon."

The tables were filling up. It was time to leave. Schmidt paid the bill. When he got up to fetch their coats, she thought of something else. "Just a minute." She waited until he sat back down before she asked him, "Why did Manfred Klau attack me in the Schlossgarten Park?"

"Are you sure you want to learn about that?"

She nodded emphatically.

"We don't know whether he tried to prevent you from carrying out the East Berlin assignment, whether he meant to avenge Kreuzer, or whether it was something else."

"Who shot him, if you didn't?" she insisted.

Schmidt looked around before speaking in a low voice. "I would have if necessary to save you. But another intelligence service beat me to it."

"Not the Brits?"

He shook his head.

"German?"

For a split second she thought she detected a yes in his eyes before he responded, "I'm not going to say any more. You're better off not knowing."

He helped her into her coat. She picked up the file on the table. When they parted company on the sidewalk, Schmidt said, "Frau Mazzoni, you have a great future ahead of you. I'm convinced of that. And when you see me in the audience, rest assured I won't be there to recruit you, but to enjoy your beautiful singing."

Sylvia wondered what made him so sure. But he wasn't finished. He hesitated, as if searching for the right words. "You got into some bad company in your student days. But from what I can see, your judgment in people and relationships is much improved."

She caught a smile before he turned his face into the wind and disappeared down the sidewalk.

Chapter Fifty-Three

Rolf wiped buttery croissant flakes from his fingers onto a napkin and sipped his coffee. He turned his chair on the hotel's sun-drenched terrace toward the panoramic view of Lake Como, the fishing village of Varenna below, and the white-capped peaks of the Alps in the distance, scenery as magnificent as he had seen anywhere in the world.

As much as he tried, Rolf could not truly savor this mild, peaceful December morning. He couldn't calm his restless mind. Half an hour past their late morning breakfast date and still no sign of Sylvia. Now and then the proprietress came to the terrace door to see whether she had arrived. Each time he shook his head and Signora Laciura withdrew.

They'd come here at his suggestion, but it had not turned out to be the romantic getaway he'd imagined. Distraught over losing the Stuttgart Opera contract and depressed about her professional future, Sylvia had been withdrawn. When she asked for separate rooms he didn't object. He hoped what he had for her this morning would lift her spirits. But where the hell was she?

While he debated whether to check on her, Sylvia appeared on the terrace in form-fitting black slacks and a red pullover and joined him. The attentive innkeeper followed, poured coffee for both of them, and after satisfying herself that the basket still contained plenty of croissants, bread, crusty rolls, butter and marmalade, went inside.

"Sorry for being so late, Rolf. My phone has been ringing off the hook." She doctored her coffee with cream and sugar and took several sips. Her face took on a quizzical expression. "I don't understand what's going on. First, the Stuttgart Opera director called to tell me he was renewing their offer for a two-year engagement and he'd fax the contract to the hotel. When I hung up, the operator gave me two messages. One from Ursula Sommer, my former agent, asking me to call her immediately on an urgent matter. The second was from the director of the Bavarian State Opera in Munich."

Rolf stifled a grin. The plan appeared to be working. "Did you call them back?"

"Not Sommer. I don't ever want to talk to her again. I did speak with the Bavarian Opera director. She wants me to come to Munich next week for an audition. I was dying to ask her how she'd heard of me, but I didn't dare. Do you suppose Schmidt could have . . . ?" She looked at him. "Why are you smiling? Did you have something to do with this?"

He reached for the newspaper on the chair next to him and laid it on the table. "Take a look at the headline."

She pulled it next to her plate. "How did you manage to get today's Frankfurt paper?"

"They sell it at the train station. I jogged by there this morning."

"And you want me to read it now?"

"Look at the headline," he repeated, pointing.

She picked it up and scanned the page until her eyes focused in the center. "Ex-Stasi Chief Mielke Arrested."

"Not only Mielke," he interjected, but his cronies, General Frantz among them. But the story I want you to read is the one to the left."

She refocused. "Opera Singer Saves Chancellor's Life." Sylvia lowered the paper and looked over its top edge at Rolf. "I don't believe this."

"Read on."

Her eyes darted back and forth as she devoured the story. She put down the paper. "But how did they learn about our . . ." She pointed a finger. "You and Schmidt cooked this up. That's what you were doing Saturday. And that's why Schmidt was so circumspect."

Rolf tried to look innocent. "How do you like that last paragraph?"

Sylvia raised the paper and read. "Delayed by her successful efforts to foil the assassination plot, Frau Mazzoni arrived for her scheduled appearance at the Stuttgart Opera only half an hour before curtain. But opera management refused to let her go on stage and withdrew its pending two-year contract offer, which it had extended after her sensational debut as Micaëla in *Carmen* a week ago."

For the first time in days he saw her smiling. "That sounds like your handiwork. You exaggerated my role and diminished yours."

"Well, it's your career we're trying to preserve."

"But how did you manage to get this published?"

"I persuaded our journalist friend Kent Ferguson."

"And he agreed just like that?"

"I gave him a draft detailing our adventures in getting the Stasi papers and saving Chancellor Kohl's life. He was squeamish about classified intelligence information and rejected the story. I told him we could revise it to take out any sensitive parts as long as he told your story."

"And . . . ? Come on, Herr Lawyer. Don't make me drag it out of you. How did you persuade him?"

"By making it clear to him that I knew his being on my flight to Frankfurt was no coincidence, nor was the fact that we were followed after leaving his office. And you should have seen his expression when I let him know that it was me who called him at the contact number intended for Dobnik. I told him I didn't care whether he worked for the CIA, Stein, Schmidt, or all of them, but if he didn't get this published, his cover as a foreign correspondent would be history."

"You're devious, Rolf." She touched his hand on the table. "Thank you."

He squeezed hers. "Remember what I told you about the AA program and amends?" She nodded. "I suppose this qualifies as my 'living amends' to you—I can't undo the past, but I can make up by my present actions for the harm I've caused."

"I like your recovery program." She studied the basket and selected a roll, which she tore open and spread with butter and strawberry marmalade. After a healthy bite and a sip of coffee, she looked at him. "Rolf, I'm sorry I've been so grouchy toward you lately."

He held up his hand. "No apologies needed. You had every reason to think you'd be singing in church choirs and weddings from now on." He let his eyes sweep the azure blue of the lake and the white mountain peaks beyond. "Speaking of singing, you've heard of Santa Fe Opera, I'm sure. Stein tells me they're looking for a Micaëla this summer. He is working his connections to get you an audition. If you go, I'll meet you there."

"Why would he want to help me?" She paused. Her face lit up. "Oh, I get it."

Puzzled, Rolf asked, "You get what?"

"When did you talk with your boss?" she asked, ignoring his question.

"Last night. He knows I had Betty sneak into his office yet he offered me a partnership." Rolf shook his head. "Then he gave me instructions on how to send the two boxes of documents to him. But first he quizzed me about the contents. And he asked again about you. You're sure you don't know him?"

She shook her head.

"He asked me the most curious thing. He wanted to know—"

"Let me guess," she interrupted. "He wanted to know if the Stasi documents said anything about me."

Rolf dropped his jaw. "That's exactly what he asked me. How in the hell did you know that?"

"Remember Stein's client, Anthony Fabrini?"

"Yes, what's he got to do with this?"

Sylvia gave him some of his own medicine, taking her time to refill her cup from the carafe and chewing on her roll. He held his tongue. Finally, she said, "The real reason your boss sent you over here was to find out if the Stasi had anything negative on me."

"But how do you know?" he asked, this time suspicion vying with curiosity in his voice.

"Because it came to me that the letters 'ARM' on Stein's folder are initials without periods." She sought his eyes. "They stand for Anna Renata Mazzoni."

Dumbfounded, he looked at her. Then it sank in. "Your mother? Her middle name is Renata?"

Sylvia nodded.

"I still don't see the connection."

"I didn't either. So I confronted her on the phone. She admitted that the money she'd been sending me to pay for college and opera school had mostly come from . . . my father." Her voice faltered as she spoke the last two words awkwardly, almost as though for the first time.

"But that means . . ."

"Yes, Stein's client Anthony Fabrini is my father."

"Whew!" Rolf studied the scenery once more taking in this revelation, then turned back. "But why didn't Stein tell me about the real purpose of my assignment? It would have made things so much easier."

"Because Fabrini started a family when he returned to the States from military service in Germany. He didn't want his wife and children to know about his German affair and . . . illegitimate daughter." Rolf noticed how hard it was for her to say the words. "But he assuaged his guilt by sending monthly drafts to my mother's Milan bank account for my education."

"Incredible. I don't know what to say."

"Not good for a lawyer," she teased, tossing her head and bouncing dark curls across the collar of the red pullover. Then she turned serious once more. "You didn't tell Stein about my Stasi file?"

"I've never heard of such a file," Rolf deadpanned.

Sylvia released held breath. "Schmidt intimated that Manfred Klau, the RAF terrorist who attacked me in the park, was shot by another intelligence service, probably German. Do you have any idea which one that could be?"

Rolf thought for a moment, digesting the news that it was Kreuzer's successors who had targeted Sylvia. "It might have been the Office for the Protection of the Constitution in Cologne. I hear it has done more than its share of bungling. Did Schmidt say what the attacker's motive might have been?"

"He didn't know whether the RAF had gotten wind of the Berlin assignment or whether Kreuzer's buddies were looking for some belated revenge when publicity about my Stuttgart engagement put me back in their sights."

Rolf did not like what he heard. He was brooding about the implications for Sylvia when Signora Laciura appeared, carrying a bouquet of lavender roses. "These are for you, Signorina."

Sylvia uttered a startled, "Grazie, Signora," and the innkeeper withdrew discreetly. Sylvia stared at Rolf. "From you? You sneak!" She bent her face toward the buds. "They smell heavenly."

Rolf felt a broad smile spreading across his face. "Gee, I wonder if there is a secret note."

Sylvia parted the stems and produced a lavender envelope, which she tore open. Out came a note card. She read, "Sylvia, No more unexpected difficulties. Meet me in Santa Fe (for old times' sake). Your greatest admirer."

Sylvia flew around the table, spilling coffee and marmalade over the white tablecloth. As he caught his breath from the long, hard kiss, she whispered, "Let's not wait till Santa Fe. It wouldn't hurt your arm if we were really careful, would it?"

Whether it would or not, for Rolf there was only one possible answer to *that* question. Without a word, he put his good arm around her waist and led her across the terrace.

♫ ♫ ♫ The End ♫ ♫ ♫

Printed in the United States
218583BV00003B/1/P